RED ZONE

by
KELLI HUGHETT

D1089172

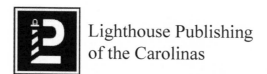

Lighthouse Publishing
of the Carolinas

RED ZONE BY KELLI HUGHETT
Published by Lighthouse Publishing of the Carolinas
2333 Barton Oaks Dr., Raleigh, NC, 27614

ISBN: 9781941103364

Cover design by writelydesigned.com
Interior design by Karthick Srinivasan

Available in print from your local bookstore, online, or from the publisher at:
www.lighthousepublishingofthecarolinas.com

For more information on this book and the author visit: www.kellihughett.com

This is a work of fiction. Names, characters, and incidents are all products of the
author's imagination or are used for fictional purposes. Any mentioned brand names,
places, and trade marks remain the property of their respective owners, bear no
association with the author or the publisher, and are used for fictional purposes only.

Brought to you by the creative team at Lighthouse Publishing of the Carolinas.com:
Eddie Jones, Rowena Kuo, and Michele Creech.

Library of Congress Cataloging-in-Publication Data
Hughett, Kelli.
Red Zone/Kelli Hughett 1st ed.

Printed in the United States of America

1

THE VOICE AGAIN.

Annoyance scratched like a t-shirt tag at the base of his consciousness as he acknowledged the caller on the other line. "This line is safe. What do you want?"

"I've got another player for you."

He poured a cup of steaming coffee, knowing he'd pay for the acidic shot of caffeine. "I told you I wasn't going to do it again. I'm finished."

Still, satisfaction warmed his blood as he remembered the control he'd exercised over NFL players. *And they thought they were invincible.*

A voice, gruff from too many late nights and cigars, barked at him from the phone. "I'm offering a bigger payoff this time."

He stroked his chin, feeling the growing stubble, considering the suggestion. Risky— especially now. In fact, he wouldn't be in his current situation if he'd just said no the first time. The injection was a simple manipulation of a mega-million dollar game, but could he handle the backlash if anything went wrong?

Another player injury offered big money and cash was helpful— even necessary at a time like this. He'd need it to cover his tracks and eliminate problem number One before he could consider getting out for good.

A Google search of the player's name put a face on the guy they intended him to take out. A rookie fresh out of college. His stats were well known. "Why this guy?"

"Don't ask me questions you don't want me to answer."

Silence. Let them think he didn't understand how NFL gambling worked—or how much money was on the line if he refused. Would it hurt to do one more? NFL players made millions in their sleep and didn't need to play the game to reap the benefits of their contracts. They'd go on to better things, even if they were forced to retire by an injury.

"I'll triple what I paid last time if he's eliminated before the playoffs."

Triple?

A sharps container, three sizes of surgical gloves, and a tumbler of Popsicle sticks adorned the otherwise empty desk. Tools of the trade. And if he used them right, he stood to make a *killing*.

The word wormed its way into his stomach. A hit on a player paled in comparison to what he'd already planned: murder.

A belch of acid scalded his throat as he wrestled memories that threatened his subconscious. He popped a chewable into his mouth and swallowed it whole. Mentally, he chained the beast that threatened his composure. He would end this. The past—and the woman who'd gotten too close to the truth—had tormented him long enough. The payoff from this injection would pay his debts and free him to move on if things got ugly after he finished her off.

This time the risks were greater and money generated from a player hit would insure his escape if push came to shove—not that he planned on leaving. If things went the way they should, he'd be putting down even deeper roots.

A cleansing breath locked the memories further away, where they belonged.

The voice interrupted his reverie. "I'm waiting."

"I'll do it."

His heart jumped. He slid the desk drawer open and pulled on a pair of latex gloves with a snap. A well-placed injection into the player's knee would hopefully sideline him for the season. Players got injured every day in this league.

And he could walk away from the memories a very wealthy man.

The heavy door of Jack's Chevy truck slammed shut, echoing through the parking lot. He glanced toward the stadium and anxiety snaked through his stomach as he scanned the area for the mob of fans or media he dreaded. Since his injury the questions they asked hurt more than a hit from Oakland's center. Didn't they understand he had nothing to offer anymore? He'd been waiting for the day he'd be labeled "old news;" perhaps that day had arrived. Not a day too soon.

No sign of a stampede. He exhaled, donned dark sunglasses and started for the stands. Worries careened off the invisible cliff in his mind like lemmings, and he let them fall. At thirty-six, he was determined to start living again—even if it was a half-life in comparison to the one he'd left behind.

The wind caught the fresh-cut-grass scent of the field, taking him back to the crack of helmets, and the palpable tension of the crowd before a game. Near the high school stadium, a line snaked around the entrance, everyone waiting for the ticket booth to open. A teenager with a blonde ponytail shoved past him carrying a white poster board cut into the shape of a fence. Her giggling friend followed carrying a matching "D." He smiled. He'd never forget the day Mom asked him, "What's 'D' gate?" *Defense, Mom.*

Mom. She believed there was life after the NFL, and pushed him to get out of the house more often. But what could possibly take the place of professional football? She couldn't understand the emptiness. How many times would she remind him it would have been an easier transition if he'd have found someone to share his life with? At least he'd dodged the marriage bullet. Lots of former players divorced within months of stepping off the field, and he understood why. Life was bleak without your heart beating in your chest.

At the ticket gate, the buttery scent of popcorn conjured memories as delicious as the grandstand snack itself. His chest compressed. Oh, to be back on the field again! To hear the deafening roar of an invigorated crowd, feel the edgy anger finally assuaged by the first hard hit of the game. He cracked his knuckles and ducked his head under a banner.

Feet clanged on the bleachers overhead as he rounded the concrete dividing wall to find his seat. He savored the view of the green field, marked with white lines, like an artist did a landscape, but a vibration from his cell phone brought him back to the present. He glanced at it and frowned. Lisa Sparks, assistant to the editor of *NFL Rush* magazine:

Could we set up an interview soon? Off the record?

Off the record? What was the point of an interview if it was off the record? This was just what he'd been trying to avoid for almost a year. Probably another gimmick to get him to endorse something, although Carter, the editor, had always been a straight shooter. He'd rather just disappear than hawk sub sandwiches or used cars. The phone sank into the pocket of his loose-fitting jeans. He'd deal with her later. Today, he just wanted to get back to the game.

He settled into a spot where he hoped his imposing frame wouldn't draw notice. Further up, the stands teemed with parents and grandparents. To his relief, only one other person sat near him. She was attractive and clearly into the game. Her faded jeans and a school t-shirt with Farris and the number 41 on the back marked her as a parent or football-loving aunt. Her knee bobbed and she rubbed her hands together as the announcer's voice crackled from the speakers.

The grandstands vibrated with anticipation.

"Give a soaring welcome to Your Thompson Valley EAGLES!"

The band erupted with the fight song.

The woman near him stood and yelled, "Go, Brant!"

Jack smiled. *Another proud mom.*

The announcer introduced the defense, and Jack strained to hear the names of the players over the bygone loudspeaker. Brant Farris caught his attention. The woman stamped her feet and hollered before she settled down for the coin toss. Brant Farris must be her son.

The team ran onto the field, and since they'd won the coin toss, he had no trouble locating number 41, Brant Farris, who played inside linebacker. He folded his legs beneath him and sat on the metal bench, anxious to study the only player he had any clues about.

After the first set of downs, he realized the kid was pretty good, covering the receiver and deflecting a pass without drawing a flag. Helmets cracked as Farris made a killer open field tackle on third down, forcing the offense to punt. The crowd roared, and Jack's feet itched for the field again.

Close to the end of the half, the Eagles were up by a field goal. More fans pushed into the empty seats around him, and Jack dreaded halftime. What if someone recognized him?

The woman near him kept drawing his attention. Maybe it was because she kept standing in her form-fitting jeans, or the fact that she cheered so passionately, but he couldn't keep his eyes from wandering back again and again.

She'd spread a black and gold stadium blanket beside her as if she anticipated someone joining her. She smoothed the blanket into place with her left hand, but he didn't see a flash of gold. Probably divorced. Not that it mattered; he'd never play back-up to another man. He tackled his thoughts midstream. Why were his thoughts straying to her relationship status? That was the last thing he needed.

He guessed her to be thirty-something despite the dimpled smile he'd seen when she turned her head to watch the last play. She opened a bag of sunflower seeds and balanced it next to her hold-everything-you'll-ever-need bag. How had she lugged that thing up the stairs? Her hazelnut-colored hair was pulled into a ponytail, he suspected, to show off the last name and number of her child.

At the end of the half, Jack stood to stretch his legs. He realized his mistake when someone called out, "Hey! I think that's Jack Briggs!"

The crowd burst into action, coming closer by the second. He dreaded the pity in the eyes of prying fans. Hiding his six-foot-four frame was difficult when seated, so standing had been a bone-headed move. He should have covered his dark hair with a hat. Beads of sweat prickled on his forehead. He couldn't face them.

Panic-stricken, he stepped over the two rows separating him from the woman he'd been eyeing. Her eyes widened as he sat down on her blanket; her whole face registered surprise when he slung his arm around her shoulders, and pulled his glasses down to meet her eyes.

"Honey, those guys think I look like Jack Briggs. I told you I'd be famous someday."

He prayed his eyes communicated his need for her to play along.

Indecision flashed in her eyes, but she patted his shoulder, "You may look like Jack Briggs, but can you play like him?"

That one hurt. Even so, it was enough to distract the crowd, and no one approached him. He remained beside her, uncommonly aware of her shapely shoulder beneath his arm. When the band began the fight song again, he loosened his grasp and dropped his arm.

A cloud blocked the fast setting sun and her features became clear. Blue eyes flashed. "Would you like to tell me what's going on here?"

Jack swallowed past the lump in his throat. Her pretty cheeks flamed with embarrassment.

"You just saved my skin."

Her eyebrows rose. "How's that?"

Jack brought his head closer to hers. "I really am Jack Briggs. I just can't stand the crowds sometimes." Did she have enough football knowledge to know his name?

She bit her lip as her eyes searched his with hawk-like precision. "You've got to be kidding me."

"Nope. I live in Loveland. Thought I'd catch the old team in the semi-final match-up. Is your boy number 41?"

Her eyes lit up with pride. Thank goodness he'd been observant earlier. No better way to flatter a mother than to ask about her son.

"Yes, Brant Farris. He's a linebacker."

"I noticed."

The marching band took the field, and Jack leaned forward, resting his forearms on his thighs, in no hurry to leave her company. "He's got talent. What year is he?"

"He's just a freshman."

He couldn't see her face from this angle, but imagined he'd heard a smile accompanying her words. "Then I'd say he's got a lot of talent. Do you think the coaching staff can handle him?"

"Handle him? With forty teenagers on the team, who's handling whom?"

He nodded. "A good coach will bring out the best in him."

She shrugged, not meeting his gaze. "I don't really know what they think of him as a player. I was so surprised when he came home and announced he'd be a starter."

Jack sought her gaze. "I really have to thank you for not freaking out on me a minute ago." He extended his hand. "Like I said, I'm Jack. And you are?"

She shook his hand. "Marcy Farris." Her smile reached her eyes, lighting her whole face. "You're not really Jack Briggs, are you?"

Jack put his hand to his chest, feigning pain. "You don't believe me?"

She bit back a smile and shrugged, shaking her head.

"What would I need to do to prove it to you?" Somehow, it mattered that she knew the truth.

Before she could answer, her cell phone rang. "Hi, honey. No. I saved you a spot."

So there was a man in her life. He edged away.

"Have Grandma drop you off. I'm in my usual spot."

He relaxed. Sounded like a kid. Man, what was he doing? She didn't have one kid, but two? Major baggage.

He checked his own phone. He'd had two more texts from Lisa Sparks. *Let up, lady! What interview could be that important?*

Marcy tucked her cell phone into the striped bag and turned back to him. "Sorry, that was my daughter. What were you saying?"

"Nothing big."

"You were going to prove your claim to be Jack Briggs."

Against his better judgment, he succumbed to her dimpled grin, baggage and all. He pulled out his wallet and flashed his driver's license.

She appraised him. "I guess you look different with a helmet on."

So she'd heard of him, at least.

"You might say that." Jack smiled. "A jersey with Briggs and number 44 doesn't hurt either."

"You mean you don't wear it around town?"

He lifted an eyebrow. "It's awfully tempting, but I prefer a little anonymity in public." Especially since retirement after an injury.

Marcy nodded and turned her attention to the game. The defense trotted onto the field for the second half.

"Go Eagles!" Marcy cheered with the crowd.

The visiting team maneuvered down the field into the red zone in a series of first-downs. The Eagles' defense wasn't able to stop them until Farris swatted the ball out of an opposing player's hands and dove for the fumble. A pile of players jumped on top of him in an attempt to recover the ball. Marcy gasped and gripped the edge of the cold metal in fear.

He glanced her way. Was she so nervous he'd be injured? Maybe all moms were that way.

The referee indicated a change of possession, and the crowd roared approval as she recovered her composure. Marcy laughed. "I imagine it's rather painful for an NFL star to watch high school ball."

"Not at all. I love the game. Brings back the good old days."

Marcy glanced at her watch and scanned the crowd. She stood and waved. "Haley, up here!"

A girl of about nine or ten with unruly blonde curls (unlike her mother's sleek dark hair) waved back and started up the bleachers.

"Cute kid." How many more did she have?

Marcy wrapped her arm around her daughter's waist. "Jack, this is my daughter, Haley."

The little girl grinned at him with a dimple identical to her mother's. "Hey."

"Hales, this is Mr. Briggs."

He stood and extended his hand to shake hers.

Haley's eyes widened. "You should have been a football player. You sure are tall."

He caught Marcy's eye and grinned as they sat down. "Man, she's good."

He was probably sitting in Haley's spot on the blanket, and her arrival provided him a great moment to excuse himself, but he felt reluctant to go. "Guess I'll leave you to enjoy the game."

"Thanks." She nodded and turned her attention to the field.

He shook his head as he stepped over the bleachers. "No, it's you I've got to thank. I wasn't up for autographs tonight."

"Any time." Marcy spun back to the game. She hugged Haley close and handed her the bag of sunflower seeds.

Marcy Farris intrigued him. All he'd have to do was turn on his ex-NFL charm and flash his famous smile, and she'd follow him like a Hamlin child after the Pied Piper. At least that's what all the guys said. But, she spelled disaster. Kids. Heck, she probably had a husband, too. Jack had swagger, but never the nerve to use it like a weapon. It was all bravado. Inside, he was as unsure of himself as anybody, especially after the injury. His fingers massaged his knee, tracing the scar that robbed him of everything that mattered.

Evening fell and the temperature dropped as the stadium lights flickered on. When the game ended, he couldn't help hoping he'd have another opportunity to talk with her. He hovered in the bleachers, but she never got up.

The crowd cleared quickly and Jack stepped over the bleachers separating them. "Is Brant's dad down on the field?"

Marcy swiveled around. "No. Brant and Haley's dad died a few years ago. Brant's meeting us up here."

Stupid. He'd asked a personal question and didn't anticipate being embarrassed by her answer. What did a guy say to something like that? Sorry your husband died?

She raised an eyebrow. "Are you waiting for the all-clear?"

"You might say that. Although this late at night, I'm not as easily recognized."

Marcy dug in her bag for a piece of gum for Haley.

"Where are the finals being played?"

Haley brightened. "Right here, since we won! I can't wait for that game."

Jack smiled at her enthusiasm. "You're into football?"

Marcy shook her head. "No, Hales just enjoys the popcorn."

Haley put a slim hand on her hip. "Mom. I like football, too. Especially since Brant plays."

Marcy ruffled Haley's blonde bangs in an intimate gesture. "You're a good little sister, you know that?" She turned back to him. "Do you have kids, Jack?"

"No kids, no siblings. Just my mom."

She brushed a wisp of hair away from her cheek. "No other family?"

He shook his head. In the silence that followed, he wracked his brain for something to say. "Hey, would you mind if I stayed around to give Brant some pointers?"

Marcy blushed. "That would make his night. But I hope you don't think I was detaining you with small talk. I wasn't trying to be manipulative."

"No. No. I'd love to stay and chat with him."

Haley dug in her mom's bag. "Did you bring the iPad?"

"No, honey. It's at home on the charger."

"Well, what am I going to do while we wait?"

Marcy winked at him. "Why don't you ask this nice man for his autograph?"

Haley looked back and forth between the adults. "Why?"

Jack couldn't contain the roar of laughter. Marcy grinned and joined him.

Flabbergasted, Haley shrugged. "What?"

Marcy took a deep breath. "Haley, this is Jack Briggs. He's a former NFL player."

Haley's eyes widened as her mother's had earlier. "No way!"

He nodded. "Way."

The cleats of Brant's shoes clanged on the bleachers as he made his way to them. Marcy jumped up and hugged him. "Great game, Sweetie. I'm so proud of you." She pushed his long hair away from his forehead, revealing the same uncommon blue eyes of his sister. Marcy thrust a lemon-lime sports drink into his hand.

"Thanks, Mom."

Haley poked him. "Brant, do you know this guy? He used to play in the NFL!"

Brant dropped his helmet.

Jack fist-bumped him. "Nice game."

Brant appraised him. "You're Jack Briggs!"

"Guilty."

"Man, this is awesome!"

Jack stood, well aware of the awe-inspiring height of his frame. "Your mom helped me out of a tight spot this evening."

Brant extended his ball. "Would you sign my ball?"

Jack beamed. This was more his speed. "Sure."

Marcy produced a Sharpie and Jack signed the ball with his name and jersey number, 44. He handed it to Brant. "You guys have time for some pie and ice cream tonight?"

Brant and Haley looked at their mom. Brant grabbed her shoulder. "Mom, an NFL star just asked us to have ice cream with him. This is the part where you say yes." Haley nodded in agreement.

Marcy looked at him with a raised eyebrow. "I don't think we—"

Jack smiled and helped her over the steps, pulse responding to her touch. "My treat."

She craned her neck to look at him and stepped away from his touch. "It was nice to meet you, Jack."

She'd managed to end the conversation without an actual rejection. Interesting. He followed them to the parking lot, ignoring the fourth vibration of his cell. Lisa Sparks was a regular bulldog. Marcy carried her shoulder bag and Brant's helmet, and still managed to look good from behind.

What had he gotten himself into? The first date he'd proposed in over a year was a foursome shared with two kids. And she'd rejected him.

Street lights caught the golden highlights in Marcy's hair as she disappeared.

2

MARCY CHECKED THE rearview mirror and pulled out of the school parking lot, thanking God she'd escaped him. She ground her teeth against memories. She'd never trust professional athletes, especially after witnessing her husband Pete put out the fires some of his clients created. As an NFL agent, he'd seen everything—affairs, drugs, you name it. Retired players were even worse. Many were bankrupt or facing lawsuits soon after they left the league. The chance of his being a Christian was next to none. And with that dark hair falling across his forehead and deep green eyes, Jack Briggs was too handsome for his own good.

The invisible knife that never left her stomach turned. As indestructible as Jack looked, she'd earned a reputation for driving men away. Heck, she'd driven her own husband to suicide. Good thing Jack played defense.

Brant spoke from the back seat of their sedan. "Mom, I can't believe you said no to having ice cream with Jack Briggs!"

She eyed her son in the rearview mirror. His thumbs flew across the keys of his phone, texting his fellow players, no doubt. Maybe she should have said yes. Brant could use all the encouragement he could get, and who better than a former NFL player?

"I'll still take you like I promised. We'll go to Dairy Delight."

Haley popped a pink gum bubble. "Did he ask you like a date, Mom?"

"I don't think so, Hales. Mr. Briggs was just being nice. He probably wanted to give Brant a few pointers."

"Then why are you blushing? Seriously Mom, he's an NFL star." Haley talked behind a film of bubble gum.

How'd Haley see her blushing in the dark car? "Haley, please talk with your mouth closed."

The kids busted up. "How'm I supposed to talk with my mouth closed?"

Marcy laughed too. Maybe Jack made her a little nervous. "Sweetie, I just meant you needn't talk through your gum."

Haley popped a bubble. "Did Dad represent him?"

Marcy shook her head. "No. Mr. Briggs wasn't one of Dad's clients. I don't know who his agent is."

Brant stopped texting for a second. "Did he know Dad? Is that how you know him, Mom?"

The knife that sliced every time she thought of Pete struck again. "I don't know if he knew him or not. I never heard your dad bring his name up. I just met him tonight."

The pink and green neon lights of Dairy Delight ice cream parlor illuminated the parking lot. This local hang-out was the last place a guy like Jack would patronize.

Mouth-watering smells of fried food hung in the night air. So much for her new diet. She flung her purse over her shoulder and closed the car door. Her heart screeched to a stop and started again as a shadowy figure flashed momentarily in her headlights. Jack Briggs leaned against the door of his truck, an overconfident grin on his face.

She opened the car door, wrestling her heart to maintain a steady rhythm.

"Thought you might come here." He leaned against the door, one leg crossed over the other, a hoodie sweatshirt under his arm.

For all their earlier excitement, Haley and Brant shied away on the other side of the car. She'd left the stadium after he had and he followed her here? The nerve.

Jack broke the ice, pointing to the red and white striped awning. "You guys here for some ice cream?"

Brant pocketed his phone. "Yeah."

Jack shrugged. "Mind if I join you?"

The pressure of Haley's tug on her sleeve brought her to her senses. "Is it okay, Mom?"

Outnumbered. She couldn't politely avoid him now, and the place was about as safe as anywhere. "We can't stay long, guys."

The door swung open, and his eyes danced as if he gloated at his victory. "After you."

Jerry Lee Lewis' "Great Balls of Fire" played on a jukebox in the corner of the 1950s themed restaurant. Red and white striped chairs gathered at small tables formed a maze as they fought their way through the crowd to the counter. Jack insisted they find a seat after asking for their order.

She swallowed suspicions. He was just trying to be nice.

Indian summer still held the night temperatures above usual lows, so she and the kids settled at an out of the way table on the patio.

Jack opened the door with a single push and smiled as he handed a banana split to Brant and a chocolate dipped cone to Haley. Then, he swung his long leg over the concrete picnic table bench to sit beside her. Jack popped a straw into his root beer float and pushed the vanilla shake in front of her. "You know, some people say a dessert choice reflects a person's personality." He cocked an eyebrow in her direction.

Flirting with her in front of the kids? The guy had nerve. She shrugged. "Then I guess I'm vanilla."

His eyes crinkled at the corners when he smiled. "Unlikely." He turned to Brant. "Awesome game tonight, man."

Brant looked up from his triple-scoop banana split, which was almost gone already. "I know I've got a lot of room for improvement."

Jack shook his head. "I reviewed the tapes after every game. There's always room for improvement."

Brant gnawed his lip, but Marcy saw anticipation, maybe hero worship in his eyes. He soaked it up like a sponge.

"So for starters, you know when the quarterback sets up in the shotgun . . ."

She and Haley shared a sigh, and Haley rolled her eyes. Her husband, Pete, lived and breathed football, but Haley was only five when he . . . died.

Marcy winked at Haley. "Get used to it, Hales."

Jack jumped up from the table to collect salt and pepper shakers from the other tables. He sat back down and constructed a makeshift offensive line with the salt shakers. She assumed the pepper shakers were defense.

He pushed one salt shaker forward. "If this lane opens up, you can get the midfield tackle."

Brant shook his head, grinning. "What if it's a blitz?"

Haley licked her ice-cream. "You rush the quarterback."

Jack stopped, turning to Haley. "Right." He grinned. "You're a smart cookie."

She flashed him a missing toothed grin. "That's what my mom says."

"Well, she knows what she's talking about." Jack winked.

The guy acted like they were old friends. He'd certainly won the kids over, but she wasn't as easily swayed. The long-sleeved T-shirt stretched across his shoulders accented his larger-than-life persona. Not bad, but in her limited experience, football players were all skin deep.

Why hadn't he married before now? Probably shacked up with a model.

Haley and Brant laughed when Jack folded a napkin and thumb-punted it through the "up-rights" of Brant's forefingers. The guy had a way with kids.

The wind sharpened, and Marcy shivered. Jack scooted closer to her. "You cold?"

Not with Jack sitting so near. "A little."

Marcy's heart drummed as Jack's hooded sweatshirt fell across her shoulders. Her mouth fell open when Brant snapped a picture of them with his phone. "I can't wait to send this to Uncle Bobby."

Evidence she'd taken leave of her senses. Bobby would eat it up. Her brother-in-law would wonder if the guy was a cardboard cutout from the mall sports shop. Marcy toyed with her straw, desperate for something to talk about. "So what have you been doing since your retirement?"

Jack coughed and glanced away. "Rehabbing the knee."

Marcy chewed her lower lip, wondering why the question made him uncomfortable. "How's that going?"

He slapped his leg. "It's as normal as it's gonna get."

Mom-o-meter kicked in. "Does it still hurt?"

Jack grinned, his in-need-of-a-shave cheek creasing in a smile. "Only when it snows."

Haley tossed her cone wrapper in the trash bin. "Did you hurt anything else when you were playing?"

"Nope. Just the knee. I always protected the moneymaker."

Haley's eyes widened. "How did you do that?"

Jack pretended to punch Brant's jaw. "Always wear a helmet, right big guy?"

Brant and Marcy laughed, but Haley didn't join them. "I don't get it."

Jack winked at Marcy, his roguish grin playing with her emotions. "I'll explain it to you later."

Marcy checked her watch. "You guys have a church workday

tomorrow at noon."

Jack collected the remaining trash. "Better listen to your mom." He looked at Brant. "And this guy's got to get ready for the championship." Jack followed them out of the restaurant.

Marcy slid into the driver's seat, and Jack leaned against the frame. "So, Ms. Vanilla. Think I could claim a seat beside you at the state game on Saturday?"

The scent of his aftershave steamrolled any resolve she'd formed against him. "Sure. I've got to reserve tickets on Tuesday morning."

"Can I call you?"

She had to shake the spell he'd woven around her. This would end in disaster, but she heard herself recite the number before she had a chance to take it back. When he turned, Marcy yanked the door shut. The breath she'd been holding trickled out.

"Mom, he's totally into you."

"I think it's a little too soon to say that, Brant."

"Still, I can't believe Jack Briggs is coming to watch the state championship. Yes!"

She couldn't believe it either. She'd eat her purse if he actually called back.

Nervous butterflies fluttered when she recognized Jack's cocky grin as he walked to her car Saturday morning. If she hadn't been waiting for him, she might not have known the man at her window. The ever-present sunglasses gave him an incognito look, while the close fitting beanie and black Under Armor half-zip sweatshirt and pants further disguised his rugged features. All he needed to complete the gangsta look was a cigar hanging from his lips.

Marcy rolled down the window and blew a frosty breath into the sky. "Hey."

Jack raised his eyebrows as his eyes swept her. "Hellooo, Vanilla. You look good in white."

Maybe she shouldn't have worn the new ski jacket. Too close fitting? She slid from the car and shut the door with a bang and gulped as she faced him. Her unadorned hands slid easily into jeans pockets.

"Ready?"

Haley climbed out, and Marcy shot her a look, hoping to remind her of the conversation they'd had before the game, no dating talk.

His green eyes absorbed her smile and he returned it with one of his own. "Ready."

A few snowflakes drifted from the sky, christening the playing field. Marcy pulled her ski jacket closer around her neck as she followed Jack through the crowd. His tall frame blocked most of the biting wind that kicked dust and frozen snow into their faces.

Marcy grabbed Haley's coat sleeve. "Let's get your popcorn before we find our seats."

As Jack picked up their tickets from Will Call, hundreds of people pushed close around them. Some forced their way toward the concession stand, while others marched to their seats. An electric charge energized the crowd. The palpable excitement tingled through Marcy's shoulders. She grasped Jack's forearm and shook it.

"You excited?"

A nervous jolt hit her midsection. "I might be more excited than Brant is."

Jack grinned. "I've not experienced the excitement as a fan very often, but I know the exhilaration of the game better than anyone."

"You miss it?"

"More than anything. Let's get in line."

Jack tucked her arm in his and Haley followed, her finger hooked in Marcy's belt loop (she'd learned that trick when her kids were toddlers). The woman in front of them moved nervously from foot to foot, her blonde hair and jacket swaying to an unheard rhythm as she checked her watch. Maybe she had to go to the bathroom. She'd seen Haley do *that* dance before.

Jack glanced at Haley. "You want anything besides popcorn?"

Haley grinned. "Nope. Popcorn is my favorite. It was Dad's favorite, too."

The familiar sadness reared its head. If she'd been a better wife, maybe Haley would still have her dad. Would a thing with Jack bring more pain to the kids? She sighed, getting a look from Jack. She tucked her hand in the crook of his arm. It would be fun while it lasted.

The line advanced, and the woman in front of them kicked her black bag along, instead of picking it up. She checked her watch again. If Marcy didn't know better, she would think the woman was a terrorist or something. Loveland, Colorado wasn't exactly a terrorist mecca.

Instead of kicking the duffel bag this time, the woman unzipped it and pulled a portable CD player from its depths. She hit the play button, and a big band swing song erupted from the speakers. Marcy jumped when the woman threw her coat off and said, "Let's swing!"

A man materialized from the crowd like a ghost and swung the woman over his head in a complicated move before they pressed together to dance. The crowd stepped back as another couple joined them. By the third bar, five couples danced to the music flowing from the CD player at Marcy's feet.

"MOM!" Haley shouted above the music. "I've heard of these! They're called flash mobs!"

Marcy shouted above the music. "What?"

Jack leaned down and talked into her ear. "A group of dancers breaks out at a planned time in a public place. They're all over the news."

"Awesome."

A swarm of people pressed into the small space in front of the concession stand. Marcy guessed there were thirty dancers now, mostly couples, swinging to the thundering brass. Haley clapped her hands to the music, eyes wide.

A pause in the music brought more dancers jumping into the fray. Onlookers held up their cell phones, recording the phenomena. Marcy glanced up at Jack. Was he nervous? Of course, this was the kind of publicity he tried to avoid, but why? He was the "Gentleman Linebacker." Everybody knew and respected him.

Jack looked at her and shrugged. "At least they're looking at the dancers, and not at me."

A cluster of unruly kids pushed forward, throwing Marcy off balance. She tried to grab Haley, but the crowd pushed in closer around her. Haley's head disappeared around the corner of the concrete divider. "Haley!" The music and dancers drowned her voice. With this crowd, it wasn't likely Haley would get far. She'd find her when the dancers stopped.

When the song finished, the audience cheered. The dancers took a bow, and melted back into the throng as if they'd never been there. Slowly, the game crowd came to life again, resuming their migration to the concession stand and their seats.

Marcy scanned the mass of people for Haley. She couldn't find her. Jack either—— which was odd because he was a head taller than most men. "Haley!"

Marcy pushed forward, like a spawning salmon swimming upstream. "Haley!"

Annoyance and a tremor of worry passed through her mind. They would miss kickoff at this rate. Marcy dug in her purse for her cell phone. She sent a text to Jack. *Where are you? Can't find Haley.* Looking around, she slipped the phone into her jacket pocket.

A blast from an air horn agitated the crowd and the motion thrust Marcy forward. She tripped over something and landed on her knees. The crowd surged again, and Marcy felt prickles of panic dance up her spine. She'd heard of people trampled by mindless crowds. In the near dark, hundreds of feet stomped, pressed, and kicked her, tossing her like waves. She attempted to crawl nearer to the wall, but her hands slipped in a sticky liquid.

Great, a spilled Slurpee would stain her new jeans and white coat for sure. Bodies blocked out any light and her heart hammered. What would it be like to die like this?

Someone's foot came down on her hand with a crunch. "Ach!" Her head took a blow from a knee and she toppled sideways. Her phone vibrated in her pocket, but she couldn't reach it. Her breath came in short pants as she tried to push herself onto all fours, but the bodies around her refused to allow her any movement.

Groping on her stomach, she grasped frantically for something to hold onto. She grasped a hairy leg but was jerked forward and struck her chin on the concrete. Another foot pounded her hand, which throbbed mercilessly. She pushed to her hands and knees again, heart hammering uncontrollably.

God, help me.

Panic strangled her throat when she tried to stand, but the crowd thrust her to the concrete again. The filthy odor of spilled snacks, feet, dirt and oil gagged her. Like a wild animal, she lunged forward, desperate to escape the barrage of people that threatened to suffocate her. Her hand slipped again in the sticky liquid, and she grasped a soft object in the dark. She pulled, hoping for an anchor.

Mercifully, the legs and feet around her parted. She pushed herself into a squatting position, careful to avoid the pool of the substance she already had on her hands. As the crowd parted, weak sunlight pierced the darkness.

Her stomach revolted. Her hands were covered in blood.

The stain of death left its mark on her cuffs and dripped from her fingers. Her ears roared. The object she'd grabbed was no anchor. A woman stared at her with lifeless eyes. A jagged hole in the woman's neck oozed blood into a puddle, smeared by Marcy's struggle and footprints from the crowd. A scream split the chilly air, but she only stopped for breath when she realized it came from her lips.

Strong hands lifted her to her feet and Jack's arms enveloped her. "Someone call 911!"

3

FLASH BULBS EXPLODED like lightning in Jack's face as they pushed through the throng of people gathered tightly around them. His palms sweat and his heart tried to beat his feet to the car. He propelled Marcy forward and held Haley's hand. After police questioning, petulant paparazzi was the last thing these girls needed. And he couldn't face them, either.

Reporters swarmed around them like killer bees, microphones for stingers. The familiar experience made his blood congeal. Marcy shivered, but he suspected it wasn't from the chill in the air. He resisted the desire to put his arm around her shoulders. Instead, he put his hand on the small of her back, guiding her through the parking lot. There were more reporters than police on the scene. By this time, they'd had plenty of time to make the drive from Denver.

A man in a jean jacket shoved a recorder in his face. "Jack, were you a witness to the murder?"

"I have no comment at this time."

They pressed closer, jabbing microphones under his nose. This time, he pulled Marcy close to him. He didn't care what they thought.

"Jack, is this your girlfriend? What's her name?"

He pushed to the right.

"Jack, what was your relationship to Miss Sparks?"

"Do you know who murdered her?"

"Did you know she was coming to the game today?"

Haley squeezed his hand, conveying childish confidence.

"I have no comment whatsoever."

Jack yanked his truck door open, pushing people away with its weight. He helped Haley into the back seat first and stared at Marcy.

"I'll handle this."

Her hand warmed his as he helped her into the car. An exhausted smile creased her lips, and she slid into the passenger seat. Jack bit back comments that bubbled to his lips before shutting the door, not caring which hands and fingers attempted to prevent him.

He put the key into the ignition, and the truck roared to life though it didn't scatter the cattle-like obstruction in front of them. Marcy put her hand on his arm. "Jack, I'm sorry. What a circus." Her colorless complexion wrung his heart out like a rag.

"Never mind. I'm used to it. Let's leave your car here for tonight. I'll bring you back in the morning. I can't face that mob again."

He stepped on the accelerator, grateful to be away from story-hungry reporters. In the past, the press had acted as a liaison between him and his fans. He wanted no more of that.

They cleared the speed bumps and the chain link fence on the north side of the stadium before he chanced a glance at Marcy. "Pretty fun second date, huh? Believe me, I know how to show a woman a good time." He flicked on her heated seat, noting the blood stains on her cuffs and jeans, a gruesome contrast to the white jacket he'd admired. A sickening reminder of the carnage they'd witnessed.

His mind strayed to the moment he'd recognized the victim's face. Lisa Sparks, the one who'd sent him the texts about the interview. Had she tracked him to the game because he'd ignored her all week?

Marcy relaxed into the seat and massaged her temples. "Flash mob and a murder sure beats dinner and a movie."

"Talk about icing the kicker." He swallowed. "Did Brant say when they'd make up the game?"

"No. I guess we'll hear later this week when it's rescheduled."

Jack glanced in the backseat. Haley slept against the headrest. Poor thing had had a rough day. But since she was asleep, he was at liberty to ask the questions that burned in his mind since the incident.

"I was surprised the police questioned you so long. Did you know Lisa Sparks?"

Marcy sighed, and closed her eyes as if resigned to telling him the truth. "Do you know the name Peter Farris?"

"Sure. Wasn't he the—?"

Realization dawned. *Farris.* Pete Farris, the NFL agent who committed suicide a couple of years ago. Oh, man.

"Pete was my husband."

"I'm so sorry. I didn't make the connection. Wow. So you know this game inside and out, don't you?"

"You might say that."

"That explains how you knew Lisa. You know Carter, then?"

"Carter's been my stronghold since Josh died. We were friends before he became the editor of *NFL Rush*. This will devastate him."

Bits of snow swirled on the ground. "From your tone, I gather Lisa was more than an assistant to him?"

His stomach soured when he thought of blowing Lisa off for the interview she'd requested. Should he tell Marcy he suspected she'd been there to see him?

She pointed to the turnoff to her neighborhood. Her hollow voice lacked the life he'd admired on their first meeting. "They were engaged."

"Oh. That's awful."

From the corner of his eye, he watched a tear escape and trickle down her cheek. He remembered the news report said she'd been the one to find her husband, overdosed on sleeping pills right next to her in bed. Pete Farris had always seemed so *normal*. And now she'd been the one to find Lisa's body. It probably brought up awful memories.

Another sigh escaped her quivering lips. "I'm glad Brant's gone to a sleepover. I can't wait to get to bed." She massaged her temples.

He thumbed the sleeping girl in the back seat. "Haley beat you to it."

She glanced in the back seat and turned when he slowed in the neighborhood she'd indicated. "That's our house, the gray one."

Jack pulled into her driveway, and an awkward silence hung heavy between them.

She patted his shoulder. "Thanks for the ride home, anyway. I can pick up the car tomorrow."

He hated to leave her like this. The fatigue and pain in her eyes struck his heart like a hammer, and he felt compelled to try and alleviate it. "Can I make it up to you somehow? You know, maybe a gang shooting next week?"

Marcy gathered her purse and shrugged. "I think I'll pass."

His hopes fell as his ill-timed humor hung between them. "On the gang shooting, or another date?"

She laughed and met his eyes. "I've got more baggage than you need, Jack. The reporters are going to be all over this story."

Had she read his mind? He'd told himself the same thing a hundred times this week, but something in that simple smile and those stormy blue eyes made him disregard it all. "I think I can handle it."

Tears shimmered her eyes. "If you want to escape the limelight, I'm not the woman you're looking for." She pushed open the car door, and a gust of snowy air rushed in, waking Haley, who blinked sleepily.

He gripped the steering wheel, unwilling to argue with her while she stood in the cold. "Stay in touch, okay?"

She helped Haley out of the backseat. "Sure." She slammed the door and headed up the walk.

He watched her go, knowing she'd had an amazingly rough day. If he were smart, he would take her advice, but somehow he couldn't see himself walking away.

Lisa Sparks thought she was slick, but he knew she was on to him like a hound dog on a fox. If she'd had the chance to complete that interview with Briggs, she'd have finally put it all together. Thank the gods he'd got to her in time.

He'd been in the shower until his fingertips were white and pruny, but the feeling of her blood on his hands wasn't easily washed away. He turned the water off and stepped out onto the scrap of terry cloth meant as a substitute for a bath rug. The hotel towel wasn't the Egyptian cotton he used at home, but it would do. He scrubbed his face hard and cleared a spot in the foggy mirror.

He smiled at his reflection, tousled his hair dry and slung the towel over his shoulders. He couldn't have planned it more perfectly, except the fact that Marcy had been the one to find the body. The look on her face etched itself permanently on his mind. The flash mob had been a stroke of luck, too, though he'd panicked at first when he couldn't escape. In the chaos, no one heard Lisa gasp for breath as he plunged the knife into her neck. She hadn't even seen him come up from behind. No one heard her fall.

Brilliant.

Hiccups threatened, and he tightened his stomach against the physical sign of weakness. His first hands-on kill rattled his nerves, but why should it matter? Pete's death was no less a murder, even if the world was convinced he committed suicide. This time, instead of guilt, pride welled in his chest. He'd gotten away with the perfect crime.

He pulled on jeans and a sweater. Something still bothered him. He still didn't know how much Lisa knew or how he'd get his hands on her records.

What if Marcy had been her contact?

But if Marcy suspected, she never said anything. That sense of justice, which was ingrained on her conscience like tree rings, wouldn't allow information like that to go unacknowledged, if she possessed it. The burning in his stomach eased. She couldn't know or even suspect. He was safe.

But life was never uncomplicated. She'd been with Briggs. And that was *not* good news.

Anyone could see why she'd chosen him. The man had it all. Money. Looks. *Everything.*

And he knew Marcy's charms better than anyone. He'd never hurt her, but he'd need to use the events to his advantage. She was rattled after finding Lisa's body, and that's what he needed. He didn't want her picking at old wounds, or especially taking a second look through Pete's files. She'd been putty in his hands since the morning of Pete's death, insecure in ways he'd never seen before.

He could play on that weakness.

The bed bounced when he plopped onto it and snatched the remote from the nightstand. He'd taken more risk this time, planned and plotted. What was the legal term?

Premeditated.

High school stadiums weren't known for good security, and he'd walked right past the police officers as they rushed to the scene, the latex gloves and the knife hidden in his pocket. No security cameras. No problem.

Channels flipped past. Nothing on. As usual.

The antacids he crunched crumbled like dust in his mouth and he coughed. His conscience tried to come out from the stranglehold he'd put on it, but he wrestled it into place just in time to watch the late news and the aftermath.

Marcy got Haley into bed minutes after Jack dropped them off, but even after a long, hot shower, she couldn't sleep. Her mind tumbled over the events of the day, and she hugged the sheets closer. *Lisa.* At first she hadn't recognized her, but now the image of her face wouldn't go away. What the heck was she doing in Loveland? And without Carter?

The police grilled her pretty hard about her relationship with Lisa, and she hadn't been totally honest with them. The last thing she needed was the resurrection of skeletons from Pete's closet. He'd made enemies along the way; every agent did.

The skin of her hands tingled. She'd scrubbed it until it burned, but no amount of scrubbing could cleanse the memory of Lisa's blood dripping from her hands, nor the memory of those lifeless eyes. She shook her head to clear the thoughts away. Maybe there was something on T.V. besides news. She plumped her pillow and changed the channel. A *M*A*S*H* rerun would do.

Wind rattled the window, and bits of icy snow pelted the glass. She clicked the dial on the heated mattress pad. Winter crept up on her during an Indian summer football season. She prayed Jack made it home before the snow hit in full force. She didn't know where he lived exactly, but she guessed his house wasn't on a cul-de-sac near the middle school, probably lived in one of those ritzy gated communities in the foothills.

The radiant heat penetrated muscles still wrestling with events of the day.

"God, how can I get this image out of my head?"

She flexed her hands. She could still feel Lisa's blood between her fingers, if only the memory remained. A prayer fluttered in her mind like an errant butterfly, but she couldn't catch it. Her disquieted thoughts refused to gel.

The broken-record memory of her husband's suicide scratched to life once again; the one burden she continued to take back after giving it to God. She had Pete's death on her record. Was she now also responsible for Lisa's? She and Pete had fought the night before, and she'd fallen asleep before they made up. In the morning, she'd awakened to a corpse. Cold and dead like their marriage had been.

Despite the heated pad, her chill increased. Though their renewed communication had been brief, had she tipped Lisa off to information that had gotten her killed? Her pulse increased; if someone killed Lisa for that information, could she be next?

Poor Carter. She didn't have to imagine his feelings. She had experienced all the stages of grief. She'd call him in the morning after everything had a chance to sink in. Carter still didn't know she and Lisa had been in contact, and she didn't plan to tell him. No need to jeopardize their friendship, especially at a time like this. She'd make plans to go to New York for the funeral.

Her cell phone vibrated on the dresser across the room. Marcy checked the clock, only ten. She scrambled out of the clinging flannel sheets. Maybe it was Brant.

A smile touched her lips when she read the caller I.D. *Bobby Farris.*

"I just saw the news. You home yet?"

Her composure cracked when his familiar voice warmed her ear. "Yes, we've been home an hour or so." Tears choked her. "I've had a lot of bad days, but this one beats most of them." He understood.

"I'm so sorry, Marce. Does Carter know?"

She snuggled down between the sheets, the phone cradled on her shoulder. "I can't face him tonight, but I'll call in the morning. I'm sure I'll go out there for the funeral. Can Brant stay with you for a couple of days? I can leave Haley with your mom."

"Of course. We have a ball when he's here." Bobby paused, his voice softened. "You sure you're okay? I know this must stir some difficult memories."

"It does. I can't help remembering." She'd never forget.

"Well, I'm here for you. Family is all we've got when the fog settles in."

That was a good way to put it. She couldn't see the way in front or behind her right now. "Thanks."

"Get some rest. Mom and Dad are coming over in the morning with some muffins or something."

"They know?" She'd dreaded reliving the experience in words.

"Yeah, I called them."

"Thanks for breaking the ice." She disconnected the call after Bobby's 'good night.'

The silence in the room scared her. Memories poked their faces out from under the bed and the closet corner. And they were the biggest enemy of all.

Jack glared at his ringing phone. Who'd have the nerve to call at this hour? Probably one of his former teammates who'd had too much to drink. It seemed that's all he did these days: talk retired players off the ledge. Kind of ironic since he seemed so close to it himself.

Jack's eyebrows shot up as he read the caller I.D. *Carter Cunningham.* "Hello?"

The strain in Carter's voice was evident. "Jack Briggs. How are you, man?"

"Carter. What can I say? I'm so sorry about Lisa."

For a long moment, Carter didn't speak. "Lisa was coming to get an interview with you."

The blow fell like a hammer. Would she still be alive if he—? "With me? She sent me a couple of texts last weekend, but I had no idea she was coming. I would have met her at my house."

"She wanted it off the record."

Jack massaged his temples. That's what Lisa indicated in her texts. "Why? I'm retired now."

Carter sighed deeply. "Listen, Jack. Would you come to the funeral? It'd mean a lot to me."

His heart went out to the guy. Something in Carter's tone expressed the words he couldn't say. Carter had something on his mind; he wanted to talk. Jack knew Carter Cunningham by acquaintance only, and Lisa Sparks even less. Carter had done a few interviews with him through the years.

"I appreciate you asking me, Carter. I'd be honored to come. Anything else I can do?"

"We can talk when you get here."

Carter gave him an address and hung up.

Weird conversation.

He clicked off the lights, but sleep was far away.

In the morning, a headache akin to a hangover hammered on his brain. His bicep flexed as he shook the health food shaker bottle which contained three raw eggs, milk and a scoop of protein powder. Breakfast of champions.

In rare moments of sleep the night before, he'd been plagued with dreams. Dreams in which he'd seen Marcy's face, lifeless and white, instead of Lisa's.

He squeezed his eyes shut. The police dubbed it a random murder, but as he'd drifted between dreams and consciousness all night, he became acutely aware of the painful coincidence. He could not have prevented it except maybe if he'd done the interview before she'd had to hunt him down. But the question remained: who else knew she was going to be at the game?

Despite her warnings, Jack grabbed his phone and dialed Marcy's number. He couldn't get her off his mind.

"Hello?" Her voice sounded as lifeless as it had last night.

"Hey, it's Jack."

"Hey. Did you get any sleep?" She yawned.

"Not really. It was kind of hard to decompress from a day like that."

"Tell me about it." She sighed. "Listen, my in-laws are here. Could I call you later?"

"I didn't call to chat. I wondered if you planned to go to the funeral."

"Yeah, why do you ask?"

"Carter invited me. I thought we might book the same flight."

"Wow. Carter called you?" He heard hesitation. "Why don't you send me your itinerary once you've booked it?"

Didn't Marcy feel the same chemistry he did? Just the sound of her voice set his heart racing. It was the first sign of life he'd felt in over a year. "Why don't I book both flights? We can sit together."

Her silence confirmed his suspicions. She planned to shrug him off. But he wouldn't take no for an answer. "Come on. Just let me take care of it."

"You're tenacious."

"Thanks." Long dormant feeling stirred inside when she sighed.

"I can't let you book my flight, Jack. Like I told you—I'm not the woman you want."

She had no idea what he wanted. For that matter, neither did he. "I'll let you think on it. Call you later."

Their game of cat and mouse stirred adrenaline through his body. He'd take it easy for a while, let her get over the shock of the murder. But he planned on getting to know her better. Much better.

4

MARCY FOLDED THE last of the laundry on the couch, a welcome mind-numbing activity after an emotional week. The events replayed in her mind whether she liked it or not. The bloodstains were gone, but they'd left their mark. The police deemed it a random hit, but she knew better. She'd asked Lisa for help just three weeks ago.

Now she's dead.

Everywhere she went, death followed. She was as dangerous as a plague.

Something about Jack's connection with Lisa blurred the truth as well. He said he didn't know Lisa. Why would Carter invite him to the funeral? She'd known Carter for more years than she cared to count; were there things she didn't know?

After his call about booking the same flight, Jack hadn't called again. It was all for the best. If what she found in Pete's files was even a shade true, the last thing she needed was another NFL connection.

A car door slammed outside, and Brant jogged into the living room wearing his iPod earbuds like a scarf around his neck. He polished an apple on his sweatshirt. "Have you heard anything from Jack, Mom?"

"What? No, greeting for your mother?" Marcy ruffled his sandy hair.

"Hey." He smiled. "So?"

Marcy shook her head, hoping her son didn't dig deep enough to tap the longing she'd hoped to keep hidden. "He called Saturday."

"What'd you tell him?"

She held a breath and slowly released it. She frowned. "I told him I had junk in the trunk."

Brant laughed at the old joke, a tinge of sadness in his voice. Pete used that statement when a player he represented had a criminal record.

"Seriously?"

She tossed a ball of socks at him. "Not really. My first try at dating was kind of a bust, wouldn't you say?" She inspected her hands.

"It wasn't your fault. I'm sure Jack understands that."

"I'm sure he does, Honey." She wasn't about to discuss this with Brant. How could her teenage son understand the emotions that warred in her mind? "Hey, will you take your laundry up while you're here?"

Brant raised an eyebrow and shrugged. "Sure." He balanced the pile and took the stairs two at a time.

Marcy smiled. Brant was a good kid. He did the typical teenager stuff, but he had a leader's heart. Could she channel that talent alone? She'd never bargained for the single-mom gig, even if she did take the kids to church by herself most Sundays when their father was alive. When she married Pete, her commitment had been for life. But she'd made his life so miserable he'd gotten out of the contract early with sleeping pills.

Alternative music thrummed down the stairs. Brant's voice boomed over the ruckus. "Is your cell phone on silent or something?"

She checked. Sure enough, she'd forgotten to take it off silent after Bible study last night. She was getting as bad as her mother who never remembered to take her phone off vibrate. "Not anymore."

She tossed the phone onto the couch and jumped when it rang immediately.

"My boy came through for me." Her heart leapt at the sound of Jack's voice.

"What?"

"I texted Brant to see if you were purposely ignoring me or if you had phone troubles."

The sound of his voice sliced everything she'd just been thinking to ribbons. "What if it's both?"

"I'm going to pretend you never said that. Did you make your plans?"

"I fly out tomorrow."

"What time's your flight?"

She shouldered the phone and carried the laundry basket back to the laundry room. "Why do you ask?" She couldn't hide the playful tone. Her heart thumped like a giddy seventh grader's. Memories with Pete evaporated when she heard his voice.

"Thought I could pick you up in New York since I fly out tonight.

Save you a rental."

Marcy tempered her excitement with a shot of reality. Ten years of marriage taught her a thing or two about the expectations of men. "Are you sure that's not too much trouble?"

Jack exhaled. "Never. I'm staying at a hotel near the airport. What time do you get in?"

"Five-thirty." She'd handle his expectations with a cool head. Anything was better than spending another day folding laundry and making peanut butter and jelly sandwiches.

Jack cleared his throat. "How have you been coping with everything?"

She searched her hands again which were raw from washing. Should she tell him she might have played a part in Lisa's murder when she hadn't had the guts to tell the police?

"I know I sound like a paranoid freak, but the idea that it was a random murder just doesn't sit well with me."

Jack coughed. "You're not kidding. I've been thinking I should tell you that Lisa was on her way to get an interview with me. " His voice trailed off.

Marcy's heart shot into overdrive. "You mean the day of the murder?"

"She'd sent me a few texts requesting an interview earlier in the week, but I had no idea she was coming to Colorado." He paused. "Did Carter say anything about the interview?"

She chewed a fingernail. "He never said. Are you pulling a Brett Favre comeback or something?"

Jack chuckled. "Hardly. I can't imagine why she wanted an interview. My endorsement for Honda of Greeley?"

Fear and worry mingled in her heart. She couldn't bring herself to mention the eerie connection between herself and Lisa. She swallowed, but her parched throat stalled. "I don't think I can process it right now."

"Agreed. Can I meet you at the airport tomorrow, then?"

Marcy bit her lip. The offer tantalized, and it would be short lived. "I'll make you a deal."

"Shoot."

"Come to church with Carter and me on Sunday." Marcy cringed. Now, he'd show his true colors.

"It's important to you?"

"It's a big part of my life."

"Then it means a lot you'd invite me. I'm in." The tone of his voice warmed her entire body.

She bit her knuckle to stifle the surge of emotions he evoked, thankful she'd hidden in the laundry room for the conversation. "Thanks."

"What hotel are you staying at?"

"I'm staying near the church where the funeral will be held. The Garden Overlook."

"I'll have it pre-programmed into the GPS."

She ran a hand through her hair, aware of a smile so big it hurt. "Thanks, Jack. I'll text you when I get in."

"Perfect. Have a safe flight."

Her heart bounced like a basketball. How could she, stay-at-home mom, driver of the minivan and bookkeeper of Girl Scout Troop 774, keep the attention of a former NFL player? He could have any woman he wanted; why pick her? She hugged her middle. The old butterflies weren't dead, as she'd suspected. She would ride this train as long as it would go, if just to break up the monotony of life. Jack wouldn't be interested long.

After repacking her suitcase three times, Marcy managed to drop Haley off at her mom's on time. Brant still had to be dropped off at Bobby's. She'd leave news of her and Jack's little fling for Brant to blab when the two of them were alone. She eyed her son in the rearview mirror. "Did you pack your toothbrush, Brant?"

"Yes, Mom. Quit worrying. I stay with Uncle Bobby all the time."

Bobby met them in the drive. He opened the car door for Brant. "I got the new X-Box *Utility Tryst* game. Think you can best me this weekend?" He winked at Marcy.

Brant launched from the car. "Plan on having your rear kicked."

Bobby's fist connected with Brant's. What would she do without him? He'd been there for her and the kids since before Pete died. He was like a second father to Brant. She shot him her most motherly look. "Make sure he gets plenty of rest, Bobby. He's got a lot of homework." She tossed Brant's gym bag at him.

Have I ever told you that you talk like a mother?

She seared his sarcasm with a withering look. "I am one."

He patted her shoulder. "That you are, Sis. You have time for a cup of coffee?"

She checked her watch. "No. I need to get to the airport. Listen, I really appreciate you letting Brant stay with you this weekend."

"It's no problem, Marce." He put Brant in a headlock. "If he gives me any trouble, I'll have to take him out."

Brant threw a weak punch and took Bobby down at the knee. Bobby grinned as they tumbled onto the grass. Marcy rolled her eyes. Boys! "See you guys on Monday. Love you, Brant."

Brant looked up from under Bobby's armpit. "Love you too, Mom. Have a safe flight."

The long flight to New York provided ample time for nerves to twist her gut into knots. Meeting Jack was a little clandestine—exciting yet frightening. She should have told Bobby about their relationship if one could call it that. Bobby would have remembered him, and probably warned her away.

She breathed a prayer to quiet her nerves. Not only was she getting into the car with Jack, but she'd have to face Carter. Should she tell him what Lisa had been doing for her?

After clearing security, she touched up her lip gloss and reached for her phone. She tamed nervous fingers as she wrote a text to Jack.

A moment later, her phone vibrated a response. "I'm on the curb at level 6. Black Mustang."

Marcy shook her head. The guy lived like a rock star and looked like an Abercrombie and Fitch model. The old monster raised her voice. *You'll never be good enough for him.*

An airport announcement echoed off the polished floors. Marcy surveyed the exits. Since the flash mob, she'd been gun shy in large crowds, and her pulse increased as she jockeyed for position in front of an elevator. As she squeezed herself into the elevator, she prayed God grant her self-control. She knew firsthand the kind of trouble people found themselves in when emotions ran high. And if her heartbeat was any indication, emotions were already there. The last thing she needed was another bead to string on the guilt necklace she'd worn since Pete's death. Loneliness and longing clouded her judgment where Jack was concerned.

She shrugged her carry-on up onto her shoulder. Jack's charm put her on double guard. He might have been called the "Gentleman Linebacker," but she still didn't know if she could trust him off the field. She sure didn't trust the flustered twisting of her own heart as the elevator door opened on level 6.

The Sports Illustrated swimsuit issue hit the wall and fluttered to the floor. He couldn't concentrate. The knot in the pit of his stomach threatened the doughnut and coffee he'd had earlier that morning. Blasted digestive issues! He fingered the antacids in his pocket. He was sick of the chalky aftertaste and even sicker of needing them. Managing this dark part of himself wasn't easy, though he'd successfully hid it from the world so far. The good guy the world knew felt more normal, but he had an unruly conscience that often got in the way.

Lisa's funeral would be difficult, especially for Marcy. And if she put the pieces together? Her connection with Jack Briggs bugged him. Too coincidental. He'd do anything to know if they were a couple.

The funeral would be crawling with NFL players and press. She'd get comfortable with the lifestyle again, maybe ask a few questions. The years after Pete's death had kept her safely out of football. His insides writhed. She'd never hinted she knew anything, but the fire ants in his stomach refused to tame until he felt sure.

He had to do something to throw her off balance without hurting her. Prey on her fear. He'd seen every weakness and been the source of the lies she now believed. A little fear would keep her focus on something other than the connections between Lisa's murder, Jack's injuries, and her husband's career.

Jack revved the engine playfully before jumping out to assist Marcy with her luggage. She only half smiled as she waited for him on the curb. If he didn't stop this macho act, he'd scare her away. During his NFL days, he'd carefully avoided a reputation as a "play-yah," but she didn't know that. Why hide behind the bravado? There was a heart in his chest somewhere.

"Let me get that for you."

He picked up her suitcase. The cloud of diesel fuel from the hotel shuttles clogged his throat.

She ducked her head. "Thanks."

He watched her slide into the passenger seat before he closed the trunk and joined her. Dressed to the nines, she would turn every head in New York. Her hair touched her shoulders in generous dark curls. He'd never seen it loose before. His pulse purred like the engine of the car. His eyes trailed to her knees. Those jeans were man-killers if he'd ever seen any. But, even from their short acquaintance, he knew she never suspected her powers. Her beauty hinted at things deeper than physical. "The Garden Overlook, right?"

Marcy grinned. "You got it."

"Do you have plans for dinner?"

She rolled her lips between her teeth in regret. "I do. Carter's picking me up from the hotel at eight. Do you want to join us?"

Disappointment ate at him. He thought he'd get some time alone with her while they were in New York. He shrugged. It wasn't like he owned her. "I'll let you two catch up. Can I offer you a ride to the funeral tomorrow?"

She turned. "I'd like that."

He wondered if the hours until morning would pass as slowly as the hours had passed while he waited to pick her up.

After breakfast and a workout the next morning, Jack convinced himself he left early to pick up Marcy in order to avoid the New York traffic. The sunshine glinted off puddles from a passing shower that morning, reflecting a sky much too cheery for a funeral.

Jack parked his car. He checked his suit in the side mirror before entering the hotel. He hoped his slight limp would be overlooked. He'd ranked among the hardest hitting, toughest men in America; to him there was nothing more humiliating than weakness. Self-pity melted away when Marcy stepped out of the lobby elevator. Even dressed in black, the sight of her sent his blood pounding through his veins. Her dark brown hair was twisted up, revealing the curve of collar bones. The neck of her dress dipped where a string of pearls kissed her throat. Man, was he jealous of those pearls.

Jack took her hand. "You look gorgeous."

His compliment hit home, and her cheeks brightened. "Thanks."

"No evidence of vanilla today." He couldn't help caressing her with his eyes.

She tucked her hand into his offered arm. "Unless vanilla is your favorite flavor."

His eyes widened, and an electric current flashed though his body. Was she flirting with him? The pink color in her cheeks said so. Oh, today was going to be a good day. Once they got past the funeral. He led her through the lobby, not trusting himself to ask. "How is Carter holding up?"

"He's a trooper."

He opened the car door for her. "You mentioned he goes to church with you. Is that how you met?"

"We've been friends a long time. We went to college together, forever ago."

Questions burned in his mind. What kind of *friends* had they been in college? "Were you and Pete married back then?"

"Oh, no. I married Pete long after that. Carter and I were college sweethearts."

Suddenly, Carter didn't seem like such a nice guy. "Really?" He started the car and merged with traffic.

Marcy shoved his arm. "Yes, really."

He shrugged. "Well. Why didn't you marry him?"

"He never asked." She inspected her nails as if he'd inquired about the weather.

This conversation was worse than the funeral threatened to be. If Carter hadn't asked her to marry him while they were in college, he had every reason to ask now that they were both totally unattached. "Why does that leave me feeling like I should punch him?"

She laughed. "It was a long time ago."

Long time or not, there was a lengthy relationship there. Carter, schmarter. Jack exhaled. "Let's try a new subject."

"I'm trying everything I know of to avoid thinking about the funeral."

"I noticed you were a little frisky today."

"You should recognize it." She grinned.

He raised his eyebrows and exited the freeway. "What else can you expect from a guy who played a game for a living?"

"Why did you never marry?"

Good question. "I was married to the game. Didn't have time to think about marriage. Seemed like an encumbrance to me."

Marcy frowned. *Maybe Pete should have stayed single, too. If he hadn't married me, he might still be alive.* "You sound very dedicated."

Jack clutched the wheel with one hand. "When I put my heart into something, I go all the way."

"I like that about you. You're genuine."

Jack got in the valet parking line in front of the church. He turned to look at her. "I know I find you genuinely attractive."

She absorbed the compliment, a smile teasing her lips. "That's another thing I like about you."

"What?" He stopped the car in front of the valet station.

She started to slide out of the car and shot over her shoulder, "Your good taste."

His laugh echoed against the stone church building. He guided her, avoiding the barrage of media reporters that snapped pictures of them as they passed.

She clutched her purse close. "I don't suppose we can skip this part."

"Are funerals hard for you?"

Her heart ached. The only funerals she'd attended in five years were for people she'd found dead. She didn't expect Jack to share her morbid thoughts. "Yes. Do you enjoy them?"

He handed her a Kleenex. "Here you go, *Ms. Sarcastic*. Let's get this behind us."

They followed others into the church where organ music played softly. Marcy inhaled the scent of furniture polish and old carpet. The scents mingled with the sickly-sweet smell of white lilies which draped the front of the church.

Carter stood alone beside the coffin. His tortured expression seared itself on her mind. She knew that look, had felt that sorrow. She and Lisa had only spoken a few times. Where had she been spiritually? There'd been rumors of wild behavior in Lisa's past, but since she'd been with Carter, her reputation had substantially improved. Just being with Carter had improved Lisa. She'd felt the same way when they'd been together. Tears threatened and the service hadn't even begun.

Jack's solid presence was an immeasurable comfort. Halfway through the service, his arm slid around her shoulders. She sank back, allowing his touch to assuage the terrible pain in her heart. She cried for Carter, but she also cried for herself. For the love she'd sought with Pete and never found. For the ways she'd let him down. For the man beside her who could never understand.

When the funeral ended, Jack accompanied her through the receiving line. Carter's red-rimmed eyes brightened when he saw them. "Marcy." He hugged her, choking back tears. She wished she could absorb some of the hurt, but prayed God would instead. When he pulled back, he stroked a tear from her cheek with his thumb. His eyes flicked to the man standing behind her.

"Jack Briggs. Thank you for coming."

The two exchanged a handshake.

"I'm so sorry for your loss." Jack's soft tone barely reached her ears.

"Thank you." Jack's hand lingered on her back. Carter glanced between them. "Are—are you here with Marcy?" His eyes flicked to her. "How did you two meet?"

She shrugged, praying he wouldn't make a big deal. "At one of Brant's games."

"So you're here *together*?" Carter's eyebrows disappeared under his brown hair. "You forgot to mention that at dinner." Obviously, he couldn't refrain from the big brother act even at his fiancée's funeral.

Jack's hand massaged the base of her neck. "We're *together*." The warm tone of his voice and the intimate gesture made her feel like a supermodel on the runway.

Carter pinned Jack with a serious look. "Will you be here long enough to come by the house? Marcy knows where it is."

Jack nodded. "Marcy's invited me to church tomorrow. Why don't we meet for lunch?"

She marveled at Jack's easy business sense. There seemed nothing he wasn't good at.

Carter nodded his voice devoid of emotion. "Sounds good. Tomorrow then."

Carter's arms slid around her again and he kissed her cheek. His eyes said what his voice could not. She understood. He'd said last night what her presence meant to him. And there wasn't anything she wouldn't do for Carter.

Except tell him she might be responsible for Lisa's murder.

Outside, the sunshine kissed her skin with warmth, obliterating the swath of sadness that clung to her like an ugly shawl.

The media mob must have gotten a tip about a current player or other celebrity because they buzzed at a side door of the church like angry bees. At least they'd leave Jack alone. "I'm glad that's over."

He nodded and pointed to the park across the street. "Me, too." Jack jammed a fist into his palm "I didn't want to have to use my signature moves on poor Carter. You sure he doesn't still think of you as his sweetheart?"

"Stop it. If we'd wanted to fan the old flame, we would have done it years ago."

"Could have fooled me when he was wiping that tear off your cheek."

They crossed the street to a tree lined sculpture park. "I assure you, he thinks he's my big brother."

"Then I hope your mom adopts me." Jack laughed and fell into step with her on the walk.

Laughing released the tension pounding in her head. The smile felt good on her lips after fighting the emotions of the day. "What do you have planned for the rest of the day?"

"I was hoping to spend some time with you."

They stopped under a tree that had surrendered almost all its leaves to the seasonal wind. "What do you have in mind?"

The wind tossed the last leaf into the air, and it landed on her head. Before she could remove it, Jack stepped close and plucked it from her hair. She craned her neck to look him in the eye. He towered above her, his smile melting her heart like a Popsicle on a summer afternoon. His hand lingered in her hair, and his eyes caressed her face. "I hated seeing you sad today." He pressed his lips to her cheek. "But your eyes are so pretty when you cry." His lips grazed her other cheek, and her body blazed with longing. His hand slid down the back of her head, and he rubbed his thumb on her cheek.

Emotions swirled, and a tear escaped her eye. He wiped it away with his thumb as Carter had done, but Carter's touch didn't leave a trail of fire on her face. He stepped back, grabbing her hand. "Have you ever seen the Smithsonian?"

She shook her head, not trusting her voice. Her heart still pounded in her ears.

"Want to go? Let's stop by your hotel, and you can change those shoes. Then we'll have lunch and see what we can."

She found her voice. "Sounds good."

While they drove to her hotel, Jack held her hand, his thumb tracing patterns on her skin.

Gathering courage, she took a deep breath. "Why don't you come up and have a drink while I change?" She prayed he didn't think her forward.

"Sure. If you're uncomfortable having me in your room, I can wait for you in the hotel lobby."

"I think I can trust you."

He pulled into a parking spot. "*Think* being the operative word."

She shrugged. "Prove yourself worthy."

He bowed and took her arm as they walked into the hotel. Once in her room, she tossed Jack the remote. "There's some bottled water on the table by the window. Make yourself at home."

She grabbed jeans and a long sleeved T-shirt. Her favorite Converse tennis shoes weren't exactly upper west side, but they would be great for a romp through the museum. The black heels she'd worn were killing her.

In the bathroom, she touched up her make-up, thankful she'd worn waterproof mascara to the funeral. She leaned toward the mirror and pulled at the tiny wrinkles at the corners of her eyes. What could a man like Jack see in her? Pete hadn't appreciated it. She ran a brush through her hair and pulled it into a ponytail. She ran a hand along her hip. Had she gained a few too many pounds since the kids? Whatever the reason, Pete's inattention wore a hole in her heart that hadn't healed. There were days she was able to find beauty in God's faithfulness, but as she stared into the brightly lit bathroom mirror, insecurities weighed her down. While Jack's admiration awakened the woman inside, negative thoughts devoured her. She straightened and steeled her heart. His admiration wouldn't last. Pete's hadn't.

Jack was sprawled on the bed, watching TV when she came out. Like a chameleon, he could blend in everywhere.

"They have ESPN." He jumped up. "Did you bring a jacket? The wind could get up while we're walking. You don't have a curfew, do you?" He winked.

She swatted him with the jacket she'd pulled from the closet.

5

JACK ADMIRED MARCY's spirit. She could laugh despite the sorrow of the last days. If he could capture what she had, he might be able to walk away from his injury and move on. He opened the car door for her. "You ready?"

For the first time since his retirement, contentment settled into his heart. Marcy's hand in his, they strolled through the vast Smithsonian. The tension in her hand eased gradually.

Marcy clasped her hands behind her back to view a scientific exhibit. "I'm so glad God created a few of us with an imagination."

He studied her profile. She was so unlike the brazen women who'd haunted his life, hungry for a piece of the NFL action. She didn't sit in awe of his career, but respected his talent. She'd probably learned that from years as an agent's wife. A smile tugged at his lips as she marveled at each display, exclaiming over the collection of Americana with childlike admiration.

"You really haven't been here before?"

She smiled up at him. "Never. It's as wonderful as people say. Thanks for inviting me."

Jack noticed she walked nearer to him than when they'd first entered the museum. He didn't want the music of her laughter to end, but noticed she stifled a yawn. He steered her toward the exit with gentle pressure on the small of her back. Outside, Jack ordered ice cream, loudly telling the vendor, "Vanilla is definitely my favorite flavor."

She licked her cone. "Very funny."

"You don't believe me?"

She ignored him and walked under the barren trees that overhung the sidewalk. "You ready for our meeting with Carter tomorrow?"

He jumped into step with her. "He's an interesting guy. I wonder what he's gonna say?"

She took another lick of her cone. "Me, too. He didn't mention anything about it when we had dinner, and curiosity is killing me."

His heart jumped. Curiosity may have been what killed Lisa, too.

Jack paced the hotel lobby waiting for Marcy on Sunday morning. A cup of designer coffee kept his hand warm in the air conditioned lobby; they were both going to need it. He hadn't been able to sleep and called to leave a message on her phone at midnight. Shocked and pleased when she answered, they'd wasted half the night in small talk.

The thought of himself sitting next to Marcy at church almost made him laugh out loud. His experience with religion had been limited at best. He'd worshiped at a shrine all his life, but an earthly one. Still, he admired anything that took discipline, and Christianity took discipline. When that phenomenal quarterback from Florida burst onto the NFL scene, many players sneered at him, but he admired the kid for what it took to stick by his beliefs. Not everything everyone said about religion rang true for him, but he held the utmost respect for Coach Black, the defensive coordinator at USC his freshman year. He reminded his players to treat everyone with respect, on the field and off. Jack grinned. That's how he'd come by his reputation as the "Gentleman Linebacker," picking players up off the field after he'd annihilated them. Coach Black's fire for religion sounded like Marcy's. They seemed cut from the same cloth.

He swirled the last sips of coffee in his cup, considering the whole religion thing. It was weakness to look outside oneself. There was nothing higher than the goals he'd set for himself, but the passion he'd poured into the game with sweat and tears now had no outlet. His future looked bleak and uninviting, and he envied Marcy's sense of purpose in life.

The elevator door opened, and she stepped out. Marcy wore the same dress she'd worn to the funeral, but today she wore a soft wrap around her shoulders. Despite the late hours they'd spent talking, she bloomed fresh as a flower. He handed her the coffee he'd purchased. "Good morning."

She smiled and tucked a curl behind her ear. She inhaled the aroma. "Peppermint Patty Latte? How did you know this was my favorite?"

He shrugged. "Sometimes, a guy's got to study the other team's playbook." He'd texted Brant that morning.

The drive to the church took a few moments, but they arrived in plenty of time for services. She slipped her hand into the crook of his arm as they walked up the stairs of the church. "Did you go to church as a child, Jack?"

"A few times before my dad died. How about you?"

"I became a Christian when I was fourteen. It's been my whole life since."

They were greeted at the door and offered a seat, but Marcy told the greeter they'd be occupying Carter's pew.

Great, sitting with Carter. Hope he nestles down between us.

Carter hadn't arrived yet, and they continued the conversation after sitting down.

"This is where I feel at home." She smiled.

"Have you been at this church often?" Probably with Carter.

"I didn't mean the place exactly. Sundays breathe new life into me."

"Always been my favorite day of the week."

She nudged him. "There are other things to do on Sunday besides play football."

He wasn't convinced.

Carter arrived looking better than he had at the funeral, but his eyes still sported dark circles. He nodded. "Morning, Jack." He pushed past Jack's knees and sat on the other side of Marcy.

He kissed Marcy's cheek. "You look pretty this morning."

She smiled and squeezed Carter's hand. "Thanks. How are you holding up?"

Their easy conversation got to him. Real friendly. *Too friendly.*

"Last night was rough, but I'm here." Carter dragged his eyes away from Marcy's to meet Jack's. "We still meeting for lunch?"

Jack nodded. They would have lunch if he didn't slug him for snuggling up next to Marcy. If he sat any closer to her, he'd be in her lap. His thoughts were interrupted as a man approached the podium to make announcements and start the service.

A jealous rhythm drummed through his frame as he sat in the epicenter of Marcy and Carter's blended voices. Her eyes were closed, but glittering drops of tears on her lashes indicated her absorption in the singing. He'd dated women that two-timed him like a broken clock, but jealousy never fazed him. Carter he could handle, but what about God? If He took her whole heart, would there be any left for him? Something else Coach Black had taught him came to mind: the best players gave everything they had. He glanced at her. God was lucky she was on His team.

Carter chose an upscale, off-the-beaten-path, restaurant for lunch. The waiter served appetizers before Carter was ready to talk. He leaned on his elbows. "Lisa was very intent on getting that interview with you, Jack. It's the reason she was in Colorado."

He swallowed a bite of shrimp cocktail. "So you said before. I figured there was something she wanted besides an autograph."

Carter wiped his mouth on a napkin and exhaled. "Lisa knew you had your medical records sealed. She wanted to talk with you about the injury that ended your career."

"Your magazine ran an article on it when I retired. That wasn't enough?"

Carter took a sip of water. "Lisa was doing a story on great defensive players and noticed a trend of knee injuries in linebackers over the last decade. Among the players destined for the Hall Of Fame, five suffered severe or career-ending knee injuries. She planned to highlight the bodily stress put on linebackers as players in general get bigger and faster."

He massaged his bad knee while memories jumped to life. His team had a shot at their second Super Bowl win the year he was injured. Their dreams and his life blew with his knee.

"I'm not surprised other players had injuries. If you aren't willing to sacrifice everything, you're in the wrong league."

The waiter delivered their food. Carter picked up his fork. "She wanted a look at what life was like after football. You were on track to become the best run-stopper in NFL history, Jack. Your injury was a tragedy to watch."

The truth of Carter's words punched him in the gut. "Nothing could ever replace my passion for the game." He eyeballed his order, appetite gone.

Marcy's eyes said she understood. She knew what it was like to lose heart. He'd left his on the field the day of the injury.

"Lisa would have killed for that quote."

An uncomfortable silence followed the ironic statement.

Marcy patted his arm. "Have you collected enough to finish her article?"

Carter looked at Jack. "That's why I asked you to come. You were her last interview. She told me she'd saved the best for last."

He wasn't buying it. Lisa hadn't come to Colorado for a petty little interview like the one he'd described. "I'm happy to help. Just for curiosity's sake, who were the other players who suffered the same injuries?"

"Isaac Johnson. Brandon Dart. Randall McFarland. Garvis Haywood."

He knew them all. "But why the urgency?"

Carter steepled his fingers. "I think she uncovered some connection."

"And you have no idea what it is?" Was it something worth killing for?

"I was hoping you could tell me," he said. "Do you know what caused your injury?"

Caused his injury? "Football." He shrugged. "It's a tough game."

Marcy frowned and searched the restaurant with her eyes. "You think there is a connection between the injured players?" Her knee bounced under the table.

Carter's eyes sagged, and he shook his head. "I don't think so. Lisa was digging into something bigger than player injuries."

They tossed around questions over dessert and coffee, but Carter offered nothing that helped him understand why a beautiful woman was killed so violently or why she wanted an interview so badly.

Laying his fork aside, Carter turned to Marcy. "When does your flight leave? You need a ride to the airport or anything?"

She licked a bit of chocolate sauce from her spoon, a sensuous move that unraveled Jack's resolve.

"Jack and I are flying home together." She met his eyes and actually smiled. She'd been pale and closed-mouthed throughout the meal.

He stopped himself from punching the air in victory as he read disappointment on Carter's face. Carter nodded. "I know you're anxious to get home to the kids. Call me when you get in, okay?"

She stood and hugged him. "You're always in my prayers. I'll call you in a few days."

Carter followed them from the restaurant, eyes on Marcy in a very non-brother way. Jack couldn't blame him. A man would have to be blind not to notice Marcy Farris.

Later that afternoon, Jack lounged on the bed, arms behind his head, watching TV in Marcy's hotel room. Someone knocked and

Marcy answered the door. A bellman stood outside.

He handed her a single white rose with a note attached. "This came for you, Mrs. Farris."

An envious stab entered his heart; it was probably from Carter.

She closed the door and put her purse on the nightstand after tipping the bellman. She brought the flower to her nose. "Did you send this?"

He shook his head. "Believe me, if I'd thought of it, I would have." The stab of jealousy grew by the minute.

Marcy pulled the card from the paper and opened it. From his vantage point, he saw the front picture was a benign black and white photograph of kids sitting on a fence.

"It's one of those recordable cards with a personal message." She grinned and pulled the plastic flag inside, throwing a playful look at Jack.

The recording was barely audible and gravelly. "You found the body. Marcy Farris, are you sure your children are safe at home? There's a murderer in Colorado."

Her eyes met his in confusion. A crunching sound came from the recording and then a little girl's voice, "Help me! Stop it! Stop hurting me! I want Mom!"

He saw the fear pool in her eyes.

"Haley!"

Jack snatched the note from her hands. "Who sent this?"

The white rose fell to the floor, and her hands shook. "It's not signed."

He gathered her into his arms, crushing her head against his chest. She trembled against him.

"Jack. Who would send something like this?" Her voice muffled against his shirt.

He stroked her hair. "A monster."

She lifted her head and looked into his eyes. "Do you think it sounded like Haley?"

"It could have been any little girl, the recording was so poor. I used to get crap like this when I played in the league. Just idiots playing a trick on you."

"But what if it's real?"

He smoothed her hair and laid his head on hers. "If someone hurt Haley, your family would be on national news by now. Your parents would have called."

She pulled from his arms, unzipped her purse, and withdrew her cell. Her calm worried him. He would have dealt better with hysterics. His skin crawled. Someone had her hotel information and knew she'd been the one to find Lisa's body. That someone was a killer.

"Brant's not answering. I'll give my mom a call."

"Mom, it's me. Hey, is Haley doing all right? She had the sniffles when I left, and I was just checking in. Call me when you get this message." Marcy dropped the phone, and it bounced on the bed. "She didn't answer. I'll call Bobby." She dialed and put the call on speaker so Jack could hear. Bobby answered on the second ring.

"Bobby. It's Marcy. How's it going up there? Is Haley okay?"

"Haley? I guess so. She's with Mom, but I think she spent the night with someone from youth group. Heston or something?"

Her voice cracked. "Heston? Really?"

"Yeah, we all had lunch yesterday, and she mentioned it."

She chewed her fingernail. "Did Mom mention when she would be home?"

"I'll bet they already picked her up. Have you heard the weather forecast?"

Stress crinkled the corners of her eyes, and she rolled her lips between her teeth. "No. Are you getting a storm?"

"First snow of the year, and it's a doozie."

Do not panic. Her chest squeezed uncomfortably. She didn't know a family named Heston from youth group, but hadn't wanted to alarm Bobby before they knew more. Her eyes met Jack's. They mirrored the concern she felt. Was the note from the killer or someone else? Panic hit her like a tractor trailer, despite her best efforts. Lisa had been but one person on the hit list. Worse yet, did the killer have his eye on her kids? "I've got to get home. God help me get home!" The prayer felt like it hit the ceiling and bounced back in her face. "Maybe I should call the police?"

Jack rubbed her shoulder with strong fingers. "I'm pretty sure it's just a prank. Your parents would have called."

"But what if they don't know she's been taken? They think she's sleeping over at a friend's house."

In seconds, Jack's muscled arms pinned her to his chest. She leaned into him, drinking from his immovable strength. "If we head to the airport, we can get a standby flight."

She clutched the back of his shirt, so thankful he was with her. Mama bear protection instincts threatened to overwhelm her good sense. "There has to be a reason besides messing with my sanity. Someone thinks I saw something during the flash mob."

Jack massaged her shoulders deeper. The heat from his hands melted the tension and sent waves of a different nature throbbing through her stomach. He held her at arm's length. "You said earlier, this was no random murder. What made you say that?"

She shook her head. Maybe it was time she told him the truth. "I'm not sure. It just seems strange that Lisa was murdered on *that* day. There are too many connections. Pete was an NFL agent. Lisa worked for Carter, editor of *NFL Rush*. Lisa was on her way to interview you, a former player. It just seems too coincidental." She hadn't begun to touch all the connections.

"I see a connection, but not a motive. Her interview seemed benign."

"I know. I don't understand any of it." She shrugged from his embrace. "I gotta pack."

He sprang into action. "Let me help you. Then we'll stop by my place before we drive to the airport." He opened the closet and pulled a Denver Broncos nightshirt from the hanger. He held it up like he was modeling it. "Nice."

She cocked an eyebrow. "Very funny. Concentrate on packing, will you?"

"Aye-aye." He tossed the other items of clothing into the suitcase while she gathered her bathroom things.

She zipped the suitcase shut. "I think that's it."

"For such a gorgeous woman, you pack light." He wheeled her zipped suitcase to the door as her hungry heart absorbed his compliment. Had Pete ever said she was gorgeous?

She closed the door behind her, praying the glow from the compliment would propel her down the hall. Her life had turned upside down in a matter of moments. She struggled to calm her heart. Mom and Bobby wouldn't let anything happen to them. Jack was right. This was just a threat meant to frighten her. Pete had some weird clients that might pull a strange stunt like this for a headline. Her heart squeezed again. Prank or no prank: no plane could get her home fast enough.

The silence of the elevator gave her a moment to observe Jack. He still wore his suit, but he'd unbuttoned the collar revealing a subtle hint of his dedication to the gym. As if she needed another reminder of how good looking he was. Maybe it was the pull of the elevator that made her a little dizzy. She glanced at him again. Maybe not. Heat climbed into her cheeks as she observed them as an outsider would; a couple leaving the hotel together. A grin teased her lips. What would Mother say?

Forgotten rebellion kicked in. Didn't she deserve a little adventure now and then? She wasn't married any longer, and Jack had been nothing but a gentleman. She'd spent too much time worrying about what other people thought—what Pete thought.

After she returned her key, Jack followed her out to the car, pulling her suitcase. "Who's Bobby?"

"Oh, I thought you knew. Bobby is Pete's younger brother. Bobby Farris."

"The trainer?"

"Football runs deep in the Farris family."

He opened the trunk and slung her suitcase in. "Obviously."

Thirty minutes later, they pulled up in front of Jack's downtown hotel. High-rise buildings flanked the striped gold and yellow awning at the sidewalk. "Why don't you wait here? I'll go check out and grab my bags."

"Okay. If you're sure you can trust me with this car." The separation would give her a moment to collect her thoughts. It wasn't unusual for Haley to spend the night at a friend's house when she stayed with Pete's parents. Maybe Bobby had gotten the name wrong. There was a new girl at church. Maybe Haley had gone to stay with Hollis Weston. She smiled. That's it. Weston, not Heston. Her pulse relaxed. Everything had an explanation. Pete's mom never, ever answered her cell phone. It was either charging at home near her nightstand or was buried in her purse. Either way, the people responsible for Haley and Brant would never let anything happen to them. She surrendered to God. The peace she prayed for melted over her like the sunshine outside. Why did she ever doubt Christ was beside her? Everything would be okay if she could get home today.

Moments later, the revolving door of the hotel revealed Jack, dressed in jeans, checking out at the counter. The woman waiting on him laughed and touched her hair. Marcy smiled. That man inspired admiration wherever he went, the same feelings and longing he inspired in her. The thought frightened and excited her, but, she knew how it was with NFL players. Women queued up outside their hotel rooms, hoping for an invitation inside. Her gut rolled. He probably had a very colorful past. Could her broken heart handle something like that if their relationship progressed? She didn't want ghosts of the past haunting their relationship. A bitter laugh bubbled in her throat. Who was she kidding? If anyone had a ghost, she did.

Jack strode to the car. "You ready?"

She twisted her hands together. "I won't feel comfortable until I know the kids are safe. Judy still hasn't returned my call." For the sake of her sanity, she dared not open the card and listen to the message again. Her heart couldn't bear it.

The traffic in downtown was miserable. Jack inched out front. Taillights stretched for miles. She calmed her nerves with a breath. "I could never live here."

He glanced at her. "No? You don't see yourself hailing a cab and eating dinner no earlier than eight p.m.?"

"I was raised in Colorado. I thought I-25 was bad!"

"This is a good day, actually. It will clear up in a few minutes."

She gasped. "I should call Carter." She pulled her phone from her purse again. "What should I tell him?" His protective nature wouldn't take the news well. He doted on the kids.

"Tell him you're dating someone else and to move on."

She shook her head. "Seriously! Should I tell him what happened?"

"Will it upset him?"

"I'm not sure. After the murder and the funeral, I wonder how much he can take."

Jack maneuvered into a lane with moving traffic. "What can he do anyway? You didn't even want to alarm your brother-in-law."

She plopped her purse onto the floor of the car. Carter could do nothing. "You're right. What he doesn't know won't hurt him."

Jack grinned over at her and grabbed her hand. "What did Carter do before he became the editor of *NFL Rush*?"

She bit her lip in sweet frustration. The chemistry between them boiled under their benign conversation. "Carter? He was a trainer, like Bobby."

6

WIND WHIPPED HIS hair as Jack dropped off the rental car and helped Marcy jump into the airport shuttle. The driver, sporting a company polo shirt with a huge coffee stain, took their bags. Jack settled down beside Marcy and noticed she twisted the strap of her purse in her hands. "We'll be there in six hours. I'm sure they're fine."

Her eyes sought his. "What would I do if something happened to them?" She chewed her lip.

Jack scrambled for comforting words. His own doubts surfaced, but he shoved them away for her sake. "It was just a threat. We don't know who sent it."

"Have you ever had one of those dreams where you're trying to get somewhere, but it feels like you're running underwater?"

The feeling was uncomfortably familiar. He sighed and grabbed her hand in a gesture of comfort as much for himself as for her. He knew, all right.

The shuttle jolted to a stop and moments later they joined the herd pushing toward the elevators. Jack pressed to the back of the elevator, and Marcy followed with her rolling suitcase. Marcy stepped back against him to get out of the way of a woman with a stroller.

The scent of Marcy's perfume lit a fire in his veins. Abandoning inhibitions, he pulled her close. The moment her body pressed against his he realized his mistake. He didn't want to let go. The gentle curve of her form fit perfectly against his chest. He wanted to protect her from everything. She relaxed against him, accelerating his pulse and sending blood throbbing in his temples. He held back, knowing the elevator was hardly the place to make a move.

The five-story ride dissolved in seconds. Too soon, the crowd pushed out of the elevator and reluctantly, he released her. She didn't meet his eyes, but he caught a blush on her cheeks as she rolled her suitcase from the elevator.

They approached the ticket counter. "Let's see what flights are available."

He left her in line to grab some coffee and joined her as she reached the ticket counter. He felt her rigidity and predicted a bad outcome. "When will you have another flight available?"

The airline clerk checked the screen. "I'm sorry. All flights in and out of Denver have been delayed or canceled."

Her body went rigid beside him. Jack leaned onto the counter next to her and handed her a cup of coffee.

"Why? What about flights to Colorado Springs?" Marcy's eyebrows knit in frustration as she met his gaze. The clerk checked the screen again. "I'm sorry, there is nothing flying within 100 miles of Denver today. The weather conditions are too bad."

Marcy ran a hand through her bangs and sighed. She looked at him and shrugged. "Have you heard the forecast?"

He nodded. "I just saw it on the Jumbotron outside Starbucks. Denver's got seventeen inches and at least twenty more are expected before the storm is over. I-25 is closed at 104th Avenue. Bobby wasn't kidding."

Marcy turned to the clerk. "Thanks for the information. I'll come back later and see if anything's changed."

She took a sip of coffee before she found a chair and slumped into it. Jack folded his legs underneath him and sat beside her. Whoever designed the waiting chairs in every airport should be shot. The northern Colorado storm was predicted to last another three days. They wouldn't get a flight after that for maybe another twenty-four hours while everything got moving again.

He glanced at her. A tear escaped and she wiped it off her cheek before turning to him with a sheepish grin. She sniffled. "I know I'm being ridiculous, but I gotta get home to my kids."

He put an arm around her shoulder and drew her close. "You're not being ridiculous. You're their mother."

She leaned her head against his shoulder. "What are we going to do?"

She jumped when her cell phone rang. "Judy?"

He couldn't hear the conversation, but worry crept into Marcy's voice before she finished the call.

"It was Pete's dad. He said they dropped Haley off at the skating rink at eleven. They'll pick her up at four." Another tear slipped, but it streaked down her cheek, unchecked.

His mind raced; they needed a game plan. The more time he spent with her, the more committed he'd become to helping her. He strolled to the departure board. As predicted, several flights to Denver and surrounding areas were canceled. Albuquerque jumped off the screen. He pulled out his phone.

She stood next to him and swirled the last of the coffee in the cup. "What are you doing?"

He pulled up the Internet. "Checking to see which way the storm is tracking."

"And?"

"Looks like it's heading north to Wyoming." He held her gaze. "Let's catch the standby to Albuquerque and rent a car and drive in. We'd beat the airlines by twenty-four hours at least."

Her eyes lit up. "Anything would be better than sitting in the airport for days. At least I'd feel like I was getting closer. I think I'll go crazy if I stay here."

"You sure you can stand being in the car with me for ten hours?"

She leaned over to kiss his cheek. "Thank you."

His heart beat like he'd just run the 50-yard dash. He held out a hand to assist her up. "Someone's got to make sure you stay awake."

They stepped onto the people mover. "And what if you fall asleep?"

No chance of that. The adrenaline produced by confinement in the car with her would be enough to keep him awake for weeks. "I think I can manage."

Marcy watched Jack return from the ticket counter. A girl could get used to that boyish grin.

"I think everyone else is headed to the same place. Got us booked, though."

Her heart plummeted. More waiting. "How long?"

He steered her through the airport. "It'll be a while, but we'll be waiting in style."

"At the airport?"

He pulled her along. "You question me?"

She cocked her head. "Never."

He paused outside the glass doors of an upscale airport lounge. "Pulled a few strings. We can wait here until our flight."

He'd thought of everything. It had been a long time since she'd had someone take care of her. Other passengers came in behind them, and she rolled her suitcase near the wall to get out of the way. They were shielded, for the moment, by the narrow wall that divided the lounge from the kitchen. Leather chairs clustered into conversation stations clustered around a well-stocked beverage and snack bar welcomed marooned passengers. And she'd imagined them crammed into vinyl seats in the main waiting area. She leaned into the strength of his shoulder for a moment, and Jack dropped his bag at her feet. His eyes sought hers as his hand landed on the wall next to her head. The masculine scent of his cologne made her pulse skip.

"It's about time someone took care of you."

She shrank back against the wall, but he shortened the distance between them by leaning on his elbow. Her stomach rolled in sweet anticipation. The heavy black lashes of his green eyes couldn't hide the desire in his gaze. Her emotions teetered close to the edge already and a kiss from Jack would melt her into a puddle on the ground. "I've never flown standby before, but I sure didn't expect this place." How lame she sounded, even to herself.

His head hovered inches from her own, and his eyes caressed her lips. "Woman, you're going to drive me crazy."

Her arms itched to wrap themselves around his neck, but she held her breath, ready to melt into his kiss when he offered it. Instead, he stood, flashing white teeth and a dimpled grin that made her knees go weak. "The closest games are the most fun to win."

He winked and stepped back. "Did I see Cheetos on the counter? I won't make it through the night without Cheetos." Behind the desire in his eyes, a challenge danced. He'd hooked her and she prayed there would be a next time.

He strode to the snack bar while she regained her balance. Regret teased her heart. She could almost taste that kiss. If she'd learned anything from Pete's death, it was to seize the moment. So much for that.

While Marcy chose a snack, Jack excused himself and plunged into the men's room. His pulse still raced, even though he never missed a cardio workout. He washed his hands and dried them on a rolled towel from a basket on the counter. It had taken everything he had not to kiss her, but, he hadn't earned the reputation of 'Gentleman Linebacker' for nothing. He wasn't going to kiss her again until she begged him. Maybe he wasn't a gentleman, but a scoundrel. The thought had him grinning.

When he returned, he found her curled up in a chair with a magazine, dark eyelashes splayed on her cheeks. She looked up and smiled as he approached. He was a goner.

He popped open his bag of Cheetos and munched one while she returned to her magazine. He wished the murder case was as easy to open. The conversation with Carter really frustrated him. There were things he wasn't saying. Because Marcy was there? An article about injured linebackers wasn't front page news, though it hit close to home for him. Injured players. Not really motive for murder. But, if not the other injured players, what was the connection? One thing was certain, Marcy was involved up to her eyeballs, if she didn't know it yet. Someone was out to get her and time was running out. His stomach twisted when he thought of all she'd been through. Her husband's suicide. Lisa's murder. His fist shook. No one was going to cause her harm if he had anything to say about it.

He grabbed a water bottle for himself and Marcy. Whoever it was and whatever his motives, they'd threatened Marcy today. His protective instincts heated up. A killer threatened her and her kids—he would do everything in his power to stop it. In so many ways football was so much simpler than life. On the field, he saw the threat and crushed it. Things got complicated when he couldn't identify the obstacle.

Football fueled his sense of justice in this case, but the game hadn't been fair to him. He'd given it everything he had. Practices in the rain, when he couldn't see his opponent until he loomed inches away. Early morning workouts charged by strong coffee. The soreness and bruises after a game. Sometimes, he couldn't get out of bed on Monday morning. Most years, he hadn't experienced a pain-free day until well after the season ended.

The sacrifice.

He'd lived on the game-inspired adrenaline for years. It filled the void when he and Francine went their separate ways after his junior year at USC. How long had it been since he'd thought of her?

His hands still remembered the leather grip of the ball when he'd caught an interception in the red zone. He'd never forget the thrill of the hunt when he saw the next move in a running back's eyes. His Super Bowl ring proved the sacrifice had been worth it.

But emptiness yawned inside.

The rush was over. A cloud of depression blackened his life. A Super Bowl ring couldn't fill the void. He'd given everything to a game that gave him nothing in return. Maybe Marcy's husband, Pete had it right. Go out in a blaze of glory. There were few distinctions in life, few reasons to carry on.

After football, there was nothing.

Marcy sighed. She crossed her legs and circled her foot nervously before looking up at him, worry in her eyes. She reached for another magazine and tucked a strand of hair behind her ear. Could the love of a woman like Marcy fill the void in his heart? Renew his zeal for life? He detected untapped passion under her mother-of-the-year persona. If he tapped it, the fire could sustain him through the empty months ahead. He'd seen glimpses of the flame when she looked at him, felt it in her touch. Unquenchable. The thought drove the air from his throat. He suspected her love, in all its tantalizing shapes and forms, would save him from the demons that pursued him. A salvation of sorts.

7

MARCY STRETCHED AND stifled a yawn as she worked the kinks from her neck. She checked her watch. She'd been dozing an hour and felt she could sleep forever. Jack's cell phone ring tone brought a groggy grin to her face. The USC Trojans fight song.

"Sorry," he mouthed.

She sat close enough to hear the conversation. If he wanted privacy, he'd have to get up.

"Hello?" He lowered his voice.

"Jack, it's Greg."

"What'd you find out?" Jack eyed her from the corner of his vision.

Her mind snapped to attention as she strained to hear the caller's voice.

"There wasn't anyone watching her house, but someone could have been there. The back door was ajar."

Jack glanced at her; a frown split his features. "Did you have a look around?"

"I peeked inside, but everything looked in order. I made sure the door was locked when I left. Glad I went when I did. We're practically snowed in. Probably won't have phone service much longer."

"Thanks, Greg. I owe you one."

"An autographed number 44 jersey will do."

Jack laughed. "You want another one?"

"The missus stole mine and sleeps in the thing!"

Jack looked at her and shrugged. "I know another woman who sleeps in NFL wear. I'll bring it over when things settle down. Thanks again, man."

"Sure thing. They're saying this is a storm for the record books."

He grinned as he ended the call. The man must take pride in embarrassing her.

She ignored him. "Who was that?"

"While you were sleeping, I called my buddy, Greg. He's with the Larimer County Sheriff's office. He offered to check your house before he started his shift today."

The words sank in. They'd been talking about *her* house, her back door. Had she made sure the door was closed?

Or had someone been inside?

Her palms moistened. She'd opened a can of worms the day she'd looked into that file in Pete's office. Now, a killer knew her every move.

The terror of finding Lisa after the flash mob crashed over her again and nausea sloshed in her stomach. Her heart felt like it would explode with pain. Something was very, very wrong, and she was incapable of intervention.

She leaned against the headrest and covered her eyes. "Lord, keep my babies safe."

"Marcy, you okay?"

She hadn't realized she was holding her breath. She clawed at her throat. "I feel so helpless."

Jack's brow knit in worry, and she forced herself to attempt to breathe more normally.

"Could Brant have left the door open by mistake?"

She raked a hand through her hair. "It's possible. The back door sticks."

"Greg said everything looked fine, so maybe it's just a coincidence."

"Lisa is murdered at Brant's game, and then my children are threatened while I'm gone? I don't see a coincidence." What hornet's nest had Lisa kicked? Pete's enemies? "I can't seem to do anything right. I've abandoned my kids. I left them alone." She clutched her stomach. "Everyone I love ends up dead." The truth sobered her.

Jack stood in front of her and grabbed her hands. "Come here."

She obeyed his command, allowing him to pull her to her feet. She fell against his chest and felt his arms encircle her.

"The kids are safe with Judy and Bobby. When we get home, we'll find out who sent the note." His muscles tensed. "I'll find out who sent it."

The beat of his heart, solid and strong, calmed her fears. What good would it do to go to pieces? She swallowed. Did she trust God with her kids? Really trust him?

She didn't know.

How could she trust God with the ones she loved when she couldn't trust herself? Hadn't she fought for her marriage, prayed that Pete would turn his heart back to her, if not to God?

She clung fiercely to Jack. A promise from the Psalms came to mind. *He is an ever present help in times of trouble.* She couldn't change one moment of the past. Couldn't change the future.

Couldn't save her kids from a murderer.

She understood the peaks and valleys of the Christian walk better than most women, and she could fake it until she found her rock again. The old adage her mother passed along would do the trick: act your way into feeling.

Jack wrapped his arms tighter about her shoulders. She looked him in the eye. "I'm forgetting who I trust to care for my kids. When they were born, I placed them in God's care. After Pete's death, I thought I could do it alone." She shrugged. "Maybe I thought I *had* to do it alone. I just need to put them back in his hands."

He shook his head, even if he didn't understand. His eyes blazed with emotion. "I promise you, those kids are safe."

He made promises he couldn't keep, but they comforted her. "Let's head to the gate."

Jack shoved Marcy's bag into the overhead bin and sat down behind her. *On the flight at last.* He stretched his back muscles and checked his watch. At this rate, they would need more caffeine. The muscles in his jaw tightened. If he ever found out who'd sent that note, there would be no unbroken bones in his body. Marcy was strong, but not invincible.

Her warm hand caressed his arm. "You getting tired?"

He stifled a yawn. "I think I can go another couple of hours. How are you holding up?"

"I'm okay. I'm glad we're on the way to New Mexico." She twisted the air nozzle overhead. "I was thinking about what your friend said about cell service in town. I'll bet that's why I haven't heard from the kids yet."

He took her hand. "They're probably drinking hot cocoa, waiting for the announcement that school is closed tomorrow."

She squeezed his fingers. "You're right."

The flight attendant gave the crash instructions and he leaned closer.

"Will they close your work, too?"

She fiddled with the window shade, even though it was dark outside. "I haven't worked since the kids were born. Sometimes I clean Bobby's house when he's on the road, but I don't work a full-time job."

"How do you support the kids?" The question popped out before he could check it.

The lights flickered off and on as they prepared for takeoff. "Pete had good life insurance, so I've basically been living on that. I got some money from the sale of our old house, too."

"Don't you want a career?" Something more than he had?

"I have a teaching degree, but I've always wanted to be there for the kids. It's bad enough that they don't have their father anymore. I can work when they move out."

"And you find this fulfilling?"

"Nothing more satisfying than cleaning toilets and doing laundry. Didn't you know that?"

He laughed. "I guess that's what I've been missing."

The plane started on the runway. "The truth is, it's not always fulfilling. When the kids were little, I took pride in those domestic duties, but sheer determination is all that keeps me going these days. When Haley comes home from school, I want to be the first to hear about her day. When Brant asks a girl to the prom, I want to be home to offer an opinion he probably won't take."

The world looked different through her eyes. "You have a point. My own childhood might have been different if someone had been home to meet me after school."

"Your mom?"

"Never missed a day at the office. She retired three years ago."

He'd known women who were more vicious in the office than he'd been on the field. Marcy didn't exactly love her duties as a stay-at-home mom but sacrificed for her kids.

"I can't wait to get to know those kids better."

When had he stopped thinking of them as baggage? Since about two minutes after meeting them and their lovely mom.

"Haley talked about you for two days after we met at Brant's game. And you know how he feels about you. Total hero worship."

"It's a blast to help him. When I talk football, I feel alive again."

"You don't always feel that way?"

She trod close to the wound. "It's hard to find life after football."

In the darkness, he sensed her nod.

"You've done pretty well for yourself. Stayed out of the headlines and out of jail." Her teasing brought a smile to his lips.

"There's a first time for everything."

"Stop." she shoved his shoulder. "You're a good man, Jack. You've done more for me than anyone has in a long time."

He stroked her hand. "I'd do a lot more if you'd let me." He hoped the duplicity of meaning in his words hit home. He yearned to offer her his strength as much as he ached to kiss her. He'd never been so lost to a woman before.

"I'm a widow. Things on this side look so skewed sometimes. I'm not sure my heart knows how to function properly anymore."

"I think people call that a broken heart." He intended to fix that, once he'd helped her through this crisis. Her love promised to fill the frightening emptiness. She didn't know he needed her more than she needed him.

"Maybe. But my marriage wasn't all that great. I've always felt kind of guilty about it not being broken enough."

A flight attendant brought them both a pillow and blanket. The low lights of the night flight forced their voices to a whisper. "What do you mean?"

"Pete was so wrapped up in his work. We'd grown apart in the last few years."

He heard the pain in her voice. "Was he unfaithful?" Silently, he thanked the darkness that allowed them this freedom of conversation.

"I'm not sure. Maybe physically." Tension reverberated from her.

He contemplated the meaning of her words. "Not emotionally?"

"I never captured his attention. He was a brilliant agent, as you know. I couldn't compete with the glittering world of the NFL."

Pete Farris was an idiot. "If it's any consolation, I think that's what I like most about you."

"What?"

He wished he could see her face. "You aren't a glittering piece of the NFL. Something sets you apart from all the women I've ever known. You're an original."

"If that's a compliment, thank you."

"You had my attention from the first moment."

She didn't answer, and the darkness didn't reveal her face for him to read.

Finally, her voice broke in emotion. "It's nice to be noticed."

He covered her with the thin blanket and slid the pillow under her head. They'd slept three hours in the last forty-eight. Maybe they'd get an hour or two of sleep before they arrived in New Mexico.

A single fixture over the washing machine at the foot of the basement stairs provided just enough light to mix the drugs. The washer thrummed on the rinse cycle, vibrating the vials like he would have in a laboratory. The clear compounds reflected the light from the bulb overhead.

He'd come upon the mixture by accident; his undergrad degree in chemistry didn't hurt. Properly injected into the tissues surrounding a large joint such as the knee, the drug temporarily weakened the muscles to the point that when stressed, they completely gave out. This phenomenon might not hurt the average person, but the extreme torque a player put on the injected joint yielded results that were almost always catastrophic.

He grinned. Much as his conscience riddled him at times, it got easier and more satisfying every time. They didn't deserve the worship of the fans any more than he did. Kind of did his heart good to see them go down.

The player was a rookie out of Stanford. It settled his stomach to know it wasn't a notable player this time. There were too many big names like Jack Briggs on his list of injured players.

His hand trembled as he dropped the proper amount of saline into the measuring beaker.

A quick glance at the collection photographs of Lisa brought a smile to his lips. He'd been conversing with her image a lot lately.

"A precise mixture isn't just practical, it's necessary for success." He held the solution to eye level. "If the solution were diluted by a few drops, it would not be potent enough to do the damage I've been paid to inflict." The basement stairs shimmied as the washer changed cycles.

He cursed the small work area and paused, careful not to leave a spot on his expensive sweater. "You thought you had figured it out, didn't you?" He toasted her with the vial.

Emptiness echoed through the unfinished basement. Memories as dirty as the clothes in the machine churned in his mind. Truth was he missed her smile and snarky comments. The ulcers in his stomach burned again. Proof he still had a conscience, though it did him no good. Their complicated relationship had ended when she'd found him out.

He'd learned early on to play the game to win—Lisa's murder being a move he'd calculated. Gambling fueled his business, and it paid him well, even if he never played the stakes. The odds were better in his favor from where he controlled a little more of the game.

He dropped the pre-measured tincture into the cup and let the washer cycle vibrations do the mixing. Marcy had probably gotten his gift by now and was churning away with anxiety. He imagined her terror and guilt burned in his gut. He cringed. The darkness seemed to win more often these days, and it frightened him. Oh well. He hadn't hurt her, and she was way too uptight anyway. Always had been.

8

THE MUSCLES IN Marcy's neck screamed, and she would have killed for a toothbrush, but her toiletries were snugly zipped into her suitcase in the overhead bin. The fasten seat belts bell sounded, and her heart jumped like a racehorse at the starting gate. She praised God as the wheels of the plane touched down at the Albuquerque airport, bringing them miles closer to the kids.

Jack must have sensed her urgency, because he stood and unlocked the overhead bin the moment the plane stopped. Fatigue showed in his features as he handed her the suitcase.

"What time is it?"

"In New Mexico? I think about one a.m. You hanging in there?"

She nodded and followed him down the aisle. Hopefully, the weatherman was right, and the storm wouldn't impede their journey. She dared not call home at this hour.

The well-lit terminal gave no indication of the day or hour except there were no passengers clogging the byways. "This is the way to travel."

Jack looked around. "Tell me about it. But, I understand the meaning of red-eye flight better now." He scrubbed his eyes, and they strolled in the direction of the signs that read Rentals.

Dull thoughts dragged through her brain, and she prayed they'd find their second wind somewhere between here and Denver; at this rate, they wouldn't make it. His hand rested on the small of her back, and he pointed to the rental car directional sign. "This way."

A yawn threatened as she followed him down the escalator.

In ten minutes time, they'd been assigned one of the nondescript rentals in the dark parking lot. Jack's step lagged. "Want me to drive? You look beat."

He tossed her the keys. "Is it safe?"

"Just don't give me a reason to be distracted." She unlocked the door and slid into the driver's seat. Jack tossed their suitcases into the back seat of the SUV.

She started the engine and pulled out of the lot. "If you fall asleep, I'm in for it. So, tell me about your college days." Marcy leaned back into the seat, but her eyes threatened to close so she pushed herself straight. A deep breath pushed sleepiness away. Strange to think of the blizzard raging at home in Colorado while the roads here were dry. Clear New Mexico skies contrasted the storm in her heart. Feelings for Jack and worry for the kids tumbled against each other like the hot and cold air of a sudden thunderstorm.

His voice shook her reverie. "There isn't much to tell. You know I hail from the great USC."

"The ringtone kind of gave it away. Besides, I remember hearing your alma mater somewhere."

"My college days played pretty much like my pro days. I did whatever I had to do to play the game. In college, it meant keeping my grades up. In the pros, it meant keeping my body at peak performance."

"Girlfriends? Dates?"

He shook his head. "I was pretty fastidious about my choices in those days. Anyone waving a foam finger and wearing a skirt would do." He glanced over and winked.

She knew the type. While she'd been changing diapers, he'd been out chasing women. How could she reconcile his past with hers? Oil and water.

Sensing her annoyance, he elbowed her. "Don't get your skirt in a bunch, I'm just kidding. Truth is, I rarely had time for dating. I lived and breathed football, which wasn't very attractive beyond the surface."

She swallowed the bitterness. Fatigue made her testy. Pete followed players' careers like ants follow honey, and she knew most of what he had and hadn't accomplished through the years. "You were on the cover of Sports Illustrated three times. I imagine the fan club is still in existence."

"Fan clubs are for current players. Mine has taken quite a nosedive."

Talking kept her sharp. "You're pretty nervous in public for a guy who nursed a fan club. I remember some pretty charismatic interviews through the years." She'd remember those eyes forever.

"The last year I played, before the injury, an elderly woman who'd brought her grandson for an autograph was mobbed by fans. She broke her hip in the fall and eventually died."

"You knew her?"

"No. But I found out her name and visited her in the hospital a time or two. Should have done more."

Not the whole truth, but she'd take it. The juxtaposition of values in his life threw her. He was the Gentleman Linebacker, the one who would pick players up off the field while reminding them he'd be back for more. He visited little old ladies, never married and had little faith in anything but the game of football. What kind of life was that?

"Do you have any regrets?"

"From my career? None."

His answer lacked that genuine ring. He was successful, was touted as a shoo-in for the Hall of Fame, immeasurably handsome—her heart jumped—and probably lived in a luxury home in the foothills. The only thing he lacked was a God to thank for all his blessings. Her shoulders drooped. Their differences were great.

His voice cut into her thoughts. "Did you ever think to call the florist and ask who'd sent the flower and the note?"

She raised her eyebrows. "I thought I had mentioned it. The desk clerk at the hotel didn't know how it had been delivered. It had my name on the card—that's all he knew."

"Too bad."

Dryness scratched her throat. The car moved at a snail's pace while her babies could be in the hands of a madman. She blinked hard. Keep pushing forward. Nothing but time would answer the worry in her heart.

Static irritated on the radio as she fumbled with the dial. Eventually, she found a Colorado channel. Power lines were down everywhere in northern Colorado. The north-tracking storm hit the front range hard, especially Loveland and Fort Collins. Last report there was 26 inches.

Jack grabbed her hand. "This storm might be a blessing in disguise. How could someone get to the kids in that weather?"

"What if he got to them before it started snowing?" Her eyes burned, but adrenaline kept her awake. *Cool it.* Worry wouldn't get them home any faster, even if there were a murderer in town. "Did your friend from the sheriff's office say anything about the murder?"

"I wasn't sure I should mention the connection. I get pretty sketchy about giving details. Something I learned in the NFL."

"You're not kidding." When Pete died from an intentional overdose of drugs, the whole world suggested it was his job that pushed him over the edge, but she knew the truth. It was her. She didn't make the grade. She didn't dress like the NFL wives, didn't have her toes polished at the salon, and she'd nagged like the proverbial dripping faucet. Drip. Drip. Drip. *Could you come home and spend some time with the kids? How about joining us at church? Would you like to lead the prayer, honey?*

She'd been reticent to approach Jack with her faith because of that reason. Pete had become a Christian shortly after they started dating, and she'd never questioned his sincerity, but once they were married, he'd given it up for more important pursuits. At least they'd been important to *him*. Hadn't she prayed for a spiritual leader in her home? Asked God to change him?

But he'd rejected God and finally rejected her.

Jack didn't know he was stepping into a minefield. Her insecurities and desires could blow at any second, especially under the current pressure.

Jack yawned, and she patted his knee. "Feel free to go to sleep. I'm good for a few hours."

"You sure?" He punched his sweatshirt into a ball and tucked it under his head. "I can't keep my eyes open."

"No problem. When you've had some rest, you can drive."

Jack's breathing steadied as he fell asleep. An hour trudged by, and headlights slashed her retinas, but she knew she wasn't going to make it. Driving drowsy was as dangerous as driving drunk.

Hotel signs reached up like hands on the roadside, each one crying, "Choose me, free breakfast. Pick me, in-room Wi-Fi." Her eyes crossed, and she fought to keep them open. If the radio were correct, they'd get stopped near Colorado Springs anyway. A few hours sleep would do them both a world of good.

Gravel popped under the tires as she pulled under the portico at the Holiday Inn. It wasn't the swanky digs Jack was used to, but it looked recently remodeled, at least, and boasted a hot breakfast. About time they had a hot meal.

Jack didn't move when she stopped the car, so she slipped out quietly.

Inside, the lights cruelly mimicked daytime. A fountain behind the check-in desk mocked her with its carefree bubbling. "I need two rooms for the night."

Cigarette smoke lingered on the clerk's uniform, and Marcy deduced she'd just returned from break.

"We're very full tonight, and I just came on shift. Let me see what I can find."

"Sure." The scent of chlorine drifted into the lobby from the pool she glimpsed through glass doors.

"I've got one room."

That would go over well with Mother. "Are you sure you don't have anything else?"

"Yes, ma'am."

The idea tickled her fancy for a moment. She'd slept alone too long. "Guess we'll drive down the road and see what they've got."

"I'm not sure you'll find much. We are hosting a large convention, and I'm guessing we've got one of a few rooms this close to the highway. If you want two rooms, head twenty miles east into town."

They needed to get on the road in a couple of hours, and each minute was precious.

"The room has a king-sized bed."

Perfect. A frown pinched her already throbbing head. The last thing they needed was an endless quest for lodgings tonight.

"Can I get a roll away bed in there?" She was a grown woman. She could handle this.

The keyboard clicked as she checked availability. "Sure. I can have it brought up in a few moments."

She slapped a Discover card on the counter. If she weren't so tired, she would have enjoyed telling Jack, but resisted the temptation, dead tired as they were.

A smile tilted her lips as she strode to the car. The scenario struck her funny bone.

He lifted his head. "Hey, did they have a couple of rooms?"

"Got us the honeymoon suite." She grinned at him.

"I wish." He stretched and pulled himself from the vehicle. "A couple hours of sleep is a good idea."

"My eyes got so heavy, I couldn't keep them open. Besides, I heard on the radio that I-25 is still closed. If we get there too early, it won't matter anyway." The handle of her suitcase clicked into position. "Here's your key. I'll follow you."

The secret almost bubbled out, but she enjoyed it while it lasted.

Jack looked at the card. "Fourth floor?"

She nodded and pointed to the brass and glass elevator flanked with greenery. He punched the button and slumped against her while they waited.

His nearness intoxicated her and complicated an already complicated situation. "You've been such a gentleman on this trip, Jack. Thanks for everything." His hand slid onto her waist and sent shivers through her abdomen. She stepped closer and tipped her chin to look in his eyes, conscious that they were playing with emotions which could easily be walking the plank to her death.

He swept the scene for onlookers and pulled her closer. His lips met hers in a kiss lazy with fatigue until she tasted cinnamon gum and Chapstick and responded by pulling his head closer.

Heat poured over her body like molten lava. Years of dampened desire beat against the walls of her heart as her hands slid up his chest and grasped the fabric of his shirt. The telescopic handle of her suitcase made a metallic click as it left her grasp.

His muscles tightened as he pulled her close. Worries tried to break through but finally gave up, and she focused on the pleasurable sensations zinging through her veins as he kissed her.

Jack was *dangerous*. And she liked it.

Then she remembered the sleeping arrangements. Her eyes flew open, and she wrenched herself from his arms.

Had she been tired a moment ago? She'd never sleep again.

He ran his fingers down her arm and stopped at her hand. He brought the palm of her hand to his lips and kissed it.

The elevator opened like a lion's mouth and they walked in together.

9

A SWEET AND strange tension rode up the elevator with them. Marcy's heartbeat refused to return to normal, and she grinned at him like a drunken idiot. A moment was all she needed to put priorities into place. But she didn't regret the kiss. Not for a second.

Jack was unusually quiet as he followed her down the hall. She prayed he wasn't having second thoughts about the kiss. He was probably even more fatigued than she was, subsisting on Diet Coke and Cheetos.

He stepped in front of her and opened his hand. "Let me get your door for you. I'll head to my room in a minute."

She smiled and handed him her room key and pointed to the door. "Thanks."

Jack held the door as she stepped inside. A mound of tasteful pillows graced the king-sized bed in an alcove off the main room. The pleasing green and gold filigree of the carpet led her eyes around the room. Double doors opened to the bathroom where granite counter tops gleamed. Opposite the bed, a mini fridge, two-burner stove and cherry cabinets welcomed guests to cook a light meal.

The door closed behind him. "Took the big room for yourself, eh?"

A crooked smile split her lips, and she shrugged. "They only had one room."

His eyes widened, and his eyebrows crawled beneath the curly lock of hair that hung on his forehead. He shook his head as a smile spread across his lips. "Didn't know you had it in you."

Her hands deflected his insinuation like a shield. "I know what you're thinking." She put a hand on her hip, hoping he would dismiss the blush that heated her cheeks. "We're not in high school anymore."

He threw back his head and laughed. "You booked us *one* room?"

She backed away. If he got any closer there would be no denying him.

His bag hit the floor, and she almost stumbled onto the bed. His eyes tracked her like a hunter tracks his prey.

She shrugged. "There was only one room available. We'd have had to drive around for hours to find two rooms at this time of night."

A raised eyebrow indicated he didn't buy her story.

A headache threatened behind her eyes. "I didn't know how to break it to you, but I promise I had no ulterior motive. I'm so tired, I can hardly see straight." The grit in her eyes burned.

A knock on the door startled her.

She answered. A woman dressed in black with a bottle of champagne in a bucket peered into the suite, "Did you order a couple's massage?"

Her face must have said it all. Oh, Jack would have a heyday with this one. "No. Thanks. You must have the wrong room."

She closed the door and spun on her heel, hands splayed. She opened her mouth to speak, but the laughter in his eyes stopped her.

"They say there's a first time for everything."

Another knock on the door broke the tension like a cue ball. She yanked it open.

"Roll-a-way bed?"

Jack peeked around her shoulder. "Yeah. In here."

The bellman pushed the sandwiched bed into the room. "Where to?"

Jack pointed to the corner opposite the traditional bed. "Put it there." He tipped the man and closed the door behind him. "Excuse me while I take a cold shower. Get to bed before you fall over." Jack got too close for comfort. "You look as exhausted as I am. I can't believe I'm saying this, but can we go to sleep?"

Dumbly, she nodded.

"Good night, Marcy." He yanked his bag off the bed and headed for the bathroom.

Her heart melted into a puddle, and she breathed. "Good night, Jack." A cold shower wouldn't be enough to cool the heat he'd generated. She reached for her bag, thankful God had provided an easy way out of the latest temptation.

Though his feet hung off the end of the mattress, Jack managed to extract a few hours of sleep from the roll-a-way bed. How low he'd sunk, sleeping on a bed that folded in half after a decade in the Hilton. Sheesh. He squinted and blinked to clear the sleep from his eyes. The king-sized bed where Marcy slept was made and her suitcase by the door.

His feet hit the floor. They hadn't exactly enjoyed the suite the way it was intended, but the sleep would help. Where was she?

"Marcy?"

The patio door squeaked open at his touch, and the highway noise assaulted his senses. Marcy sat on a plastic lawn chair, legs drawn up, staring at the parking lot. She didn't stir when he joined her. "You okay?"

Her shoulders rose.

Had she been out here all night? He'd been so tired, he'd hit the bed sleeping. He felt bad about taking advantage of her fatigue and worry last night. He owed her an apology. "About last night—"

She turned. "Did you sleep well?"

The plastic legs of the chair scraped the patio as he moved closer. Dark circles hung below her eyes. "I'm guessing as good as you did."

Her voice softened. "Have I soiled your reputation by spending the night with you?"

He laughed. It wasn't like he hadn't entertained the idea, if only for a minute. He scraped a chair closer and put his arm around her. She leaned into him as he spoke. "I don't think Carter would forgive me."

A smile teased her lips. "I imagine the offensive line pales in comparison."

Relief flooded him at the return of her humor. "I hope the couple got their massage after all."

"I think I may have heard them. The walls are pretty thin."

He squeezed her shoulders. "You didn't sleep well."

"Thinking about the kids."

His heart went out to her. "You can sleep in the car. Ready to hit the road?"

She stood. "Yep, I gotta get back where I belong." He heard deeper meaning in the words.

As they neared the Colorado state line, snowflakes plastered the windshield, and the wipers worked overtime to keep the view clear. He turned to Marcy, who'd been lost in thought most of the day. "They weren't kidding when they said it was the storm of the decade. Looks like slow going from here on out."

Jack fumbled with the radio, looking for road closure information.

They needed to clear Raton pass before it closed again. His foot pressed the accelerator. Marcy would be with her kids in no time. "Have you tried to call Pete's mom again?"

Her hands pulled on her face. "Can't. My battery died last night, and I didn't bring my car charger." That explained her resignation today. The unknown surrounded them like the storm.

The memory of their kiss practically drove him crazy as the miles passed. The soft skin of her hand on the console next to him only increased his agitation. His desire could melt the snow building up on the windows. He wanted her for her quick wit, her dedication to her family. Dare he give a thought to her body and his reaction to it? Not if he wanted to stay on the road.

The strain of the hours in the car picked at her mind control like a vulture on dead meat. Another hour and they'd finally be home. The blizzard had moved on, but a wall of snow on either side of the road made horizontal visibility impossible, like they traveled through a white tunnel.

Visibility might be limited, but the truth was clear. When the excitement was over, she'd be as desirable as overcooked potatoes. Perhaps the things Pete did while they were married miswired her feminine heart. Oh, she wanted to throw all sense to the wind and return the passion she'd felt in Jack's embrace, succumb to the tidal pull of his eyes. But she was old enough to understand that physical fires burned short if not fueled by the soul, and hers was in pieces. She liked Jack too much to hurt him.

Much as she wanted to get home, the unknown scared her to death. Her imagination ran wild. What if—?

Her hands tightened when she thought of Lisa's blood on them. The jagged stab wound in her neck. The lifeless eyes. It didn't take much to put her kids in Lisa's place.

She swallowed a desperation, clinging to control by a fingernail. Tremors of anxiety shook her and Jack glanced at her. "You're thinking too hard."

She hugged herself. "This is not thinking, it's obsession."

"Want to sing ninety-nine bottles of beer on the wall?"

She laughed. "If it could take my mind off the kids, I'd agree." Her insides squirmed. "What if the killer got them, Jack?"

"Slow down a minute. You are the one who said God was taking care of them. Do your thing and let Him do His."

"What's my thing?"

He shrugged. "Pray?"

Here she was being reminded about prayer by a non-believer. She took a deep breath. "You're right."

"Assuming the kids are safe, are you going to call the police about the note?"

She strangled her cell phone. "Not with this useless hunk of junk."

He rescued the device from her hand. "Give the poor phone a break."

As usual, his humor disarmed her. "I'll cross that bridge when we get there. I just want to know the kids are safe. Let's head to Bobby's first, he's closest."

The snow scrunched beneath the tires when they pulled into the drive at Bobby's house fifteen minutes later. She left Jack in the car, and her heart galloped out of control as she ran up the drive and burst inside.

"Bobby? Brant?" Her voice echoed in the room.

Cords and wires snagged her feet and the television blared, unattended. The couch had been overturned and papers littered the floor. The curtains hung crooked. A piece of uneaten pizza peeked from a greasy box on the floor. A dining chair lay on its side.

He's been here.

10

JACK CAUGHT HER as she swayed, shocked at the state of the house. The place looked like an animal had come through and tore it to pieces. She would have gone down if he hadn't decided to join her in the house. Her feet stumbled around the corner to the kitchen like a sleepwalker.

Brant and Bobby looked up from a game of Monopoly at the kitchen table, shock on their faces.

Brant's chair toppled. "Mom! What are you doing here?"

Marcy flew to his side, strangling her son in a hug. She trembled, but he saw her body relax.

Bobby's chair scraped the floor as he stood, his face shocked. "How'd you get here? I heard all the flights were canceled. Figured we wouldn't see you for a few days yet." His face colored as he cast a glance at the carnage around the room.

Marcy stepped back, allowing Brant to come up for air. So far, Jack had gone unnoticed in the doorway. Their heads turned when he spoke. "We got here, however we could. I couldn't stand waiting in the airport."

Brant jumped up and fist-bumped him. "Hey, Jack. Good to see ya."

"Same here, man."

Bobby stepped forward, hand extended. "Jack Briggs! How did this happen?" Tension built in the room like thunderclouds; his eyes locked on Marcy.

Brant's explanation saved him a lengthy excuse. "Mom and Jack met at one of my games. They went to the funeral together."

Bobby ran a hand through his hair and grinned at Marcy. "Wipe that grin off your face, Marce. You didn't mention you were meeting anyone there."

A telltale blush climbed to her hairline, and she shrugged. "Guess it slipped my mind."

Bobby's thumb shot out. "This six-foot-three NFL linebacker just slipped your mind?"

The blush deepened. She clunked her cell phone on the table. "Have you heard from your Mom? Is Haley okay?"

Bobby opened the fridge. "Jack, you want a beer or something?"

"No, thanks. I've still got to get Marcy home."

Bobby handed a Dr. Pepper to Brant and got Marcy a glass of water. "We've been holed up here for three days. No phone service. No Internet. They just plowed the street this morning. I still can't believe you got here so quickly."

Brant rolled his eyes. "We ordered pizza the first night before the power went out."

Judging by the state of the front room, they'd had plenty of bonding time, despite the lack of modern conveniences. It reminded him of college.

Marcy didn't leave Brant's side. "What did you guys do? It looks like a train went through here. I thought the house had been ransacked."

Brant and Bobby had no idea what they'd cost her in worry moments before.

"I didn't expect you home so soon, *Mrs. Clean*. Real men don't clean during snowstorms."

Brant toasted him with his can of soda. "If you say so, Uncle Bobby."

Bobby tossed an oven mitt at Brant's head. "Suckah."

This family had obviously spent a great deal of time together. The fear on Marcy's face dissolved. She put her empty glass in the sink and hugged Bobby. "Thanks for everything. I want to get over to my mom and dad's house and get Haley." She turned to Brant. "Get your stuff, honey."

Brant jogged to the back room and Marcy followed.

Bobby raised his eyebrows. "You live around here, Jack?"

"Yep. In Loveland."

"How cool. So, you and Marcy—did someone say you two met at one of Brant's games?" He scratched his head and pointed. "Did Pete represent you?"

He fired questions off like a semi-automatic weapon. Marcy was as protected as Peyton Manning in the pocket; first by Carter, now by Bobby.

"I didn't know Marcy until we met at one of Brant's games."

Bobby nodded. "So you guys drove here from where?"

Brant appeared with his gym bag. "Ready."

Marcy touched Bobby's shoulder. "Thanks again. Do you head back to work in the morning?"

"Maybe. The airport's gonna be a nightmare. I won't get back for a day or so."

"Okay. Call me before you head out, if phones are back up."

Bobby kissed her cheek. "Glad you're back. Take care."

No wonder she didn't lunge at the opportunity to kiss him. She got more male attention than—well—more than he was comfortable with. He touched the small of her back on their way out the door. Just a little something for Bobby to think on while he was gone.

Brant climbed into the back seat. "How was the funeral and Carter, Mom?"

"He's holding up. You have a good weekend?"

"Sure. Did you see anything in New York while you were there?"

"Jack took me to the Smithsonian."

"Cool. One of my coaches called before my phone died. The championship is rescheduled in two weeks. They've got to find the field again after all this snow."

Sunshine flooded her soul as they arrived home with both Haley and Brant in the car. Whoever had sent the threat was just blowing smoke, but they'd given her a turn she'd never forget. Jack insisted on shoveling her drive, did a sweep of the house and found the offending back door locked as his friend had assured him he would.

He opened the car door for her. "Everything look right here?"

"I think so." She hugged Haley to her side, a subtle warning for him to keep his distance. "Thanks for everything, Jack."

"Can't wait for a hot shower and my own bed. Night." Snow scrunched under his tires as he slowly pulled from the driveway. *What a storm.*

The frigid air inside the house hit her as they entered. The power hadn't been on in days, but she heard the furnace humming away in the basement now. Thank goodness they had power again. She flipped a switch. She'd dreaded returning in the dark, but home welcomed her with its familiarity in a bath of light. Nothing looked out of place. She wasn't housekeeper-of-the-year, but kept things neat and clean. Their family portrait, taken a year before Pete's death, greeted from its place over the couch in the den. Their Persian cat, Nana, curled around her ankles, but nothing compared to having both the kids safely in her arms. Marcy squeezed Haley's hand. "Did you miss me, sweetie?"

"Um-hum. Grandma bought me a new dress while you were gone, and I went to Christy's skating party."

"Sounds fun." She slid her arm around Brant's shoulders. "I'm so glad to be home. I missed you guys so much."

"So, how come you didn't invite Jack to stay a while?"

"I think he was pretty tired. We'll see him around, I'm sure."

"He promised to coach me before the game next week."

She squeezed him. "Then, I'm sure he'll call. Let's head up and get ready for bed." She hefted her suitcase. "We've all got a lot of laundry."

Jack may have gone home, but he wasn't far from her thoughts. She sighed. It was fun while it lasted, but her heart was too wounded. Pete left her that legacy. Truth was, she couldn't trust Jack, if he did light a fire in her that she never wanted extinguished. Jack could have arranged for the note to be delivered, and she hadn't actually seen him during the flash mob since she'd been on the ground. Was there a chance he—? Her stomach clenched. She dashed the crazy notion. Fatigue had left her melodramatic.

When the kids dawdled, she growled and chased them up the stairs like she used to before they were too grown up for such play. A mother's heart never forgot how to play. She wished she could chase the worry from her mind as easily.

After she made sure Haley showered before putting on her favorite pajamas, she called to the kids. "Hey, guys. Come in here before you go to bed."

Brant's almost-man frame filled the doorway. He'd inherited height from his father, along with blond highlights. "You called?"

"Come in here for a minute." She tossed him a wooly throw blanket. The furnace worked overtime to heat the house, but the temperature was still frigid.

Haley snuggled in front of her, and she finished braiding her hair while Brant sat Indian-style on her bed. "Nothing strange happened while I was gone, did it?"

Brant shrugged. "Because the back door was left open?"

"Do you remember me locking it?"

Brant scratched his head. "You know how it sticks sometimes."

She nodded. Nothing was out of place, and the door *had* blown open several times in the past when they'd forgotten to lock it. "I'm just glad no snow got in. Looks like the wind was blowing the other way."

Haley's downy head landed in her lap. "I'm glad you're home, Mommy. Do I have to go to school tomorrow?"

"Nope. The school bus won't be able to get out tomorrow."

Her heart soared. A whole day to spend with the kids would be the best medicine for her frazzled nerves. She could forget the note, and the murder, and move on. "Want to play games and watch movies? I've got popcorn, and there might be some hot chocolate in the cabinet."

Haley beamed and squirmed on her lap. "Love you, Mom."

She looked between their faces. "I love you guys, so much."

The note and the dreaded journey afterward had been more than enough to remind her how precious her kids were. God's gift. She didn't want to waste a single minute. Like she had with Pete.

The days following the storm sparkled with sunshine and temperatures in the sixties. Typical Colorado weather. The front range communities awoke slowly as the plows mounded mountains of snow where it would be least intrusive to traffic and pedestrians. If winter visited again anytime soon, the piles of snow could remain until spring. Of course, the kids made the most of their time off, building a snow monster in the front yard and making trails in the hills with their sleds. Their cold-burnt cheeks gleamed at the sliding glass door.

She pushed the door aside. "Come in and warm up."

Brant stripped his snow clothes and grabbed the mug she handed him. "Don't tell anyone, but I'm glad we have school tomorrow."

She smiled at him. "Ready to get back on the field again?" She'd practically gone crazy waiting, but Jack hadn't called, even after phone service had been reestablished. It was true; she couldn't keep his interest past the urgency of the moment.

"Definitely."

After school the next day, Marcy snapped pictures at practice, determined to capture the rare moment on her digital camera. The team practiced on the frozen turf which was literally in a snow bowl due to the high walls of packed snow that surrounded the field.

She and Haley waited for Brant after practice, and he slid into the passenger seat. "Jack called me. Is it okay if he comes over tonight?

We're going to go over some plays."

Her heart shot off like a rabbit. "That's fine with me, but I'll be at Bible Study."

"No problem. He's coming after dinner."

Haley looked up from a book she'd gotten from the library. "Do I have to go with you, Mom? I could stay home with Jack and Brant."

OK, so she'd pay good money to be alone with the man again, but that didn't mean her daughter should. "Maybe I'd better call him before we make any plans."

He hadn't heard the gruff voice on the phone since the day he'd agreed to the final hit. "Is everything ready? I have millions riding on this one."

"The drug is ready, and I've got a spot as interim trainer in Sunday's game. Watch the headlines Monday morning."

"I'm counting on this one."

Of course, he was. A guy didn't pay millions to manipulate the game without getting a few gray hairs in the process. "Don't worry about it. I've never failed you before."

He'd never considered failure before, but the situation accelerated when he'd been forced to kill Lisa, and Marcy got involved. This candle was literally burning at both ends, and he didn't want to be caught in the middle.

Marcy should have arrived home by now, accompanied by her white knight, Briggs. Didn't she understand by now that she belonged to him?

He paced the floor, hands knotted behind his back. Jack's feelings for Marcy were clear. And that complicated everything. To make matters worse, she hadn't called him when she received the threat. He'd anticipated her quavering voice describing the chilling likeness to Haley's voice that she'd heard on the scratchy recording. He couldn't remember a crisis they *hadn't* shared since Pete's death. His stomach burned when he thought of her sharing her troubles with Jack. Another undeserving king of the sport.

But he knew she'd received it. He'd gotten confirmation from a hotel employee.

How long before they started piecing things together? From his perspective, the connection was uncanny. Of all the guys on the planet, why'd she have to date *him*? Maybe it would be short-lived. The last person he could touch was Briggs. Too many connections there. He'd have to stick with Marcy. Was she off-balance enough to neglect the truth that stared her in the face?

In light of current circumstances, she wouldn't expect the same degree of communication, and he needed this week to focus. This Sunday, in the midst of benign injections to other players, he'd make the hit. It'd been his practice for years to label each player's injection and have them ready at game time. No one would notice any difference in the player that had been chosen for the serum. They'd all line up for Toradol, a powerful anti-inflammatory drug that made the serum even more effective because it blocked pain to the point of injury. The players would thank him.

All but one.

That player would get the magic injection that could end his career in one hard cut on the turf. A shredded ACL should do the trick, at least for one season.

He stopped pacing. Maybe he'd made too much of the whole Marcy-Jack thing. There was no reason for Jack to suspect his injury had been intentional any more than other players had. Their relationship was what got under his skin like a splinter. Even before Pete died, he'd spent years fantasizing about having her all to himself.

He felt assured if he played on her see-saw emotions and pushed hard enough, she would run into his arms like she'd done in the past and forget Jack Briggs ever existed. But if he was too heavy-handed, she might snap. And where would that leave him? He'd go back to playing the good guy. That's where he felt safest. And it was the man Marcy knew best.

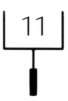

11

JACK SET HIS teeth and cranked out the final rep on the bench press. His shoulders and pecs burned as he sat up, wiping sweat from his brow. He'd kept up his routine of an early workout, even after retirement. When rookie players asked, his advice was always been the same: "Hit the gym early and let your performance on the field do the talking." How many times had he been the one making coffee before the rest of the team arrived? Passion for the game consumed him. It made him great, drove him to succeed.

Passion played him dirty in the end. Without it, he was dead.

Blasted knee injury.

He missed Marcy and the high she offered, and the depression that clogged his mind returned with a vengeance. He stared at the newspaper headline. Another player committed suicide over the weekend. Many were attributed to CTE, a brain injury caused by repeated concussions. His insides squirmed as he faced every player's nightmare. The walls of the weight room pressed closer, and the scent of rubber and sweat turned his stomach. CTE wasn't diagnosed until death, when the brain could be examined for the telltale buildup of protein. Depression was frighteningly common among ex-players, and sometimes, the emptiness in his soul yawned so wide he thought he'd fall right in.

He might have but for Marcy.

He slung the towel over his shoulder and lowered the volume on the stereo. The phone rang so he clicked the music off and answered.

"Jack, it's Morgan Brewers." The old coach's voice brought back memories.

"Morgan, how are you, man?"

"Doin' good. Hey, I've got a favor to ask."

Who didn't? "Shoot."

"I've got a rookie that needs some pointers, needs to get his head straight."

Jack understood. Some players didn't handle the transition to the NFL well. They'd grown up on the streets, in gangs, and the glitz and expectation of the NFL could be overwhelming. Heck, some players didn't handle retirement well, either. Look at him. "He got a name?"

"Drew Shaw. Running back out of Stanford. If he settles down, we think he could bring us over a hundred yards per game. Injuries have got him down."

"That good, huh?" His pulse responded in the old way. Anytime a back was touted as a great player, he'd seen it as his duty to annihilate them.

"We hope so."

Jack scrawled Drew's number on a scrap of paper in the weight room and hung up. A smile touched his mouth. He knew what made running backs tick. As a linebacker, he'd prided himself on knowing just how they thought and reacted in order to predict their next moves. There was nothing so satisfying as knocking the stuffing out of a back before he knew what hit him. If he could help Drew, he'd give it his best shot. The kid must have potential, or Coach Brewers would have left him to figure it out on his own.

He eyed the phone jealously. He'd expected Marcy to call after he'd sent a text to Brant, but what did he have to offer?

He could almost taste the subtle strawberry sweetness of her lips again as the memory of their kiss snaked through him. For a second, he'd tapped the woman under the surface; a raging river held back by a dam. Marcy held herself away from the world. Hiding something he couldn't identify. It was almost as if she was afraid of the woman inside. Afraid she wouldn't measure up.

He'd had Silly Putty women in his life before, the kind he could manipulate with heat and the pressure of his baby finger. Marcy's hard exterior intrigued him rather like granite called to the sculptor. He saw the goddess inside.

His thoughts touched the edge of a satisfying fantasy before reality snapped him to the present. *Get your head in the game.* Thoughts in the passion department were anything but helpful. If he intended to win her, he'd need to take it slowly. One false move, and his muse would leap from the table.

His fingers itched to call Marcy, but he dialed Drew's number, instead. "Drew, this is Jack Briggs. Coach Brewers asked me to give you a call."

"The Gentleman Linebacker. The warden send ya to work yo' magic?" The accent dropped clues to his origin and breeding.

Cocky little punk. Probably one of those kids who kissed his bicep in front of the camera. He'd help if he could. "It's not magic. Hard work."

"Sure was for you."

Jack grinned. His reputation preceded him. "Tell me what time you got to the gym this morning."

A call beeped through during their conversation, *Marcy*. He didn't answer, but continued questioning Drew about his work ethic, recent diet, and workout plans.

"What does all this have to do with my injury?"

"Shaw, if football isn't in your blood, this league is going to kill you. There are players who play the game and those who live it."

The fog of depression lifted; football and Marcy. Looked like it was going to be a good day.

Marcy massaged her temples and grabbed the pan of lasagna she'd finished layering. The idea that Jack could be the killer left her confused and her heart unresponsive. The pan scraped on the hot racks as she pushed it into the oven. If Jack was a killer, why not take her out on the trip home? He'd certainly had opportunity. Maybe he liked to play with his prey like a cat plays with a mouse before he sinks his teeth in. She shivered at the image and righted her thinking. Jack Briggs was no killer. Oh, he had a reputation for toughness on the field, but she would have sensed something more sinister in the hours they'd spent alone. No, someone else had killed Lisa Sparks, and she had to find out why, if not who, as quickly as she could.

She hung up the dishcloth. If she continued along this vein, she'd go crazy. Longing and fear made a sour cocktail. But which would she give in to?

Neither.

She was no stranger to longing. How many nights did she lie awake listening to Pete's quiet breathing next to her, knowing he was so close, yet unreachable? The hole in her soul yearned for his touch, but she'd been left empty, night after night.

He'd been a decent husband and something inside wanted to believe the best of him. He'd left her and the kids enough money to get through a couple of years without her working, and also provided college funds. He had seen to their needs but had never seen her with the eyes of his heart.

Because she wasn't worth noticing.

The longing sliced through her like a machete. She'd done everything to make him happy. She followed his clients, cooked and cleaned, and wore spicy nightgowns, only to lie awake while the tears dried on her cheeks in the darkness after his rejections.

She shook the despondency and turned to the salad, rejecting wilted leaves of spinach the way Pete cast her aside.

Jack's attention stirred these emotions. He drew out the woman inside like a vacuum, despite her resistance. She swallowed and started wiping the counters. He wouldn't like what he found. She swept up a broken eggshell that lay on the counter. The translucent shell was as empty and useless as her life. On the outside she looked whole, but when someone cracked through the shell, there wasn't much worth having inside. Pete had been disappointed.

Her breath caught in her chest as the memories crashed in. The morning of Pete's death, she'd awakened with a start, annoyed because he slept through his alarm. When she shoved his shoulder, a chill crept up her arm. His unyielding form did not respond to her touch as the sickening moment of realization struck her. She shook him and called his name, but his face was etched with eternal sleep. An empty pill bottle lay on the bedside table. She'd been sleeping with a dead man.

The chill of the memory paralyzed her with hands from the past. She opened the fridge and put the Mozzarella and cottage cheese in the drawer. If she'd been more, Pete might not have killed himself. Jack didn't deserve to make that discovery. Why not leave him wondering what he missed?

Hot water soothed her hands as she washed the bowl she'd used to mix the filling. She rebelled against this well-worn train of thought. What was the minister's advice in their last session? "Everyone plays a record in their head. Be careful what's playing on yours."

She repented. *Lord?* Could He find beauty where there was none? *You are clothed with Christ.* How could she miss the beauty in that statement? She glanced at her reflection in the kitchen window. Maybe God brought Jack into her life for a reason. It did feel good to be wanted.

As if her thoughts summoned him, the phone rang.

"I'm returning your call."

"Brant said something about you coming over tonight?" She eyed the impressive dinner in the oven.

"Yeah, I told him we could work on some strategy before the game. You okay with that?"

Um-hum. "Yep. Why don't you come for dinner?"

Hadn't she baked the lasagna with the secret hope he'd be there to enjoy it? She and Haley would miss Bible study tonight. After the threat, she didn't dare leave the kids alone for a second.

"I'd love to. What time?"

She checked the oven timer. "How about quarter to seven?"

"See you then."

She raced from the kitchen; if she hurried, she'd have time to touch up her makeup and change her shirt. She'd passed over the Broncos jersey in her closet with a grin. No use baiting him.

The doorbell rang, and her heart responded like it had when her first date showed up at her parents' house. She swung the door open. "Jack. Come in."

His eyes swept over her with a satisfied expression, "Brant home from practice yet?"

She hid her disappointment. "He's in his room."

Jack started for the stairs.

"Warning. You may need a bio-hazard suit."

He laughed, taking the stairs two at a time. The jeans he wore— never mind—she left the entryway to set the table.

Moments after she called them to dinner, she heard Jack's voice in the hall with Brant. "You'll see it in their eyes."

Were they talking football or women? She didn't want to know. The oven timer rang, and the mouth-watering scent of mozzarella and garlic silenced the guys as they came into the kitchen. The sides of the dish bubbled with melted cheese as she pulled it from the oven.

"Haley! Time for dinner, honey."

Without being asked, Jack poured water into the glasses from the pitcher she'd put on the table. He folded his legs under the table and grinned when she brought the bubbling lasagna to the table. Haley clapped her hands. "Ummm. My favorite."

Jack met her eye. "Mine too. Smells good enough to eat."

She cut a steaming piece and lifted it high to break the tantalizing strings of cheese that pulled at it. "Tastes good too, so they tell me." She slid it on his plate. "Brant, will you say the prayer?"

When Brant finished, Marcy passed the bread basket. "You like cracked pepper, Jack?"

He looked up from a bite of lasagna. "Sure do."

She ground pepper into a shallow dish in the center of the table, added minced garlic, salt and topped it with olive oil. The kids dove in without ceremony, and her cheeks warmed.

Haley spoke through a mouthful of bread and olive oil. "Mom always makes this bread and dip when we have Italian food. Have you had it before, Jack?"

Marcy tried not to blush at her daughter's naivety. This simple meal was nothing compared to the five-star restaurants he usually dined in.

"I've had it before, but your mom's lasagna is the best."

"Um-hum." Brant grunted his agreement, too busy shoveling food in his mouth to answer. Where did that kid put it all?

She enjoyed a man's presence at the table; there was something satisfying about watching him eat. Satisfying or sensuous?

His fork balanced in front of his mouth. "This is great, Marcy. Thanks for asking me."

She dabbed her lips with a napkin. "You're welcome. It's the least I could do after you drove me across the country."

His eyes danced. "I'd do it again in a second." He turned to Haley. "Are you interested in sports, Haley?"

She twirled a string of cheese on her fork before it met her mouth. "I run track in the summer. Last year I got second place at the state track meet." She grinned, ignoring a smear of marinara sauce on her cheek.

Between his second and third slice of lasagna, Jack peppered the kids with questions and they beamed under the attention.

Marcy pushed back from the table when the meal was finished. "You want some decaf, Jack? I'll bring dessert out to the living room if you and Brant want to talk out there."

The boys got up, and Jack followed Brant to the living room after handing Marcy his plate. He mouthed, "I'll thank you later," and winked.

Was it hot in the kitchen? She'd open a window if the temperature outside wasn't single digits.

The kitchen swam with the warm aroma of coffee. After it finished brewing, Haley put brownies on a plate and followed her out.

Jack took the mug she offered. "Just what I ordered." His magnetic eyes pulled her, and she stepped back, glancing at the kids, lest they suspect her feelings. She didn't know where they stood. Or her own mind where Jack was concerned.

Jack's voice took on excitement as he continued their conversation. "Make it your goal to never miss a tackle. Your mission is intimidation until they give up."

"What did you used to say to them?" Brant stuffed an entire brownie in his mouth.

Jack used his fork. "Let your action speak louder than words. When you knock the wind out of them, they'll get the message."

Marcy leaned on the couch with her hip and sipped her coffee. Did Jack understand how parental he sounded?

"Wish I had a playbook."

She scanned her memory. "Any playbook, or something specific?"

"Any one would work. I just thought I'd give him a visual on certain plays."

Her coffee cup clinked on the table. "I think Pete kept some old playbooks. Let me look."

She hefted the box from the closet and slid it across the table. "This is some stuff from Pete's office. See what you guys can find." She turned to Haley. "Let's go finish the kitchen and then we'll read together."

The warmth of Jack's touch on her arm stopped her. "Let me help you in the kitchen later." His eyes begged. "You can read with Haley while Brant and I talk for a while. I want to help you wash the dishes."

Sure he did. "Okay. Come on, Hales." She grabbed her hand.

Haley tugged her up the stairs. "We're starting book three of the Little House on the Prairie series."

Feeling like he'd violated the Holy Grail, Jack flipped through the papers in the box that Marcy had thrust at him. He stole a glance at Brant. Would digging through his dad's stuff make him uncomfortable? "You want to have a look?"

"It's cool. You know what you're looking for." Brant drummed his fingers on the arm of the chair he was sitting in. Not a care in the world.

He scanned a scrap of paper with frizz from a spiral notebook. In pen, *Injuries* followed by a series of numbers. Probably Pete keeping track of his clients. His eyes rested on another scrap. More random notes. Why'd she keep this junk?

He found the playbook she'd mentioned and pushed the box away.

Brant could see what he meant in action.

After an hour, Brant's responses slowed. Jack never tired of talking of the game, but the kid had school in the morning. "You have an early class tomorrow?"

Brant nodded. "Yep. Chemistry."

That subject had been on his schedule ever since he met Marcy. "I'll come by practice on Saturday. That cool?"

Brant stood. "That would be so awesome!"

Jack fist-bumped Brant and tossed the football at him. "Get some sleep. I'll see ya Saturday."

Marcy passed Brant on the stairs. "Night, sweetie." She squeezed his cheeks and ruffled his hair.

Brant tossed a look at Jack. "Mom! What was that for?"

She continued down the stairs. "Oh, just a little something I learned in Smothering Parent Magazine."

Jack swallowed a chuckle.

Brant rolled his eyes. "Not cool." His door clunked closed.

She paused at the landing and tucked a strand of hair behind her ear. What was so exhilarating about women's hands?

"Haley's in bed."

He jumped at his chance. "Let's tackle that kitchen."

12

JACK'S EYES FOLLOWED Marcy from his perch in the doorway. She ran water into the sink, and suds rose up in a mound. Her jeans transmitted every movement of her hips. One hot mama.

She glanced over her shoulder and pushed her bangs off her forehead with her wrist. Water glistened on her bare arms. "You just going to watch?" She turned back to the sink.

Not a bad idea.

Jack crossed the kitchen in three strides. He came behind her and submerged his hands into the water on top of hers. She melted back against him, but her hands never stopped moving.

She trailed the dishrag through the water, but they both knew she wasn't washing dishes. Jack shivered. Amazing where the mind could take a man. He joined her in the fluid motion, their fingers tangled beneath the bubbles. A crescendo of emotion drowned him, and he grabbed her shoulders and turned her to face him. Water dripped on the floor from the rag in her hand, so he grabbed it and tossed it into the sink with a plop.

Breathless, he crushed her against the counter and claimed her lips with his. He kissed her until the mask slipped, and she returned his ardor with a taste of what she hid from the world. The feather-soft skin of her neck begged his attention, but he pulled back and stroked her cheek with the backs of his fingers. "Dinner was amazing."

She trembled against him and exhaled a ragged breath. "You know my limits, Jack."

He knew. She'd explained the rules without a word in every conversation they'd had. He buried his lips in her hair. "You're testing mine."

Her sapphire eyes sparked. "Be good." She plunked a towel into his hand. "You dry."

Her eyes darted to the doorway. The kids. She'd cook his goose if they caught them that way. He touched her forehead with his. "I forgot about the kids. I'm sorry."

She turned back to the sink, sloshing water at him. "I've got more baggage than you need."

He handed her a plate. "Not baggage. More like a signing bonus."

Her hand left a wet spot on his shirt where she shoved him, but her eyes smiled.

They left the kitchen sparkling clean, and he followed her into the living room. "Thanks for coming tonight, Jack. Brant thinks the world of you."

"He's a great kid."

She pushed the box of papers she'd brought out toward him. "Can you gather these up and put it back on the shelf in the closet? I'm gonna run up and check on Haley."

Two unruly papers curled out from the top of the pile he tried to straighten. He patted them with his hand, but they rolled under his touch. He tugged the corner into alignment with the edges of the other documents, but paused when he got to the second dog-eared paper. The scrap stuck out because it was stapled to a medical report from a doctor. He'd recognize those anywhere. The player's name was blacked out, but the stapled scrap read: *Another one bites the dust. # 3.*

Jack scanned the document. Familiar phrases drilled into his consciousness like nails in the coffin of his career. Torn ACL. Reconstruction. Cadaver tissue. Proprioception. He'd learned the medical terminology. Did many agents keep records of their clients' injuries like this?

Jack held the document to the light. The marker couldn't hide the imprint of the name on the paper. Isaac Johnson.

Marcy's foot sounded on the stairs, and Jack folded the paper and crammed it into his pocket. Pete wouldn't miss it.

She walked him to the door, and he leaned against the frame with his shoulder. He hated leaving, but the temptation was going to his head. "Can I see you again?"

She bit her lip between her teeth. "After tonight, you have to."

Jack's headlights reflected off the snow on the front lawn as he pulled away. She swallowed her heart. A siren blared in her heart, but she wouldn't heed it. She turned to her ringing phone. "Carter."

"Hey."

She snuggled under a shaggy throw on the couch. "How ya holdin' up?"

"Not so good."

Her heart twisted. Would it ease the pain if she told him she'd asked Lisa to look into Pete's records? "I'm so sorry. Time is all you've got right now."

"And it's time that's killing me slowly."

Grief used time as a stranglehold. "Just mark off another day. And then another."

"I had no idea a person could hurt this bad."

You can. Emotion in Carter's voice churned to life the memories of Pete's suicide and the aftermath to life. Sometimes the pain didn't subside, especially when things were not cut and dried. "It's gonna get better." A tear slid down her cheek. An empty promise.

"How am I going to get through this?"

He'd asked the wrong woman. A guilty pang stabbed her stomach. Telling him would solve nothing. She had no proof that Lisa's death was somehow related to the papers from Pete's office. "Cast all your cares on Him. He's the only one who can handle them."

Bitterness strangled Carter's voice. "Where was God when someone stabbed Lisa in the neck? Where was He while she bled to death?"

"He was right there with her, crying. And later, welcoming her home."

"It's so hard."

Death didn't discriminate, and pain lingered no matter how a person died, but suicide and murder were harder to swallow. Just so *unnecessary.* "Just get through this minute. Then get through the hour. Then get through the day." The hollow echo in her offering of comfort sickened her.

"My stomach feels like it's eating me alive. I'm surviving on Rolaids and coffee."

"Sounds like a better diet than we had in college."

He chuckled softly. "I'd give anything to go back to those days. If I hadn't been so blind—"

There was no going back. They each had their cross to bear. "Even with everything that happened, I wouldn't give up my years with Pete. Without him, I wouldn't have Haley and Brant."

"Lisa wanted kids."

What response soothed that wound? She breathed a prayer of thanks for the kids Pete had blessed her with. "You might still get that chance."

"I'm not getting any younger." He paused. "So you and Jack Briggs? You guys getting serious?"

Don't go there. Her stomach jumped at the mention of Jack's name. Their kiss had been serious. *Seriously amazing.* "After my experience with Pete, I think he's bitten off more than he can chew."

"Hope he understands the kind of woman he's getting."

She frowned. "He's not *getting* anything or anyone."

"Cool it. You know what I meant. So, what's he doing after his retirement? Bought a car dealership yet?"

"Very funny. I don't think he's doing anything. Seems like he's got his head on straight." She chewed her lip thoughtfully, smiling at the possibility of getting to know everything about him.

"I'm thinking of getting out of media."

She raised her eyebrows. "You'd leave *NFL Rush?*"

"I've had a few offers."

"Would you go back to training or something?" Carter built *NFL Rush* from the ground up. It was nearly impossible to imagine him giving it up. "Don't make any big decisions for a while."

"I've kept my license current. Done a few rounds on the floor when teams needed a substitute."

Bobby would die. He'd roll his eyes and make a gagging motion. The two hadn't exactly seen eye to eye over the years. Carter's jealousy (his one fault) irked her and made the gulf between them bigger. "Give it six months before you do anything, okay? And what about Lisa's article?"

They chatted about Brant's game and Haley's plans for the winter months. Fatigue weighed on her limbs. Wrestling the emotions Jack stirred drained the last drop of energy the day afforded.

"You sound tired, Marce. Call me before Brant's game and tell me what channel it's gonna be on."

She tossed the throw aside and turned the lights off. "You got it." She started up the stairs. "You are in my prayers, Carter. I know this isn't easy."

His sadness permeated the miles between them. Sometimes life's hurt was unfathomable. "Night."

The next morning arrived all too soon. Marcy rubbed the grit from her eyes. She'd dreamed of Pete and their wedding day. A surge of happiness warmed her when the minister said, "You may kiss the bride." But when her lips met his, he'd turned into the cold corpse she'd found the morning after he'd taken his own life. The kiss of death. She'd stumbled backward in revulsion, and Jack caught her.

Just a dream. She swung her legs over the bed and glanced at the clock. Ten minutes to get the kids out the door. Thankfully, life offered little time for reflection on the emotions stirred up by her dream. Instead of getting dressed, she grabbed the luxurious wrap Bobby had given her for Christmas and slid her feet into the pink knit slippers she'd worn every year since Pete died. They'd seen better days.

A horn blared from the front yard. Brant's friends must be picking him up this morning. Good. One less thing to worry about. She tapped on Haley's door. "You up, baby girl?"

"Yep."

Marcy jumped when Haley tapped her shoulder from behind, grinning. "What's for breakfast?"

When would a tooth replace that gap in her smile? Her baby was growing up too fast. She pulled her into a hug. "How about instant oatmeal and milk?"

"Sounds good."

The memory of Jack's kiss teased a smile to her lips as she arrived in the kitchen. The pressure of his body as they'd leaned against the counter. Her lungs refused to fill. Jack Briggs threatened to destroy the wall she'd built around her heart.

"Mom, can I play with Michelle after school?" Haley slurped milk from her bowl. "We want to sled down that snow pile at the park."

A whistle shot from the teapot, and she poured boiling water over loose green tea leaves in the pot. "Why don't you ask her to spend the night? I'll call her mom later this afternoon."

Haley jumped up. "Thanks, Mom."

Dressed in a Columbia jacket and matching beanie, Haley waved from the drive as the bus pulled to a stop outside their house. What a cutie. Her little girl seemed to grow up a little more every day.

The exciting prospect of laundry and toilets loomed ahead in her alone hours. She should have homeschooled the kids. At least then she'd have something to do with her days instead of facing alone domestic duties that ate at her like a vulture on carrion.

The bus disappeared. Her Bible rested on the desk in the kitchen. Excuses pulled her away as she poured a cup of tea. Maybe she'd find some answers in those worn onion skin pages.

The doorbell interrupted her prayer. Good thing she'd grabbed the cashmere wrap to cover her pajamas this morning. A delivery man handed her a cellophane wrapped basket of chocolate-dipped strawberries. A huge red bow balanced on the top.

Jack.

A smile kissed her lips as she eyed the array. A sprinkling of coarse sugar on the chocolate winked at her like diamonds. The wrapping crinkled as she put it in the trash, and her mouth watered as the tempting aroma of fruit and chocolate burst forth.

Breakfast.

She fingered the card hanging from a golden cord on the handle, but plucked a stick from the bouquet and bit into it before enjoying the card. The coating cracked and strawberry sweetness exploded on her tongue, like the kiss they'd shared. She licked her lips, amazed at how sensuous certain movements were, and unfolded the card after swallowing another bite.

Please accept these as a parting gift. The poison will take effect in under two minutes. Less messy than Lisa, but just as satisfying. Wouldn't you think, Mrs. Farris?

The strawberry in her hand tumbled onto her Bible, leaving a wet red stain across the page. She staggered backwards. Her skin tightened like shrink wrap, and green tea churned in her stomach. Could the note be true? She eyed the glistening, sinister sprinkles as the room tilted on its axis.

God, help me.

Her back slammed into the seat, and she knocked a tea cup off the table, her nerves shattering. Cotton clogged her throat, preventing her from swallowing as she read the note again, ingesting the death-sentence. Words blurred on the page as the poison took effect. Thoughts in her head swirled like the ashes from the fire that burned in her throat. Her heart fought to escape her rib cage as her fingers reached for the phone and fumbled over the emergency numbers.

Who would take care of the kids when she was gone?

Drew Shaw grimaced as his legs dangled over the edge of the table in the training room of the Oakland facility. He cringed as the trainer taped his ankle, and he caught his expression in the chrome paper towel dispenser that hung on the wall. Not the face of the carefree running back that caught the winning passes from the quarterback at Stanford. The same dark skin and heavy jaw he'd inherited from his grandfather, but his eyes lacked the cocky gleam he'd worn when he entered the NFL as a second-round draft pick.

"This isn't going anywhere." The trainer—what was his name again?—squeezed his ankle to assure him it was tight. "Ready for the other foot?"

Drew groaned. He'd never suffered injuries in college, but his first months in the NFL had been brutal. *Welcome to the pros, Rookie.* "Get 'er done, man. Let's hope my body cooperates."

The trainer ripped the tape with his teeth and started on the arch of his cleat. "We have a state-of-the-art facility here and top-notch trainers. The best the NFL has to offer is at your fingertips."

The whole NFL gig wasn't what he'd expected. He'd been on top of the world after college, but one dropped ball in his first preseason game, and sports reporters smelled blood and sank their teeth in. Criticism was the one thing he couldn't handle.

The tape squeezed his ankle like the pressure to perform squeezed his life. He hadn't expected this injury.

"You're all set."

"Thanks." He jumped from the table, ignoring the encouraging smile from the trainer.

"Hang on a minute, Shaw. Let's think about some pain injections before the game. The team doc ordered Toradol, and Marcaine. I'll have another look at your MRI."

Drew shook his head. He wasn't going to line up for his cough syrup like the old fogies. He stepped gingerly against the confinement of tape and cleats. "I want to see how this feels in practice. I'm good. Thanks, man." The older players got regular pregame injections, but he wasn't about to let on how much the pain affected him. He jumped to work in the tape despite the pain in his ankle.

Living the dream, baby.

His feet worked a hole through the floor as he waited. Had she taken a bite before she read the card? The whole thing balanced on this question. If he knew her as well as he thought, she did, she didn't wait for words—she dove right in. He chomped an antacid. It *was* a cruel way to manipulate her, but it kept her off balance and away from the truth.

He thumbed through a file or two, preparing for an interview. It took seeing her with Briggs to awaken his heart. He'd loved her forever, but a new urgency burned inside. The threats would push her into his arms, finally. How long had he been waiting? He'd been the one to hold her hand since Pete's *suicide*. Now, he wanted to hold every part of her.

Committed suicide. He'd told himself the lie so often he'd started to believe it. Pete committed suicide. The ulcers in his gut churned. That's how lies worked. Say them often enough and they became truth. Pete committed suicide.

Panic swept through his limbs like the chill of death. What about Lisa? Could he cover her blood with a lie? Yes. He'd done it already. The cops hadn't found a connection. Marcy wouldn't either.

Why didn't the blasted phone ring? RING! She'd be rattled when she learned the effects of the poison were temporary. Hysterical. He flipped through a sports magazine to distract his thoughts.

Ah ha. His eyes scanned a picture of the rookie whom he'd targeted. Drew Shaw.

Another silver-spoon player who had it all, but did anyone notice the trainers who kept them in the game? He may have been overlooked when it came to football, but the game he played exhilarated him. "He's in the red zone, poised to score the game winning point." His best sports announcer's voice echoed around him.

He tore the photo of the running back out and pinned it to the wall. Shaw fit the criteria. Superstar potential. Early season injury. An easy idol to topple. The whole world watched millionaires try to knock each other's heads off every Sunday afternoon in the fall. Why not take his cut? And manipulate the game in the process.

The ringing of the phone sliced through the silence.

13

THE ALARM BLARED and Jack silenced it with a push of a button. He should get up. He'd already hit the snooze button three times, but his mind was more agreeably occupied this morning. A workout could wait. Nothing to get up for anymore except Marcy. He grinned and rubbed his eyes. If she was with him now, getting up would be the last thing on his mind.

The alarm went off again. "All right. I'm up." Jack's feet sank into the sheepskin rug. He grabbed the remote that controlled the blinds. He hit the button, and a sliver of light sliced through the room as the blinds rose. The house echoed with emptiness. Maybe he should get a dog. At least something to greet him with kisses every morning.

He pulled on his favorite muscle shirt and shorts and grabbed his shoes on his way to the weight room. The fluorescent lights flickered on in the weight room when he hit the switch. His equipment greeted him like an old friend; the weights anchored his life. Produced dependable results. He scanned his play list for something to match his mood after last night with Marcy. Frank Sinatra? Maybe later. Brant listened to some pretty cool stuff. What was that band he'd mentioned? Casting Crowns?

He downloaded a few of the songs Brant recommended and cranked the volume. After a warm-up on the Treadclimber machine, he stretched his hamstrings. The muscles served him well, he should treat them well. The red scars on his knee faded to white lines, but the damage they'd left behind still stung. Maybe it had been a mistake to make football his whole life, but he'd do it all again. He hefted the dumbbells to the rhythm of the song blasting from the speakers. Adrenaline pumped through his veins, but the contractions couldn't push the depression from him.

Marcy would soon see his inadequacy. He squatted deeply. He'd put his heart on the line. Her smile had already wormed its way into his heart, there seemed no cure. Warmth, not from exertion, rushed over him. Risks and all, he was willing to play this one out.

After his workout, Jack jumped into the shower, enjoying the six massaging heads that shot water from every angle. The roughness of football taught him to appreciate the finer things in life.

He slid his jeans on and buttoned them before pulling Pete's note from his pocket. He held it to the light again in his office and pulled the keyboard toward him. Isaac Johnson yielded a few pages of information on Google search. Jerseys for sale. Sports articles. Trash about his divorce and subsequent bankruptcy. And his agent?

He clicked the second page. *Agent: Horace Treadwell.*

Jack scanned the paper in his hand again. A simple MRI read from a radiologist in Chicago. A second opinion?

He scanned his contacts and dialed Isaac's number. "Isaac, this is Jack Briggs. We met at a fundraiser a few years ago. Listen, I'm sure you heard about the tragedy with Lisa Sparks. I heard you did an interview with her and wanted to get your take on the whole thing. Call me when you get a minute."

He checked the clock. Drew Shaw would be calling in fifteen for his pep talk. The housekeeper was due any minute, so he strode to the kitchen to stash the dishes in the sink and then returned to the office and closed the door. When would he learn not to be such a slob?

In his office, he logged in again and flipped his TV to the sports channel.

The phone's ring turned his head.

"Jack, this is Isaac Johnson."

His office chair creaked as he leaned back with a pen in his fingers. "Isaac. How you been, man?"

"This side of football, what can I say?"

"I get you. Kinda leaves a hole, doesn't it?"

"Uh-huh. The thing with Lisa was tragic. Carter's a good guy. Sorry to hear about it."

"Me too, man. So, did you have an interview with Lisa recently?" The front lock turned. Must be the housekeeper, Mrs. Nelson.

Had he hung up his robe?

Isaac continued, "Yeah. She wanted to know about my injury and what my life was like after football."

"Same here. Did you get the impression she was on to something else?"

"Not really. She asked about injections I'd been given throughout my career, stuff like that."

"You kept track?" Jack's forehead creased as his eyebrows crept up.

"Na. Trainers made recommendations. Docs wrote prescriptions. I followed their advice."

Dishes clanked in the sink. Mrs. Nelson must have started in the kitchen. "How's the knee these days?"

"Doing good, though I've put on a few pounds since playing days."

More than a few pounds, judging from recent photos Jack had seen online. "Tell Alice I said hello."

Silence lengthened between them. "We're split up. Some things never change."

"Sorry to hear that." The Internet reported Alice was Isaac's third wife.

"She signed a prenup. I'm good with it."

Jack cringed. *Nice.* "Thanks for calling me back. Let's play eighteen holes next time you're in Colorado."

"Sounds good. Great to talk to you."

He laid the phone on his desk after ending the call and massaged his temples, nowhere closer to an answer.

Wait a minute. What is the connection between Isaac and Pete Farris?

He'd expected to find Pete was his agent. Jack picked up his phone to call Isaac back, when Drew called.

"Drew, how are you?" The young man's voice held a strain of panic. He spun the pen in his hand like a pinwheel.

"Coaches are threatening to pull me from the starting lineup."

A couple of dropped passes last game were bound to ruffle feathers. "How many workouts did you get in this week?"

"Three or four. The bum ankle is really holding me back. You got any suggestions?"

What held Drew back was his mind, his focus. After twelve years in the pros, he knew they'd find the solution. "Listen, I'll come out and train with you for a week. You've just lost your edge."

"Whatever you say."

Jack rolled his eyes. The cocky little rooster also had an attitude. "How bad is your injury?"

"Just a sprain, but the minute I make a hard cut, it flares up again.

I've never been hurt in my life. What gives?"

Hadn't he wondered the same thing? "I'll be there Wednesday."

Blood throbbed in Marcy's ears, and her lungs refused to fill. Where was the oxygen? A chill penetrated her cheek, and she detected the faint odor of Pine-Sol. If she'd been run over, her body could not have ached so deeply.

Thoughts spinning into focus, she wrenched her eyes open.

How did she end up on the kitchen floor? Her hand throbbed as she pushed herself upright. She passed her palm in front of her limited vision. Blood coursed from a clean wound near her thumb, jagged pieces of shattered teacup littered the floor, the obvious cause.

Gripping her hand, she blinked at the benign scene before her.

Strawberries.

Her stomach revolted, and she clutched her middle, hoping she'd feel better when she got rid of the contents of her stomach.

She leaned against the counter and dialed Jack, but the call went to voice mail. A kitchen chair caught her as she stumbled backward, weak with whatever she'd eaten. The chocolate-covered orbs on the table mocked her with their beauty. Pure poison. Her head hung like dead weight from her neck. Her thoughts were foggy and nothing came to a logical end. Should she call 911?

She stood and heaved into the sink again. Not knowing how, she found herself at the table again, head against the cool wood. She would call the doctor when her arms could move.

Why was she being targeted?

Because she'd been the one to find Lisa's body.

She stifled a cry, struggling against the memories she'd wrestled for four years. She'd had blood on her hands since Pete killed himself. It was partly her fault, wasn't it? If she'd been more in tune to what he was doing, would she have had the chance to intervene? Fear cut through her. The person sending these threats knew her. Could they get in her head so easily they knew she'd take a bite before reading the card?

The never-ending nightmares she'd struggled through in the first few months after Pete's death slithered into her mind. She'd dreamed of waking over Pete's body with a bloody knife in her hand, or holding a gun, standing in a pool of Pete's blood.

The animal gnawed in the pit of her stomach as the poison wore off.

Thoughts like these took on a life of their own. She'd pushed the thought away so long, but it reared its head without warning, dragging her back into the terrifying cycle of doubt and guilt.

She remembered the preacher's words from long ago. "What you feed will lead."

Don't feed it! She would lose her mind completely.

She gripped the table, bringing her head up. This was about *Lisa's* blood. She still felt it slipping through her fingers. Still pictured the smeared handprints she'd left on the concrete.

Someone thought she knew more than she did. She knew *nothing.*

The clock showed she'd been out twenty minutes or more. This morning, she'd skated through the kitchen on a cloud of anticipation.

Avoiding the mess on the floor, she tripped to the kitchen sink for a glass of water.

Dust motes in weak sunshine drifted in the rays. She must not have gotten enough poison to kill her, though her head felt as if it was cleaved open with an ax.

Thank God.

She slumped against the counter as her phone rang. "Jack?"

"You, okay? Your voice sounds like you just got up."

"Could you run over for a minute?" She didn't want to explain on the phone.

"Sure." The warmth in his voice would change when he saw the note.

"Thanks. Let yourself in. I'm in the kitchen."

A thought seized her. The papers she'd sent to Lisa implied Pete had been involved in some kind of gambling. She'd been busy raising the kids while he built his career as an NFL agent, not acting as Pete's secretary. Her anxiety simmered into anger. What did someone hope to accomplish by sending threats when she knew nothing?

Drew stared at the blank TV screen after his call with Jack. Jack Briggs didn't understand him. Fool thought it was all in his head? The pain slowed him one step necessary to be in the target zone when the quarterback threw the ball. So what if Briggs was the greatest run stopper in the game? Briggs had never played against him. His chest puffed out. Even Jack Briggs couldn't have stopped Drew Shaw.

At least until he'd been injured. He cursed and threw a ball of socks at the wall.

Maybe he should consider an injection or two. Toradol was known for its anti-inflammatory properties and game time pain relief. If the pain weren't so bad, he'd get his speed back.

His pride rescued him from such thoughts the minute they'd arrived. The older players got injections. Not Drew Shaw, the eagle claw from Oakinaw. He flexed his biceps. He'd show them all. He was a first-class player without the crutch of an injection.

Working out with Briggs would be a good thing. He wouldn't allow the old goat to show him up on the field, or in the gym. It had been said that Briggs crawled into the mind of the running backs he faced.

When they faced off, the only place Briggs would want to crawl was under a rock.

The thought sustained him as he walked down the hall to the training floor to get his ankles taped for practice.

14

Jack exhaled. He'd heard fatigue in her voice. Had she lost sleep thinking of the other night, as he had? One more call and he'd head to Marcy's house. He cracked his knuckles and dialed Isaac again, clicked a pen into motion and pulled a notebook from a pile.

Isaac answered after three rings. "Hey, Briggs."

"Sorry to bother you again, Isaac, but I wondered if you'd answer one more question."

"Shoot."

Jack licked his lips. "Did you know Pete Farris?"

"The agent who committed suicide? I knew who he was."

"You mind me asking what your relationship was?"

"I never met him. Just knew his reputation."

Jack's brow furrowed. "You weren't working a deal with him toward the end?"

"Nope. You got the hots for his widow or something?"

More than the hots. He was panting. "You know her?"

"Nah. Saw her picture in the paper when her old man did himself in. Pretty nice package."

Jack rolled his eyes. "Thanks anyway, man."

"This got something to do with Lisa's murder?"

He hoped not. "No. I was just curious. Truth is, I have been seeing Marcy Farris."

"I knew it. Jack Briggs never had a shortage of women pounding down the door."

Whatever. "Hey, thanks for the time."

Isaac was still chuckling. "No problem, Briggs. Catch you later."

Jack pushed back in his chair. Why would Pete Farris have a medical record for Isaac Johnson? Weren't medical records private? He'd had his own sealed from the public. Didn't need every reporter in town doing a write up on the injury that brought Jack Briggs to his knees.

After a protein shake and a handful of berries, he jumped into his car for Marcy's house.

He waved to Mrs. Nelson. Faintly, he could hear the tune of the music she listened to on her iPod. He pointed to the door. "Going out for a while. Did you find your check?"

She removed it from her back pocket and waved it. "Got it." She smiled and went back to work on the bathroom.

Jack eyed the rearview mirror, which offered a stunning view of the Rockies. After the blizzard, the weather had been cool and sunny. Typical Colorado.

Now that the real storm seemed to have subsided, it was time for the next move. He'd order a nice dinner and have Mrs. Nelson make the dining table up for two. it was time he and Marcy had a real date. His gut twisted as he thought of the flavor of her lips against his, and his mood lightened and he smiled to himself.

Before he could ask her, he had some explaining to do. He shouldn't have taken that paper from Marcy's house. Worse, it belonged to her husband. Maybe his stuff was kind of sacred or something. *Crap.* If he wanted to know more about Isaac and Pete, he'd have to confess to taking the paper. He'd yet to encounter Marcy in a foul mood, but better risk it. Like it or not, this thing with Pete and Isaac wouldn't leave his mind alone.

The front door pushed open, and he called into the room. "Marcy, you there?"

A weak voice quickened his pace. "In the kitchen."

The paleness of her face brought him to her side. "What's wrong?"

"You think you could run me to my doctor's office?"

He crouched beside her, resting his hand on hers while the clammy texture of her skin alarmed him. "Are you sick?"

Hand shaking, she pressed the note into his hand and pointed to the strawberries. "Check this out."

Panic struck him as he noted the red stain in her Bible and the discarded strawberry missing a bite. "How long has it been since you ate it?"

"I think I'm going to be okay. Just need to be checked out." She pushed to her feet with his help. "I'm a lot clearer than when I woke up."

His heart galloped. "You passed out?"

She shook her head as he helped her to the car. "I feel a lot better, really."

He balanced her weight and the feelings that fought for prominence in his heart. "I can see that." The note fell into his pocket where it would make it to the hands of the police as soon as they arrived at the doctor's office.

"Did you get the lab results?" The concern in Bobby's voice warmed her. It was nice to have so many caring friends. Marcy clutched the paper in her hand with a tremor. "The lab results were inconclusive, but the strawberries tested positive for a mild hallucinogen. The police will get the report, too." Little good it would do.

"I wish I had been home a couple of days sooner."

"Jack took care of everything, and I'm feeling much better. Headache is totally gone. We can still do our yearly trip to Pete's grave."

"I wouldn't miss it. Take care."

Unlike years past, she looked forward to the tradition. She hadn't sought the journey she was on, but wanted to face it with a clean heart. Pete squelched the passion she'd been so ready to display, but it'd been awakened by Jack. Time to say good-bye to the past and embrace the future, whatever it may hold.

Marcy checked her watch. She was the room mom in Haley's class this afternoon and still hadn't dressed. She climbed the stairs two at a time. Bobby had so many good qualities, except for the fact he ducked Christianity like a boxer.

Because of Pete. She guessed Pete's heart was parable-like. The Word had sprung up in his life quickly, but as soon as trials came, the wind blew it away because it had no root. Bobby saw his brother dive in headfirst, only to see him floating on the surface sputtering profanities. No wonder he avoided God.

She remembered the black looks from some church members when they learned her husband ended his own life. Maybe she'd thought that way about suicide at first too, but losing Pete the way she had changed her perspective. Grace was as big as God, and a person had to be in desperate agony to end their life. Even a spider ran out of the way when she tried to stomp on it. God placed life within the hearts of His creation, but sometimes life was just too much to bear. She'd never judge anyone the same way again. The aftermath of suicide taught her at least one thing. *My grace is sufficient for you.*

She opened her closet door, seeking jeans and a T-shirt. How would Jack react to the Gospel? He hadn't been against attending church and even reminded her to pray after receiving the threat. Rocky soil? She slid the jeans on and jumped a few times to distribute the respective body parts before buttoning them. Good old body had given her two children. She tried not to disrespect it, but it'd become a habit. Jack didn't seem to mind that she'd once been a size six, but was now an eight. Not that she'd tell him.

A long-sleeved T-shirt with an ACU logo completed the outfit. Nice. Other women coordinated pants and tops with jackets and vests, but she was lucky to put two things together for Sunday morning. Good thing her job required casual dress. Most days she stayed in her pajamas until eleven or twelve.

Marcy stared at her reflection in the full-length mirror behind the door.

Words from the strawberry note echoed in her head: *Less messy than Lisa, but just as satisfying.*

Her blood ran cold in her veins, and a lump the size of a baseball returned to her throat. She turned away, unable to look at her reflection. Did the person who sent the threat want her dead or nearly so? He'd taken Lisa out in one stroke. Why wouldn't he just end it?

Weather-beaten headstones in the cemetery dotted the brown grass. Marcy pulled her jacket closer about her body as the brisk December wind thrashed around her. Her scarf threatened to come loose, but she clutched it at her neckline. With her other hand, she covered her eyes as she scanned the area for Bobby. His silhouette, in contrast to the naked trees that stood like guards over the graves, filled a space in her vision.

Haley stayed behind with Brant. They made their own pilgrimage at another time.

Avoiding headstones, she hurried to Bobby's side, craving the meager warmth his body would provide.

"Morning." His breath came out in clouds as he rubbed her shoulders.

She smiled. "Hi."

Together, they turned to Pete's grave. The engraving looked new, as if it'd been cut yesterday, but the pain was fading.

Peter Gene Farris
April 4, 1961-December 6, 2004
God give you peace.

They spent a moment in solitude, each wrapped in private thoughts. Bobby grabbed her hand and trembled. "It's harder this year."

She swiveled. "Why this year?"

He shrugged, but his eyes looked wild with grief. "I'm afraid my memory of him is slipping. Afraid I'll forget him."

She nodded. She feared he'd be forgotten, too. She patted Bobby's arm. "We won't forget him."

Wordlessly, he wrapped a supportive arm around her shoulders and pulled her close. They stood silent at the grave again. The billowy puffs of their breath a testimony to life even as they paid tribute to death.

She was ready to close this chapter, but Bobby's obvious sadness weighed heavily on her heart. He'd lost his only brother that night, and he didn't seem to be holding it together as he had in years past.

"Marcy." The husky tone of his voice broke her heart.

She leaned onto his shoulder. "Yes?"

"He was lost too soon, but I don't want to lose you."

"I'm right here, Bobby. We're doing this together." She squeezed his forearm.

He turned, the usual teasing light gone from his eyes. "I mean it Marcy. In the years since Pete's death, you've come to mean so much to me."

Where would she be without Bobby? He was the best brother, but the look in his eyes suggested something more.

Something she'd never suspected.

She felt him tremble against her, his grief—and something else—dizzying in its fierceness.

"I've been in love with you, forever." The words spilled out, and he spun her in his arms. "I'm losing you. Pete had his chance. Give me one, too." He gripped the back of her head with his hand and kissed her hard, crushing her lips in a furious expression of the emotion he'd held in check too long.

She struggled away from his kiss, breathless with the intensity of it. "You won't face life without me. I'm here." She splayed gloved hands against his chest.

His gaze penetrated her heart. "It's not enough, Marce. You should know that. I know how lonely you've been without Pete." He hungrily claimed her lips again, groaning out all the emotion of the years in a single expression.

It was too much. In that surreal moment, she might have melted against him, clinging to him for strength, but for Jack. Her head said this was natural, expected. Her heart denied it.

Jack inspired a passion she could not express. A yearning that she'd never felt, even for Pete. This complicated her life beyond words. Her father always said, "Men and women can never be *just* friends." Why were the lines always getting blurred? Judging by Bobby's kiss, they'd erased them all.

Bobby leaned his forehead on hers. "I love you. I always have."

The biting cold couldn't compete with the emotion boiling in her heart. Sadness crept in and nested. She couldn't pursue this with Bobby. Much as the kids would love it. As natural as it seemed. Her lip quivered. This decision hurt someone she loved. "I can't do this, Bobby."

"Yes you can. I know it's a new idea. But I can love you better than Pete ever did."

She stifled a chuckle. That wouldn't be hard. Especially for a man like Bobby who'd been the rock in her life. A pang pierced her heart. He was one of her best friends, a father-figure to Brant and Haley, and a rock of stability in her own life. If she kissed him back, what road would they travel together?

He disregarded her words and loosened her scarf. His breath warmed her neck as his lips roved toward her ear. Her body responded, but not the way Bobby would appreciate. This was no "fake it 'til you make it" moment. "This isn't right for us, Bobby."

He pulled away from her neck. "Why?" A cloud of cold air accompanied his question.

"This place brings every emotion to the surface for us. You're going to fly back to Houston or wherever and regret it happened."

"I will never regret loving you." His green eyes pierced hers.

How could she explain her heart when she didn't understand it herself? "Pete did."

His eyes clouded. "My brother never appreciated you. Haven't I shown you my heart?"

He had, indeed. She swallowed. If she broke his heart, where would her rock be? "Give me some time."

He masked the emotion in his voice. "This about Jack Briggs?"

Marcy nodded. Would her heart respond to Bobby if Jack hadn't got there first?

"You'll come around." He tipped her chin. "I have faith in you."

Faith? He should put his faith in God who would never let him down.

God, what do I do? Give me the words! "There is only one person who will never let you down."

He smiled confidently and turned back to Pete's grave. Had Pete been alive, Bobby would have a black eye for kissing her. She found the situation almost comical, the kiss over his grave. He never wanted her himself, but wouldn't have wanted to share.

Typical brothers, Bobby and Pete were in constant, friendly competition. Some of her fondest memories were of Christmases when Bobby and Pete would play ping-pong at their parents' house until sweat dripped from their shirts. Neither was willing to give in until the last.

Surrounded by the ghosts in the cemetery, her own loss hit her harder. How would Haley or Brant feel? There was a unique bond in that relationship, one she didn't understand.

He tossed a coin on Pete's grave, a symbol of the game of football they both loved. Heads or Tails. "Love you, brother." The emotion in Bobby's voice sent a wave of tears to her eyes. Good thing tears were salty, it kept them from freezing on her cheek. She leaned into him and cried for everything they'd both lost. For her kids' dad. For the man Pete could have been, and the man standing next to her.

15

DREW'S FINGERS TAPPED the steering wheel while he waited for Jack to arrive at the airport. He grinned as Briggs stepped from the terminal into the California sun. "Les get the party started." Briggs stood a good five inches taller than him and wider by far, the guy looked like he was pure muscle, even after retirement. He turned down the Lil' Wayne song that vibrated the windows.

Drew texted his license plate number to Jack and saw recognition dawn on his face. Jack shouldered his duffel and stalked in his direction. Drew rolled down the window, making sure his bicep showed above the door. "Bout time." He stuck his hand out the window.

Jack shook it. "Drew, Jack Briggs. Glad to meet you." He swung his bag into the back seat and slid in next to him. "Nice weather. I left thirty-two degrees in Denver."

"I'm from down south. Never seen much snow 'til I played for Stanford."

"You'll see your fair share playing in the AFC west."

He pulled out into airport traffic. "That's what I hear. How you stand livin' in Broncos country?"

Jack grinned. "Some say it's God's country."

His head bobbed with the music like he'd been charmed by a snake charmer. The rivalry between the Raiders and the Broncos went way back. "Whatever you say, man. So, whatcha doin' now you're retired from the league?"

"I'm thinking of buying a car dealership."

What the heck? Drew glanced at Jack. "You messin' wi' me?"

Jack flashed him a perfect smile. "Yeah."

His head swayed back and forth as he laughed off the joke. "Pretty funny, for a white guy. You been to the training facility before? It's near the beach. Pretty nice."

"Did you get in a workout this morning?" Jack lounged in the leather seat.

He shook his head. "Thought that's why you was here."

Briggs leaned forward. "Listen, if you want to play this game, you've got to give it everything you've got. Hold nothing back."

What did he know? His college years at Stanford were nothing to sneeze at. "Look, man. I think I know how to play the game."

"There is more than knowing how to play."

What was this dude about? "Don't know what'cher sayin'."

"Do you wake up every day thinking football?"

Drew thought for a moment. When had football stopped bein' fun? Somewhere between Pop Warner and Stanford.

"If it's not magic off the field, you won't have magic on the field. I was the first one in the team weight room every morning. Made the coffee for my teammates. I would get up and say to myself, 'You get to play football today.' Attitude makes all the difference. It's like I said when we talked yesterday, the heart of a player wins the game. Gotta find the magic."

Who did Jack think he was, Tinkerbell? "Oakland is a long way from Disneyland, bro."

"You think I'm kidding? Look at the profile for most great players, and you'll see magic there. They loved the game. Loved the smell of the grass. You gotta feel it before you step on the field."

Maybe the guy had a point. Drew took the exit for the training facility in Alameda. He couldn't remember the last time he'd enjoyed anything about football. He sure wasn't enjoying it now with a bum ankle and bad press.

"Tell me what you like about the game, Drew."

"The fame. The money when I signed my contract." Wasn't that enough?

"You grew up with little?"

Little didn't begin to describe the way his mom had scraped for cash his whole life. "Mom never had two dimes to rub together. Don' know how I woulda gone ta college if I hadn't had the scholarship."

"And your dad?"

What dad? "I think he's living on the streets down in Nashville or somewheres. Who knows?"

Jack nodded.

"Don' you go judgin' my past." He was getting all up in his face like some preacher man.

"Knowing your background helps me know you. I'm here to help you find the magic. I don't care if you were raised by Barney the dinosaur. It's part of who you are."

Drew pressed on the accelerator and peeled into the parking lot. He glanced at Jack from the corner of his eye, but the guy wasn't fazed. This wasn't his first rodeo.

Salty sea air blew in through Jack's open hotel window, a perfume he'd almost forgotten. The week with Drew Shaw went better than he expected. Immersed in the NFL, he'd felt life creep back in. If he could teach the kid to tap the magic, he'd have a winner on his hands. Question was, could he find it himself. Facing the nothingness of life at his kitchen table, he wasn't so sure the magic ever existed.

His shoulders creaked from their hard-hitting workouts. It felt good to be sore again. Felt really good to show that rookie what a hard hit was.

Jack slid the window closed and grabbed his bag, anxious to be on his way home to Denver where Marcy promised to join him for dinner.

He sent her a text. "Leaving Oakland in a few minutes. Can't wait to see you tonight."

She texted back. "Meet you at the airport at six."

Jack bounced his eyebrows. Hadn't he imagined this night when they'd first met? A quiet dinner somewhere, just the two of them? Normally, reservations at *Fruition* were hard to come by, but he'd pulled a few strings, and they had the best table in the house tonight at seven.

When he spotted her at the baggage claim, his heart did a back flip. Dressed in jeans, high heeled boots and a sweater, she could have knocked him over with a feather. Even his good knee was weak. A charm bracelet on her wrist tinkled as she waved.

Had it only been a week since he'd seen her? He wanted to memorize every line of her body as she walked across the crowded room. In two steps, he closed the gap between them, sweeping her into a hug that communicated what he wouldn't dare in such a public place.

"Glad you're back." Her muffled voice sounded delicious against his chest.

"Me too. Colorado gets better every time." He winked at her.

He threw an arm around her as they walked through to the parking lot just outside the baggage claim to her car. "How was your week? We hardly had time for a conversation in the midst of our schedules."

She leaned into him. "Brant's game is tomorrow, and we could hardly contain the excitement at the Farris house."

Exhaust choked them in the parking garage. He coughed. "Let's get on the road before we get lung cancer. Tell me about your week."

She spun the keys on her thumb. "Sure you trust me to drive?"

"I'm sure the minivan is more can than I can handle."

Once she'd pulled out of the parking garage, he relaxed. The hideous, but iconic, red-eyed horse outside the airport flashed past. "So, what's up lady?"

"I'm so frustrated. The police haven't found anything. Someone put the strawberries into the truck or exchanged them."

"You didn't get another threat, did you?"

"No."

He half turned to look at her. "Something else happened. I can hear it in your voice."

"Murder, threats. Nothing new."

"Never a dull moment." He grabbed her hand, but traffic demanded she drive with two.

"Tell me about your week in Oakland. Pete used to hate going to the Black Hole."

"It's not so bad. We had some good practices. Felt great to be back in the action."

"Not enough action at home for you?" The teasing in her voice brought a smile to his lips.

"Plenty. Did you hear anything more about Lisa's murder?"

"To quote the sergeant in charge of the case, 'The threats may or may not be a connection to Lisa's murder.'"

His anger burned hotter. "There's a connection. You were the one to discover the body." He cringed at the memory of finding her in shock, covered in Lisa's blood. "I think that's the problem. The killer thinks I saw him or something."

"Did you?"

She squirmed in her seat. "No. I saw nothing until the crowd parted, and I could stand. I haven't slept all week."

"Why didn't you call me?" He hadn't noticed the dark circles under her eyes until now.

Her knuckles whitened on the steering wheel. "I just didn't want to bother you."

Didn't want to bother him? Had he made their relationship seem like bother? He tempered his anger a little. Who was he to guess what motivated her decision? "Wish you would have told me. We're in this together, you know." He thought of the paper he'd taken from her office.

"Are we, Jack? I'm just not sure of anything anymore."

He laced his fingers with hers. "We're on the same team. Trust me."

A few miles passed, and Marcy followed directions from the airport to *Fruition* on her GPS. "Tell me more about Drew? Did you get through to him?"

"I think we made some progress. Did you see his game on Sunday?"

"Nope, it was an early game, so I missed it for church."

"That has nothing to do with the fact it was a Raiders game?" He ribbed her.

She grinned. "It could have. You know I can't stand them. Does Drew fit the whole Raider persona?"

Jack chuckled. "He'd like to, but it's not going to happen. Rough on the outside maybe, but he's got a good heart."

When they pulled into a Sixth Street parking spot, he jumped from the car to open her door. When she gave him a puzzled look he said, "It is a date, after all. Our first official, I think."

She bit her lip and sighed as she took his hand. "I'd like to forget this week ever happened."

"That's my plan." He kissed her fingertips, which only fueled a desire to kiss more of her. He tucked her hand into the crook of his arm as they crossed the street. Something deeper than she'd admitted to was bothering her, but he would get to it later.

Once they had ordered drinks, he relaxed, trying to put all the disconnected pieces of the puzzle from his mind. He raised his glass. "To a peaceful evening."

Her shoulders straightened. "I'll drink to that."

Light brightened her eyes by the time dessert arrived. Jack loved the easy way she laughed and the curve of her smile. He could watch her for hours.

If this was life outside the game, he could grow to like it.

Marcy licked melted chocolate off her spoon, though she thought she'd never eat it on strawberries again. After a tough week, she'd almost dreaded the evening with Jack. Bobby's words felt like a barrier, but without knowing her burden, Jack coaxed her mind to relax. The food at *Fruition* was amazing, but it was Jack's presence that made the evening perfect.

"Thanks for asking me, tonight. I needed to get out of the house. I felt like a caged animal after awhile."

Jack leaned back in his chair, eyes roving her face with pleasure. "You should get out more." He toyed with her fingers.

He raised an eyebrow. "I can see a list of excuses in your eyes."

She ducked her head. He read her mind more easily than she cared for. "Let me get back to you."

She'd said similar words to Bobby last week at the cemetery. Sheesh. Life was a real mess.

"Okay."

After Jack paid the bill, he took her arm, "Let's walk a bit." His hand warmed the small of her back as they exited. "I love downtown at night."

"Me, too." She took a confident step outside. Thugs beware, she was walking with Jack Briggs. Now was as good a time as any to bring up what she'd debated telling him all night.

"I think I've made a connection between the murder and something I found in Pete's office."

He stopped. "You have?"

Her stomach dropped. "I found some files taped to the bottom of Pete's desk a few weeks before Lisa's murder. Because of Carter's relationship with Pete, I didn't want him to find out, so I asked Lisa to look into what I'd found." She shivered. The words sounded so damning when said aloud.

"What was in the files?"

"Player profiles, some point spreads and betting books, but the only reason I thought it might be significant is because of its secret location."

"And you didn't tell Carter?"

A chill wind bit through her jacket, making her wish she'd remembered her gloves. "No. Carter and Pete didn't exactly see eye to eye all the time, and I didn't want Carter tempted to take the opportunity to run Pete's name in the mud."

"I thought you two were pals."

She shrugged. "He's one of the best friends I've got, but when it came to Pete, he was a little jealous. I didn't want to make things worse."

A string quartet warmed up under a circle of lamplight near an alley. Jack pressed her against the wall to block the wind, though they stood outside the circle of light. "So Lisa was murdered after you ask her to look at some of Pete's files. What do you suspect?"

People stood in front of them, leaving them in the semidarkness and the protection of the alley. Despite their snug vantage point, vulnerability left her soul exposed to the elements. She took a breath. Should she open this subject with Jack? Did she trust him to handle her heart with care? Much as she loved Carter, he would have run wild with her suspicions. "I think he was being paid off to ignore some kind of fraud. The players listed in the files weren't Pete's clients. Their names were followed by sums of money." Her heart slammed against her ribs when she felt Jack stiffen.

He faced her. "Do you remember the players' names?"

"No. I barely looked at it before I sent it off." A knife of pain stabbed her heart. If she'd have taken more care, looked closer. "The murderer got her instead."

Jack's arm slipped around her waist and the warmth of his body instantly soothed her. "We don't know she was murdered for that reason."

"Poor Lisa." *Oh, Pete, what were you involved in?* Whatever it was, it sure shed light on why he committed suicide.

Strains of spirited music carried out into the frigid night air, clear notes flitting to the clouds like fireflies. If they could just press pause on life, she'd stay here in his arms forever.

"Did you keep a copy of those files?" Jack's thoughts hadn't received her subliminal message.

"Nope. I assume they're still at Lisa's house."

His grip tightened. "If someone found those files, they might think you were connected with what Pete was doing. Maybe that's why you're receiving threats."

A lump the size of a grapefruit lodged in her throat. "I stayed as far away from Pete's business as he did from me and the kids in the final months."

He met her gaze. "So you saw the signs?"

"You mean of him committing suicide?" She drew a quavering breath. "I guess I did." She shrugged a shoulder. "He'd been 'experimenting' with pills for months. If he were involved in something illegal, it would make more sense. Pete didn't seem like the depressed type."

And therein lay the root of her personal guilt. The chasm between them had grown so wide, she didn't recognize the danger signs in her own husband.

"It wasn't your fault, you know." Jack's thumb traced her cheek and his fingers lingered in her hair. Suddenly, the night wasn't so cold. He stepped closer to her. "I'm not going to let anything happen to you. Not like Lisa." He held both bare hands.

Her heart cried to believe him, but no man could protect her. He was the strongest man she'd ever known, but Jack's strength might not be enough to keep her from a killer. Still, his promise wrapped her like a hug. "Thanks."

His eyes held hers as he brought her hand to his face, and her whole body shivered when he exposed her wrist and pressed his lips against the tender flesh of her inner arm. A wildfire roared up her arm at his touch.

"You are too precious to lose."

Her eyes slid closed as his lips found hers in the darkness. She thought she should resist in light of what happened with Bobby this week, but the magnet of Jack's kiss pulled her in. He pushed her against the brick wall and dug his fingers in the hair at the base of her scalp. This was no Bobby Farris kiss. Suspended in his embrace, the need for him weighed heavily in her stomach, and she drew a ragged breath when he lifted his head.

Jack's voice tickled her ear. "What?" He stole a kiss near her ear.

She'd never admit to comparing his kiss to Bobby's. "You make me smile, that's all."

"We're gonna get to the bottom of this. I promise."

She inhaled the aroma of his cologne. "Where do you get your strength?"

They turned back to the music. He shrugged and sighed. "Tell you the truth, I don't feel very strong anymore."

"Who is stronger than Jack Briggs, number 44?"

"Exactly."

He read the puzzled look on her face. "I felt strong when I was wearing a number and a jersey. Outside of football, I feel like I'm about to drown."

She chewed her lip. After a person experienced the pinnacle that life offered, where did they find fulfillment? "When we look for strength inside ourselves, we come up sorely disappointed."

"I think I read that Gandhi quote on the Internet."

She jabbed him in the gut. "It's no Gandhi saying. It's an original Marcy Farris."

He bowed in front of her. "Allow me to offer you my apologies. You are one wise woman."

"A wise man is strong, and a man of knowledge increases power."

"Now, that's gotta be Gandhi."

"King Solomon. The wisest man in history."

He cocked his head in consideration. "So strength is attributed to wisdom."

She leaned on his shoulder. "The Bible tells us to be strong in the Lord and the strength of his might." The verses came easy to mind. *Not so easy to follow.*

"I don't trust any strength but my own."

"Maybe that's the problem." She shivered. "I'm freezing. Can we head to the car? I think my toes are going to fall off." She'd dropped the provocative statement like a bomb and took cover in safer words. Sometimes that was the best attack. She'd tried head on with Pete for too many years with nothing to show for it but a bruised cranium.

When they arrived at the car, Jack tucked her into the passenger seat. "Your hands are like ice. Let me drive home." He kissed her nose and took the keys.

A giggle threatened as he folded his long legs into the driver's seat of her Honda minivan. "Takes a real man to drive a minivan."

Pete wouldn't do it. He made her chauffeur him all over town when they went out with the kids. Jack Briggs was a puzzle she'd enjoy piecing together.

16

He ground his teeth in frustration and gripped the phone. "Drew Shaw refused further injection treatment?"

Unbelievable. Without a Toradol injection, the chances of injury lessened. He needed the superman effect the drug created in order to make his own plans possible.

"I think he's trying to man up without it. I suggested Toradol, of course, before the game next week. You know how these rookies have to work to prove themselves."

If the trainer in charge of Shaw's care had any idea what was riding on this . . .

"Thanks for keeping me informed. I'd love to see the kid succeed."

He would succeed at warming the bench, if everything went according to plan.

"Jack Briggs came out and worked with him this week. I think we'll see a different running back this Sunday."

Great.

The static hum of the furnace in his office mimicked the throbbing of his pulse in his left temple. "Probably just what he needed."

Briggs blighted his life like the plague. He chased a roll of TUMS across his desk with his finger, and his office chair creaked under his weight as he leaned back. If Shaw wouldn't take injections, the serum was useless. He'd have to move quickly, profiling Shaw with greater diligence, so as to complete the task before the deadline and the post-season. Once the bets were in, the curtain would fall, either on his life, or Shaw's.

He opened the week's press releases. Just as the caller said, Briggs had spent the week training with the young running back as a favor for the coach. He rolled his eyes. Briggs was no philanthropist. He was a weenie, trying whatever trick he could to get up Marcy's skirt. That lowlife scumbag.

Insulting Briggs improved his mood, even as his guts squirmed.

Marcy wasn't herself these days, but even if she found out *everything*, she couldn't know Drew was the final victim. He cursed Jack Briggs, his meddling, and his good looks. Finally, he cursed Marcy for falling for a stud like him.

Heat warmed his palms as he rubbed them together. Right now, he had to forget about Marcy. If anything could get her off his mind, it was work. He needed to focus on Shaw and how to coerce him into some treatments. The sooner this job was completed, the sooner he could move on. His stomach burned like fire. The stress was killing him.

Bright sunshine filtered through the picture window in Jack's kitchen. At ten Saturday morning, his heart already galloped like a runaway stallion as he pulled on a sweatshirt and beanie for the game. His palms sweated. The high school state championship was on the line, but to him, it felt like the Super Bowl.

And he wasn't even playing.

He licked his lips and applied balm before heading out the door. Shaking as he was with adrenaline, he'd be lucky to arrive at the stadium without a fender bender. Adding to his excitement was the woman he'd be sitting next to. He hadn't seen her since their night out, but she roved through his thoughts constantly. Especially today.

He grinned as he imagined her chewing her nails off in anticipation. Brant was a great player, but there was always a risk of injury, and Marcy was almost neurotic. But his heart raced in the face of danger. It was all worth it. He'd faced injury every time he stepped onto the field. Brant would be fine.

The new car smell in his truck bolstered his good mood as he pulled out of the garage.

He nodded at a police officer when he pulled into the school. A mounted policeman patrolled the parking lot and uniformed officers flanked the stadium entrances like a blue picket fence. He breathed a sigh of relief. One less thing he'd have to worry about.

A line of people snaked from the ticket gate, all waiting at tables for their bags and person to be searched. A metal detector stood guard, looking more like a guillotine on the horizon than a safety device. State games brought an increased security risk, but this was overkill because of the murder.

He scanned the crowd for Marcy and Haley waiting in one of the lines. Haley waved her black and gold streamer stick when she spotted him. "Jack! Over here!" She danced with excitement, and his heart warmed despite the chill temperature. That kid was irresistible.

He grinned as he approached, catching Marcy's eye. She wore her dark hair in low pigtails covered with a pink ROOTS beanie. Cute and sexy. His kind of woman. If the two words could ever go together, they described Marcy Farris. If Haley weren't here, he'd start the pregame show right there in the parking lot. "Hey."

Marcy craned her neck and smiled into his eyes. "We saved you a spot in line."

Jack massaged her shoulder through her ski jacket. "Things have changed since the last game. This place is crawling with security."

Her eyebrows disappeared beneath her beanie. "Does it bother you?"

They stepped forward and Haley thumped her bag onto the folding table to be examined.

Jack put a hand on her waist while Haley was occupied explaining the contents of her purple unicorn bag to the officer in front of her.

"I'm glad there's more than one person looking out for your safety."

She nodded and placed her purse on the table. "He could get you, you know."

When they passed security, the cinnamon scent of churros mixed with buttered popcorn and people. His mouth watered, but it wasn't for the food. "How was Brant before you dropped him off?"

"Pretty sure the carpet in his bedroom has a path the size of the Grand Canyon in it from pacing. I heard him going back and forth all morning."

"You feed him a good breakfast?"

"He wanted one of those green shakes, and I added eggs and bacon."

Haley's head whipped around as she shouldered her bag. "You made Brant bacon? I didn't get any." Her lower lip protruded.

Marcy shrugged. "I'm pretty sure he ate the entire pound."

Jack laughed. "Gotta feed the animal."

"Speaking of animals, Brant's such a pig. He should have saved me some." Haley thumbed the straps of her backpack in disdain.

Marcy ruffled her bangs. "Leave him alone. You're eating popcorn today at the game, and he isn't eating at all. Follow Jack, he's got our tickets."

The ant-like procession took a few minutes, but soon Marcy had spread her stadium blanket for Haley and pulled out the sunflower seeds from her enormous bag. "Here." Haley took the bag and smiled.

Marcy handed him a black and gold decorated stadium seat. "Thought this might be more comfortable than metal bleachers."

With yellow electrical tape, she'd written Farris and Brant's jersey number on the backs of three cushioned seats. He imagined Haley had added the gift wrap ribbon curls in black and gold on the support bars. "Thanks. Haley, aren't you going to sit on one?"

She glanced at him. "Nope. Mom brought that one for Uncle Carter."

His mood plunged. *Oh, goodie.* He tackled the sarcasm. "Carter's coming?"

Marcy nodded. "He called at the last minute, and I had an extra ticket. Bobby was coming too, but Brant got to invite one person to sit on the sidelines with him, and he asked Bobby. I think most kids asked their dads."

Jack nodded and watched in disgust as Marcy set the stadium seat up on the other side of her. She rubbed her hands together. "We never made it to the stands last game. I think this is a good sign."

Haley jumped up. "Mom, can I go say hi to Nate and his dad? Nate's brother is on the team."

Marcy smiled. "Sure, but stay where I can keep my eye on you." She watched Haley bound down the bleachers and slid a hand onto his knee.

He brought her fingers to his lips. "Your hands are freezing."

She pulled out black gloves. "Brought my gloves this time."

Too bad. He would have offered to keep her hands warm the entire game. That'd give Carter something to stare at.

"You can keep them warm for now."

She tucked her hand into the crook of his arm, and he melted. She scooted her seat closer to him and leaned on his shoulder. Thank goodness for the cold temperatures.

"Brant's invested so much in this game. His dad would have been so proud."

"He's a hard worker. Any father would be proud of a kid like Brant."

The flag team and band took the field for the pregame, and Marcy tensed. "Pete would have eaten this up, but I worry about Brant. I know he's at that moody age, but I'm sometimes concerned." Her knee bobbed up and down.

She worried about Brant following in his father's footsteps. "Did Pete have a diagnosed condition?"

"Nope. But you have to be pretty messed up to commit suicide, right?"

He squeezed her shoulders. *Not as messed as you'd think.* He frowned. Pete Farris had an amazing wife and two beautiful kids. He was well respected in the league. Why kill himself? Maybe he did have some kind of mental condition. Or could it have something to do with the files Marcy found? Maybe Pete was involved in some dirty business, and the guilt ate at him until he couldn't stand it any longer.

He checked to be sure Haley wasn't within earshot. "I was thinking. Maybe we should sort through some of Pete's stuff together this week. Maybe we'll find something. Any luck getting those files from Lisa?" He'd rather tell her about the paper he'd taken over a cup of coffee at her house.

She shrugged. "I looked through everything before except that box you saw the other night. I'm kicking myself for not making a copy of those files now." She glanced around the stands. "I, uh, didn't exactly tell Carter I'd asked for Lisa's help. I'm not sure that information would be helpful while he's grieving."

He agreed. They couldn't involve Carter in this.

On cue, Carter mounted the bleachers, taking the stairs two at a time. Great. He forced a smile. "There's our man now."

Marcy stood a smile glowing on her face. "Carter!" Dressed like he was attending a casual business meeting, he climbed up the remaining bleachers and into her embrace.

Carter's eyes swept her slowly, and a smile reached his eyes. Oh. Jack knew that look.

She gestured to the seat Haley decorated. "Saved you a seat."

Before he sat down, he stuck out his hand. "Good to see you, Briggs." He settled into the seat as the cheerleaders took the field and Haley returned from her visit.

"Uncle Carter." Haley threw herself at him, and he wrapped her in a hug that lifted her off her feet.

"How've you been, squirt? You're as pretty as a princess, you know that?" He tugged her ponytail, earning a smile.

"You know what? Jack promised to buy cotton candy at halftime. I'll bet he'll get you some too. I know blue is your favorite."

He'd be sure to remember Carter's favorite color of cotton candy. He could barely restrain his eyes from rolling into his skull. Instead, he focused his attention on the cheerleaders who were tossing girls into the air.

Carter doffed the tip of her nose with his index finger. "Do you ever think about anything besides food?"

"Yeah." She squirmed to sit beside him. "Want to know what else? Brant says Jack is Mom's boyfriend. I think he's my boyfriend, too." She turned to him. "Aren't you, Jack?"

Marcy stiffened. "Haley!"

He glanced at Carter. "I wouldn't trade that title for a spot in the Hall of Fame, Haley."

Carter narrowed his eyes but turned to Haley. "And all this time, I thought I was the boyfriend."

The man spoke the truth.

Haley bit her lip in contemplation. "You used to be, 'til Jack came. Right, Mom?" Haley turned to her imploringly.

Oh, this was getting good. Both men eyed Marcy's face.

Her lips pursed into a circle and pink sprang to her cheeks. "Just to be fair, why don't we split them? You take Carter, and I'll take Jack." She met his gaze boldly.

Jack gripped the metal seat to stop himself from dancing. Take that, Carter Cunningham!

Carter's face twitched, and Marcy patted his knee. "I haven't talked to you. This week better than last?"

"Yeah. I'm not sure I can handle a career change right now, but I may take a sabbatical. I've got some other stuff lined up that should get me through a year or two."

Jack's interest peaked. "You leaving *NFL Rush*?"

"I've got some plans. After what happened with Lisa, it's hard to focus on the things that used to matter so much. I need to step out of the limelight for a while."

Jack understood. After his injury, he'd needed a year without the flashbulb of society constantly blinding him in order to heal, if you could call this healed. People said time healed all wounds. He'd gone from hero to zero in one play, but it took a heck of a lot longer to get the status back. He couldn't face the press as a zero. His esteem slipped when he left the league limping.

A voice boomed from the speakers, and Marcy clutched both hands together and bit her bottom lip. "Ladies and gentleman. Welcome to the Colorado State High School 4A Football Championship between the Thompson Valley Eagles and the Northglenn Norse."

The stands rumbled with stomping feet, and Marcy clutched his arm. Excitement vibrated through his bones. Unforgotten nerves welled up in his stomach as he watched the big tunnel of balloons to see which player would rip through the paper first.

An electric current passed between them when the announcer said, "Number 41, inside linebacker, Brant Farris."

Marcy jumped to her feet and hauled Jack with her. "Go Brant!" She jumped up and down, her pigtails bouncing with her. She put her fingers to her lips and whistled. "Number 41! Whoo Hoo!"

She turned to him, excitement glowing on her face. "I think I'm gonna be sick. I'm so nervous."

He took his hat off and held it open to her. "Be my guest. It wouldn't be the first time I've used this hat for something other than keeping my head warm."

She shoved the hat playfully back into his chest. "Gross. Keep your hat on, Briggs. Someone is bound to recognize you." Her eyes danced as she reminded him of their first meeting.

He pulled her back down. "Jack Briggs? You mean the greatest run-stopper ever to play the game? I haven't seen him, but get his autograph if you do because it'll be worth big money one day."

She shoved his shoulder and settled in to watch the kickoff, knee bobbing like a kite in the wind.

Carter glanced at Marcy. "So Brant still wears Pete's old number. His dad would have been proud." His gaze flicked to Jack's and seemed to say, "See? We've got a history."

There was more than one game being played today.

Words failed him when he read nostalgia on her face. "Pete would have loved this. I was just telling Jack how proud he would have been."

Carter spoke first. "He's got the best mama in the world." He patted her shoulder.

She grinned. "You're totally biased, but I'll agree with you."

The tension between Jack and Carter couldn't bruise the excitement that surged through Marcy's mind as the Eagles kicked off.

Her heart twisted. *See what you missed, Pete?*

Her chest tightened in fear as Brant stood behind the line for the first play. *Lord, protect him.* The Northglenn quarterback handed the ball to their running back; she held her breath as Brant tackled him before he'd run three yards.

"Yes!" Jack clinched a fist. "Go gettum, buddy!" He turned to her, his eyes bright with excitement. "Did you see that? I told him to watch that middle lane."

Was that pride in Jack's eyes? She knew now why she liked him so much. A man could never admire her kids enough.

"You should consider coaching. You'd be great at it."

TV cameras and news crews crammed onto the practice field beyond, adding to the surreal feeling of the day. Brant's big day had finally arrived.

Three plays later, the Norse were forced to punt, and the stands erupted in a furor as the Eagles' offense took the field. Brant said their quarterback was already getting calls from big name colleges. The team had the talent this year to take the title. She grinned at herself. She wanted it as badly as they did.

Haley dug in her bag. "Did you bring my hat, Mom? My ears are getting cold."

"I made a list and checked it twice. Dig a little deeper, sweetie."

Carter pulled a stocking cap from his pocket. "Here, Haley. Use mine."

He pulled the hat over Haley's ears, making sure it was snug on her head. She smiled. Everything considered, Carter looked pretty good today. The brown leather of his jacket brought out the color in his eyes. He leaned on his thighs, eyes fixed on the game. Even dressed down, as he was today, Carter had an air of refinement about him, like he belonged in New York instead of Colorado.

A pang of sadness cut through the joy of the day. Things were not right in the world. Jack had brought so many churning emotions to the surface. Thoughts of Jack and Bobby and even Carter swished in her heart like garments in a washing machine. Should she remarry so the kids could have a father? Jack awakened *certain* longings she'd missed about marriage, but Carter would fit into their lives like a lost puzzle piece. He had always had a soft spot for the kids and often remembered special days. He'd been a part of her life since before she'd met Pete; irreplaceable in some ways. Her eyes flicked down field as the quarterback threw a pass which was dropped by the receiver. A collective sigh rippled through the crowd.

Her mind continued its trek through the muddy recesses of her circumstances. Then there was Bobby. He'd said he wanted more, but he was family already. Best to keep him in the role of uncle and not complicate matters. They'd parted on good terms, but her stomach still turned when his insistent kisses came to mind. They had a fun, competitive relationship. Why mess it up trying for more?

Why couldn't things be simple? Like football?

Marcy asked Jack a question about the game, but he was so engrossed he didn't answer. Her eyes slid over the muscled curve of his shoulders. She'd always had a thing for big shoulders. What was up with his jealousy today? Did he think she'd choose Carter Cunningham? He was Jack Briggs, for heaven's sake. Any woman in the world would give their nail-polished big toe to sit this close to him.

Maybe they weren't that different. She'd struggled so long to see something beautiful when she looked in the mirror. She'd spent too much energy seeking the approval of a man. One specifically. And when he rejected her for other pursuits, her worth fell into pieces. Maybe Jack put his worth in football. Now that he couldn't play, he found little value in his life.

The possibilities of a future with Carter dimmed in the light of Jack's glow. His eyes followed the players on the field, locked in concentration like a laser beam. Carter warmed her heart, but Jack lit the fire in her soul. He'd be perfect if he were a Christian.

Northglenn called a time out, and Jack turned to her. "Did you ask me something earlier?"

"It was nothing. I was enjoying you watch the game."

His eyes danced with hers. "What I wouldn't give to be in high school again. Those kids haven't a care in the world. They get to enjoy the game for the pure fun of it."

"Brant could have used that advice before the game. He was pretty tangled up emotionally."

Her son put a lot of pressure on himself, and now he wanted to prove to Jack he was worthy of his attention.

"I should have called him this morning and given him a Briggs pep talk."

She cocked an eyebrow. "We wanted him to win the game."

He shook his head and grabbed her hand when play resumed. "Think you're so smart, don't you?"

The half passed with no score from either team, but none of the excitement in the crowd dissipated. When the band took the field, Jack jumped up. "Ready for your cotton candy, Haley?"

She took his hand. "Sure."

"That's the way, Jack. Win her heart with sugar. What if someone recognizes you?"

"So I sign a few autographs." He shrugged. "I'm finding it's not as bad as I thought it would be."

Jack took Haley's hand, and they started down the stands.

Carter leaned nearer. "I can't tell you how good it is to see you, Marce. I've missed you."

"I know. Why don't you stay a few days since you're here?"

He checked his cell. "I'd love to, but I've got to fly to Oakland."

"Seriously? Jack was just there. Is it something for the magazine?"

"Not officially. You know how it is."

She smiled. "Yes. Everything in the NFL is a potential story."

Emotion flickered across his face, but she couldn't identify it.

His hand warmed her arm. "Why don't you take a break and come with me? The weather won't be warm, but I'm sure you could use the time off."

Wow. Did stay-at-home-moms get breaks? They'd spent some fun times on the beach in college, but it was Jack she envisioned when she thought of a break on the beach. Had she replaced her friend so easily? "Bobby's working and Mom and Dad already had Haley this month so I could come to the funeral. Christmas is only a couple of weeks away. Why don't you stop back by and stay for the holiday? It will be better than sulking at home."

"I don't sulk." He pushed his lip out in a pretend pout.

Good. A glimmer of his old humor. "You seem like you're feeling better. Have you been to her apartment?" What if he found the files Lisa had been working on?

"I can't bring myself to go there, yet. Her sister said she'd go by next month. Maybe I'll be ready to sort through some stuff by then."

"I didn't go through Pete's files for two years. Some stuff is still in a box in the closet."

He sat up. "You didn't get rid of all Pete's things? I thought Bobby took care of the office stuff."

"He did, but some things got left. I threw them in a box and shoved it in the closet. Someday, I'll let Brant look it over for anything he'd like to keep." More than likely, she and Jack would be tearing into it later this week. But, the less Carter knew about her involvement with Lisa, the better.

Jack and Haley returned with the bags of fluffy cotton candy in hand. Jack grinned devilishly and handed Carter a blue cloud of cotton candy. "Haley insisted."

Carter nodded. "Thanks, Hales. I like the way it turns my tongue purple." He stuck his tongue out at her and she giggled.

She snatched her bag from Jack's hand.

Horrified at her daughter's behavior, Marcy gasped. "Haley. Did you thank Jack for the cotton candy?"

"Sure I did." She hid the bag behind her back. "Jack says you have to share his." Haley sat on her blanket and turned on the iPad. "Uncle Carter, come see the new app I've got."

He jumped over the metal seat and joined her, pressing his head on top of hers.

With a gleam in his eye, Jack loosened the twisty-tie, pulled a pink cloud of sugar from the fluff and smiled as he put it in her mouth. It melted instantly on her tongue, and she pushed the rest in with two fingers. His gaze never left hers. She licked her lips, but laughed at her fingers, which looked like dolls wearing pink wigs. Jack seized her fingers and licked the cotton candy off. The sensuous movement lasted less than a second, but a hot rush bottomed out in her stomach at the touch of his mouth. She pulled her hand away. "Think of the germs."

"You haven't been picking your nose or anything?"

She shoved his shoulder. "I should have. That would teach you." They'd buried the emotions that surged between them in humor and sarcasm. Safer that way with all the other people around.

Her breath caught as Brant trotted onto the field, carrying his helmet.

"Go Eagles!"

She remembered the binoculars she'd packed in the bag and offered them to Jack. "Want a front seat view?"

"Thanks."

Carter sat with Haley until the Eagles defense returned to the field and then he joined the adults. "Scoreless in the third quarter. Quite a matchup." He settled into the stadium seat she'd brought.

The Norse offense threw a fifteen yard pass, but Brant jumped and intercepted the ball on the thirty-yard line. A wave of total panic and excitement smashed into her and she stood, screaming. "Go! Go! Go!"

Brant tucked the ball under his arm, his legs churning on the grass. Jack's and Carter's shouts drowned her own vigorous yelling. She held her breath as the confused Norse offense reacted to the interception. Brant's feet seemed to move in slow motion as he made his way toward the goal line with two huge players on his tail. The screaming crowd quieted as every nerve ran with him down the field.

"Come on!" Her heart urged him forward. At the fifteen-yard line, she cringed as the players trailing him made a running leap for his feet, and the three of them rolled like a tumbleweed on the prairie.

17

PRIDE SURGED IN Drew's chest. He'd beat Bomanski to the gym this morning. The week with Briggs reminded him how much he loved the game—not that he'd let on. A new energy pulsated through his limbs. He couldn't afford to throw away another game if he wanted to keep playing.

Grabbing his clothes and waterproof mp3 player from his locker, Drew headed to the showers, passing a wall of mirrors on the way. He flexed. *Still lookin' good.*

His confidence rose a notch. They'd have home field advantage this Sunday, and he'd rock the joint. Something in him came alive and growled as he anticipated the game.

There were no other players in the bright shower bays, so he turned up his music and cranked the hot water. During their meetings, Briggs opened his eyes to the mind of a linebacker. His message was clear. They want to kill you.

As a running back, avoiding the three hundred pound dump trucks that wanted to steamroll him was priority number one. He internalized the beat of the song and visualized himself, as Jack suggested, making a great catch, running for a touchdown. If there was something to the whole sports psychology thing, he'd capitalize on it.

After showering, he wrapped a towel around his waist and dressed near his locker. He clenched his sore hands. During one of his training days with Briggs, he'd spent four grueling hours catching passes, perfect ones and not-so-perfect ones. He'd shaken his head in defiance at the time, ready to beat the crap out of him, but the reps had done him good.

Being drafted second round made him think he'd arrived; talent on autopilot. But an ankle injury and five sucky regular season games later, he was willing to take some advice.

Drew checked the time. He was due for a session with the trainer in ten minutes. He'd head to the cafeteria and grab a snack before their meeting. He intended on working extra hard today to be ready for the game tomorrow.

Coach stopped him in the hall. "Jack Briggs help you sort some things out, Shaw?"

He tempered the rebellious swagger that threatened to leap out. "Yes, sir. The guy is brilliant."

"You got that right."

He rolled his shoulder and kept walking. He'd never get used to taking orders or swallowing his pride. Briggs said, in the NFL, you had to do both. That would take some practice, but he'd made a start.

The scent of cornbread and smoked sausage made his southern taste buds tingle, but he'd promised himself he'd eat clean six days a week. On his way out, he grabbed a whole wheat turkey wrap with guacamole, which filled the hole in his stomach so he could focus on the session ahead.

"Come on in, Shaw." The trainer on duty held a clipboard in his hand.

"Let's start with some exercises on the Powerplate today, then we'll get you iced down. If we can control the inflammation in your ankle, you'll heal faster."

"Powerplate?"

The trainer gestured to a machine with a large platform. "The magnetic vibrations cause fast-twitch muscle fibers to fire during static exercise. The result is better circulation and improved balance. It's our new toy." He punched the digital display, and the machine whirred to life as Drew stepped on. His eyeballs vibrated.

"Keep your knees soft to counteract the vibrations. You'll get used to the pulse."

Fifteen minutes later, Drew stepped off the machine, muscles twitching in the backs of his legs. He wiped his brow. He'd worked as hard in therapy as he intended to in the game Sunday, thanks to encouragement from Jack Briggs.

The trainer settled him into a chair and packed ice around his ankle. "Looked strong today. How'd it feel?"

Drew flexed the ankle as the ice began to burn. "Pretty good. Sore still."

"I think Toradol is the way to go tomorrow. It's gonna take the edge off the inflammation while providing pain relief throughout the game."

Time to swallow his pride. The last thing he wanted was to mess this up. "Sounds good, man."

"I'm in the locker room Sunday at nine. See you then." He made notes in his chart and nodded a good-bye as Drew headed for the door.

The whistle's shrill blast cut through the air to end the play short of the touchdown. Marcy's heart stood still as the seconds ticked by. Brant was trapped somewhere in the unmoving pile of arms, legs and helmets on the three-yard line. She held her breath, clutching Jack's arm in fear as the coaches ran onto the field.

Her pulse pounded in her ears as a player rolled off Brant and staggered to his feet. Brant crawled onto his hands and knees and faltered forward, his head buried in the turf in a display of obvious pain. He fell to his stomach and beat the grass with his left hand. She swallowed fear, he'd moved his arms and legs: a good sign he wasn't seriously injured.

Bobby joined the coaches on the field as the other players trotted to the sidelines. The voice of the crowd hushed as the coaches and trainers made a circle around Brant, blocking their view. Soon, Brant's head appeared above Bobby's as they pulled him to his feet.

The crowd cheered as he made his way to the sidelines, obviously favoring his right hand. Bobby walked alongside him, asking him questions. She turned to Jack, her face on fire.

"Probably a broken hand or fingers." He flexed his own hands as if feeling the injury himself. "Hands get caught between two helmets. Hurts like heck, but he'll be fine."

"Can he finish the game?"

Jack nodded. "Probably. Bobby's with him. They'll get him a cast in the locker room and send him back out fourth quarter."

Her stomach turned, and Carter patted her arm. She'd almost forgotten his presence. "Want me to run down and check it out?"

Relief flooded through her. Two NFL trainers were better than one when it came to Brant's health, and he could bring back a report. "Would you?"

He shook his head and headed toward the locker room.

She clutched her hands together. "Tell him I'm praying for him."

Carter nodded. "Will do."

The injury time out ended, but the Eagles couldn't push past the three-yard line for the touchdown. They settled for a field goal. The ball sailed through the uprights, and a roar of approval erupted from the stands as the Eagles took the lead.

Sunshine pulled the temperature out of the teens. She struggled with her coat until Jack slid the jacket off.

"He's going to be fine. Don't worry."

She sighed. "I can't help worrying. Pete would have handled this better than I do."

He pulled her close and whispered on her head. "You're doing fine. His PlayStation game will suffer more than his football." He gestured like he was playing with the controller.

She laid her head and her worries on Jack's massive shoulder for a few moments, breathing in his masculine scent and the calm he exuded.

"Is Brant going to be okay, Mom?" Haley twisted a strand of hair between her fingers.

"Come here, baby." She pulled Haley into a hug. "Carter went to check on him. He'll be fine." She wanted to believe it, too.

By the time the fourth quarter rolled around, Jack's prediction came true. Hand in a club-like cast, Brant lined up behind the defensive line for the first play of the quarter to massive cheers from the crowd.

Carter returned to their space on the bleachers. "I think he broke his hand in two places, but we've got him fixed up. Took some Motrin for the pain and insisted on getting back in the game."

Marcy hugged him. "Thanks for checking on him." What would she do without these men in her life? "It's safe to play?"

Carter pulled her close. "Sure. If he was a receiver it would be a different story, but he should do fine for one quarter."

Her hand fluttered to her heart. "Glad it wasn't something more serious."

"He's got his dad's fighting spirit. That boy won't quit."

Bitterness washed into her throat. Fighting spirit? Pete was the biggest quitter she'd ever known. She swallowed it where it didn't hurt so much. "Is the bone going to need to be set?"

"Bobby and I took care of it. I think it will be fine. Felt good to be working like that again."

The light in Carter's eyes warmed her. It was good to see life in his smile again. She squeezed his arm before settling down to watch the game.

From the sidelines, Brant raised his clubbed hand to show one of the cheerleaders his plaster badge of honor. She grinned and waved a pom-pom in his direction. Marcy shook her head. A mother's worries never ceased.

Jack elbowed her. "You're not the only one interested in Brant's injuries."

She nodded. "I noticed."

"You know her?"

"Nope. But Brant knows the rules."

"What rules?" His eyes teased.

"Brant understands there is a season for relationships with the opposite sex. And even then, she has to be a Christian."

He talked while he watched the game. "Interesting. Do the same rules apply to Mom?"

Her heart dropped. She thought of Carter, who'd shared her faith through the hard times. Maybe she should apply those same rules to her own life, but one look into Jack's eyes told her otherwise. "I'm still holding out for you, Jack."

He ignored her comment. "The measure of a man is tested on the field."

"Are you saying I'm too protective?"

He tweaked her nose. "You're a fast learner."

She sighed. Jack had a point. Brant would never develop his own strong faith unless she let him try it out for himself.

Thin clouds covered the sun, but Jack turned his attention to the game. Brant was a stud, going back in when most kids would come crying to Mommy. He'd played a few games in a cast himself, and while it wasn't comfortable or easy, he applauded Brant for his determination. He grinned as the Eagles completed a fifteen-yard pass. Sometimes, an injury fired the team up like a steam engine, pushing them forward until they were unstoppable.

He eyed the coach talking to Brant. Maybe Marcy was on to something. He might make a good coach one day. Brant couldn't say enough about the school coaching staff. It seemed like they were a close-knit group. He could stay in the game while maintaining some distance from the league. His week with Drew and the Raiders reminded him what it was like, and he didn't miss the pressure of the press.

He glanced at Marcy's profile, bottom lip rolled between her teeth in anticipation as the team neared the goal line. She mumbled encouragement to the team with her fingers tangled nervously. It revved his engine seeing her so into the game he loved.

Everyone jumped to their feet during a Norse third-down conversion. The defensive line bent over in their three-point stance, puffs of steam blasted from their mouths. Jack's heart hammered his chest wall as the quarterback shouted the count. His stomach clenched, and he held his breath as the play came into motion. Marcy jumped to her feet and yelled as Brant batted down the pass with his club-hand. Northglenn was forced to punt, and the crowd exploded as the minutes on the clock ticked away. They'd done it. The Thompson Valley Eagles were the State champs.

Someone from the crowd pumped his fist in the sky. "We won!"

"Whooo Hooo!" Marcy jumped up and down in excitement, turning to Jack with a grin a mile wide. "They did it."

He scooped her up in a hug. "Yeah." He shared the thrill of victory as if it were his own. Brant and his team clustered in the field, raising helmets and voices in unison. Soon, the famed Gatorade dump crashed over the coach's head and he reacted as if he didn't know it was coming. Good stuff.

Marcy landed on her feet still screaming and crying as the teams passed each other in congratulations. She raised a hand to the sky. "Thank you, God."

Movement on the field attracted his attention. Obviously emotional, Brant searched the stands for his mom. He nudged her. "There's Brant." He stood back.

When she saw him she waved and blew a kiss. He grinned and grabbed his jersey with both hands, pulling it from his chest. His dad's number. Brant kissed his fist and pointed to the sky, dedicating the game to Pete. She laid her hand on her chest and smiled through a veil of tears, nodding her appreciation through a watery smile.

The moment stamped itself on his heart. This win was a victory over grief as much as it was a victory on the field. He glanced at Marcy. For mother *and* son.

Carter watched the exchange, as well. He twirled Haley on his arm, but his eyes never left Marcy's face. Her eyes met Carter's, and he reached for her shoulder, his face chiseled with emotion. An understanding passed between them, leaving Jack the outsider. Carter understood the impact of the victory in Marcy's life. Jealousy and competition fell away. How could he hold a candle to the years they'd spent together? Maybe she would be better off if he just threw in the towel and let Carter win.

He almost jumped in surprise when Marcy turned to him, tears streaming down her face. His heart jumped into his throat. Carter may have understood the emotional moment, but she'd turned to *him*. He pulled her against his chest, tears wetting his shirt. He stroked her back in an effort to comfort her, even if he couldn't understand the emotion like Carter did. He wrapped his arms about her, wishing to guard her from every hurt she might face in the future. And hurts from the past, too.

She pulled her head from his shoulder. "I'm sorry." She wiped her eyes. "Brant needed this more than anything." A tear streaked down her cheek, and she swiped it away with the back of her hand.

He wanted to kiss away every tear, but felt Carter and Haley's eyes on them.

"Mommy. You should be happy. Brant's team won." Haley stroked her mother's arm.

Marcy turned and slid a finger down Haley's cheek. Emotion quavered in her voice. "Sometimes moms cry when they're happy."

Haley shrugged and continued to cheer with the crowd as the news crews took the field for interviews.

She sniffled and leaned back into his chest as he wrapped his arms around her. His chin nestled on the top of her head while they watched the team celebrate. The warmth of her body seeped through his jacket, but this was her moment. He wouldn't muddle it with his own desires.

The black look on Carter's face said he hadn't missed the way things went down. Jack met his eye, and he turned quickly away. They both held a piece of the same woman.

18

MOST OF THE crowd cleared, but Marcy still paced the bleachers, waiting for Brant. She gritted her teeth against the memories. Pete missed all this because he gave up on life just when they needed him. Why? The question hurt as much today as it had the morning she'd discovered he'd overdosed on pills. She might never understand the 'why' of her husband's suicide, but she refused to let his choices muddy her future any longer.

Jack must have sensed the edge in her, because he stood behind her like a rock.

This victory brought the losses into perspective. Her kids needed a faith example, not more rules, not more should and should-nots. Jack was right. Pete's faith piggybacked off her own, and she wasn't going to let that happen with her kids. Brant and Haley would see *her* celebrating a victory over the past, starting now. If Pete was involved in a scandal, she prayed her kids avoid the consequences. He'd left them for her to face, and at this moment, she knew she'd been ignoring the truth: Lisa had been killed because of the files she'd sent. They were connected; she felt it in her gut. Even in the face of the threats, she'd been more terrified of the truth and its consequences, but it was time to face it before the game was up. She would conquer if it killed her.

Jack knew something wasn't adding up, and she'd need his expertise to put the pieces together. She felt the strength of him from behind her. They were on the same team now.

Brant and Haley were too precious to risk.

She twisted her hands in anxiety. What was taking Brant so long? Was his injury worse than they'd expected?

Jack put his arm on her shoulder. "When the adrenaline wears off, he's gonna feel that hand."

She nodded. "That's just what I was thinking. It's going to be a long night."

"Will you allow him to go to the team party?" Jack's eyes challenged her.

"I'll leave that decision up to him. He's old enough to make up his own mind about those things, I think."

"Rules about dating, but not about partying?"

"His choices will determine his destiny. My rules won't change his heart. I think it's time he gets the chance to show his faith."

He hugged her. "And what if he goes down the wrong track?"

"I'll be here to help him find the right one again. Everybody stumbles along in this life." She knew that better than anyone.

Bobby finally jogged up the stairs toward them, warm brown eyes focused only on her. The smile on his face warmed her heart. If anyone understood the significance of this day, Bobby did.

"Hey you." He caught Haley and swung her into a hug. "How is my little ankle biter? Did you see the game? Pretty awesome, huh?" He caught Marcy's eye again and grinned. "He'll be up in a minute. The Reporter Herald was interviewing him."

"Really? How's he feeling?"

He shrugged. "He's gonna hurt for a few days, but he's doing great. Keep that cast on three weeks at least. We'll take some x-rays tomorrow. Make sure there's no breaks we didn't detect."

She hugged him. "Thanks for looking after him. What would we have done if you hadn't been with him?"

"They probably would have pulled him from the game. I was able to cast the hand in the locker room, and he was itching to get back onto the field." Bobby noticed Jack. "How are you, Briggs? Good to see you again."

Jack shook his hand and smiled. "You were in the right place at the right time tonight."

"Glad I was on hand." He turned to Marcy. "Did you see him dedicate the game to Pete?"

She lowered her gaze. "I did. Thanks for being here to sit with him. It meant a lot to him."

"Proud to take Pete's place."

Surrounded by the three men in her life, emotions competed for a place in her heart. An awkward silence followed.

Soon, Haley spotted her brother. "Brant! Up here." She jumped down two or three bleachers and met him in a bear hug. "Eww." She backed away. "He's sweating like a pig."

Brant scrubbed her head and raised his armpit to her face. "Didn't wear deodorant, either."

Haley shoved him, but stayed close, a smile beaming from her face.

Jack stepped forward and fist bumped him. "Congratulations, man. How does it feel to be the state champions?"

"Feels awesome." Brant's gaze swept the group. "Thanks for coming."

Marcy couldn't stand it any longer and pulled him into a sweaty hug. "I'm so proud of you!" She pushed his wet hair from his forehead. "How's your hand?"

He raised it like a trophy. "Uncle Bobby fixed it up."

Bobby winked at him. A bubble of joy nearly lifted her heart from her chest as she witnessed the closeness of their relationship. She'd been so blessed with the men in her life. She squeezed Brant's shoulder. "How does it feel, honey?"

Brant shrugged. "Feels okay now."

Bobby pounded on his back. "Take it easy for a couple of days. Ice and Advil will work wonders."

She turned to Bobby. "Are you working this week?"

"I fly back tonight, but I'll be home for Christmas. You have plans?"

She glanced at Jack who was engrossed by Brant's game play-by-play review. Would he want to be part of their holiday? He'd mentioned his mother, but she didn't live nearby. "I was thinking of asking Jack to join us. Do you mind? We'll do our traditional Christmas Eve at our house. Carter's coming, of course."

The sting of her words showed on his features. How quickly she forgot the minefield of her life. "If it makes you uncomfortable, we'll just make it family."

His eyes, so like Pete's, begged her. "Give me a chance, Marce."

A chance at her heart? Wouldn't she know if there were sparks between them before this? But didn't he deserve a chance? He'd supported them through everything. "I'll ask Jack for New Year's. Let's celebrate as we always have this Christmas."

He narrowed his eyes. "What about Carter?"

Carter heard his name and stepped nearer. "You were saying?" The challenge in his eyes heaped burning bricks of guilt on her shoulders.

Bobby smiled oily. "We're discussing the *family* Christmas we were planning this year."

Carter looked at Marcy. "What time is dinner?"

Her cheeks flamed and she sighed. This was one game she wasn't going to win. "Around noon as usual." These guys sure knew how to take the triumph out of the day.

Haley called Carter to her side and when his attention was engaged, Bobby grasped her elbow and whispered, "I'll be there. Where I belong." The significance of his words wormed in her stomach. Why couldn't she just love him? Her eyes flickered to Jack, who was riveted on Brant's every word.

There's your reason, girl.

Marcy shook her head, focused on the one man she knew her heart couldn't live without. "Brant, do you have plans to go out with the team tonight?" The calmness in her voice surprised her. *Good job, mom.* She was giving him the choice.

"You'd let me?" He nearly dropped his helmet.

"Sure. I think you know what kinds of things honor God and what kinds of things don't. I want it to be your choice."

He searched her face. "Seriously?"

She smiled. "Time to give you some freedom, don't you think?"

He grinned from ear to ear. "Thanks, Mom."

His hug warmed her like the sun. "Love you, Brant. I'm so proud of you. Your dad would have been so proud of you and your dedication to the team."

"I wish he were here."

"So do I, sweetie." She leaned her head against his shoulder pad which smelled of sweat, dirt and grass. The party began moving toward the exit.

"So, I can go out with the guys tonight?"

She bit her bottom lip between her teeth. This was a leap of faith. "When do you think you'll be home?"

"How about 11:30?"

His conservative estimate surprised her. *Good boy.* "That sounds fair. Call me if you need a ride. I'll be up. Haley and I are watching the Anne of Green Gables series."

He rolled his eyes. "And to think I'll miss that for the team party. Derek said he'd drive me home."

Jack stopped him at the bottom of the bleachers. "A sober driver only."

Brant grinned. "Got it."

She looked at him, praying for some other bits of wisdom. "Any other advice?"

"Coach Black from USC always reminded me to be a gentleman."

"Is that how you got the reputation as the Gentleman Linebacker?"

He nodded. "That's where it started. And it's good advice, on and off the field."

Bobby, Carter, and Haley had been straggling behind, but caught up with them. "I'm ready to go, Mom." Haley's pink cheeks registered the chilly temperatures.

"Okay, honey." She glanced back at Bobby and Carter who brought up the rear. "Haley and I have a movie date tonight."

Carter smiled. "Not Anne of Green Gables, is it?"

Haley's mouth hung open. "How did you know?"

"Your mom used to watch that in college."

His wink brought heat to Marcy's cheeks. Carter probably knew her better than anyone, but she'd been keeping secrets from him. Especially after Lisa's murder.

Their feet clanged on the metal bleachers as they descended the last stairs, and Marcy hugged Brant one more time before they parted ways. "I love watching you play, Brant." She fished in her purse. "Here. Take these Advil with water at about five. That should get you through the night. Don't hesitate to call me if something comes up or you're in pain."

Brant clutched the pills. "Catch you later." He hugged Bobby and Carter. "Thanks for coming, guys."

"Great game."

"Made us proud."

"Check out my interview in tomorrow's paper. I mentioned a few people you might know." He winked and walked back toward the stadium.

"Our boy is growing up fast, eh, Marce?" Bobby shrugged. "Couldn't have imagined this moment when he was born. Watched him pee in his face the first time I changed his diaper."

Haley snorted and covered her mouth. "Brant peed in his own face?"

"Yep. I learned real quick to have the clean diaper ready before I took off the dirty one."

Carter and Jack laughed. Marcy shook her head. Boys!

Carter ribbed Haley. "You've got to add that story to the arsenal."

She pointed to her temple. "It's all up here."

The group chuckled, breaking tension that mounted as good-byes loomed.

Marcy put her arm around Haley. "Come on, Haley. We're going to stop at the store for some snacks before we settle in."

She waved at the guys as she and Haley walked to the car. She regretted not saying a proper good-bye to Jack, but a round of hugs would have put the last nail in her coffin. Seriously, why couldn't God have blessed her with sisters?

Jack slid into the driver's seat and slammed the door. Well, that was interesting. Marcy bounced from man to man like a pinball. Heck, she'd given out more kisses and hugs than a clown in a kissing booth. He was on the outside looking in when it came to Carter and Bobby, and if he guessed right, they both wanted a piece of the action. He ground his teeth. He should have paid attention when his head told him she carried major baggage. Two men worth, to be exact.

His phone vibrated in his pocket. He'd forgotten to turn it back on after the game ended. He grinned when he read the text from Marcy. "Didn't get to say good-bye properly. Sorry."

"Define properly." He imagined her blushing as she read the text.

"Sudsy."

Whoa. His stomach somersaulted. Could she get any closer to what he wanted to hear? "How about Monday night?"

"You got it. The kids can go to Bobby's house."

"Sudsy. I like that."

"We have work to do, remember?"

He laughed out loud as his thumbs typed the response. "Yes, I remember." He'd offered to go through Pete's box of papers looking for some answers. "I'll bring dessert."

"Deal."

He pulled out of the parking lot and guilt hit him. He shouldn't be so hard on her about her relationships. He was the newcomer, and Marcy had been through a lot. She'd done nothing more than build a good defensive line.

He whistled a long note. Marcy was worth the effort.

Carter and Bobby were tough competition, though. Heck, they grouped around her like moths to a porch light. She and Carter obviously had a long friendship, and Bobby was her brother-in-law, the kids' surrogate father. Yep, tough competition.

A jolt of adrenaline shot through Drew's body as he entered the stadium on Sunday morning. He sucked in a breath of salty sea air as the door closed behind him. This was the day he would put the name Drew Shaw in the mouths of football fans again. He could feel success knocking on the door. He flexed his ankle. It felt good after the Powerplate workouts, but he'd still go in to see the trainer like he promised. The injection might make up the step he needed to be a playmaker today. He picked up his pace, eager to get to the game. He strutted to the beat of the song on his iPod, a practiced frown on his face. He approached the training office and pulled his ear buds out.

"Mornin'."

He should learn these trainers' names. The guy lifted his eyes from the computer screen and reached for the latex gloves. "Shaw. Let's get you warmed up."

He followed him into the gym where other players worked with light weights or on the treadmill. No one pushed the heavy pounds on game day. After ten minutes on the stationary bike, he jumped down and did some calf lifts on the end of a board.

The trainer approached with a clipboard. "How's the ankle today?"

He jumped a few times to feel it. "Feels pretty good, man. Can't complain."

The trainer eyed the ankle. "Do you feel any pain?"

He licked his lips. "Yeah, still sore."

"Did you think about a Toradol injection?"

He nodded. "Cain't hurt."

The trainer smiled. "You're right. The side effects are minimal. Mostly benefits, in my opinion."

Drew splayed his hands on his thighs. "Shoot me up."

The trainer went to the back room and Drew inspected his hands. Jack Briggs' voice came back to him. "Greatness happens before you hit the field on game day."

He imagined his hands poised to catch the spinning ball and the perfect catch he'd make on the ten-yard line, felt the ball tuck deep into his ribs as he rolled right for a running play. Today, he'd bring greatness onto the field.

The trainer returned and held a couple hypodermic needles to the light. "Drop your drawers. You take this one in the butt."

He tapped the syringe with his middle finger. A sting followed by a cool sensation flowed through the glute muscle as the medicine took up residence. The trainer pressed a cotton ball to the injection site.

"I can put some pain reliever into the ankle itself." He held up the other syringe.

Drew nodded. "Good."

The familiar sting, followed by the cotton ball.

He patted his ankle. "Let's get your ankles taped up. Let me know how that worked for you when I see you Monday."

19

JACK LEANED AGAINST the frame of Marcy's front door and rang the bell Monday night. He puffed frozen breaths of air into the black sky while he waited for her. The paper with Isaac Johnson's name on it burned through his hip pocket like a hot coal. If he were a praying man, he would pray she took the truth well.

She opened the door with a smile, and he let his eyes drink in every detail of her from the green T-shirt she wore over jeans to her bare Christmas plaid painted toes. He wanted to kiss her off her feet, but opted for a peck on the cheek. "How was your day? You look comfortable."

"Come in."

She took the cream puffs he handed her to the kitchen. "Ready to get to work?" Black and gold streamers hung from the fixture over the kitchen table. "Haley and I had a little party for Brant yesterday afternoon before church."

"Did he get home on time Saturday night?"

She washed her hands at the sink. "He surprised me. His hand was hurting, so he came home early."

"Good boy."

"Did your high school win any championships?" She pulled two bowls from the cabinet. "I made chili. You want some?"

He settled at the table. "Sure. Smells amazing." Competing nicely with how amazing she looked tonight. "I won two championships in high school. Acted like a pure idiot after each one. I'm glad Brant has a better head on his shoulders than I did."

She handed him a fragrant bowl of steaming chili. "You want a tortilla with that?"

"Sure." A tortilla with chili? Where was the cornbread?

She poured two glasses of tea and gestured for him to follow her. "Thought we'd eat and work."

She plunked her bowl onto the desk in the office. "Why don't you pull down that box from the other night?"

Should he start in about the paper in his pocket? He took a spoonful of chili and watched her from across the room. He'd bide his time for a better moment. "Are the kids with Bobby tonight?"

"Yep. He's bringing them home at nine."

He put the box on the desk. "You guys are really close, huh?"

Was that color in her cheeks? "Bobby is like a brother."

"You said that about Carter."

She shrugged and fanned through the papers. "Where should we start?"

"We can group things once we get started. See if anything jumps out at us."

She pulled a spoonful of cheese-laden chili from her bowl and heaped it on her tortilla. So that's how she expected him to eat it. She took a bite and dug into the box while she chewed. She plunked a pile in front of him. "I don't even know what we're looking for."

He had to tell her what he'd found. It was the reason he'd suggested this hunt in the first place. He swallowed a gulp of tea. "Remember when Brant and I looked for the playbook the other night?"

"Uh-hum." She concentrated on her pile of papers.

"I have a confession to make."

She looked up, bite of chili suspended on her spoon.

He took the folded page from his pocket. "This happened to catch my eye, and I took it home to investigate."

Her eyes widened. "Why?"

"I don't know, exactly. Something Carter said when we met with him at lunch." He handed her the folded paper.

She read it quickly. "Isaac Johnson. What's he got to do with anything?"

"He's one of the injured players Lisa interviewed. I wondered what Pete's connection to him was."

She took a bite of chili. "What did you find out?"

"It turns out they weren't connected at all. I don't know why Pete had his MRI reading."

She pulled a manila file from the desk drawer. "This is his client and potential client list." She slid it across the desk.

He opened it, but knew he wouldn't find Isaac's name. "I called Isaac. He said he hadn't even met Pete. There's no connection I could find."

"Well, that gives us something to look for, then. Things that seem unusual. Documents that have no obvious connection to Pete."

He blinked. Had he skated by so easily? She hadn't even questioned him.

The warm scent of chili tempted him, and his stomach growled. With cheese melted on top, it wasn't hard to give in.

"What does this memo from Pete mean?" She held up the paper he'd taken and read the writing. "Another one bites the dust."

"Pete jargon?"

She shrugged. "No. It's not something I heard him say often."

They finished their chili while thumbing through other papers, most of which had no significance other than Pete's business.

Marcy collected their bowls and took them to the kitchen. When she came back, she put a hand on his shoulder. "Why not tell me about the paper the night you found it?"

Here it comes. "I'm sorry. I wasn't thinking, I just took it, thinking I'd make the connection on my own."

"Did you find anything else?"

His palms sweat. He didn't know her well enough to predict the severity of the impending storm. Best defense: grovel.

He swiveled in the office chair. "Look, Marcy. I realize it was stupid. I didn't want to question you about it in front of Brant. It didn't dawn on me that it was wrong until I got home."

"You admit it was wrong."

"Utterly." He put his hand on hers and met her gaze.

She sighed. "I understand why you did it. Thanks for telling me."

Just like that? No typical female manipulation? "You are an amazing woman."

A blush crept onto her cheeks. "Why do you say that?"

"Here I was, dreading telling you, and you don't bat an eyelash. I think you're the first woman I've met who didn't take the chance to punish me like a dog when given the chance."

Marcy sank into her chair. "I've been that woman more times than I'd like to admit. Forgiveness isn't as easy as it looks, but it's worth it."

What a woman. She made life so simple. Forgiveness.

Her fingers drummed the papers. "I thought this would be difficult. Going through Pete's papers."

He looked at two dry cleaning receipts and put them in the "trash" pile. "You didn't go through the other papers in his desk?"

"Bobby handled it for me. He put most of his stuff in those filing cabinets. But this is what was left."

"Let's make it worth it." He pulled the stack toward him, new purpose filling his chest. If this brought them no closer to the truth, he'd still help her close out the past.

Fifteen minutes later, she held a paper out to him. "What do you make of this?"

He scanned the paper. It was another MRI read with #2 written on it in Pete's handwriting. He put the two papers on the table side by side.

"He's keeping track of injuries." Marcy leaned forward.

"I think you're right." They met eyes. "Just like Lisa was."

"Isaac Johnson was number three. This guy is number two."

She opened the folder cataloging his clients. "Is he a client?" She ran her nail down the list and shook her head.

"So Pete's tracking injuries? Why?"

She shrugged. "Not a clue. We didn't talk much about his work. But, I think the file I gave Lisa had something to do with injuries, too. I didn't give it much thought at the time."

Jack's mind raced. He pulled another stack from the box. "Let's keep looking."

An hour ticked by, and they hadn't made any more discoveries. Marcy put her hand on her neck and massaged. "Let's have some dessert before the kids get home."

She bit her lip and grinned at him. The office light touched her dark hair and brought out the blue in her eyes. He'd be satisfied with that sweetness all night long.

A candy cane added a festive touch to the tray Marcy prepared with a plate piled high with cream puffs and two cups of coffee. She pushed the French door of the office open with her toe and balanced the tray on her hip. "Hope you're hungry."

His dark eyebrows pinched together. "I found something else."

The tray clattered as she set it down. "What?"

He handed her the paper, and her eyes scanned the document which was a spreadsheet with handwritten notes by each entry line. Across the top it read: *Call George Barker Re: Isaac Johnson.* She met Jack's gaze.

"Who is George Barker?"

"He's the Player Safety Commissioner. Or was at the time. Keep reading."

"What would the Player Safety Commissioner have to do with anything?"

A list of players followed by a list of medication names. Jack massaged his chin. "I'm guessing Pete suspected the injections they were given might be causing their injuries."

She shook her head. "Meaning—?"

His Adam's apple bobbed up and down. "The drugs are dangerous."

She handed him a mug of steaming coffee and sat down. "How would he know?"

He shrugged. "I don't know for sure, but this list is eerie." He took a sip of coffee and tossed a couple of cream puffs into his mouth. "They've all got similar injuries, but I still don't know how he made the connection."

Marcy eyed the plate of cream puffs. In moments of stress, she could eat the whole plate herself. Good thing Jack was here to quell her compulsive behavior and save her the extra pound or two she'd regret in the morning. Even the luscious scents of coffee and chocolate could not calm her nerves. What the heck was Pete looking for? She picked up the paper. December 14. Her bottom fell out of her stomach as it hit her. "This was dated a few days before Pete's death." The cream puffs lost their appeal.

Jack's eyes held hers.

Was this the scandal she'd suspected? Bad drugs used on players? "Why else would a normal guy commit suicide?" She swallowed around the lump in her throat, trying to decide how much to tell Jack about her suspicions. If she trusted him this far, it would be worth it for him to know everything. "The files I found and sent to Lisa had similar lists to this with more detailed information about injuries and drugs."

Jack's fingers traced the veins on the back of her hand. "What do you suspect?"

Some of the tension melted. "I wish I'd taken a closer look at those files. He'd gone through a lot of effort to conceal them, and I was just looking for a way out of the guilt."

He pulled his hand away. "Guilty? Why would you feel guilty?"

Her throat closed around the words. "The night Pete died, I accused him of having an affair. We had a huge fight. And I'd been nagging at him for months." She mimicked her own voice in a piercing whine. "Pete, you need to spend some more time with the kids. Where were you last night when your office was closed at eight? Why haven't you been to church in over a year?"

He looked like he was fighting laughter.

It *was* comical to say it out loud. Like a rerun of *All in the Family*. She shrugged. "At the time I found the files, I was desperate for answers. I wanted another reason *why*, all the time knowing *I* was the reason he'd killed himself."

She hadn't exaggerated. "The Bible says a nagging wife is like a dripping faucet. Drip. Drip. Drip."

Jack stared into her eyes. "Did you ever find out if he'd had an affair?"

"No. I felt so guilty about the fight we'd had, I never investigated further. I remember going to bed wishing I didn't have to put up with him any longer." She bit her lip. "Guess I got my wish." Hot tears squeezed out from the corners of her eyes.

He pulled her to her feet and into his arms. "No one deserves to live with guilt like that, Marcy." He pressed his forehead against hers. "I'm no psychiatrist, but I'm pretty sure guys don't kill themselves because they've got nagging wives. They'd choose divorce first."

She laughed and lay her head on his chest. Airing the ghosts that plagued her heart wasn't as scary as she'd imagined. At least with Jack's arms around her. "So that leaves scandal."

"And it might explain why Lisa was killed."

Her skin tightened as a cold tingle crept down her spine. "Lisa's killer has linked me to the information." Sweat broke out on her head and panic set in. She'd practically led Lisa to slaughter.

Jack left her and paced the small space. "But what does it have to do with me? She wasn't here to interview me as a coincidence."

"The timing makes sense. Maybe he just saw a good opportunity."

He shook his head. "Maybe." He sat down in the leather office chair and ran a hand through his hair.

She brushed the hair back from his face. "We have to get that file back from Lisa's office."

He raised his head and met her gaze. "What?"

"The file I gave to Lisa. We have to get it back." More tears escaped.

Seeing her distress, Jack grabbed her shoulders. "This is not your fault."

She buried her head in his rock-solid shoulder.

He brought her head up with gentle pressure on her chin. "How could you have known what would happen when you asked her to look at the files?"

"She'd still be alive if I hadn't."

"Maybe, but we have a pretty patchy case. You're right. If we had the file, we'd know more. Could Carter get it for you?"

"I haven't told him about the file. Or the fact that I gave it to Lisa."

Jack paced again. "How well did you know her family?"

"Not at all. She was just Carter's fiancée."

Jack sat again. "Why ask her to look into it, if you didn't know her well?"

She stood near him, and he slid an arm around her waist. "That's just it. I asked her because she was the only one whom I wouldn't have to face on a daily basis. I knew she'd been in touch with Pete, they were friends and that she worked for *NFL Rush*." She massaged her temples and settled into the other chair. "I figured if Pete was involved in scandal, the less Carter knew, the better. He's a wonderful friend, but he never had any trouble sniffing out Pete's faults."

Jack raised an eyebrow and nodded. "The guy does seem to have a jealous streak."

He stacked papers against the table. "Let's finish the papers in the box and see where we stand. I don't see how we're going to get anything from Lisa if Carter's not involved."

"You understand why I can't tell him now? I practically ordered her murder."

Jack's look sliced through her. "Would you stop? You are no more responsible for this than Haley is. If anyone is responsible, it's Pete. He's the one who left it all on your shoulders."

A new thought sickened her. "What if he was the one causing the injuries? Or ordered them?"

He shook his head. "Pete was already dead when Lisa was murdered. There's someone else involved."

A vehicle revved in the driveway, and Marcy hurried to put the box and its contents back in the closet before the kids came in.

Brant's voice rang from the entry. "Mom? You home?"

Jack nodded almost imperceptibly. "We'll come back to this."

"In here, honey."

Things were finally working out the way he'd planned. He rolled his neck in the hot water of the shower to release the tension that had been building there. Drew Shaw had an incredible game on Sunday, scoring the game-winning touchdown, and he'd submitted to pain shots and Toradol. He cranked the heat higher, loving the burn of hot water on his skin. The plan was flawless. Shaw had to see the benefits of the injections before he could use the serum that would end the season for him. He'd been asked to cover the game Sunday, which created the perfect window for the serum injection. Right on schedule.

The scent of the shampoo he used reminded him of Marcy. She'd commented on it once, and he'd used it ever since. She had to see they belonged together. Admittedly, he couldn't compete with Jack's looks, but he counted one very big detail in his favor. They had a past together. And Briggs had all but acknowledged it at Brant's game Saturday.

Reluctantly, he turned the shower off and stepped onto the plush rug. He grabbed a towel and rubbed his skin 'til it burned. Routine kept the proper thoughts in their place. He'd managed to keep the dark man from plaguing him too much lately and wanted to keep it that way. The wrestling was killing him.

The phone rang, and he stepped from the bathroom to check the caller ID. Why was *he* calling again? Hadn't he said he would take care of Shaw? "Hello?"

"He had a great game Sunday. You have anything to say about that?"

Shouldering the phone, he wrapped the towel around his waist. "The guy had a great game? So what?"

"I've paid you good money to eliminate him."

"And so I shall. The plan is in place for this Sunday. Raiders road game."

"You sure this serum of yours is foolproof?"

He rolled his eyes. He had over twelve players to prove it. "Nothing is foolproof. If the torque on the muscles isn't sufficient, the damage might not be significant. But look at Jack Briggs. He retired the year he got the injection."

"The season is flying by. Take Shaw out while the playoffs are still in contention."

"Like I said, Sunday." The bed bounced as he landed on it and grabbed the remote. He never missed a game.

"Sunday."

The line went silent, like his conscience. For once, he didn't experience the pang of guilt that rose up when he talked to *him*. He hated being a puppet for the men who controlled the gaming ring, but the money was more necessary now than ever. Let them gamble their customers' fortunes away, manipulating the game to their advantage. It was an obvious win for him, and there was no paper trail. Even the nosy Lisa Sparks hadn't totally unearthed the connection.

He smiled to himself. He'd go through the papers he'd *retrieved* from Lisa's house later. He'd stored them in a safe in the basement, no one the wiser. Her family could go on looking for her Pulitzer prize winning article. They wouldn't find it.

A syndicated woman sports reporter rarely made Pulitzer material. Her picture appeared beside her daily newspaper article, *NFL Dirt*. She was good at digging dirt, and even dirtier when it came to her personal life, as he well knew, but she was no Pulitzer prize winner. What sports writer aspired to that?

His stomach lurched when he thought of Lisa's own dark side, but he'd learned the triggers and steered his mind to thoughts that didn't increase the terrible burning in his stomach. Thoughts of Marcy were always calming.

Hadn't she singled him out at the game? Even with Briggs watching? Oh, yeah. Their relationship clock was ticking. Christmas was his chance to capitalize on what they had going. He had a lot of things Briggs didn't have: memories, personal jokes, time. When he boiled it down, he stood a pretty good chance in the long run.

Of course, she wasn't exactly falling into his arms, but she wasn't pushing him away, either.

When he'd finally gotten his hands on some of Lisa's files and put together a fairly good picture of how deep Lisa had been digging, he felt guilty about the strawberries. From the looks of things, Marcy knew nothing. Maybe he shouldn't have scared her they way he did.

He pulled his feet up to watch the game. *Life is good.* He could sit back, relax, and dream of finally finishing his business with Drew Shaw.

And Christmas with Marcy.

20

DREW DIALED JACK'S number, hoping to catch him in person instead of his answering machine like he had since Sunday evening. He smiled when Jack's voice answered.

"Drew Shaw, how are you?"

"Did you see the game, man?" Even as he stepped from the shower, his hands still tingled from the long pass he'd caught for a touchdown. The bathroom mirror reflected the new sparkle in his brown eyes.

"I said it would come back. Nicely played."

The words soaked into him like water on desert sand. "I've never had so much fun in my life."

"How's the ankle?"

"Dude, that Toradol or whatever they gave me is amazing. Didn't feel pain at all for, like, twenty-four hours."

"Not just for us old guys, is it?"

"I'm hooked. Listen, man. I just called ta thank you for coming out to Cali. Helped me get my head straight." He wouldn't mention how grateful he was for all the training Jack had given him on the field and off.

"My pleasure, but it's a constant battle. You'll have bad days, injuries, and crappy press that sets you back. Just keep pushing forward. Goal setting is important at this stage. Hall of Fame? Longest career of a running back in NFL history? You name it."

"I like the sound a' that. Maybe they'll retire my jersey in the Black Hole."

"First things first. How many workouts do you plan to get before then?"

"I've been first in the weight room all week. Been going to my therapy sessions, too."

"Then I'm expecting you to be the playmaker again this Sunday."

Drew cracked a half smile at himself in the mirror and laughed. "Tune in, my friend. I own the game."

He disconnected, a grin lingering on his lips. Somehow, Jack had wormed his way into his calloused heart. Been a long time since anyone cared a stitch about him. Jack may have been the one guy in the world who could have cracked his shell. *Good call, coach.*

Jack hung up with Drew and hurried to shower, heart hammering in anticipation for his date with Marcy. Despite Drew's bravado, he saw potential in him. A little modesty would do the kid a world of good. An NFL career wasn't handed to great players on a silver platter. *One thing at a time.* At least he'd finally decided to put in some work on his game.

He stepped out of the shower and ran a comb through his hair. In his closet, he slashed hangers aside, looking for the perfect shirt. When he'd found the one he wanted, he shrugged it on and checked the mirror to see if he'd buttoned it correctly. Marcy was finally coming to his house, and he wished the minutes away, even while hustling to get last-minute details done before she arrived.

The bell rang at his front door, and his heart did a somersault when his eyes captured her form in the doorway. She'd let her hair down in dark waves at her shoulders. Her candy-red lips begged him to taste them and matched the clingy sweater that drove him crazy with longing. He wiped sweaty palms on his jeans as he took her coat and hung it in the hall closet. They'd spent so little time truly alone, he felt like a teenager on a first date.

The feminine tang of her perfume filled the room as she gazed at the fourteen-foot Christmas tree in the entry, decked with white lights and gold decorations, all the housekeeper's doing.

She spun on her heel, taking in his home. "Nice place."

He studied her face for signs of nervousness. The last thing he wanted was for her to be uncomfortable. Maybe he should have asked Mrs. Nelson to tone it down with the decorations.

Her face shone. The tree paled in comparison to the light she brought to the room.

He shrugged. "Thanks." His home was significantly larger and certainly grander than hers, but it usually echoed with loneliness.

"You've improved it." He kissed her cheek and planned to step back, but she slid a hand onto his chest and detained him.

"I've missed you." She stood on tiptoes and pulled his head down for a kiss, his pulse responding instantly to her forwardness. Her lips tasted like sugar cookies, and he inhaled the scent of her hair as he pulled her close. The heat she created in his body could have set off the smoke detectors.

He regretted the space between them as she stepped back. "What was that for?"

She shrugged and bit her lip. "Tell you the truth, your house intimidates me, and I wanted to be sure I still had some control over the situation." Humor and feeling radiated from her.

He took her hand and led her to the kitchen. "Maybe you'll feel more at home in here." The lights flickered on when he flipped the switch. The music he'd put on earlier filled the room with sound. "But, I'll have to remember your response to intimidation and make it happen again."

She tossed him a look and grinned. "Smells delicious. Do you cook?"

"The housekeeper is responsible for the meal, I admit. I did help with dessert." He wasn't about to tell her 'help' meant he'd run to the grocery to pick up ingredients.

She closed her eyes as if listening to the music. "Music in the kitchen."

He nodded. "Andrea Bocelli."

"PBS almost got me the year they ran his outdoor concert."

A laugh bubbled up. "You're impossible. You should have sent them a donation." He grabbed her waist. "Just to see those phones light up."

Her eyes lit up at his touch, and his whole body responded. He could so easily forget dinner.

"The kids are off school this week and next. Do you have plans for the holiday?"

He frowned. "Visiting my mom in Florida for a few days."

She toyed with the buttons on his shirt. "Will you join us for New Year's Eve? Haley is determined to stay up and watch the New Year come in. She thinks there's actually something to see, like a huge rainbow or flash of light or something." She swiped her hand in an arc across the room.

He buried his face in her hair and made his way to the soft of her neck. "Why don't we watch the ball drop at ten and put her to bed?" The oven timer clanged, and Jack reluctantly pulled away.

She smoothed her jeans. "Can I help with anything?"

He grinned as he donned oven mitts. "Light the candles in the dining room, will ya?" He pulled the oven door, and the rich aroma of his favorite dish, seafood ziti, filled the kitchen. His taste buds watered as the pan slid from the oven. Mrs. Nelson had a wire rack waiting so that he could carry the dish to the table.

She returned to the kitchen. "Anything else?"

He shook his head. "Lead the way." He'd never come clean about the ulterior motives for asking her to go first. *Ai-chi-wah-wah.*

He put the pan on the table and hurried to pull her chair out and push it in as she sat down. "First-class service."

She folded the black napkin across her lap. "I see."

He pulled himself soundlessly to the table. "I've used this table maybe three times since I moved in."

She took a sip of water from a stemmed glass. "It's an honor to be invited, then." Her teeth flashed in a special smile, reserved just for him.

He raised his glass, noting how her eyes caught the candlelight and his attention. "To a beautiful evening."

A lovely crystal note rang through the dining room as their glasses touched. Jack served the salad first, followed by the ziti.

He raised a mouthful of ziti to his lips careful to stab a large scallop or piece of crab with each bite. "Tell me about your week."

She smirked. "Not much to tell. Brant's hand is doing much better." She thought for a moment. "Haley lost another tooth. All she wanths for Christhmath ith her two front theeth."

"Shouldn't she have lost them before this?"

"The dentist said so, but God plans these things. She didn't cut teeth as a baby until she was fourteen months old."

Jack lingered over a sip of water. "I'll bet she was a little cutey at that age."

A faraway look touched her features. "Yes." She toyed with her water glass. "Those were special days."

For the first time in his life, he wondered what it would be like to have children of his own. He brushed the thought away. "Did you find out anything new about the file you sent Lisa?"

She bit her knuckle. "I told a little white lie to Carter to get Lisa's sister's number, but I haven't had the nerve to call her yet."

"Because of the white lie you told to get it?" *Miss Goody Two Shoes.*

She nodded. "A white lie is still a lie."

He shrugged. "So, what are we going to do?"

A smile crept onto her fair features, illuminated in the candlelight. "Enjoy our dinner together and forget we've ever heard of Lisa Sparks or Isaac Johnson or Carter Cunningham."

He raised his glass. "I'll drink to that." There was so much he wanted to enjoy with her, but it seemed every time they got together, tragedy struck.

Tension melted as the meal progressed, but Marcy steeled herself for the battle she knew was coming after dinner. If she didn't prepare now to resist him, all her defenses would come crumbling down. He wasn't making her job easy. His fingers traced the veins on the back of her hand as they finished dessert, a chocolate peppermint cake with white candy cane icing.

He stirred his coffee with a whole candy cane. "Candy canes are the best part of Christmas."

"Really? Not the tree or the carols or the lights?"

He crunched a larger crushed piece between his teeth. "Nope. You gotta love the simplicity of the candy cane. My favorite."

"Haven't really thought about it before. They've always just been trimming."

He pushed his chair out and came to her side. Taking her hand, he pulled her up. Her heart jumped into her throat at his nearness.

His eyes danced. "Help me enjoy my favorite candy." Jack took a bite of the candy cane, but left a quarter inch hovering on his lips. He lowered his mouth to hers, offering the stick of candy—and something else. Their teeth played tug-of-war with the bite, lips grazing until he bit his end off and surrendered the piece into her mouth. The peppermint was as sweet and hot as his lips as they continued what he'd started. She melted against him, swallowing a moan. His perfect body molded to hers as he deepened the sweetest kiss ever. She lifted her head for breath. "You've given me a whole new appreciation for candy canes." Her pulse drowned out the music overhead. If she didn't stop now, there would be no turning back.

"I have a whole box in the kitchen." He kissed her again, the delicious heat of mint still on his breath.

Oh, he was so tempting, but she must stop. She took a big step backward and held her palm up.

Disappointment deflated the room like she'd poked a pin into it. She sought his eyes. "I'm sorry, Jack."

He squeezed her upper arms. "I think I understand." He motioned for her to follow him to the living room, where dozens of bright red Poinsettias contrasted with a humungous Christmas tree. He fell into the gray leather couch and beckoned her to sit beside him. "Let's just sit for a while."

She sighed and sat beside him. With a remote control he dimmed the lights, and the picture window caught her attention. "I'll bet you have an incredible view of the mountains."

"Yep. Will you come back and see it in the daylight? The snow on Twin Peaks this time of year is stunning."

She smiled. "I'd love to."

He wrapped her in his arms, the warmth of his body radiating through her. She rolled her neck and relaxed against him. Did they really have a shot at a lasting relationship? They'd certainly had a rocky start. Nothing like a murder on a first date and threats thereafter to put a damper on things. She took a deep breath. She hadn't received a threat in over a week. Whoever sent it must have realized she didn't know anything and given up, but fear still rippled through her stomach. They'd hit too close to home, been too personal.

Jack must have felt her tense. "You okay?" His green eyes probed hers.

"I was thinking about everything that's happened. The threats, Lisa's murder."

"I thought that was taboo tonight."

"I haven't gotten another threat."

He tensed. "Doesn't mean the creep has given up."

"Bobby said it was probably some college kid doing a prank after reading I'd been the one to find Lisa's body."

"Did you tell the police?"

She nodded. "I did, and they took the information I gave them. They're still stumped on the murder."

"At least the cops are involved. We should get a restraining order or something."

"On whom?"

He shrugged and shook his head. "Drives me mad that I can't stop it, figure out who's sending them."

"My own strength gave out long ago. God's strength is what keeps me going."

His muscles rippled. "It isn't strength I lack."

No one would question that fact. "Maybe not physically, but what about emotionally? Even the strongest man can't support me. Men were not created to meet every need a woman has."

He squeezed her closer. "There are a great many people who would disagree with you. What about the statement, 'you complete me'?"

His words awakened some truth. "We're too imperfect to complete anyone. That was my problem with Pete. I put him as the idol in my life, and he let me down. Over and over. I looked to him to fill the hole in my heart, but no one can fill it but God."

His eyebrows rose. "God's filled the hole?"

"I'm starting to let him."

Jack nodded with fire in his eyes. "That takes surrender, and I never surrender."

Her stomach soured as his words sank in. He was so sure of himself, so confident. He was further from turning to God than she'd thought. She'd read a quote on a bookmark that morning: "A man who isn't after God's heart, shouldn't be after mine." The truth stung. Jack wasn't after God's heart.

She'd already let things go too far; invested emotionally where she had no business investing. Half-heartedly, she tried erecting a safe wall in her heart. She didn't want to hurt him for anything in the world, but she should have set better boundaries—been more guarded.

A strand of her hair fell through his fingers and he sifted more. "Let's go up to Estes Park tomorrow, do some window shopping, and look at the lights? Could you get another sitter?"

The internal siren went off. Pawn the kids off again? She'd almost called to cancel already. "I promised Haley we'd start our Christmas baking tomorrow. And Brant's home, too."

"Couldn't you do those things a day later?"

"Thanks for the offer, Jack, but we have special traditions leading up to Christmas. Call me old-fashioned."

His eyebrows raised, and she detected a note of annoyance in his voice. "We could start our own tradition."

She couldn't break her promise to the kids. "I'm not mitigating annoyances. I'm raising human beings."

He rolled his eyes. "I never said they were annoying."

She wasn't being totally fair. "I know you didn't."

The clock ticked the silent minutes away. She checked her watch and stood. "I should get home. It's pretty late."

"Don't go." His eyes begged, and his fingers trailed down her arm.

His touch left a trail of fire on her skin. "You know I have to. I have responsibilities. Obligations." Not to mention she'd promised to honor God with her body under every circumstance, and she was close to an epic failure in doing so.

He sighed. "I understand."

How could he? He'd never been married or had the pressure of kids. "Thanks for dinner. It was perfect." She meant it from the bottom of her heart. She hated to leave him after they'd argued. She sought his eyes and slid closer.

He pulled her close again. "Any chance you'd share another candy cane?"

She cocked her head, anticipation shooting through her stomach. The man reeled her in like a rainbow trout. She knew she shouldn't bite, but—he tugged her over the edge with his eyes.

"Maybe a small one."

She'd build that safe wall later.

21

THE COLD PENETRATED Marcy's fingers as the heater in the car went head to head with the night temperatures. Jack watched her leave from his front porch as the first snowflakes of the night tumbled in the wind. Her breath caught at the sight of him. She blew a final kiss and backed out, careful to avoid his massive brick mailbox decorated with fake greens and Christmas lights.

Christmas carols played on the radio and headlights flashed as she made her way east to her home near the high school, the bubble of happiness fueling the trip.

The drive gave her time to think, to reflect on their conversation before their passionate good-bye. He'd been angry when she wouldn't go to Estes Park with him, annoyed that she had special traditions with the kids. Worse still, Jack's comment about God. *I never surrender.*

Her heart fell into her feet. Why did some things seem so clear in the dark?

She'd been ignoring the tugging of her conscience, struggling with surrender herself. Now, her heart responded. She hated to acknowledge it, but some of Jack's comments brought the truth to her mind as clearly as the beams of those headlights in the left lane.

She was in for a heartache.

Jack showed no interest in her faith, and without that, she wasn't free to pursue a real relationship with him. Weren't these the same feelings she'd ignored when dating Pete? Her stomach flip-flopped. This was not the life she'd planned.

But what moment of her life *had* gone as planned?

Since Pete's death, maybe years before, hurt followed her like a swarm of killer bees, bent on breaking her spirit, if not ending her life.

There were so many things Jack didn't understand about being a parent. The selflessness of loving someone more than oneself. Submission.

The car was warm now, but she exhaled a breath laced with pain. She'd done it again; put her feelings for Jack in front of her relationship with God. She scowled and shook her head. When would she get it right? Had she prayed for his soul? For the opportunity to reach him with the good news of Christ?

No.

Her chin quivered. She'd plowed in head-first because he made her feel desirable again.

But he couldn't fill the hole. Ah, but she wanted him to. She never wanted him to stop trying.

A tear on her lashes caught the lights from an oncoming car, and she wiped it away, remorse coursing through her like a raging river. When would she ever get her priorities right?

White-knuckled, she gripped the steering wheel like she'd been gripping the control on her life. And therein lay the problem. She'd fought for control when she should have given the wheel to the One who knew her plans before she made them. The One who'd promised her the desires of her heart if she delighted in Him.

She pulled to the side of the road, blinded by tears. It had been so easy to get off track, but she knew the way back.

Lord, I will delight in you.

Goosebumps prickled her arms. Suddenly the verse wasn't just a plaque in her kitchen, it was a promise. If she delighted in the Lord, what else could she desire? He was a generous Father that wanted to bless her. What was that verse? *He seeks to bless you even as you sleep.*

Peace flooded through her, and her shoulders dropped an inch as the muscles relaxed. His arms encircled her heart, numbing the pain and the fear that boiled out of control just below the surface. She'd surrender the desires of her heart to God. He would keep them until the proper time. Fears were harder. She still wrestled with the threats she'd received. With memories of Lisa's murder and her own part in it. She wiped tears from her eyes and prayed. For her relationship with Bobby and Carter, for Jack and his spiritual discovery, for Haley and Brant and their spiritual development.

One by one, the burdens fell away. Ashamed as she was for being so hypocritical with Jack, she was glad she'd had all the right things to say to him in the past days. It just hadn't gone heart-deep until now.

Spent with tears, she put the car into drive and pulled back onto Highway 34. She headed home, ready to face what lay ahead with more strength than she'd possessed before.

A dark movement in her rearview mirror caught her attention. She reached up to adjust the mirror, and a bolt of fear shot through her chest as a gloved hand clamped around her mouth.

A man's hoarse voice grated in her ear. "Keep driving and you won't get hurt."

Thirty minutes after she left, Jack still tasted Marcy's lips as he piled dishes in the sink for Mrs. Nelson, but the flavor was bittersweet. Was it so hard to make sacrifices for the relationship? His mood was on a crash course after the amazing way she'd said good-bye.

He filled the sink with soap and hot water to soak the dishes overnight. Marcy's whole "trust in God" theme was off base. A man didn't need to trust anyone but himself. He'd learned that in the NFL. Make your own success. Hadn't he just said that to Drew Shaw?

Jack returned to the dining room and grabbed the plates from the table. Just because she didn't agree to go with him didn't mean he couldn't make the trip himself. That'd show her.

Emptiness filled the house, and the familiar blackness took over. She should still be here with him, still wrapped in his arms, saving him. But she was too stubborn and bent on pleasing an impossible God who asked for weakness and surrender and offered nothing in return. He submerged the plates in water. Tiny soap bubbles drifted in the air, but his mood sunk further. He'd spent his life sacrificing for football. He'd sacrificed his time, his body and especially relationships. He'd let Francine walk away because of his dedication to his career, the same dedication he'd been trying to impart to Drew.

Why couldn't she see that?

In his heart, he knew he wasn't being entirely fair, but the reigning emotion of the hour wasn't compassion. When the dishes were all soaking, he sat down at his computer and booked an overnight reservation at the Stanley Hotel in Estes Park, knowing all the time it was a petty way to pay her for her choices.

No use waiting until later in the week. I'll head out in the morning. I'll celebrate with or without her.

An anvil of fear crushed Marcy's chest, and her muscles recoiled at the touch of smooth leather gloves at her throat. Reactions on autopilot, she steadied her hands on the wheel even as her heart tried to escape the cage of her ribs. What had the self-defense teacher on the news spot last week said? Crash the car? A fog settled into her brain.

She snatched a look at him from the mirror but couldn't make out a face.

He loosened his grasp on her mouth, and she whispered, "What do you want?"

"To teach you a lesson."

The insignificance of her life crashed over her as unsuspecting cars passed while she trembled in the presence of a madman. "I don't understand."

"A slow learner? You got my threats."

Synapses weren't firing, her brain was black and cold as the night. "I don't know what you mean."

A four or five day stubble from his chin scratched her cheek as his fingers cut into her cheeks with a vice-like grasp. "Keep sticking your nose where it doesn't belong and it's liable to get cut off." He pronounced every consonant fiercely. "Pull over."

A cold sweat broke out on her upper lip as she scanned the car for a weapon to defend herself.

He grabbed her chin harder and pulled her cheek close. "You heard me. Pull over." His voice was as rough as his face against hers.

Tires threw gravel as she slowed onto the shoulder into an unlit area. Air refused to enter her lungs as she imagined his next move.

Three CDs and an empty McDonald's cup weren't likely to prevent what was about to happen. She'd tossed her purse in the back seat when she left Jack's house.

As soon as the car stopped, his hand clamped around her mouth again, pressing the blood from the tissues. The distinct smell of cowhide and dirt from his gloves suffocated her and prevented movement. Coffee-laced breath burned her nose and seethed into her ear, and she shivered as his free hand slid down her neck and—lower.

Her stomach rolled when he spoke again. "Stay away from Jack Briggs."

Every muscle in her body tensed as he caressed her hair while breathing heavily in her ear.

God, help me.

His intentions were clear, but she wasn't going down without a fight. With all her strength, she thrashed, arching her back to escape his grip, but he held firm and her arm hit the steering wheel hard as he pulled her head into the headrest until she couldn't move an inch. Her scream penetrated his glove and died along with all hope of escape. A sickening chill danced across her skin as he breathed into her ear. "It's your fault she's dead."

Her heart withered in her chest like a dying vine. What was he talking about? His breath seared her ear again, and she braced herself. She had one advantage on him. He was behind her, and it would be a struggle for him to get into the front seat or pull her back. She gritted her teeth for a fight, but his hand slackened and he released her, jumped out of the car, and ran. She turned as he disappeared into the darkness, leaving her quivering and alone, wondering if she'd just imagined him.

A gust of wind blew the door shut, and her hand flew to the button to lock it.

Her jaw ached with imprints of his grip, proof she wasn't dreaming. The pressure from his fingers would probably leave bruise marks. Her body shook, so she clutched her stomach, too dull to attempt an escape, lest he return.

Her head spun like the siren lights on a police car, and the black landscape teetered to the left as she swallowed around the grapefruit in her throat. A wave of relief washed over her as she thought of what *hadn't* happened. *Thank you, Lord.*

The tremors lessened, and she checked traffic over her shoulder and pulled onto Highway 34. She should call the police, call Jack, or Bobby, but her brain couldn't connect thoughts with decisive initiation. She just drove, entranced by the terror that still held her in its grasp.

The idea that a man lurked behind her for so many miles churned fear in her stomach. He'd waited for the right moment and found it. She'd even pulled over before to catch her breath after the revelation she felt sure God had given her.

Nothing about the attack made sense.

She stopped at a red light. While she waited, she stared at the ceiling of her car. "Is this a test for saying I'd put my trust in You?" Her words hit the upholstered surface and disappeared.

The light turned green and the motion of the car helped her mind kick into gear, as well. She found the best-lit parking lot OR most well lit parking lot, ironically McDonald's. *Lot of help that cup was.*

Her fingers fumbled on the keys as she dialed 911. Why had she thought she could handle this on her own? All the threats, the murder, Pete's files? She should have surrendered everything to the police long ago.

"What is your emergency?"

It took effort to put words to what happened. "I – I was attacked in my car."

"Is your attacker still in the vehicle?"

"No. He ran off."

"Are you hurt?"

"No." Not physically, anyway.

"Ma'am, stay where you are. I'm sending an officer out to check on you."

She nodded, but did not verbally respond. Should she call Jack? After the way they'd parted, she wasn't sure that was a good idea. And her attacker had warned her away from him. Why?

Moisture dampened her cheeks, and she blinked away tears.

She could trust no one.

The policeman filed a report and took some samples from the car, but she knew he hadn't left a trail. And besides, this wasn't CSI. This was her life. Not everyone left a single hair that could be traced through a national follicular database. She almost smiled at her own sarcasm.

"Can I escort you home? You've had a terrible night." The officer's eyes scanned the back seat, as if looking for someone else to jump out.

She gripped the wheel with both hands. "I'm only a few miles from home. I think I'll be fine."

She put the car into gear and started forward, anxious to get home. Her matted hair scratched her neck, and she imagined her face looked worse. The kids would be worried if they weren't already asleep. Bobby was entertainment for Haley and motivation toward homework for Brant, but he never stayed past bedtime. Brant watched over things after he left.

An elephant of fear sat on her chest, brought on by the feeling that someone might still be concealed just behind her. She snatched a view of the back seat and shivered. Empty.

The garage door obeyed after she punched the button. The car rolled in, and she closed the door before turning the ignition off. She raked a hand through tangled hair and stepped out, praying the kids were asleep.

The house was dark and filled with ghosts. Floorboards creaked as she tiptoed to check the kids. Brant lay twisted in his sheets like a haphazard burrito, and Haley slept with her hands under her chin like a cherub. She breathed a sigh of relief and scurried to her bedroom. She gasped as her bathrobe flew out of the closet as if to choke her. She let out a breath as she stripped, pulled on the offending robe and slippers and turned on the shower to scour away the feeling of panting breath in her ear.

Nothing could scour away the memories. The blood on her hands from Lisa's murder. The white rose. The strawberries. And now, his voice telling her she'd gotten too close to the truth.

After the shower she curled up in a ball on her bed, but sleep was as elusive as the man who'd waited for her in the back seat of her car.

22

A LONG OVERCOAT and scarf kept the frigid temperatures at bay and helped Jack maintain a low profile. The streets of Estes Park teemed with people, some holding hands, others chasing kids away from candy shop windows. He checked his phone again. He'd missed her call when he'd gone out running last night.

The moment he arrived in town, regret weighed on his chest. Marcy had a life, and she shouldn't have to sacrifice it for him. He was the one who'd been selfish. Matter of fact, he'd been selfish enough to ask her to sacrifice holiday traditions. If he'd come to his senses earlier, he would not have sent that text telling her he'd gone to Estes for an overnight stay. She hadn't responded. He'd deserved her silence; he'd put it right in her face to make her feel guilty for refusing him.

He walked a few blocks and glanced at his phone again. There was a chance he didn't have good service up here. As forty crept up on him, there were days he wondered if he'd ever grow up. Maybe that's why Marcy hadn't called. She had experience with all this long-term relationship stuff. The only thing he'd been committed to since college had been the league.

Not any more.

Penelope's Old Time Burgers, a favorite restaurant, lured him from the opposite side of the street. He jaywalked and ducked into the restaurant that smelled of frying oil, burgers, and ketchup, all of which were ground into the wood plank flooring by thirty years of tourists. It was the kind of place where he couldn't help feeling at home. Not a swanky joint, but he didn't know a guy on earth who would pass up a chance at a great burger and fries or a Coke in a Styrofoam cup—and they had that special ice, irresistible crunchy pellets. His mouth watered as he stared at the menu, and he knew in an instant he'd order the bacon double cheeseburger and a large side of fries.

Fast food was a special luxury after years of strict diets that emphasized nutrition and healthy calories. He left his name with the clerk and weaved among the others crowding the restaurant to the seats that faced the windows offering a view of the street. Brant would appreciate this place; a no-frills restaurant with sticky tables, napkin dispensers, and the best burger in Estes Park.

Jack toyed with a bottle of Tapatio in a basket on the table, waiting for them to announce the name he'd given: Jesse. Since Marcy and the kids weren't here, it was a perfect time to nab their Christmas presents. Mom, too. She'd love a wool scarf, though when she would need it in Florida, he'd never know. He ticked off his list. There were several jewelers in town that did one-of-a-kind pieces with semiprecious stones and glass beads. Marcy would love something like that.

"Jesse, your burger is ready."

He jumped up to get his tray and returned to his seat, munching a fry, to watch the people on the street. Estes Park had a 'Christmassy' feel even in June, but this time of year was special. He should have waited until Marcy and the kids could have joined him.

The first bite of the double-decker bacon cheeseburger brought a smile to his face. He wiped the grease from his lips with a napkin. The smile didn't linger long. Since the night he and Marcy had sorted papers from Pete's desk, questions plagued his mind. He'd thought of every angle, but still couldn't understand how the players were injured intentionally. Perhaps with drugs given before the game? He'd certainly taken his share of injections. Could a drug do that?

Where did Pete fit in?

He'd begun compiling a list of injured players of the last ten years and had noticed an alarming trend. An overwhelming number of the injured players were Pro-Bowl players, but wasn't that normal? The players that play the hardest fall the hardest.

Or was it intentional? A bite of burger lodged in his throat. Could his own injury—

Jack washed the bite down with a swig of Coke and forced himself to think of other things as his palms grew moist. If he went down that path, he might not ever recover. His brain shut down against the thought of an intentional injury. Better ignore it than face it.

Dusk fell as he finished his shopping and lights of all colors twinkled from trees and people milled the streets, their fingers pointed at particularly pretty displays in certain windows. He'd done his shopping, but couldn't help checking his phone just once more to see if Marcy had called.

Last year, he'd done this alone, moping and limping. This year he'd planned to spend it with Marcy. Marcy Farris changed everything. Because of her, he'd gotten his lease on life again. She'd given him strength to carry on. His salvation.

And he'd jeopardized it by being selfish and childish.

Jack strolled up and down one side of the street before climbing the hill to his hotel. He couldn't help thinking how Haley would react to the lit-up polar bear or the giant tree with a beautiful star on top, and his stomach clenched as a couple rolled past in a horse-drawn carriage. The night held no magic. Might as well end it peacefully with a beer in the hotel bar before bed. A little alcohol might keep the thoughts about his injury at bay. How would he tell Marcy his suspicions?

The lobby of the Stanley Hotel was stunning, decked in Poinsettias and greenery amid the old world loveliness of the setting. Jack turned the corner and bumped into a woman coming from the bar.

"Pardon me."

Brown eyes, fringed with long lashes flashed recognition. "Jack Briggs?"

He looked up, dreading an interaction with a fan or media. "Francie." He stopped short. Of all the people to run into tonight. He smiled and scanned the girl-turned-woman he used to know. "Wow, it's good to see you. What are you doing in Estes Park this time of year?"

A blush crept onto her dark skin. "I'm here for a conference for work."

"What are you doing now?"

She tucked a strand of hair behind her ear with an unadorned hand. "I'm a professor at USC, actually."

Wow. He raked a hand through his hair. "How long has it been? Ten years?"

She rolled her lips between perfect white teeth. "You played in the NFL for what—eleven?"

He nodded. Eleven years, two months and three weeks, but who was counting? "Give or take."

She cocked her head. "Then it's been that long at least."

Had she kept track? Still had the same smile with a dimple near her left eye. "Listen, you want to have coffee or something? Catch up?"

A quick check of her watch. "Sure. I've got a few hours before my brain turns off. These conferences are bully."

He laughed as they strolled into the room. "I haven't heard that expression since college." They entered the elegant bar together, and he pulled her chair out at a table that offered a view of the mountain.

She scooted in. "I was sorry to hear about your injury. How has retirement treated you?" She appraised him with appreciation. "I don't see you taking time off from life."

That's exactly what he'd done for a whole year. "I've done some consulting. Met with a player from the Raiders last week."

"Can't get the game out of your system, can you?"

Jack frowned. "You would know that better than anyone."

Sitting with Francie again, he could almost see the past pull up a chair at the table. A waiter asked for their drink orders.

"Decaf, please." The white bar napkin flicked between her elegant fingers. No wedding ring. Why hadn't an amazing woman like her married long ago? Divorce?

Jack ordered. "So, what do you teach at SC?"

"American studies and Ethnicity."

He stifled a yawn. "Sounds interesting."

She grinned and ran a finger along her lip. "Um-hum."

The waiter arrived with their drinks.

She hadn't changed from their college days, same brown eyes, same tall, slender build, though instead of long blonde hair, she wore it in a short cut that fringed her face. A thousand memories vied with each other. "Did you ever buy that beach house you dreamed of?"

Her face brightened. "I close on it at the beginning of the year. Right on Huntington."

"Good for you. I live here in Colorado. Mom has lived here in the summer for years, and I just couldn't get the Rockies out of my system."

Her gaze swept the landscape outside the window. "I can see why."

Jack wiped the sweat from his glass and nearly choked as his eyes registered the form of someone else he knew standing at the registration desk. He'd know those movements anywhere.

Marcy leaned against the check-in desk, listening to the clerk give directions and point toward the bar. Jack's limbs froze as she thanked the clerk and started for the bar. The drink bit his throat on the way down as he swallowed his surprise. She'd given up the ponytail and

T-shirt for a soft red shirt and high-heeled boots. Silver earrings caught the light and played between strands of dark hair that framed her face. His heart collided with his esophagus.

Francine touched his arm. "You look like you saw a ghost or something."

He sipped his drink and grinned. "Someone much prettier."

Francine swiveled around to see who he was looking at.

Marcy straightened the silver scarf at her neck and scanned the restaurant. His blood raced as her smile reached him, but it quickly turned to confusion as her eyes slid to Francine. He felt he understood what it felt like to be an animal in a hunter's sights. "Marcy."

Even though she plastered on a smile, he saw the storm in her eyes as she approached. Was she holding back tears? She stopped at their table. "Jack. How are you?"

At this moment? Not good. "I'm good, but surprised to see you. Marcy, this is Francine."

She extended her hand in greeting, and Jack caught sight of a deep purple bruise on her forearm. "Good to meet you."

His stomach recoiled. Where'd she get that bruise? He pulled out a chair wishing the floor would swallow him. He guessed she was here to surprise him, and it hadn't turned out the way she'd intended. He gestured to a chair. "Sit down and join us."

Francie urged her with a smile. Not a viper smile, but he still cringed.

Marcy shook her head. "I'd just seen you through the lobby and thought I'd stop in and say hi before I head out." She tapped her watch. "I'm headed home before the snow flies."

A weight dropped into his stomach. He was in deep mud. There was no other reason for her to be over an hour from home today. "I wish you'd stay. We could order dinner or something."

"That's okay. I'm pretty tired already and—" She gestured to the road that stretched out the window. "I'm on my way home to the kids."

He admitted defeat, reading the warning in her eyes. "Drive safe, okay?"

The silver earrings tinkled as she turned. "It was good to meet you, Francie. Night, Jack." She shrugged her coat on and tucked the scarf in as she walked away.

What an idiot. Paralyzed, he watched her walk away with his heart.

Francine smiled at him innocently. "That was an awkward moment. Do you know her well?"

"Not well enough."

A puzzled look crossed her face. "What does that mean?"

He sighed and toyed with the salt shaker. "Does 'it's complicated' give you a hint?"

Nodding, she said, "Sure does."

New resolve filled him. He couldn't let her walk away. This was his fault. "Do you mind if I run out for a minute? I'll be right back." Something told him this was a do-or-die moment.

She wrapped her hands around her coffee mug and smiled. "Sure thing."

He skidded to a stop in the parking lot and watched as Marcy cupped her hands around her face and peered into the back window of her car. What was she doing?

She jumped when he touched her arm. "What are you doing?"

"Oh, just checking something. I'm on my way, now." She pressed past him and unlocked the door with the clicker.

"Marcy, wait."

She looked at the mountain to the west, not meeting his gaze. Was it a shadow or did he detect a purple mark on her chin, too? Every nerve stood at attention. His eyes narrowed, and he cupped her cheek and turned her face to inspect the spot. "What happened here?"

She turned her face from his grasp. "It's nothing. Just got bumped."

He'd become accustomed to the honest light in her eyes, now absent. His eyes surveyed her face further. Thumb-print on one side, two fingers on the other. Rage burned in his stomach. A strong hand had left its mark on her face. He gripped her shoulders. "Tell me how you got those bruises."

A tear glistened on the edge of her lashes, and her expression softened for a moment, but then closed down as she glanced back at the hotel. "You should go back inside to your guest."

She yanked the car door open, but he caught it and wouldn't let her pass. "She's an old friend from college. We just happened to run into each other tonight."

Only inches from him, her scent played tricks with his emotions, and his eyes flicked to her lips.

Her eyes mirrored the menacing sky overhead, but she didn't step away as if they were pulled closer magnetically. "As my mother used to say, 'a likely story.' I came all the way up here to see you." She attempted to pull the door shut. "Bad idea."

"Would you wait a minute?" They had unfinished business. He wasn't going to let her go with those bruises of her face.

She buckled her seat belt. "One."

Which was more important, finding out where she'd gotten those bruises or smoothing over the mess he'd created when he came on this foolish trip? "I know this didn't go the way you'd planned."

Her resolve crumpled, but her fingers whitened on the steering wheel.

He pointed to the hotel where Francine waited, condemning him. "There is nothing to this. She's just an old friend."

"Convenient that you met here at the hotel. What would you call me, a *new* friend?"

The quicksand question. One wrong move . . . "Marcy, listen—"

She gripped the door handle. "I'm freezing. Will you please let me shut the door?" Her eyes shot icicles colder than the night air. "Hurry inside, it's pretty cold out here."

He stepped back, allowing her to pull the door shut, the echo slicing through the parking lot.

She cracked the window. "Is this how you punish me for not coming?"

He sighed, cringing from the daggers of her gaze. "No. I never should have come at all. I missed you all day." How lame that sounded.

"I see." The glass rolled up, and she put the car into gear and drove out of the parking lot.

The town below glistened with Christmas lights, but his world had just turned upside down.

The dark man was winning tonight, and he couldn't stop it. He refused to answer the phone when he read the caller I.D. The very sound of that voice right now might send him over the edge. Everything had fallen apart.

He'd almost conquered the dark man, until he'd followed Marcy to Jack's house the other night. He'd only wanted to check on her and make sure she was safe. But he'd never forget the look in her eyes when Jack kissed her good night, or the way her hands played with the curling hair at his neckline. Everything went black and his stomach flamed, igniting jealousy which exploded in his brain in a gut-wrenching vibration. He'd jumped into her car, red-eyed with anger at Jack Briggs and even at

Marcy for being so gullible.

He'd never meant to hurt her.

He'd almost lost his nerve when she pulled over in tears, but the vision of them together beat a tribal rhythm in his brain, urging him forward. The way she bit her lip with longing as she held Jack's hand as long as she could as he walked her down the stairs. The nauseating sigh that escaped her lips when she blew him a good night kiss. Every gesture was fuel for the fire that consumed him.

He could kick himself now.

Blasted ulcers erupted like volcanoes in his gut as memories of what he'd done rippled through his mind. He'd risked everything getting so close to her. She'd been too scared to put it together at the time, but the moment would come when she would recognize something familiar about him. When she did, he would lose everything.

The lies he'd built failed to sustain him.

He rolled the lid on a bottle of Mylanta. The chewable antacids weren't cutting it anymore. Only hell could burn hotter than the lining of his stomach.

A precursor to his eternal destiny.

A shiver niggled his spine, and he took a swig of the chalky white liquid.

Tomorrow, he'd finish what he started the day he'd got the call. Drew Shaw's season would end during the game tomorrow, and he'd have enough money to erase his life completely if his last bet ended the game. He wasn't a gambling man, like those he worked for, but he had one last shot at Marcy's heart—and he held the ace.

Cobwebby boxes of Christmas decorations from the basement stood in a pile in the corner of her living room. The musty smell of the cardboard sent Marcy's mind marching backward. Ornaments collected through the years, things the kids made at school, presents from grandparents. Pete holding Brant up to put the star on the tree. Haley crawling under the tree and knocking it over. She smiled and stacked the last ornament box on top. Tonight they'd decorate the tree, just like they'd done since Brant was a baby. Other families put their tree up earlier, but Pete had always insisted on the week before Christmas. And she'd put it off even longer to drive up to Estes and surprise Jack.

Fool.

Even the precious memories of past Christmases could not staunch the flow of blood from the wound in her heart today. The heartache she'd feared came much sooner than predicted. The first time she'd really disappointed him, Jack turned to another woman. A pain ripped through her.

What was wrong with her? Was she so uninteresting that she couldn't keep a man's attention for more than a few weeks? She ran a hand down her thigh. Nothing was the same after kids, but she wouldn't trade them for the younger, sleeker version of herself. Why couldn't men accept her the way she was? The hall mirror reflected her empty gaze. Dark hair with only a stray silver strand here and there framed a face with a smattering of freckles that never faded from childhood. A tiny scar above her eyebrow from an accident playing laser tag in high school. She yanked her head away. Ordinary. Nothing *captivating*.

A lungful of air pushed the tears away. Hadn't she promised to trust God with her future? Surrender. Forget it. The emptiness swallowed her. She was nothing.

Marcy tromped down the stairs, hauled the last box up. At the top she arched and stretched her back. God hadn't ordered the heartache. That, she'd accomplished herself.

Her nerves were raw after the attack. She hadn't been able to sleep without feeling that leather-gloved hand clamping down on her mouth. There was something so *familiar* about his voice, or was it his scent? Her spine crawled with the memory. She couldn't place it, but that didn't mean it didn't drive her nearly mad thinking of it.

She'd been so weak since Lisa's murder—no, before that. When she found that file secretly hidden in Pete's desk, she hadn't even stopped to read it, but sent it off to Lisa as if it were a poisonous snake. Relying on fear hadn't been a good defense, but it seemed the safest way to go. She understood the logic of the ostrich, head in the sand.

After the attack, there was no other choice. She needed the truth or she'd go crazy looking behind her all the time. Jack provided a barrier of safety, but that safety net crumbled. Time to take care of this herself.

She slid into her favorite chair in the living room, begging God to heal her damaged heart; fill the hole. He had something good planned for her if she had the patience to wait for it.

She dialed the number she'd managed to get from Carter, but Kendra Sparks didn't answer. Marcy left a message with her request, feeling the emptiness of her own life against the sadness the Sparks family must be feeling at this time.

She ended the call and exhaled. She'd made a step in the right direction. Her faith was on crutches, bruised and broken, but she was upright, making strides to end the nightmare that started the moment she put her hands into Lisa's blood.

23

THE SOUNDS OF the crowd trickled into the locker room when the outside door opened, and Drew's blood warmed. This close to game time he always got jittery. He could taste another opportunity to show his potential to his coaches, Jack Briggs, and the world. He'd arrived a little late this morning and hadn't had time to calm his nerves.

He felt good. After every training session this week, he'd felt his ankle strengthening, but it was still stiff, so he'd get the Toradol injection again, just in case inflammation got the better of him during the game. Heck, he'd even heard guys brag that it helped ward off a head injury— or at least the headache that followed. Couldn't hurt.

He jerked his head in greeting as inside linebacker Will Roggen passed him in the locker room. "Let's do this, Shaw."

Muscles in his jaw churned. "Bringin' my 'A' game, Bro."

He scanned the training room for the familiar face of his trainer. A guy in a white coat motioned him from behind glass as he pushed the door open.

"You're Drew Shaw?" Drew didn't recognize him, but the familiar badge hung from his neck.

"Yep. Ya got my records?" He chewed a toothpick, a nervous habit he'd picked up in college.

The trainer tapped the clipboard. "Got them right here. I haven't seen you before, have I?"

Drew shook his head and hopped up on the table. "Usually see them team trainers. You fillin' in or somethin'?"

"I'm often on call on game day. Surprised we haven't met yet. Are you comfortable with me taking over for Jason Yarrow? He's the trainer you usually see."

So *that* was his name. He really should get to know the guys who took such good care of him. "Get 'er done, man. I got no problem."

The stainless steel table reflected the label on the box of latex gloves, a couple of Popsicle sticks, tape, and a bottle of Mylanta. Preloaded syringes and a bottle of medicine lay on a tray, ready for action. He tried to quiet his mind like Briggs suggested, to envision the passes and the runs from the playbook, but blood pounded in Drew's skull, and he blew a nervous breath into the air. This was his moment, and he wasn't going to blow it. The game meant too much.

The trainer looked up with understanding in his eyes. "Game time nerves?"

"Gotta get those butterflies flying in formation. That's how I plan to dominate."

The trainer's eyebrow rose at Drew's cocky prediction, but he nodded with a smile of appreciation. "Let's get you in top shape, then." He filled a syringe from the bottle and tapped it to release the bubbles. "Toradol has changed pregame treatment options for players in a big way."

"True dat. I dint have pain for like twenty-four hours after the game las' week."

He hoped there were no bad side effects because he intended on lining up for an injection before every game. He wondered why he'd held out so long. Toradol and whatever else they injected into his ankle did amazing things for his game, and his self-confidence.

The drug burned a little more this time, but he couldn't wait for the pain relief that would follow. He'd looked it up on the Internet at home and found it was a powerful anti-inflammatory. No harm in that.

The trainer held up the second syringe, smiling. "Have you had joint injections before?"

"You mean Marcaine?"

He tapped the needle with his middle finger. "Something like that." He smiled and pushed the needle deep into Drew's ankle. The trainer exhaled like the weight of the world had just come off his shoulders. He looked him in the eyes. "That should take care of it." He grabbed the tape from the table and finished taping both ankles, ripping it with his teeth and applying it with expert strokes.

He jumped from the table, favoring the ankle as he flexed his foot. Thank goodness the tape wasn't as tight as the last game when he'd lost circulation before the fourth quarter. Whoever he was, this guy was good. "Thanks, man."

The trainer turned back to his clipboard with a smile. "Anytime."

The football hit Drew squarely in the gut as the quarterback handed it off. He buried the ball deep into his side. Muscles tensed as strong hands grabbed his jersey in an attempt to rip him to the turf, but he spun, avoiding the tackle, the white line of the end-zone drawing him like a magnet. With a surge of energy, he jumped over a fallen player and stretched his body to break the plane of the goal line for the score. A heart-pounding rush of adrenaline surged as a deafening roar filled the stadium. Drew jumped up and spiked the ball. His first rushing touchdown of the season. The quarterback ran at him and jumped in the air, pounding his helmet and shoulder pads in celebration. Drew inhaled the energy from the crowd as he screamed exultantly at the fans who smacked his helmet from the stands.

"Yeah baby! That's how ya do it!" The exhilaration fueled him.

The flexibility in his ankle had returned and allowed him the lightning-fast movements he'd been famous for in college. Whatever the trainer had injected, it was a miracle. He hadn't felt this good since the first days of training camp.

Sweat dripped from the tip of his nose as he bent over his knees waiting for the snap. His eyes shifted left and right, watching the defense as Jack had taught him, never giving any indication to which side the play would run. A linebacker grunted an insult from the line and Drew smiled. Just like Briggs said, they wanted to eat him for lunch.

Not today.

After the snap, the quarterback dropped back like he was going to pass, but Drew was there waiting for the ball. A split second later, he saw the cutback lane open and shifted for the hole in the other direction, the goal line in sight. Legs churning, heart on fire, he cut through a tackle and jumped over a pile of players. He cut hard left, but a safety tackled him from the side. A sickening crunch from his ankle jolted up his leg as players piled on top of him. Pain seared through his foot, and he tried to wiggle his toes, but they refused to move.

An anguished roar tore from his lips, but the ground seemed to throw it back in his face. He cursed as the ankle throbbed. There was no mistaking this injury.

It's over.

For the first time in his life, a football game couldn't hold Jack's interest. After Marcy left him in the parking lot, he'd returned home, locked again in the same depression that cloaked his life after leaving the NFL. This time, he deserved every pang his heart endured. It hadn't been his fault he'd run into Francie at the hotel bar, but he wouldn't have been there if he'd been more understanding about Marcy's time with the kids.

The unexplained bruise marks on her face haunted him, but he couldn't force her to return his calls. At least she wasn't unprotected. She had Carter and Bobby. What would she need him for?

Despite the gloomy remembrance, he flipped the channel back to the Raiders game, which was in commercial break, so he could watch Drew play the fourth quarter. The kid had had a game for the record books so far, averaging seven yards per carry.

But watching Shaw's success hadn't dampened the regret that wedged its way into his heart.

The commercials ended, and the NFL logo flashed as the cameras cut to the field announcer. Jack's heart squeezed as the trainers loaded Drew onto a motorized cart to carry him from the field. Jack scooted to the edge of his seat and grimaced when the replay showed Drew's ankle crumple in slow motion. Drew's expression said the same thing his had the moment his knee gave way; he'd *known* it was over.

A familiar sensation punched him. Poor kid. He hated that Drew faced a serious injury this early in his career. The video cut to a female sports announcer on the field. "Drew Shaw is questionable for return this late in the game. We'll let you know when we have an update."

Another one bites the dust. Pete's words rang in his head.

Jack sank back into the couch to watch the fourth quarter, but the replay of the injury repeated in his mind. Is this what Pete Farris had done with his contracted players? Agonized over their condition, waited for the phone call? Maybe he'd turned normal concern with his own players into obsession over all injured players? He would never know now. The thought crossed his mind that, without knowing the truth behind Lisa's murder, Marcy really wasn't safe, but he reminded himself that that's what the police were for. Marcy wasn't unprotected. She had more men around her than flies on honey.

Maybe someone should protect him from himself. If his suspicions were true, he didn't think he could face another day. But how would he find out? Had Marcy contacted Lisa's sister as she'd hinted?

His mind skipped back to Drew's injury. The technology offered by the NFL was second-to-none and Drew was young. He might have been able to rehab his own knee if he hadn't had eleven years of battering already stacked against him. Maybe it wouldn't be a career-ending injury for Shaw, though he hoped the kid could keep it together during the grueling months of rehabilitation.

His head pounded. The depression was making him crazy. Players weren't injured by anything but the harsh nature of the game. He trusted the trainers. There were regulations and securities in place to prevent things like this from happening. *Shake it, Briggs.* He sounded like a conspiracy theorist. Next thing he knew, he'd be picketing at the wreckage of the Twin Towers with a sign that said, "Bush should pay."

He'd give Shaw a call in a few days, see how he was doing. That is—if he could find his phone. Jack sighed and flipped the TV off as the Raiders took a knee to end the game. They'd won a spectacular victory largely due to Drew's contribution, but none of that mattered anymore. What did any of it matter when the whole thing could blow up in your face in one play?

He wiped his hand across his T-shirt and tried to muster the energy to get off the couch and pack for his trip to his mom's house, but picked up the remote instead. He didn't pay for the NFL package for nothing. Might as well watch the whole day. He could pack before his plane left tomorrow.

The night game kicked off before he got off the couch again. Stretching his muscles after the day of inactivity, he rummaged on his desk for his phone and turned it on. His heart jumped when he read the screen. *Five missed calls.* Hopefully one from Marcy.

He flipped to the call log and scanned the list. Nothing from Marcy, but his mom had called and left a message. He raised his eyebrows when he saw an additional message from Coach Black at SC.

His heart fell as he listened to the message from his mom. She said she'd just come down with a case of the flu and asked him to postpone his trip a week or two. Since she lived in an assisted community, he wasn't worried about her care, but regretted not spending the holiday with the woman who'd made every Christmas magical.

The message from Coach Black lifted his spirits, though. *It's been too long, Jack. Janice has been asking about you. I know you probably have plans for Christmas, but why don't you come out to California for a few days in between? I know it's last minute, but I've got some time off and the kids are off on a holiday cruise this year.*

A smile tugged at his mouth. Coach Black had been the closest thing he'd had to a father back in the day, and he would give anything for a man-to-man chat right now. Jack changed his flight from Tampa to L.A. He dialed Coach Black's number. "Hey, Coach."

"Jack. When you didn't respond to my message earlier, I figured you were celebrating the holiday already."

"Sorry it took me so long. If the invitation still stands, I'd love to come out for Christmas."

"You don't have family plans this year?"

"Mom's got a case of the flu. She'll be fine, but asked me to come in a few weeks when she can slave over the stove for me."

Coach Black laughed, a familiar sound that warmed Jack through. "No woman was ever so proud of her son. Sorry she's been ill, but we'd love to have you for the holiday. You can have Kenny's old room."

Jack smiled. "I'd like that. You sure it's not an imposition for the holiday?"

"Tell you the truth, we were hating facing the day by ourselves. It'll be good to have one of our boys home again."

Our boys. The words chased away some of the gloom he'd been under. "I booked a flight for tomorrow. Can you pick me up at the airport?"

"As O'Reilly says, 'Name and town, Name and town. Name and town.'"

Jack shook his head. The old man always had a strange obsession with the political talk-show host. "L.A. At 3:45."

"See you then, Jack. Looking forward to it."

Maybe a holiday at Coach Black's house would help him get through the holiday without thinking of Marcy snuggled under the mistletoe with her brother-in-law and Carter Cunningham. The thought pierced his heart and he wondered, just for a moment, if he'd made a narrow escape.

But he realized that, if given a chance, he'd be right there, elbowing for victory.

24

THE CHRISTMAS TREE glittered in the living room, flashing on and off in multicolored rhythm. Haley sat cross-legged under the tree singing along to the Chipmunks Christmas album playing on the CD player. Brant lounged on the couch in his Broncos sweats, flipping through last month's copy of *NFL Rush*. Marcy leaned back into her favorite chair and snuggled under the throw her mother-in-law knitted for her last year. This was the kind of cozy Christmas Eve she craved, but she struggled to enjoy it. The bruises her assailant left on her cheeks faded to the point she could cover them with concealer and foundation, but the bruises Jack left on her heart were still raw. Somehow, she'd make it through the holiday preparations, though her feet ached from baking six dozen cookies with Haley this afternoon. The warm smells still lingered in the house and brought the holiday close.

She tried to push the memories, of Jack and the attack, down deep and enjoy the moments with her kids, but Jack's betrayal throbbed like a bee sting. She'd gone to him for help when she needed it most and found him with another woman. She pulled the shawl closer. At least she only suspected her husband of being unfaithful. She'd seen Jack with her own eyes. Nightmares plagued her since the incident as she remembered her attacker's warning. She'd been a fool to trust Jack, especially with her heart.

The phone rang and Marcy grabbed the handset from the table. She didn't recognize the number. "Hello?"

"Mrs. Farris? This is Kendra Sparks. I'm Lisa's sister, I got your message."

Kendra's accent came across hard as nails, but her words were not unkind. Stereotypically East Coast.

Marcy's throat closed around the words she forced herself to utter. "Hi." She wanted to add how sorry she was for their family's loss, but the words wouldn't come.

"Listen, the police took some of Lisa's files after the murder, but I knew she kept a special stash. I decided you should have the packet I found. I have a feeling this might shed some light on your questions. Can I send them to you after Christmas?"

"Was there a manila envelope among the documents?" Marcy chewed the nail of her first finger.

"Yes, it's addressed to Lisa from you."

Marcy suppressed any excitement from her voice. "That's just what I need, and anything else is a bonus. I really appreciate this. I know your family has been through a lot."

The sound of shuffling papers rippled over the connection. "From the looks of this stuff, Mrs. Farris, you've been through as much as I have."

The bottom dropped from her stomach. Was there more? "Let me give you my address."

The call ended cordially, but even through the East Coast harshness, Marcy detected a note of pity in Kendra's voice. A shiver rocked her stomach.

Her mind ran wild. Sounded like she was getting more than she bargained for. Was she strong enough to handle the answers? What about the kids? Would they be able to hold their heads high if their father was a criminal? She would soon have answers, although it would be two whole days until Kendra could post them and even longer for them to arrive.

Bobby's face appeared around the corner. "Knock. Knock. Merry Christmas!"

Dressed in khakis and a navy blue sweater, he looked the picture of laid-back Christmas. The haggard look she'd seen in his face earlier in the month seemed to have melted away. Looks like he's found a way to leave work behind. Because of the strain between them, she'd kept news of the attack to herself. If she put her fear into words, it might materialize and consume her. She'd gone to Estes Park that night to tell Jack, but after seeing him—

Haley squealed and jumped into his arms. "Merry Christmas." She hefted the largest gift from his hands. "Let me help you with that one." She grinned at Marcy. "Maybe I'll just see whose name is on the label here . . ."

Bobby mussed her hair as the cat curled around his ankles. "You know exactly who it's for, Squirt." He pulled a quarter from his pocket and tossed it at Brant. "I'm giving you the first quarter 'cause you're gonna need it."

Brant caught it and tossed it back. "Oh, no you don't. You're the one who's gonna need it."

Marcy laughed at their joke. The year after Pete died, Bobby bought Brant a Sony PlayStation. Every year since, he'd bought him the newest Madden game and they spent the greater part of Christmas Eve trying to whoop up on each other. They both put in two quarters and the winner took the whole dollar. High stakes, indeed.

She yawned and stretched, splaying her toes in her fuzzy socks. "Still playing that game?"

Bobby nodded and held up the game. "Oh, yeah. It wouldn't be Christmas without it."

Brant jumped to his feet. "Can we play in here by the fire, Mom?"

In years past, she'd been adamant about keeping all media in the basement, but this year it might be a welcome distraction. The last thing she wanted was to be alone with her thoughts. "Sure. Why not? Haley and I will cheer for you."

Bobby walked over to her chair and caught her gaze. "I could use encouragement from a good cheerleader. A whole dollar is on the line here."

Behind the teasing remarks, his eyes spoke volumes and her stomach squirmed. Maybe the time had come to give him the chance he'd asked for, trust herself with him like she'd never allowed before. Maybe she'd missed the point entirely. A relationship built initially on friendship might be stronger than one built on initial attraction. "Haley, you cheer for Brant. I'll help Uncle Bobby." She put her hands out, and he pulled her to her feet.

He kept pulling, and she bumped into his chest. He held her a moment and whispered, "Some cheerleaders can be a serious distraction."

Her cheeks felt warm as she pulled away. "I'll try to behave myself."

He tossed the game to Brant. "You've been doing that for ten years."

She rolled her lips and stepped away. Too many emotions swirled around her. She'd always been so careful. Always Miss Goody Two Shoes. Pete had called her that a time or two in a fit of anger when she'd asked him to attend church with them. Okay, nagged him to attend church with them.

She grabbed the phone. "What do you guys want on your pizza?"

Annoyance crossed his face at the distraction, but he checked it and winked. "The usual. Gumballs and anchovies."

Haley frowned. "Eww. I want pepperoni."

She picked up the phone. "Gumballs and pepperoni it is."

"Moooom!"

When she'd ordered the pizza, she settled back into her chair. The game loaded on the screen. "Bobby, Bobby! He's our man; if he can't do it, no one can."

He'd made it obvious he wanted to be her man, but could she see him as more than her brother-in-law? He was no Jack Briggs, but that was over. He hadn't called since they'd met in Estes, and she figured it was all for the best. God had something great in mind for her—a blessing. And as long as nothing else knocked her down, she'd accept what He had in mind.

Brant scored and gave Haley, who'd brought down her shiny pom-poms, a high-five.

Bobby shrugged. "Where's my cheerleader when I need her?"

Could Bobby be that blessing?

Coach Black's house still resonated with a special glow, just like it had in the bygone days of Jack's college career at the University of Southern California. He spent the bigger part of the hour locked up in the den, which was a Cardinal and Gold shrine to the good old days when Coach Black ruled like a king over the SC football program.

Janice's kitchen held a tang of spice and the sweetness of baking as he entered. A red and white checkered tablecloth with green rick-rack reminded him of the decorations his mother had saved through the years. A smile tugged his lips but quickly fell away.

Janice held a mug out to him. "Coffee?" Jack clasped a mug of hot coffee in his hands. "Thanks." He leaned onto the kitchen table where Coach pulled up a chair.

They'd both aged in the twelve years since he'd seen them, but Coach's weathered face still held those intense eyes that had burned lessons of life and football into his soul. Janice had a grandmotherly blanket of white hair on her forehead but retained a youthful gleam in her eye. Despite the years, they'd welcomed him back as if he'd never been absent, but nothing could lift the tentacles of depression that threatened to strangle him every second.

Janice brought a plate of perfectly decorated sugar cookies to the table and sat down. "Tell us what you've been up to since retirement, Jack." Her faded smile hadn't lost any of its warmth, either.

He snatched a Santa Claus cookie from the plate and took a bite. "There isn't a lot to tell."

Coach leaned his chair back on two legs. "I'm almost glad. Seems like a whole lot of big-time players get themselves in some mess or another shortly after retirement. There are exceptions, of course."

Jack nodded. He'd made his share of mistakes if they weren't as public as some of his counterparts. "It's harder than I thought it would be." He sipped coffee. "Nothing takes the place of the NFL."

Coach nodded, and it dawned on Jack that Coach had probably faced a similar situation when he'd retired from coaching.

Jack continued, "I spent my whole life leading up to my career in the NFL and it left a hole I can't seem to fill. Of course—" He chuckled. "I haven't bought a car dealership or been brought up on charges of murder yet."

Janice nibbled a cookie. "And you've managed to stay single all this time? I kind of remember you going with a girl while you were in college."

Ouch. She couldn't know how fresh that wound was. "I'm better suited for football than the game of love."

"Methinks there's a story here." She turned to her husband, a gleam in her eye. "What do you think, Ralph?"

"If there is a story, it's Jack's to tell."

They both waited as he stared into the depths of his cup. "I'm afraid the story has an unhappy ending."

The hall clock ticked in anticipation.

Drew stowed his crutches on the arm of the chair in the examination room as the doctor dimmed the lights and flicked on the computer screen. Black and white MRI scan results seared themselves on his brain with their stark revelations. Obvious misalignment of the ankle joint brought fresh waves of nausea. The doctor pulled a pen from his pocket and pointed at the image on the screen. "Three fractures and multiple ligament tears—here." He swirled the tip of the pen. "See the white edge here?"

The rest of the doctor's words blurred into a Peanuts monotone Drew could or would not understand.

"Permanent injury . . ."

Drew's head snapped up. "Wha'd you say?"

"Even with extensive surgery, I fear you may have suffered a permanent injury."

The room spun around him. "Permanent like I can't play football anymore?"

Doctor Brower tapped his chin with the pen. "I can't say until we get you through surgery and therapy, but I consider it a possibility. Your season is certainly over."

One time in high school, Drew had gotten in a fist fight. The kid sucker-punched him in the gut before he knew what was coming, but it couldn't have been as painful or surprising as the news he'd just heard. The world shifted in and out of focus as he attempted to wrap his brain around the news while the words pierced his ears. *Your season is certainly over.*

The doctor talked about the surgery for a few more minutes, and his assistant came in to finish the paperwork and get him on the schedule. The day after Christmas.

Jason Yarrow, the trainer he'd seen regularly since coming to play in the Black Hole, met him in the hall. "Once we get you home, I'd like go over some of your records. I want to have a thorough report before surgery."

Drew swiped a hand across his eyes. "Whatev."

Yarrow nodded and turned down the hall.

His crutches beat a creaking rhythm on the short nap carpet, and his ankle throbbed in time to the beat. Even Toradol hadn't been strong enough to quell the pain after the injury on the field.

"Do you have plans for Christmas?" Yarrow asked.

"I planned to go home to Oakinaw for a day or two, but I guess I'll miss it." His heart twisted. "Merry Christmas."

The bitter sarcasm didn't change anything, but it did help him cope. What was he missing at home anyway? Usually, Mom got more lit up than the tree on Christmas Eve, which meant she slept past noon on Christmas Day and woke as cranky as a yellowjacket that'd been kicked from its nest. Yeah, he'd miss *that.*

His phone vibrated, but between navigating the hall and his

crutches, he couldn't answer. Probably his agent. Wouldn't that be a fun conversation? *They say I'm out for the season. Maybe for good.*

When Yarrow settled him into the car, his leg propped against the front seat, he checked his missed call log. *Jack Briggs.*

There was one guy who would understand what he was going through. He redialed the number.

"Jack, it's Shaw."

"Drew. How are you, man? Have you seen the test results?"

Obviously, Briggs knew the drill. "Just came from there. Ain't good."

"What are they going to do?"

Drew leaned back into the seat as Yarrow started the car. "Ankle reconstruction, I think. Wasn't really listening—" He swore.

"What did they say about next year?" Briggs knew enough about injuries to assume surgery meant his season was over.

"Les jest say it's questionable." Saying it aloud brought a stinging wave of pain as the ankle throbbed in response to his increased pulse.

"They can do miracles with injections, therapy, and stuff like that."

Drew swallowed. "Sure helped you."

Briggs laughed off the wicked comment like it was a joke. "I'd played eleven years in the NFL when I blew my knee out. How much longer did you expect me to go? You're young enough to make a full recovery and a great comeback."

His guard slipped talking to Jack. "This isn't how I saw my career ending."

Briggs sighed. "I know it's rough now. Heck, it's like hearing a family member died when they show you the films, but remember about being positive and working hard. We'll get you through this."

Drew's heart perked up at his use of "we". He could do it if Briggs helped him get through the recovery.

"When's the surgery?"

"Day after Christmas."

"Good. I'm in town for the holiday. Care if I come up to hang with you before you go in for surgery?"

Mom wouldn't be sober enough to make a bus out here, and who else is there?

"That'd be cool, man. I got nobody here."

25

"Can't tell you how long I've waited to get you alone like this."

The fire played tricks with light and shadow on the walls of the living room while Bobby's words played tricks with Marcy's heart. There wasn't a sprig of mistletoe in sight, but that didn't stop him from claiming her lips in a warm kiss. Bobby's long frame stretched beside her, and her lips burned hotter than the flames in the grate, but her heart was cold.

"You won't regret this, Marce." Bobby caught her hand to his lips. "This is right." The moment hung like a smoky breath in December air. His eyes reflected the flickering fire and the lights from the tree. She knew it wasn't a simple statement, but a question, a request to move forward. She bit her bottom lip. It would be so easy to lean into him, absorb the love he so freely offered. What else did she have?

A red velvet ribbon slipped through her fingers as she tied it on a package for Haley. So many years they'd been family, friends. Could she make the transition as he obviously had? There was nothing to fear, but her heart hammered. Bobby would be a good provider, even if he did travel as an NFL trainer. The kids loved him, despite his occasional mood swings. Heck, even the cat loved him. Bobby offered her everything she needed; why didn't she want *him*?

Would she have felt differently toward Bobby if he'd made the proposition before she'd met Jack Briggs?

Bobby stuffed a blue and silver wrapped gift into Brant's stocking and turned to her. "You're quiet tonight. I thought you loved Christmas Eve."

"I'm just a little tired tonight, I guess."

He knelt behind her, thighs pressed into her back, lean and strong.

His thumbs melted into the muscles of her shoulders, wrestling with the tension she'd been building for weeks. She rolled her head and could have dissolved against him. It would be so easy, but something stopped her.

She'd promised herself to think before she jumped into things. To give God a chance to speak to her. "I need more time, Bobby."

He squeezed her shoulders. "Pete's been gone for five years."

It wasn't Pete she was thinking about.

"Is this about Jack Briggs?"

She shook her head, but if it wasn't about Jack, who was it about?

He stiffened and stood up. "I don't know what's wrong with you, Marce."

"If I knew, I would tell you. This—" She gestured between them "—is too much to process."

He grabbed her arms and pulled her against him roughly. His lips sought hers with a desperation that almost scared her. "I have loved you for years. You don't have to process anything. You *know* me."

Janice retired early, leaving Jack and Coach Black with a plate of gingerbread cookies to keep them company. They'd listened to him tell what had happened with Marcy, but Coach still looked at him from time to time with a question in his eyes.

"Tell me what's on your mind, Jack." Coach Black leaned back in an armchair by the fire.

"You mean besides Marcy Farris?" Jack gazed into the flames. His earlier conversation with these two had only confirmed the mistakes he'd made with Marcy, but it wasn't his only concern.

Coach waited.

"I thought I couldn't get any lower after my NFL career was cut short by the knee injury." He'd left out the details about Pete and the injury scandal when he'd told them what happened with Marcy. He figured he'd communicate his deepest fears in manageable bursts.

Coach lifted his knee and crossed his other leg. The old man was getting on in years.

"There were times in my life I thought I'd hit bottom, but realized I hadn't been falling long enough. Did I ever tell you about what happened my first year at SC?"

Jack looked at the man who'd coached him. The legend. "Nope."

A shaky breath preceded the tale. "When I landed the head coaching job at USC, I thought I'd reached the pinnacle of my career. The fulfillment of my dreams. I was as high as a man could get."

Jack understood the high.

"Then, our baby daughter was born."

The blow fell. Jack hadn't known the Blacks had a daughter. "What happened?"

Coach stared into the flames. "She was born with half a heart. They couldn't save her. It was 1970, and they just didn't have the technology they do now. She was with us for one precious day."

Jack swallowed around the lump in his throat. What did his problems compare to the tragedy of losing a child? "You must have hit bottom, then."

Coach shook his head. "That's when I *thought* I'd hit bottom."

Jack watched the old man's face relive the memories. "I'd spent years teaching my players that football was about strength. If a man could dig deep enough, he should find the strength to bear up under anything."

The logs crackled and shifted in the grate. There was nothing more soothing than the smell of a wood fire. Jack waited for the story to continue.

"But, I started to feel the pressure building when the season began a few weeks after Hannah's funeral—that was our little girl's name—and I felt my nerves beginning to shred. The football program at SC wasn't what it is now, but as an untried coach, the press was breathing down my neck. I knew I'd cracked when I made some offhand comments in an interview after an especially trying practice."

Jack laughed. "Some things never change. They probably deserved it."

"It was like a different man made those comments. But, I took the heat after that. Hate mail. The whole nine yards. Almost lost my job over it, but the worst thing was, I'd hurt Janice terribly."

"Janice? I guess I don't understand."

Coach nodded. "The reporter asked me if the family tragedy would have an effect on the coming season. In addition to some choice insults I flung at the reporter, I told him to leave the 'little things' in the past. That I'd moved on and they should, too. I said the university wasn't interested in halfhearted coaching and neither was I."

Jack cringed. Talk about the wrong choice of words. He could imagine Janice's heartache.

"Yeah. I'd made a public mess of things. Because the truth was, despite what I'd said, I hadn't moved on. When the hate mail started coming, and I had to answer to the university board, that's when I hit rock bottom. There were some dark days when I even contemplated suicide. It's like a different man was living my life, wearing my skin. In about five minutes, I'd ruined my reputation with the press, tore at my wife's open wounds with my sarcasm, and given the university a bad name all in one interview. I'd been trying to get through it with my own strength, and I couldn't do it."

Jack understood. A man's strength just wasn't enough sometimes. "But, you kept your job and look at the program you built."

"I did keep my position, but the man who'd landed the head coaching job wasn't the same man who led the team that year. Or any of the years afterward."

"How did you change? You were the one who helped me earn the reputation as the Gentleman Linebacker."

Coach grinned. "I never would have changed if I hadn't realized I couldn't change myself. God was the only one with the strength to bear those kinds of burdens and change my heart."

Should have known the old man would bring religion into the discussion. "I know someone else who would agree with you."

"Marcy?" Coach picked a raisin button from the jacket of one of the gingerbread men and popped it in his mouth before he bit the head off, seeming to relish every bite.

"She's pretty religious and all that." He ran a hand through his hair.

"I've never been a religious man, Jack. Just trusted God to see me through."

Not religious? The guy lived and breathed by the Bible. "So maybe I'm at rock bottom. My mind's playing tricks on me."

Coach finished his cookie with a sip of milk from a red and green striped mug. "Santa won't get here for another hour or so, yet. I've got time."

The plate of cookies disappeared as Jack wove the choppy details together. Seeing Marcy covered in Lisa's blood. The murder. The trip to New York. The threats. He detailed the things he'd found in Pete's papers.

"Why was Pete Farris following injured players?"

"I think the players were being injured *intentionally.*"

Coach's face grew serious. "That's a heavy allegation. What's the motivation for such a thing?"

Jack stopped chewing mid-cookie. "I don't know."

Coach exhaled. "Something like that happened when I was assistant coach at Ohio State. Players were attacked behind the stadium before the game and beaten pretty bad. Good way to make sure they didn't play."

"Did you find out who was behind it?"

"Sure did. Member of the board at Minnesota paid students at Ohio State to do it. Paid well, I understand."

Jack sighed. "But the NFL players weren't beat up. They were all injured playing the game. It's a long shot to look at it this way. I certainly haven't told anyone but you. I've got a list of injured players and it's pretty convincing. You'd think with some of these crazy stats, people would have noticed the trend. There's upwards of twelve Pro-Bowlers on the list. I think that's what Lisa was looking into." Jack didn't give voice to his fear that his own name was on the list.

"Maybe someone paid the trainers to take the players out. What is Pete Farris' involvement in all this?"

Coach's insight had his mind spinning. "That's where everything gets blurry. Marcy is convinced that her husband would not have committed suicide if he hadn't been involved in some kind of scandal. And when she found the documents in Pete's office, she shipped them off to Lisa Sparks to investigate."

"Could he have paid the trainers?"

He shrugged. "I don't think he made the kind of money it would take to coerce someone into a crime of this magnitude, but I never saw the papers she had. She'd be devastated to find her husband involved in something illegal." Jack slugged down his milk. "She's been beating herself up for years thinking he killed himself to escape her nagging." He struggled with memories of Marcy.

Coach nodded. "The human heart can be deceived into thinking anything."

Jack poked the fire. "I guess you're right." Deceived by whom? Themselves?

The cuckoo clock on the wall didn't sound, but the little bird came out of the door to silently announce the midnight hour.

"We'll get to the bottom of this. Don't worry. I'll be praying about it." Coach rose slowly, and Jack felt guilty for keeping him up so long.

"The strength to succeed is rarely found inside oneself."

Jack remained in his chair by the fire. "If I don't have strength within myself, I don't have anything."

Coach strolled into the kitchen, and Jack heard his mug and the empty plate go into the sink. "Strength from a higher power never dwindles." He poked his head into the den. "Don't sleep too late, now. Janice will have something special for breakfast."

After staring at the flames until they dwindled, Jack made his way to Kenny's room, where Janice had laid the bedcovers down and put a candy cane on his pillow. He smiled. Even her kindness couldn't cut the worry and fear that clouded his vision. Coach was right. They'd overlooked motive when trying to understand what had happened to the players.

He prepared for bed and thought of Coach Black. The man exuded strength even as his body broke down. He embodied it. But looking to God was a sign of weakness, a symptom of something missing inside. There'd been times when he'd dug deep inside and found a well of strength to win a game. He would just need to dig deeper.

Marcy hadn't slept well. How many times through the years had Bobby spent the night, sleeping across the hall in the guest room? Usually, it gave a feeling of safety, but Bobby was anything but safe these days. She walked a tightrope. One false step and she'd lose a friend she'd come to rely on.

She'd wrestled thoughts of Jack until they were safely buried under other worries. She had no time to think of him anymore. In a day or two, Kendra Sparks' package would arrive and she would know the truth about her husband. And hopefully put an end to the threats. Didn't they say knowledge was power?

All night, Bobby's good night kiss boiled in her heart like percolating coffee, bringing memories, long forgotten, to the surface. Love had many faces, wasn't easily pinned down. She'd loved Pete. Loved Carter. Could she love Bobby? The way he wanted?

The heart could be *convinced*, couldn't it?

A bump and giggle in the hall signaled Haley was up uncharacteristically early. Marcy smiled. One year, Brant got up at four a.m. to see if Santa had arrived. She and Pete couldn't go back to sleep, and they'd opened presents before dawn's first light. She sighed. Sweet memories.

The French braid she'd put in her hair last night now resembled a robin's nest from tossing and turning, so she brushed it out and re-braided it over her shoulder. The giggling sounded just outside her door. She twisted the wrap Bobby had given her around her body and flung the door open. "Merry Christmas, Hales."

Haley fell back on her heels, grinning her toothless smile. "Merry Christhsmas."

Marcy had promised not to make fun, but a smile escaped before she could turn her head.

"You're laughing at my lithp."

She ruffled Haley's sleep matted hair. "'Cause you're just so stinkin' cute." She kissed her cheek, still warm from sleep. "Let's wake up Brant and Uncle Bobby before Uncle Carter gets here."

She jumped up, eyes wild with mischief. "Yeah. Let's do it."

The kids wanted to dig into their stockings before breakfast, but it had been their tradition to wait until after breakfast to open gifts. Pete's parents would come for lunch, and they expected Carter any moment.

The bell rang, and Haley ran to answer it. "Uncle Carter! Merry Chrithmath!"

A few snowflakes had landed in his dark hair which showed just a feather of gray above the ears. "Merry Christmas!" He gathered her in a hug while keeping his gaze on Marcy.

Carter shook his head, and a few flakes of snow drifted onto Haley's cheeks. "Did you know it's snowing?"

She ran to the window, pressing her face against the frosty glass.

Bobby entered dressed in a tight fitting T-shirt and flannel pants. His sandy hair stuck out in all directions, and he grinned as he flung an arm around Marcy's shoulders. Any other year, the significance of the moment may have been lost of her, but humiliation burned her face as she shrank back from the possessive gesture. To anyone else, it would have looked like they spent the night *together*. The heat in her face increased as Carter noticed with raised eyebrows. "Good to see you, Bobby. Merry Christmas."

They shook hands, and Marcy breathed a sigh of relief that Bobby's arm no longer trapped her.

"Come see the snow, Mom."

She peered out of the window next to Haley. "I see, honey. Even a few flakes count for a white Christmas."

Carter handed Haley the festive packages under his arm. "Where's

Brant? Sleeping in?"

Brant moseyed out of the den, the shine of victory still on his face. "Uncle Bobby should have been the one who slept in. I beat him at Madden even with my cast." He held up the club hand.

Carter glanced at Bobby. "Keeping the old man in his place, huh?" He moved to Marcy's side. "Merry Christmas." A warm kiss landed on her cheek, and he whispered in her ear. "Bobby spend the night?"

His insinuation hit its mark and the heat flashed into her cheeks again. She frowned at him and rolled her eyes. "I never kiss and tell." That should shut him up.

The party followed the kids into the den so Haley could show them what she'd found in her stocking. Marcy wandered into the kitchen.

Despite the weather, light danced in the kitchen window, spilling onto the floor in a weak stream. In the span of a few months, everything in her world had changed. Jack entered the scene and opened her eyes once again to the real purpose—potential—of friendship between men and women. Things may not have worked out between them the way she would have liked, but here were two men she now viewed in a different light.

She'd spent Christmases with Bobby and Carter and, except for Carter's occasional jealous streak, never felt any tension. Of course, she'd always known the two weren't best friends, but the tension hung in the air on every meeting nowadays.

Carter sat on the ottoman near Haley. "Christmas coffee." She handed him a hot mug.

"Thanks. Can I help you in the kitchen?"

"Sure."

He stood and followed her. When they'd arrived in the kitchen he turned to her with a serious expression. "Kendra told me you'd called and asked for some files." His eyes flashed. "Why didn't you ask me to get them?"

Marcy wiped her hands on a dishcloth. It was time to come clean. What did she even care anymore? She'd tried to avoid hurting Carter and endangered herself in the process. "I know I should have asked you, but I knew you were hurting and didn't want to make it worse."

"Why would something like that make it worse for me?"

How much should she tell him when she didn't have all the facts herself? "Kendra has some information about Pete's clientele that I wanted to see."

His eyes narrowed, and he stepped forward. "What kind of information?"

This was a side of Carter she'd rarely seen. "She didn't say on the phone."

Carter stood so near she could feel his breath on her face, anger in his hazel eyes. "You're not telling me the whole truth. What did Kendra tell you?"

Marcy swallowed past the lump in her throat. "It's unlike you to get so upset. You sure you're okay?"

"I've tried to protect you. Tried to make the way so smooth. And now you go behind my back and get files that will only end up hurting you."

She met his eyes. "Protect me from what?"

Bobby appeared in the doorway. "Are you guys okay?"

Carter let her go and stepped back. He massaged the bridge of his nose. "We were just having a discussion."

Bobby looked between them and refilled his mug from the coffee pot on the island. "She and Pete used to have *discussions*. I'm not sure I like the sound of that."

Carter snapped. "If you think I've ever treated her the way your brother did, you're dead wrong. Don't fool yourself into thinking you were the one she called when they'd had a fight."

Bobby set his mug on the kitchen table and faced him. "And where were you when she needed a shoulder to cry on? Writing that fancy magazine a million miles away."

Brant and Haley shuffled in, confused expressions on their faces. Could this morning get any worse?

Carter flung his hand at the kids. "You want these kids to hear my reasons for staying away? They're a bit more honorable than yours."

Marcy held her breath. She would not let these two men ruin the kids' holiday. "End of discussion." Her tone must have gotten her point across because they both softened.

Bobby came to her side. "She's right. I'm done discussing anything with you."

Curiosity burned in her to hear what Carter was about to tell her when Bobby came in, even if he'd been more angry than she'd ever seen him. She should make allowances.

"Let's give him a break, Bobby. He just lost Lisa. You and I both know grief does strange things to people. He wasn't hurting me."

Bobby's eyes darkened. "He'd better not."

She thought of Jack then, of the wounds that still stung. Perhaps life would be better off lived alone, where no one could touch the tender parts. "Carter and I have been friends long enough to forgive and forget."

Carter nodded, remorse evident on his face.

"Hales, come and grab these plates and get the table set, please." She handed her the special Christmas plates, which had been a gift from her mother-in-law the year Pete died. "Brant, show Bobby where the candelabras are and get them lit for breakfast. We'll make this a special meal."

Bobby left reluctantly, and she and Carter were alone in the kitchen again.

He wrapped her in his arms. "I'm sorry. You know what Pete was. Why do you have to go digging up more dirt now? It can only hurt you."

"Something just feels unfinished." She dare not add, "Since Lisa's murder."

"What's the latest with Jack Briggs?"

Her heart sank. In the past, they'd shared an open relationship. "He was never more than a friend." *Liar, liar. Pants on fire.* The childish taunt haunted her.

"Something happened?"

Marcy filled his coffee cup again and loaded sausages onto a platter. "I was warned not to trust him, and I should have listened."

"He hurt you?"

"Not in the way you're thinking. I'll be fine."

The oven door screeched open and the cinnamon aroma of baked French toast, a family favorite, billowed out.

Haley came from the dining room. "Done, Mom. Do you want me to use those new napkins you bought?"

"Yes. I almost forgot. Thanks, Sweet Pea."

A knock on the door interrupted the preparations. Marcy tossed the oven mitts at Carter. "Who could that be?"

A delivery man held out a long white box tied in a red ribbon. "Special delivery."

She signed the electronic pad he held out. "You're right about that. Christmas Day delivery!"

"Yes, ma'am. Merry Christmas."

"Merry Christmas." She closed the door. Her hand shook as she reached for the lid. Every time she'd received a gift in the past month, it'd been a threat.

MARCY'S HEART JUMPED into her throat as she opened the card. *Merry Christmas, Ms. Vanilla. Hope your holiday is as beautiful as you are. Jack*

Who was she fooling? Her heart was putty in his hands. A day following a minor disagreement, she'd seen him with another woman. But there was little reasoning where her heart was concerned. The fragrance of the long stemmed roses pillowed in tissue paper brought a tiny smile to her lips, but it vanished as Bobby snatched the card from her hand. "What's this?"

It was unlike him to invade her privacy, but he'd already begun to read, a brotherly grin on his face. His expression clouded. "You sure you should trust this guy?"

A prickle of sweat broke out on her upper lip. Did everyone distrust him? She narrowed her eyes at him. "What do you know about it?"

Carter stepped in and read the card. "I know NFL players like the back of my hand. If you remember, I'm the editor of *NFL Rush* and was engaged to be married to a woman who wrote a daily column on NFL dirt." He stepped close to her. "You of all people should understand why there's reason to doubt him."

All eyes in the room bored into her. She put her hands up. "Give it up, guys. You can't throw the challenge flag in this game. Jack wished me a Merry Christmas. No penalty." She flung the roses on the hall table and stalked to the kitchen, lest her face betray her.

A zoo animal had more privacy. Why did they both think they could run her life? Hadn't Pete controlled her long enough?

Bobby found her in the kitchen. "Can I see you in the den?"

She sighed. "Can't it wait? Breakfast is ready, and the kids are anxious to open their gifts."

"I think it's best to have this conversation now."

Her heart froze. When the roses arrived, she knew what her answer would be. She could never love Bobby the way she loved Jack.

As they arrived in the den, he glanced over his shoulder. "I've offered you a future, but I can't have other men, especially Briggs, sending you flowers. I need to know where we stand."

Anger and frustration built like steam as he pressed her. "You want to know where we stand? You are my dead husband's brother and my friend. That's all I can offer." *Especially when you back me into the wall.*

"So you're saying there's no chance for us?"

At the moment, she didn't feel there was a chance for anyone. What could she do? He'd placed her and their relationship on the chopping block, and she held the ax. She could cut it in half with words.

No. She was not that woman anymore; the one who used words to cut and wound. She stroked his shoulder. "Bobby, I love you as a brother and permanent member of our family, but my heart can never belong to you."

"If you think Jack's going to treat you any better than Pete did, you're fooling yourself." His voice cracked.

"I'm not thinking of Jack." *Yeah, right.* "I just want *our* relationship to stay the same. Lots of things have changed since Lisa's murder." She'd told no one but the police about the attack in her car, and they'd done very little. She had to acknowledge she was on her own.

"How naive you are, Marce."

"About what?"

"Don't you know what Pete was doing behind your back?"

She'd suspected, but never had evidence. She couldn't imagine what it would be like to know for sure. "What does it matter now that he's gone?"

His eyes darkened. "The past can kill you. Believe me, I know."

The day couldn't get any worse. If she could crawl into bed and start over, she'd do it. She'd lock the door, barring the door against the men in her life. The room closed in and a painful rhythm beat in her temples. "Breakfast is on the table. I'm heading out for a walk."

She cruised past the kids and Carter, who stood in the kitchen staring at the food, which grew cold as they waited. "You guys eat. I need some air."

Marcy shoved her arms into her jacket and banged the door shut. Ignoring the snowflakes that bit into her face, she pounded the sidewalk toward the school as emotions swirled. She'd promised to trust God, but could see no end to her suffering. Three months ago, she had support from Carter and Bobby with no strings attached. Enter Jack Briggs and everything fell apart.

She pulled her coat tighter around her. The crisp scent of snow tingled in her lungs. Of course, that wasn't exactly fair. Jack hadn't been responsible for Lisa's murder. Her own part in it had really ignited the downward spiral. Some decisions made tiny ripples on the lake, others sent waves crashing to the shore. She'd reacted in fear when she'd sent those files to Lisa, and she prayed she and the kids would survive the onslaught of consequences.

Her cheeks tingled and her hands lost feeling, but she walked to the school and back before she felt ready to return. The door cracked open, and she peeked inside, ashamed to face them after such an outburst. No one lingered at the dining table. A quick trip to the bathroom to dry her eyes and apply makeup helped her put things into perspective. She wasn't going to miss Christmas Day, no matter what happened. She straightened her shirt and smiled at the woman in the mirror. *That's better.*

Haley and Carter played Connect Four in the Den, but Brant and Bobby weren't around. "Where's Brant?"

Carter glanced at her. "They've been locked up in Bobby's room since breakfast."

She missed Brant's smile. They hadn't really talked since his game. Maybe she should go knock on his door and ask them to come down.

The repentant look in Carter's eyes softened her heart. "You okay? I'm sorry you felt attacked about the flowers."

Haley grinned from her place on the floor. "I put them in water for you, Mom." She'd never doubted Jack's integrity. "Is it time for presents?"

"Thanks, honey. Take your time and finish your game. We can open presents later. Or wait for tomorrow, even." She knew exactly what her daughter's response would be.

Haley grinned and crinkled her nose in disagreement. "I'll go find Brant."

Carter's capable hands massaged her shoulders. "I'm worried about you."

She turned and met his gaze. "I'll figure it out."

"You're going to give me an ulcer with all these men around. Jack and Bobby have gotten the scent and are howling like bloodhounds."

"What's happened to us? Last year we were a regular family. This year, I'm living a soap opera." The only thing that wasn't new, the veiled resentment between Bobby and Carter—that'd been a part of her life for years.

His eyes softened as they trailed the curve of her face. "You have a certain something about you that men can't seem to resist."

She pushed him. "Tease."

His eyes darkened and locked on hers. "I mean it, Marcy."

Sure he did. She shoved him. "Thanks for the shot in the arm."

A cockeyed grin followed, and his eyes brightened as Brant and Haley entered chanting, "Time for presents."

Jack massaged the scars on his knee while he waited for the nurse to call him back to Drew's room. Christmas with the Blacks raised his spirits, but the sights and sounds of the hospital waiting room pressed on him like a weight. Drew would be fine. He was young and strong.

Was his watch working? The nurse had promised to allow him to come back after Drew was prepped for surgery, but it seemed she'd forgotten him.

His phone vibrated. "Come on back to the locked double doors. I'll meet you there." He met the nurse and followed her to Drew's cubicle.

She pulled the curtain closed as she left, and Jack turned to Drew. "Ready for this?"

"Ready as I'll ever be, man."

Jack squeezed his shoulder. "Who's your doc?" Drew's toes poked up from beneath the blanket. Were the woven blankets on the bed the same at every hospital?

"Dr. Cowers, the orthopedic surgeon for the Raiders. I've heard good things about him."

He sat beside the bed. "The trainers are the miracle workers after surgery."

"Guess I better start learning their names."

"Thought you'd already be on a first name basis."

Drew fiddled with the blanket. "Should've been a little more observant, but I can describe the guy who worked on me before the last game perfectly if I can't remember his name."

"He wasn't your usual trainer?"

"Nope. I'd never seen him before. Seemed to know what he was doin.'"

A nurse and doctor came in, and Jack stood. "Trust your trainers. They are a player's best friend. I'll see you when it's over." He patted Drew's shoulder and ducked behind the curtain. If the surgery went well, he'd be on the field, instead of the bleachers, next year.

Jack settled into the vinyl chair he'd vacated to wait through the long surgery. A digital board on the wall indicated Drew's exact movements through surgery and recovery. Pretty cool technology, especially for nervous family members.

As the moments ticked by, he played their conversation over again. What was wrong with that kid? He'd been seeing the trainers for weeks and didn't know their names? Someone should slap him when he gets out of anesthesia.

Jack still kept in touch with some of the trainers he'd worked with through the years. They'd developed a special relationship. Along with team physicians, trainers were a trusted member of the NFL system, and without them, players wouldn't play at the high level the game required.

He picked up a copy of *NFL Rush* from the side table and flipped through the pages. He frowned at the head shot of Carter Cunningham. He'd never known the guy well, but always had a respect for him until witnessing his insane streak of jealousy when it came to Marcy. He wasn't so sure what he thought. People were complex creatures. Maybe he should give the guy a break. The only time he'd seen him recently was following Lisa's death. Must be hard to lose someone you love.

A volunteer passed with a tray of snacks; Jack grabbed a warm cookie from the cart and turned back to the article. Did Carter really have designs on Marcy? Sure seemed like he'd already marked his territory, but what kind of guy went after a woman so quickly after the death of his fiancée? He could have had Marcy anytime since Pete died.

His skin prickled in fear when he thought of Marcy and the way he'd seen her last. He'd been a fool for allowing the threats to go this far and felt certain she wasn't out of danger, yet.

His eyes scanned the bio at the end of the article.

Before becoming Editor for NFL Rush, Carter worked as an NFL trainer, serving time with the Cleveland Browns, the Indianapolis Colts and the Houston Texans. Carter graduated with a degree in biology from Abilene Christian University and later studied journalism at NYU.

He nodded as he remembered the facts of Carter's past. The guy was knee-deep in the NFL even before he started *NFL Rush*. He'd experienced greater success with the latter career choice, and Jack couldn't help thinking Carter might have made the right choice. He just didn't seem the trainer type.

Intrigued, he Googled details on Carter's career as a trainer. They'd spent some years on the same side of the grass, but they'd never crossed paths until he made his name with the magazine. If anyone had a pulse on the league, it was Carter. His magazine was a must-read in every barber and lube shop around the country. Here was a guy who might have some of the answers he was looking for.

His stomach sank when he thought of Marcy's fears in regards to Carter. She hadn't wanted to involve him because of her associations with Lisa before the murder, but if he was going to get answers, it was time to rush the quarterback, so to speak. Carter was a big boy. He could handle it.

Something stopped him from dialing. Involving Carter could hurt Marcy terribly and though the possibility of a relationship seemed a thing of the past, he was still the Gentleman Linebacker and should consider her feelings.

The memory of bruises on her cheeks wouldn't leave him alone. If the person who'd sent the threats had accelerated to physical violence, she could be next on his list. Panic rose in his throat. He'd been such a fool to walk away so easily, leaving her vulnerable.

Chastised by his own guilt, he dialed Carter's number. Marcy may not like it, but someone had to do something before this got out of hand. Something told him it was already out of hand. He'd been so wrapped up in his own problems, he'd missed the clues.

"Carter Cunningham."

"Carter, it's Jack Briggs."

"Good to hear from you, Jack. How was your holiday?"

He could have smacked his forehead. It was the day after Christmas and he was probably at Marcy's house. *Idiot.* "It was fine. I'm sorry to interrupt your family time, but I have a couple of professional matters to discuss with you."

"No problem. Let me step into another room, and I'm all ears." His tone was certainly all business.

Papers shuffled, and Jack's heart sank when Haley's laugh rang in the background. Would it be bad manners to ask about Marcy?

"You're on speaker, but I'm in a private room. What's on your mind, Jack?"

He bit back questions about Marcy. "I've been doing some digging into past NFL injuries and had some questions."

"Shoot."

"Would a trainer have any way of predicting a player's injury?"

Carter paused. "That's a difficult question. There is emerging technology that could help predict a weakness, but nothing can predict injury."

"So a trainer would have no warning before a player is injured?"

"Not unless he caused it."

His ears perked up. "What could a trainer do to cause an injury like that?"

"Well, overtraining or use of stimulants can injure players."

"What about medications? Injections?"

"Not sure there's anything that could cause serious injury. Certainly nothing the industry's familiar with. Everything is prescribed by the team doc."

"You've heard of Drew Shaw?"

Carter coughed. "Shaw? Yes. I've heard of him. He was injured in the Raiders' away game last week."

"Yes. I'm sitting in the hospital waiting on him to come out of surgery. I happened to be in the area for the holiday and thought he could use a friend."

"That's real good of you, Jack. The holidays can be real tough when you haven't got anyone to share them with. So, anything else you want to know? I'm not sure I answered all your questions."

Could he trust Carter with the accusations he harbored? "What do you think about the injuries Lisa tracked in her article before she died?"

Carter cleared his throat. "I'm not sure we should continue this conversation here. Could we talk later?"

Alarm bells went off in his head. They were on to something. "Sure thing. Before you go, how're Marcy and the kids doing?"

"We've had an interesting holiday, but she's okay. Whatever happened between you guys left its mark."

Did he think the bruises were the result of rough treatment from him? "I didn't lay a hand on her if that's what you're asking."

"I wasn't asking. Nice roses, by the way."

A mixture of worry and elation crashed over him. "Good. I hope they added some color to her holiday."

"It was pretty colorful."

What the heck did he mean? "But everything's okay?"

He clipped his words "Yep. No lasting damage. I think our nerves are a little raw this year."

He understood that feeling all too well. "Well, Merry Christmas. Thanks for giving me some time."

"No problem, Jack."

The stomach acids that had been churning since yesterday increased as he processed the news he'd just heard. His eyes darted from side to side; when he was certain he was alone, he let the mask fall. Jack Briggs was close to the truth about the injured players. He cursed and jammed a hand through his hair. Cornered, he had two options. Make Jack Briggs pay the same price Pete paid for nosiness or cower in the corner and wait until he got his money. He could simply disappear with all that cash. Like the man he worked for, he'd gambled his life on this job.

He remembered, with mingled guilt and satisfaction, the moment he'd silenced Lisa with a single stab into her neck. The knife left its mark with a deft stroke, and she'd fallen before she knew what hit her. He'd have no regrets about slitting Jack's throat open from ear to ear. Why did regret over Pete's death entangle his heart like a spider in a web when he hadn't even touched the man?

As far back as he could remember, he'd been in competition with Pete. He always had the hand up, rubbing it in, mocking. No matter the game, he won every time. He scored the elite agent's job, he won Marcy's heart. Pete stole his life. Perhaps Pete's death wouldn't haunt him if he'd stayed around to see the life leave his eyes instead of hearing of it secondhand from Marcy. He may have different views as a matter of conscience, but he'd loved her for years and her reaction stayed with him. It all began when he'd spent that weekend in Vegas, living the high life with illegal bookmakers, something his own salary could never afford. He'd been fascinated how one man changed the tide of 300 million dollars with a single stroke. Gamblers were a major contingent of the NFL demographic, and when he'd been offered a part of the action it fueled his desire for power and significance. Every hit had been worth it, even if they did come at a price.

His stomach threatened to erupt, time was running out. Enough nostalgia. Of course, no one suspected him or his serum. Shaw was out for the season; when the money arrived in a day or so, he could head out with or without Marcy. Her refusal yesterday stung and, for a moment, the thought of making her pay as Lisa had, tickled his fancy.

Didn't she understand how he'd always protected her, first from Pete and now from Jack? He'd tried to warn her when he'd waited in her car, but she wouldn't listen. Jack was his next target. Maybe with him out of the picture, he'd have Marcy all to himself.

27

MARCY PAINSTAKINGLY APPLIED decals to a toy Haley received for Christmas when Bobby and Brant came bounding down the stairs. Bobby's hand squeezed her arm. "Brant and I are going to the mall for a while. He's got some things to return."

She missed the warmth in his voice. "You're nuts going into that mob. It's worse than Black Friday."

Brant shrugged and tossed her an unusually black look. They'd hardly exchanged a single word yesterday. "We know."

She lifted a mirrored sticker with her thumbnail without looking up. "Take my car, if you want. Be careful." The sooner Bobby and Carter went home, the better. Brant's attitude was unusual. He seemed stressed. She guessed they all were.

The garage door slammed behind them while Carter bounded down the stairs after completing a phone call he'd received earlier.

"Guess who that was?" He slid his phone onto the side table.

She looked up and lowered the sticker onto the toy. "Who?"

"Jack Briggs."

Her cheeks flamed. Had he called to check up on her? "Really? What did he call you for?" *Shoot.* The sticker was cockeyed and she'd have a terrible time getting it off and repositioned, now.

"He had some questions about NFL injuries. You know anything about it?"

Her heart fluttered, and she checked the room. Haley was in her room playing with her new toys, leaving them alone. No time like the present to come clean. "Why don't I get a plate of those mint brownies I made and we'll talk."

"You always know how to make a conversation palatable."

She smiled and returned from the kitchen with a plateful of brownies. She pointed to the chairs next to the fire. "Have a seat."

If she had swallowed sand, her throat could not have been as dry. There was no easy way to begin. She blew a breath out through pursed lips and grabbed a brownie. Why care about her figure now with Jack out of the picture? She'd never possessed the ability to hold a man's interest very long. Might as well make the most of it.

Haley bounded into the room, bundled in her snowsuit and new hat with the tassels on top. "Whatcha doing?" She spied the toy in Marcy's lap, and her eyes lit up. "Oh, is it done yet?"

Marcy shrugged. "Not quite yet." Next year, she'd pay extra money for toys not requiring parental involvement.

"Uncle Carter promised to take me sledding. Can we go now?"

She put the toy aside. "I think you need to wait until later, Hales. Could you go watch your new Barbie movie while Carter and I talk a while?"

"Aw, Mom. Uncle Carter promised, and he leaves tonight." Her long-lashed eyes sought him from across the room.

Haley's cheeky insistence strained already frazzled nerves, and she was about to flatly refuse to let her go, but Carter interrupted. "She's right. I did promise." He jumped up and grabbed his coat and scarf while eying the enormous stack of brownies on the plate in front of her. "Try to leave one for me, Marce." He winked.

She snapped him with a dishtowel as he opened the sliding glass door, and they slipped out into the cold afternoon. This was more like it. A true holiday. No silly romantic ideas. Bobby hadn't said a word to her, but she'd seen that look in his eyes before. He was upset. And the longer they delayed their discussion, the better.

Exhaling, she settled onto the couch, grateful for the time alone. The flowers Jack sent seemed to speak to her from where Haley put them on the mantle; just the sight of them brought a smile to her lips. If she forgave Jack the *incident* at Estes Park, would he be a repeat offender? Her breakfast threatened to find its way back up again when she thought of her own doubts about her husband's infidelity. The familiar stab of doubt weakened her further. Would she ever get this monkey off her back? Always wondering—dreading—the possibility she'd find evidence of his unfaithfulness. She swallowed against the fear that held her captive. The package from Lisa's sister was expected to arrive tomorrow. Would it contain more than she could handle? She steeled her heart. Maybe it was time to face this head on and be done with it.

The garage door slammed, and Brant filled the space in front of her. She must have dozed off. She smiled at him, but her grin died when she saw the dark look on his features. "I want to know how Dad died." His knuckles turned white in a death grip on the arm of her chair.

She blinked and rubbed her eyes. "What?"

"You heard me. I want to know how he died." Brant never dared use such a tone with her before.

She sat up straighter, looking to Bobby for backup, but he'd vanished into the kitchen. She ignored his attitude—for the moment. Hadn't they been over this before? "Your father took too many pills and died in his sleep."

His throat croaked. "Why?"

"I don't know, honey." Hadn't she spent the last five years of her life trying to figure it out?

He stepped forward, cheeks red with fury. "I think you *know* why. It was your fault."

A slap in the face would have hurt less. Sweat moistened her palms. She'd blamed herself often enough, why shouldn't Brant? "I don't know what you mean, Brant. I didn't kill your father. He committed suicide."

His voice gained volume. "But you drove him to it. He never would have done it if you hadn't been so mean all the time. Nagging and yelling at him."

Marcy schooled her voice. "Perhaps you're right, Son. I admit I wasn't always kind, but do you really think he killed himself because he had a mean wife?"

She gritted her teeth against her surprise and anger. Brant wasn't usually moody and accusative.

"Maybe you switched his pills."

Something inside snapped when Bobby waltzed in from the kitchen wearing a smirk. She pounced. "Is this the trash you've been feeding Brant while you spend all that time together?"

He held up his hands to block the verbal attack. "What? What are you talking about?"

She jumped to her feet. "Telling my son I'm the reason Pete killed himself." Her pulse pounded in her ears, and she felt her nails dig into her palms.

His brow pulled together. "Marcy, this isn't a good time to have this discussion."

"Oh-ho. Really! You are really—"

Brant stepped in for his uncle. "It wasn't his fault, Mom. Don't blame him."

She silenced her son with a hand in his face and turned back to Bobby. "Why not talk about it right now? It's been a poisonous holiday. Let's deck the halls with some accusations."

Bobby's eyes shot icicles at her as he took a step forward. "I don't have to listen to this from you, Marce. We don't have that kind of *relationship*, remember?"

The words hit their mark.

Brant pulled a hand through his hair. "I've had enough of this. I'm outta here."

The world pitched out of balance. Where was her son, and who was this boy who'd replaced him? She'd missed the warning signs and been completely sideswiped. "Brant, you've never treated me like this before. What's wrong, honey?"

She'd seen that stubborn, angry look before, in Pete's eyes. It was frightening. "Maybe I finally see the truth." He edged closer to Bobby.

"Son, I know we've had a rough couple of years, but we can get through them together. We always have."

She reached for his arm, but he shrugged it off. "I'm going home with Uncle Bobby."

She stood her ground. "You are not." The whole exchange had the quality of a nightmare.

Brant glared. "Watch me." He snatched his backpack from the hanger and slammed the garage door in her face.

She spun around and attacked Bobby again. "This is your fault."

"I just made some innocent suggestions when we started talking about Pete, and he went off like a rocket. Ain't my problem if he's been thinking the same things other people have."

She ignored his last comment. "What *innocent* suggestions?"

His eyes locked with hers. "Look, Marce. Maybe if my brother hadn't met such a cold witch in bed every night, he wouldn't have turned to other women."

His dagger found its way into her heart. "Shut your mouth! What do you know about it? Oh, I see. You can't have it your way, so you go for the kill shot? Fine. Get out of my house!"

His fists vibrated, and she wondered for a moment if he would strike her. Instead, he bowed. "Gladly."

The door slammed a second time, and she heard the tires of Bobby's car peal from the driveway. Her shoulders cramped as she sank to a chair. Bobby spoke lies, but opened a terrible wound with his accusations. Pete's rejections through the years left her more full of holes than a sieve. Pete had been the cold one, leaving her craving his touch night after night. Bobby's words pierced her. *Such a cold witch.* The venom in Brant's voice dropped the final stroke on her sanity. She covered her face and wept.

The truth danced just out of Jack's reach, but he wouldn't be in the dark for long.

The board on the wall indicated Drew had been moved to a room where he'd be welcome to visit, so he made his way through the maze of hall. Drew's dark face, framed by white linens, looked haggard. "How're you feeling?"

"Nurse gave me somethin' in the I.V. that's pretty good."

Jack nodded. "Probably Dilaudid."

Drew's words came out slurred. "Thas' what she said, man."

His phone vibrated from his pocket and his heart rocketed, hoping it was Marcy. Jack leaned closer to the face on the pillow. "You have someone to drive you home and get you set up?" Drew's eyes grew heavy, but he had to ask the question that had been plaguing him. He gripped Drew's shoulder. "You remember telling me you had a new trainer before your last game?"

He lifted his head. "Yeah. I can't remember his name, but I can describe him."

Jack paused, wondering how lucid Drew really was. "Could you describe him for me?"

The Dilaudid must be taking effect because Drew flashed him a crooked grin. "He had blonde hair and a goatee. Couldn't have been over six feet tall, kinda scrawny."

The description matched his suspicions. "You get some rest, buddy. I'll check in on you when you get settled at home."

"Thanks for comin', man." Drew's eyes fluttered closed and Jack escaped, his heart in his throat with mixed emotions on how to tread next.

His mind chewed the possibilities as the elevator closed behind him. A smile spread his face when he saw who'd called. *Marcy.*

He ground his teeth when she didn't answer his return call. How were they going to figure this out if they couldn't communicate?

The familiar scent of Hibiscus and hot asphalt assaulted his senses as he exited the hospital and headed toward his car in the parking lot. A few clicks on his laptop would point him in the right direction, and then he'd have something to report when she finally called back.

28

AFTER CARTER LEFT for the airport, Marcy turned her phone off, got Haley to bed and crawled between the sheets for a good cry. Nothing hurt more than reliving the accusations Brant had shot at her, but as morning dawned, anger replaced the hurt. She wasn't going down without a fight.

At nine, she dropped Haley at an indoor pool for a birthday party. "Bye, honey. Be sweet."

Haley waved and trotted into the Hatfield Chilson Recreation Complex in Loveland. At least she was on good terms with one of her children. She'd called Brant's phone, but he hadn't answered. Forgot who pays the bill, hadn't he? She'd suspend his phone, but then how would she contact him?

It was times like these she missed Pete most. A father would know how to handle these situations better than she did. In the past, she'd confided in Carter or Bobby, but recent circumstances made that impossible.

On the way home, she stopped the car at the mail box. Her heart thumped as she pulled a manila envelope from the slot postmarked from New York.

It bounced as she tossed it on the passenger seat and headed home.

There was nothing menacing about the envelope itself, but she trembled when she thought of the contents. The garage door screeched when she punched the button, and she scrambled into the house and tore the envelope open. She slapped it on the table before she pulled the papers out, breathing a prayer to handle what she found with grace.

The white paper slipped from its binding, and some photographs fluttered to the ground. She bent to pick them up, fingers shaking. The white Kodak backing of the photos hid the images against the floor.

Pete's smile greeted her as she turned the photograph over in her hand. Strong jaw, slightly shadowed with whiskers. Big, white teeth in a smile she'd never forget and Lisa Sparks smiling beside him in a bikini. Blonde hair curled onto her shoulders and those familiar green eyes smiled into the camera. Her heart fell into her feet, and her mouth grew dry.

The next picture pierced her heart and confirmed her fears. An orange sunset touched the background as Pete and Lisa stood on a bridge, locked in a passionate embrace. A silver scrawl in the corner: P&L Atlanta.

The proof she'd dreaded for years hit her like a baseball bat to the stomach. Her husband had been unfaithful, that she could believe. But with Lisa Sparks!

His business trip to Atlanta. She remembered it with surprising clarity. He'd been gone just a weekend, but seemed so happy when he'd returned. Even offered to go to worship with them the next week. Probably out of guilt.

The words on the papers quivered in front of unshed tears. Letters and emails. Sickening evidence of her husband's infidelity. She blushed, feeling like an intruder reading intimate details of their affair. Judging from the dates on emails, it'd been lengthy. No wonder he hadn't been much of a husband at home.

Lisa must have treasured these emails, seeing she'd kept them on her desktop. But she'd found no record of correspondence in Pete's things. Of course, Lisa wasn't married and had nothing to hide. A question jarred her. Why not just ask for a divorce? He'd never loved her though she'd been more than willing, but never wanted to lose her, either.

She sank into a chair as the truth washed over her. Ugly words she'd become so accustomed to hearing from inside her head screamed at her. She'd provided indispensable services: childcare, maid service, you name it, but her husband gave his love to another woman because she was undesirable, unlovable. Her offering of herself wasn't good enough. She lacked that quality in other women of attracting men and keeping them. An anguish she hadn't felt since Pete's death sliced her heart. How could she have thought herself worthy of any man's love?

She swallowed around the pain in her throat and opened the envelope she'd sent Lisa. She allowed herself a deep breath. The affair was in the past. The contents of this envelope affected the future, if not the present.

The papers slid from the envelope with ease, and her eyes scanned the black and white words for clues. Nothing familiar, though these were the documents she'd sent Lisa to look into. A sick terror washed over her when her eyes hit a list of twelve players' names, written in Pete's handwriting. Isaac Johnson. Terry Versacoma. *Jack Briggs?*

Thunder pounded in her ears. Could Pete have been responsible for Jack's injury?

Attached to the list were Pete's records on each player on the list. They pointed to one thing: they'd all been injured in similar ways following an injection of a drug she didn't recognize. She flipped to the last page. There were odds makers' spreads, including the names of the injured players. So they were betting on the players being taken out? Her thoughts galloped ahead. Pete had no medical knowledge, so he must have been involved on the gambling side.

She shivered as she thought of the threats she'd received. The organization behind high stakes sports betting was known for being unforgiving and ruthless.

Pete and Lisa were both dead. And she was next.

Jack knocked and tested the door to Coach Black's study.

A voice came from the desk. "That you, Jack?"

Coach's white head bent over an empty photo album. "Come in."

He flipped a chair around backwards and straddled it. "What are you working on?"

Coach fingered a photograph. "These are some pictures of our last mission trip."

He leaned forward and grabbed a stack to flip through. "Where'd you go?"

"Sudan. We were part of a team who ministered to the community while another team drilled a water well." He pulled a picture from the pile and handed it to him. "Taught the boys some American football."

The scene depicted a dusty field and six or seven almost naked boys laughing with great wide grins as Coach explained the game with a football in his hands. Coach's gestures hadn't changed. He'd always had that intense look when explaining the game he loved. "Did they get to play?"

Coach handed him another picture. "See for yourself."

A young running back stiff-armed another boy as a stray dog barked his approval of the play. The kids all looked thin and malnourished, but seemed to welcome the excitement of the game. Jack grinned.

Coach smiled, nostalgia in his voice. "Most of those boys have been drinking from a mud puddle all their lives. Many of the kids die before they are as big as these boys. Diseases in the water kill them."

"I guess we take something like clean water for granted."

Coach stared at the picture in his hand. "They are so trusting. So easy to teach." He slid the picture into the three-slotted album page.

Jack handed him another photo. "Have you gone before?"

"Uh-huh. We've been going to villages in Sudan for several years. The church sends a team every other year."

Jack's eyebrows rose. "Not a football organization, then?"

"No, we weren't really there to teach them football. I can't seem to help myself, and the boys love it." He handed him another photo of little black heads bent over Bibles. "They've watched their family members die, watched the water dry up, and yet they are so strong. It humbles me to see their trust in God." He slid the photo into the slot and turned the page.

Another picture caught his attention. Coach stood next to a stock tank of muddy water, sleeves rolled up to his elbows. A Sudanese woman sat in the water with her hand cupped over her mouth. "What's this one?"

"After the well was dug, we had four baptisms." His eyes shone with pride as he took the picture from Jack. "We can't wait to get back there. We've made plans to go back to that village this spring. They kinda stole our hearts."

Jack flipped through many other pictures. Kids smiling. Babies. Village life. "I can see why." Maybe this is what he should do with his retirement. Lots of NFL players did charity work.

The chair squeaked as Coach put down the album and leaned back, massaging his neck. "How did Drew's surgery go?"

Jack shrugged. "As good as can be expected."

Coach patted his knee. "You look worn out. Must have been a long morning."

He sighed. "You have no idea how long. I think I've got a theory brewing."

Coach stood. "Sounds like a coffee and pie discussion." He motioned with his head toward the kitchen.

Jack stood, patting his stomach. "If I keep having these discussions with you, I'm likely to gain fifty pounds."

"Voltaire said, 'Nothing would be more tiresome as eating and drinking if God had not made them a pleasure as well as a necessity.'"

Jack shook his head and smiled. Coach was famous for his unusual quotes.

The scent of fresh coffee filled the air, and the gurgling of the coffee-maker added a cheery air to the already neat kitchen. Coach peeked under a towel on the counter and grinned with raised eyebrows. "She never lets me down."

He cut two generous slices of pumpkin pie, poured the coffee and sat at the table. "Grab the whipped cream, Jack."

Jack put a generous dollop of cream atop both pieces and had taken his second bite of melt-in-your-mouth pie before he began. "Tell me what you know about NFL gambling."

Coach took a sip of coffee. "I never was a gambling man, myself, but I understand it's big business."

"Imagine the kind of money a guy could make if he had some control on the outcomes of games."

"I've been told there's over a hundred million dollars bet on each game in the season, not counting the Super Bowl."

Jack nodded and pulled a list from his pocket, his heart pounding. "Each of these teams had a winning record before a key player was eliminated from the roster by injury."

Coach's eyebrows rose as he read the list. Their eyes locked. "Your name's on this list, Jack."

And his life was crash landing. "Yep."

Coach's lips thinned into a line. "Who's the trainer?"

"I'm not sure, but I'm thinking it could be Marcy's brother-in-law, Bobby Farris."

They sat in silence a few moments. "What makes you suspect him?"

"Bobby was listed as a trainer at every facility where an injury occurred. He also has a background in pharmaceuticals."

"Makes sense. But you know him, don't you? Wouldn't you have known it was him giving you the injections?"

He nodded. "That's what I can't figure out. I'm on the list, but I would remember Farris. I spent the morning calling the names on the list, and the rest of the guys on the list confirm Bobby gave the injections, even Drew Shaw."

"So why's your name on the list?"

"Maybe there's more than one trainer involved."

"You have someone in mind?" Coach's eyes narrowed, trying to read his thoughts.

He grimaced and stared at the ceiling. No one came to mind. "I keep reading my name on the list and wincing."

"Does it change anything?"

His head jerked up. "I could still be playing ball if it didn't happen."

Coach smiled sadly. "Hemingway said, 'It is good to have an end to journey toward, but it is the journey that matters, in the end.' You had an incredible career, but it's not the end."

"I never saw any road but football."

"When football is your life, nothing fills the void when it's gone. God's the only one who filled the void when my life fell apart."

His heart rebelled. God was a good guy, taking care of kids like those he'd seen in Coach's photo album, but why would an all-pro NFL linebacker need His help? "What is there in trusting God?"

"Trust breathes new life into old things."

He raked a hand through his hair. "Like my life?"

"And your heart, son."

Jack considered his words. His heart had been empty for so long, expect for moments when he and Marcy had been together. If God could fill that horrible void, why not give it a try? "I'm worried about her." He couldn't help but think of the things that had happened since they met. The roses, the poison—

Coach waited for him to continue.

"What happens when Bobby finds out she knows? He's already threatened her. Could he be capable of more?"

As if reading his mind, Coach stood and allowed him access to the computer at his desk. "Sounds like you're playing the game again."

The stakes were so much higher. "I just hope I'm not too late."

29

ALL DAY, MARCY contemplated calling Jack, but the news about Lisa and Pete ate holes in any confidence she'd had in his fidelity. Best leave him out of it. At this point, she didn't know who to trust. She paced the kitchen, wringing a dishcloth to death. Someone knew she had this information and had tried to scare her away from putting it all together. She remembered the leather glove on her face and the stabbing fear she'd felt when she hadn't known whether the kids were safe or not. One thing was certain, she couldn't tell Carter. Grossly ironic, they'd both been deceived when it came to love.

He hadn't become engaged to Lisa until after Pete's death, so maybe it wouldn't hurt him. But deep down, she knew he'd be devastated. If not for himself, then for her. No, she couldn't tell Carter.

Bobby was still her closest ally. He could make sense of the papers she'd received from Kendra Sparks, but they weren't exactly on friendly terms. She flung the dishrag at the stove and caught a look at herself in the microwave door. She'd been indecisive and weak long enough and her life showed it. She'd cowed to threats, let her husband's memory hurt her even in death, and she'd let her son walk out the door. She'd again trusted in her own strength, which was obviously nothing.

God, give me strength to do what I must.

She glanced at the taut features in the glass again. Time to take this problem head on. A quick phone call to a friend made sure Haley had a place to spend the night. She called Bobby to let him know she was coming to his house, but he didn't answer. No matter. It was time to get her son back and find some answers, whether Bobby was ready to forgive her or not.

No one answered her knock on Bobby's door, but she knew where he kept the key and let herself in. A frown pinched Marcy's forehead as she read the note Bobby scrawled on a greasy napkin left on his kitchen table. He'd taken Brant for a private tour of the Colorado Mountaineers Stadium today, even though she'd asked him not to. Frustration ate at her as she reached for her phone. Who knew how long they'd be gone? Enough was enough.

Kicking the empty pizza box in frustration, she rubbed her palms until they tingled; she hadn't come all this way to leave before having a chance at resolution—and some answers. Bobby made it quite obvious he didn't want to see her after Brant walked out two nights ago. Her head throbbed, but she refused to cry another tear.

The relationships she'd counted on since Pete's death had crumbled around her like the ancient ruins of Greece in a matter of weeks. What happened to her strong support system? Her teeth squeaked as she bit down against the emotion. Facing all the facts about Lisa and Pete still left a bitter taste in her mouth, but she couldn't do anything about it now.

The past could take care of itself. She was bringing her son home today.

Marcy yanked open the fridge and pulled out a bottle of water, disgusted with herself for avoiding the truth. Lisa's murderer was still out there somewhere. A trainer was injuring players. If she could reconcile with Bobby, he'd be the one who might shed some light on the things she'd uncovered. The car keys jingled in her hand as she formed a plan. She'd surprise them at the stadium this morning. They couldn't be more than forty-five minutes ahead and she'd miss much of the traffic that swelled I-25 thirty minutes ago.

Before she left, she noticed a light on the basement and ran down to shut it off. She stopped short at the bottom of the stairs.

Why the makeshift laboratory?

On closer examination, she noticed glass bottles and a hypodermic needle.

He must keep his training supplies here.

She turned to flip the switch and came face-to-face with a picture of the last woman on Earth she ever wanted to see again: Lisa Sparks.

Lisa's head shot, held to the naked drywall by a thumbtack, was surrounded by framed articles clipped from the daily newspaper.

A crawling fear tickled her spine.

She stumbled back and glass bottles clinked. Why would Bobby create a shrine for Lisa? She shivered. Maybe she didn't know him as well as she thought. For years, she'd chided him about his questionable taste in centerfold wall art, especially with Brant growing up, but this was creepy.

Apparently, both brothers had the same taste in women. The thought sickened her. All the men in her life had contact with the same woman. Pete and Carter, and now Bobby.

She sought something to kick, something to lash out at. "Why God? Why is *she* the common denominator?"

She turned in disgust, a metallic taste in her mouth.

The sooner she got Brant home, the better. She took the wooden stairs two at a time and slammed the door behind her. She thrust her arms into her jacket and grabbed her purse. A surge of strength pressed her onward. Once they'd cleared the air, things could get back to normal.

The way they used to be.

Getting Brant back home was her first priority. She'd deal with the details of the scandal later. Something about all this just didn't feel right.

She locked the front door behind herself and laughed at her foolishness. Return to normal life? After Jack Briggs, things *could never* be the same. Some part of her wanted to forget everything she knew and just run away with him to the oasis she'd discovered in his arms.

No. There's no point even thinking about it. That relationship is permanently broken.

Her relationship with Bobby, on the other hand, was tarnished by their disagreement, but she knew he would eventually put it behind him. They'd been friends long enough to get through a little thing like his being in love with her.

She unlocked the car and slid in. *Yeah, right.*

Marcy started the car and pulled onto the street. A red light stopped her at the end of Bobby's street, but traffic lessened and she eased onto the highway at 120th Avenue. Fifteen minutes and she'd be at the stadium. She hit the dial on the radio and tried to relax. Since the Mountaineers hadn't made the college playoffs this year, the stadium wouldn't be in use. She'd have no trouble finding the boys.

The stadium loomed ahead directly west of the highway, glass and metal shimmering in the early morning sun. A part of her wished she'd never heard of the game of football, never set foot in the law office where Pete worked with that Broncos jersey on. She'd never expected how it would define her life, how entrenched she'd become in this world.

She drove past the Broncos stadium, smiling at the familiar white bronco gracing the top. *Invesco Field at Mile High.* She always rolled her eyes when she read the new signage. What was wrong with *Mile High Stadium?*

Money.

That's what was wrong with it. The new sponsor hadn't bought the naming rights for nothing. People said, "Money talks." She swallowed against the bitterness in her mouth. In the NFL, money *tackled.*

She arrived at the college stadium, entered through the tour door and flashed her ID to the security guard, heart pounding with every step. He affirmed her identity after offering her condolences for Pete's death. It seemed her husband was well known even all these years later. Helpful, since she needed free reign of the stadium today. Her future balanced on this confrontation, and she prayed it would clear the air rather than muddy it.

The empty halls echoed her footsteps as she followed the map the guard had given her to the training rooms, where she assumed Bobby and Brant would spend the most time. She ambled toward the weight room but saw no sign of either of them. The place was ghostly quiet.

Bobby's stomach objected to the alcohol he'd downed while Brant munched chili-cheese fries at the bar. Stupid. Drinking aggravated his condition, and after three glasses of wine, his stomach soured faster than his mood. He swallowed acid and elbowed Brant, but he ignored him while texting on his blasted phone. Poor baby boy wanted his mama already. Hadn't tasted his freedom an entire night before he'd regretted what he'd said to her.

That's not what he needed. He needed Brant's hate and misunderstanding to grow, not diminish. Brant was his last weapon against Marcy.

Might as well get moving. He staggered off the bar-stool and motioned for Brant to join him. "Let's get the tour shtarted."

Brant must have noticed his slur because he cocked an eyebrow and said, "You sure you're up for it?"

Bobby nodded and shook the cobwebs from his head. "I'm fine.

Let's get going." He hoped to get Brant's mind off making up with his mom and back on the track he'd effectively started. That Pete's death was *her* fault. He'd played the part of doting uncle and Brant trusted him. This was the best chance he had.

Brant took pictures with his phone as they toured the facility, but his attention was focused on messages that came to his phone incessantly. He did get Brant's attention when they stepped out onto the playing field. Brant's eyes widened at the awe-inspiring expanse of chalk-lined grass, but knowing Brant's aspiration to become a trainer himself, he saved the training facility for last. Brant scuffed along behind him, unusually intent on his stupid phone. *Teenagers.* The lights flickered on in the training room, a place he'd hoped would catch Brant's attention "Over here is the machine I was telling—"

Brant's large form filled the doorway. He held his phone in his left hand and glared. "I've been thinking about my dad's death. I want to know the truth."

A jolt of shock rocked his body. He put his hand in the air. *What the—*"I've told you everything I know about it. We talked about how your mom . . ."

"But it wasn't the truth, was it?" Brant stood next to him, almost a foot taller, but he lacked intimidation in his stare. Maybe not intimidating, but unnerving just the same. It seemed Pete's eyes looked at him from Brant's face, accusing him, laughing at him. Would his brother's legacy ever leave him in peace? Pete still had everything that should have been his. A son. A daughter. The illustrious career. Marcy.

But not for long.

Bobby took a calming breath. The boy just wanted answers about his dad. He could handle this. But why *now*? The payment posted to his bank account three days ago, and he was tired of the guilt and the baggage he'd been carrying since Pete's death. If only he could convince Brant to lay off. Brant glanced at his phone yet again.

"Did your mom tell you this?" He should have followed through the night he'd waited behind her in her car.

"No." Brant scuffed the floor with his toe and toyed with his phone. *Not man enough to look me in the eye.* He could handle Brant. This could work in his favor. "Why do you think you don't know the truth?"

Brant looked him square in the eye. "I called the coroner's office. They told me there was a mixture of medicines in his bloodstream."

He cringed as the dart hit home. He'd never seen the coroner's report. "And that little detail made you think he'd been murdered?"

Brant's head shot up at the word. "Murdered?"

Yes. He'd better rein in his foggy thoughts before he gave Brant more ammunition.

"Mom said he took painkillers. A whole bottle of them."

His heart squirmed in his chest, and he regretted the vodka he'd added to the wine he'd had at the bar even more. He toyed with the purple latex gloves like they were discussing the weather or the latest and greatest video game. "Pete killed himself. I guess that's kind of like murdering yourself." He repeated the lie he'd told himself so often. *Pete committed suicide.* He believed the lie, why couldn't Brant?

"But what if someone added some pills to his? Made the mixture toxic? I know he'd taken some pain pills, but what about the other stuff they found?"

The stuff he'd put in on purpose, knowing Pete's fondness for pain pills.

Bobby fired the last arrow in his quiver. Might as well use the angle that had been working up until now. "What about your mom? Maybe she put something else in his pill bottle?"

The color drained from Brant's features, and he shook his head. The stubbornness of the past days had faded. "She wouldn't do that."

"Seems to me I remember you accusing her of just that when you left."

He blew some air into a latex glove and tied it at the end, creating a grotesque floating purple udder. He batted it at Brant who grinned as he batted it back. The boy didn't have a clue. He was just being a teenager. Flip-flop.

The alcohol was taking its toll, and his head spun. At least his stomach was cooperating so far.

He batted the inflated glove at Brant. "You and I both know your dad was messing around on your mom."

The grin disappeared as he caught the balloon. "That's not what you said earlier. You said he'd been good to her."

"I didn't want to mess with your image of your dad, but the fact was, he was unfaithful to your mom. And she knew it. Maybe she thought it was the best way to protect you? Maybe we're all better off."

"So she killed him? Mom's a murderer?" Brant's eyebrows disappeared underneath his hat at the laughable statement.

Better her than me, bud. "You're the one who thought of the idea, not me." He grasped Brant's shoulder. "Listen, I'm not saying anything. I wish I knew what happened as much as you do. All I'm saying—"

Brant shrugged his embrace off. "How do you know he was unfaithful to my mom?" The question cut the air like a knife.

He'd known Lisa's darker, kinky tastes and introduced her to Pete in hopes of causing a rift between him and Marcy. It backfired when they'd begun a legitimate affair; he'd lost both women.

"Brothers know everything about one another."

And that's how he found out what I was doing to the players. The plan was backfiring. Time to get off the subject before the kid exploded. "Hey, you want to see the weight room while we're here?"

Brant got another text and stood his ground. "Where were you the night my dad died?"

Tension shot through him, and his patience snapped. "What are you driving at, Brant? Come on out and say it."

The whirling of his head wasn't helping. Normally, he'd see a way through this. He'd always been an ugly drunk, and the booze was in full effect.

"I think you were jealous of my dad. He told me you always wanted to play football, and that you loved my mom. I think you know something you aren't telling me."

The anger burned in his stomach, but he suppressed it. Where were his TUMS when he needed them? "Lots of people were jealous of your dad. It doesn't mean there were people lining up to kill him. What about Carter. Why not pin it on him?" He walked toward the weight room. "Come on. Let's see what you can bench with the cast on."

Brant followed slowly, checking a text as they walked.

Distracted for the moment, he breathed a sigh of relief and massaged his burning stomach. All his little hints had backfired on him, and he needed to get the ship turned around fast.

He rummaged through his pockets and found an antacid. He blew the lint off and popped it in his mouth. His esophagus roared fire with flames from the pit of his stomach. Once he'd paid off his loans, he'd see a doctor about the cursed heartburn. It was time for relief.

"Can I try the Powerplate while we're here?"

"Sure. Jump on, Cowboy." He pressed the buttons and set the time. The motor buzzed into motion.

"What do you know about mixing medicines? Is that part of a trainer's job?"

He was unable to quench his obvious irritation. "Why?"

Brant's eyes revealed nothing. "Just curious. I saw some medicines in the basement and thought maybe you'd come up with something new."

The fire in his stomach became fire in his veins. The kid knew too much. "Thought I told you to stay out of the basement."

Brant stepped off the plate and faced him. "You'd never experiment on players, would you?"

The unveiled threat in Brant's eyes shattered his composure. He gripped the kid's arm. "You're making wild accusations." He swore.

Brant's gaze never wavered. His bicep flexed beneath his grasp. "Am I?"

A buzzing anger welled up and blocked out everything. If Brant went home, everything he'd done would be for nothing. He yanked Brant forward. "You don't know what you're talking about."

Brant's phone vibrated with another text. Bobby snatched it from his hand and read the screen. It was from Jack Briggs. Four words that ruined everything.

Bobby could be dangerous.

The game was over. He smashed the phone against the tile floor. "I see where you've been getting your information. You'd trust Briggs over me?" He tried to sound hurt when the fury built up like a steam engine.

"Jack's my friend. And he loves my mom."

Rage exploded in his brain, and he punched Brant across the jaw. Brant toppled backward and Bobby stood over him, shaking, sweating, drooling. "I loved your mom, too. Why couldn't anyone understand that?"

Brant's eyes mirrored rage and pain. A trickle of blood escaped the corner of his mouth. "What the heck is wrong with you? I just told Jack you'd never hurt me."

"Let's hope Jack believed you." He kicked Brant in the side and yanked him to his feet while Brant was still reeling and dragged him to a treatment table. He fought the kid with super-human strength, but had to knock his head against the tile wall behind them to subdue him. He arranged his limbs on the table and searched the room for something to secure him. He'd played the game long enough.

He grabbed the large roll of tape and peeled a strip off, ripping it from the roll with his teeth as he'd done so many times. Brant rolled his head. Bobby hurried to get him pinned to the table. "What else did Jack tell you?"

Brant's speech didn't seem affected from the blow. "I told him he was wrong. Told him you didn't cause those players' injuries."

A moment of loyalty from his nephew did little to contain the fury that raged in his head. "That's funny. I'll bet he still doesn't know I was responsible for his injury, too." He laughed at the boy, useless on the table.

Brant turned his head away.

He grabbed Brant's chin and pulled. "Look at me, boy."

Brant's eyes, so like Pete's, bored into his gaze. "What did you do to those players?"

"You want to know? You really want to know?" He pulled his kit from his pocket. "Maybe it's time I showed you."

Jack sent another text to Brant as he walked through the airport in Denver. Why didn't he respond this time? He'd been responding in seconds to his previous texts, but hadn't responded in at least five minutes.

Since Brant didn't answer, he tried Marcy's number again. Since he'd made the connection he was being driven crazy at a gallop to see her. He'd settle for her voice.

After days of trying, he almost jumped when he heard her sultry answer.

"Hello?"

His heart melted. "It's good to hear your voice."

"Uh, thanks."

He hated the strain between them, but knew it was his fault. He deserved her coolness. Although, just hearing her voice, cool was the last thing he felt. He inhaled. First things first. "Listen, are you with Brant?"

"Not yet, but I'm hoping to find him."

"Where are you?"

She laughed. "You probably won't believe me, but I'm at the Mountaineers stadium."

"What are you doing there?"

"I'm looking for Brant. Bobby's giving him a tour this morning."

His mind raced. He'd been feeding Brant information about Bobby, and they were *together*? *Idiot.* "How long have they been together?"

"I'm sure you didn't call to hear the Farris sob story. What can I do for you?"

The chill in her voice hurt him. "Marcy, tell me what happened."

She sighed. "Brant stormed out the day after Christmas. He's been with Bobby ever since."

Crap. "You have a fight or something?"

Her voice broke. "He accused me of driving Pete to suicide."

The more he heard, the higher his fears soared. Maybe Bobby wasn't as benign as he thought. "Whoever put those ideas into his head?"

"People talk, I guess."

Bobby. He should have called her earlier. The effects of a tough week took their toll and he heard them in her voice. "I was just trying to text him. I found a connection between Pete and Lisa. Can I call you back when I find him?"

Genuine panic set in. "Listen, Marcy. Are there a lot of people at the stadium today?"

"No—oh, I found the training facility. Let me call you back in a few minutes."

The line went dead. *Shoot.* Jack shook his head as he slid his phone into his pocket. Marcy, alone with Bobby. Nerves snaked through his stomach, but she'd be safe with him. He hadn't done anything more than injections, as far as they knew.

The conveyer belt delivered his baggage, and he stepped out into the chilly air to find his parked car. He couldn't shake the nervousness of Marcy and Brant being alone with Bobby now that his suspicions had a name. Horns blared and vehicles raced past as he rolled his bag to the place he'd parked his truck. He found his truck, loaded his bags and merged into DIA traffic. He wasn't far from the stadium and would have no trouble getting in. It was time Bobby knew he'd been cornered. He would give him exactly three seconds to prove his theory wrong.

The blue Bronco statue with the red eyes flashed past. What if Brant confronted Bobby first? His head throbbed at the thought, and he stepped on the accelerator. If anything happened to Brant or Marcy, he'd react with something like the rage expressed in that hideous sculpture.

He took the I-25 South exit, hoping Marcy wouldn't be disappointed to see him. He left a message with Brant. *Call me right away.*

He drove three miles and got no response. *Darn.* There was good cell service in the stadium. He stepped on the accelerator. He was overreacting in his need to see Marcy, but if Bobby was ruthless enough to inflict injury on players, was he a danger to Brant? Jack sighed. If he ever got his hands on Bobby's neck, he'd be the one in danger.

The anger that burned against Bobby boiled up, but Jack wrestled it. Coach Black's words when he left came back to him, "You're not a lawman, Jack. Let God take care of the vengeance." Bobby had been a fixture in Brant and Marcy's life for years. He wasn't dangerous. But he sure had some explaining to do.

Jack turned into the parking lot at the stadium and looked at the gleaming building. An orange banner snapped in the breeze, but the parking lot was empty.

Coach said he prayed when he lost control, but God wasn't interested. He couldn't ask Him for things he didn't come close to deserving: a woman like Marcy, number one on the list.

He strode to the famous college stadium.

The security guard, Randall, recognized him immediately. "Jack Briggs. Haven't seen you in a few years." He extended his hand for a shake. "How are you?"

Jack smiled, though he wasn't sure where they'd met before. "Couldn't be better. I'm here to chat with Bobby Farris. Is he here today?"

Randall checked the clipboard. "He's not listed as a guest today, but he might not have come in here. I do have Marcy Farris listed."

"Is she with a tour group?"

"No. She said she was looking for her son, so I let her go on back."

Jack nodded. "Mind if I look for them?"

Randall paused. "Sure thing. I can page you if I see Farris come this way."

Jack started for the far door. "That'd be great."

He should have known Bobby would not have had to use the tour entrance. He was a licensed trainer, although he did not work for the Colorado Mountaineers organization. Randall caught up to him and punched a code into the pin-pad by the door. "Have a good one, Jack."

"Thanks Randall."

A metallic click followed him as the door closed. A clean scented hall stretched ahead of him, and he checked his phone. Four bars of service meant he wouldn't miss a call from Brant or Marcy. They could be anywhere in this massive place, and his nerves crackled with impatience as he quickened his pace.

A woman's scream pierced the silence as he turned the corner.

30

MARCY HAD SEEN no sign of Brant or Bobby, so she had sat on one of the benches to wait for them a few minutes. If she didn't miss her guess, they'd spend a lot of time here on the tour. When she stood to catch a glimpse from the window, a strong hand grasped her neck. But the moment she screamed, the familiar scent of Bobby's aftershave relaxed her. His hand slipped from her mouth as the rigidity left her body. She sagged against him.

"What are you trying to do? Scare me to death?" She shoved his shoulder, glad her playful brother-in-law had returned. "You got me."

The fierceness in his gaze raised goose pimples on her arms. "What's wrong?"

His eyes narrowed, and his fingers dug into the flesh of her upper arm. "What are you doing here?"

She frowned at his expression, but pasted on a smile. "I came to surprise you and Brant." She put a hand on his other arm. "You okay?" His eyes were bloodshot, and a spot on his chin quivered.

When he didn't answer, she frowned. It must have set him off more because he shoved her through another door. A movement from the corner of the room caught her eye. Restrained on a treatment table, Brant struggled to move beneath yards of athletic tape.

She lunged toward Brant, but Bobby pinned her to the wall, his eyes wild with an expression she couldn't place. His eyes pierced hers and then he shot over his shoulder, "Your mommy came to rescue you, Brant."

Her heart slammed into her ribs. Bobby had been drinking, his breath burned her eyes. "Stop it. You're hurting me." She pushed him back. "What's wrong with you?"

"I've already given him the injection."

Her skin crawled. "What?" Brant struggled on the table, and she lunged for him, hands ripping at the white tape that bound him to the table like a mummy. "What are you talking about?"

Bobby grabbed the back of her hair and yanked her to her knees. Pain slammed through her thighs on impact with the hard floor.

"I started with his hand."

Brant's eyes, wide with fear, reminded her to stay calm. Bobby had obviously gone over some kind of mental cliff. She would need to tread carefully and not panic. "Was his hand hurting?" She dug in her purse, an attempt to appear casual as she scooted toward the far wall. "I think I have some Advil in here."

"It's not hurting anymore."

She turned to him, surprised at the wildness in Bobby's eyes. "Bobby, you seem upset. I know we had a disagreement, but—"

"Give me one good reason I shouldn't be upset." He grabbed a filled syringe from the counter, blocking her from getting to Brant.

A sweat broke out on her upper lip, and her heart hammered her ribs. "I'm here now. I can take Brant home so you can get back to work."

"You're right." He stood directly in front of her with the syringe. "I'm glad you're here, too."

She stepped backward to avoid the frightening curl on his lips and the needle in his hand. If she couldn't get Brant free soon, she'd go crazy, herself.

Brant thrashed against the tape that held him.

"Your son accused me of experimenting on players."

"He's just fifteen years old. Didn't you just remind me to take everything he said with a grain of salt?"

She prayed he'd drop that needle. The dual lights overhead reflected off the solution in the vial like two white eyes.

"Your *friend* Jack tipped him off."

"I'm sure it's nothing. Let's get Brant up and talk about it on the way home."

He pointed the syringe at her like a gun. "Don't move."

He punched numbers into the key pad on the wall and automatic locks screeched shut.

Trapped.

The muffled sound of Brant's voice against the tape that bound his mouth brought rage to the surface. She ran to his side and began clawing at the tape. When she felt Bobby approach, she set her teeth and snarled at him. "Get away from us."

"Sorry. We're family. Guess you're stuck with me." He flung her from the table and stared down at her. "Aren't you going to ask me what Jack told him?"

She shook her head. She didn't want to know.

"The men in your life are all trouble, you know."

"Don't forget to include yourself." She tried to stand, but he kicked her back down.

"I'm the one who set you free."

She paused and stared at him. "What?"

"Pete never appreciated you. He despised you, cheated on you. I got him out of your hair."

Her lungs refused to fill. If this was about guilt—"You don't mean that, Bobby. It was Pete's decision."

"I told him to take the pills and gave him an injection to finish the job."

The room spun. Her brother-in-law wasn't a murderer.

"I don't believe you."

He laughed. "You're about to get a demonstration." He lunged toward her with the syringe, but Brant struggled and broke through the bond of tape on his hand and he grasped Bobby's pant leg before he reached her. Brant's eyes narrowed, but Bobby pulled from his grasp. He leaned over Brant's head and slapped him. "There's no use in struggling."

She sprang to her feet. "I thought you loved us."

"Love has nothing to do with this." He poised the syringe over Brant's leg.

"No!" She pounced on him, clawing and kicking. The syringe clattered to the floor, and he grabbed both her wrists and squeezed until the fingers tingled.

"I've lived with the truth of what I did to Pete for years. It's time you bore some of the burden, too."

"Some of the guilt for his death? You know I've carried the greatest guilt."

"Nothing like what I've borne. He forced my hand that night. You remember? You'd had a fight, and he'd been drinking. He came over in a rage and confronted me about the injections."

Bobby was the one? She twisted her hands and arms in a futile attempt to escape his grasp. Frustration snapped her control. "Finish it, then. You've got me right where you want me. So do it." Their eyes locked.

She kicked the syringe; it spun under the table where Brant lay captive, but Bobby held her unmoving and blood pulsed erratic in her ears.

Poisoned breath laced with liquor burned her eyes. "You chose Pete over me. Now Jack. We could have been happy together, you know."

"You think I'd be happy with a murderer?" She tried not to move her eyes in Brant's direction as he broke through more tape bonds. Together, maybe they could take him.

He brought a hand to her throat and squeezed. "Why are you calling me that?"

"You just admitted it yourself. You killed Pete."

His expression changed and he paused, considering what she'd said. He whispered. "Pete committed suicide."

Jack's mind spun as he sprinted down the hall. He bolted through the hall but skidded to a stop at another PIN-padlocked door. He jiggled the handle and slammed his hand against the door as frustration beat along with his heart. Was it Marcy's scream he'd heard?

He took off in another direction, praying the next door he encountered wouldn't be locked. The halls were sickeningly silent after the scream, as if no one else had heard it. He'd been so foolish to text Brant the details of what he'd discovered. Put both him and Marcy in danger.

God, help me find them. The prayer came so naturally that he let it linger and push him on.

His heart urged him forward down the hall to the weight room opposite the training room where he felt the best chance of finding them. The equipment blocked a straight line of advance, but he spotted movement through a window in the door ahead. He breathed a sigh of relief as the back of Marcy's head came into view. He moved further and panic surged as Bobby's hand went around her throat.

His body slammed into the door which divided the training room from the weight room. Bobby spun and loosened his grasp as Marcy's head snapped like a rag doll, and she collapsed onto the floor. Every nerve tingled in frustration as the handle refused to move in his hand. A smile curved on Bobby's lips, and he turned back to her. Jack's ears strained to hear the words, but even the barrier between them couldn't disguise the intent of the sneer on Bobby's face.

Jack turned back to the cavernous weight room. "Is anybody there? Help me!" His voice rebounded off concrete walls. He slammed his shoulder against the door but only bruised the muscle. The door held fast. His brain worked overtime. There must be another entry. Most training facilities had multiple entrances. Torn between watching Bobby and Marcy and getting into the room, he turned and sprinted toward the visiting team's locker room, thanking God he'd been there before.

His throat refused to swallow as he imagined what Bobby might be doing to Marcy. And where was Brant? Every beat of his heart urged him: get there in time.

He rounded the corner and flew through the locker room. The steam shower, cold baths and other therapy rooms opened into the training room. He rounded the corner, and his heart squeezed when he saw Brant, immobilized on the table to his right. Bobby and Marcy were nowhere in sight.

He ran to Brant and ripped his arms and legs free. Brant sat up and pulled at the tape on his face. Jack searched the drawers for scissors and gently cut the tape from Brant's lips. "Uncle Bobby's got Mom!" He pointed to the open door Jack had just come from.

Brant's pupils were dilated and his breathing was fast. "What happened?"

"Shot me in the hand with something. Didn't say what."

The fear in the boy's eyes brought a lump the size of a grapefruit into his throat. He couldn't leave him like this. "Lie down. I'll call for help."

Jack pulled his phone from his pocket and dialed 9-1-1.

Brant stuck his hand out. "I'll talk to them. Find my mom."

There was little he could do for the boy, so he agreed. "Stay here. If I can't find them in five minutes, I'm coming back." He raced through the door Brant indicated.

A crash ricocheted through the locker room, and Jack changed directions. Brant's description of their location helped spur him on.

Steam poured from the door of the steam room, and Marcy's scream hit his heart like an offensive lineman. Jack yanked the door open but raised his hands as a wall of hot steam blinded him. "Marcy!"

"Jack! Look out!" Her cry came from somewhere deeper in the room. To his left, maybe.

He gritted his teeth and plunged through the wall of blinding steam.

His tennis shoes slipped on the slick tile floor as he struggled to make out even a shadow in the cloud he'd just walked into. "Talk to me Marcy, where is he?"

The steam choked his lungs as the door slammed behind him. A loud hiss signaled a blast of steam that enclosed them in another hot white cloud. Acting on instinct, Jack turned and tackled the shadow looming in front of him. Their bodies squeaked and cracked as they hit the tile floor and slid to a stop at the first set of tiled seats. Jack shook Bobby's frame. "What did you do to her?"

Rage seethed through his pores. If he'd hurt Marcy—"Answer me!" He realized why Bobby didn't answer. His body flopped like a limp rag. He'd probably knocked him out on impact. Tile floors weren't exactly football turf. He left him on the tile.

Jack slid up from his knees and groped for the dial to stop the steam. He kicked the door open to allow the steam to escape but couldn't find the stopper. When he'd located the dial and cranked it counterclockwise, he followed Marcy's whimper.

Relief flooded him as his hand felt wet skin and hair. "Jack." She clung to him.

"I'm here." He stroked her tangled, soaking hair. "I'm here." His hand roved the length of her body, but with all the steam, he couldn't tell what was hurt. At least he'd heard her voice; that was a good sign.

"Thank God I found you." He whispered against her hair. "Tell me what's hurt. What did he do to you?"

Her head lifted an inch. "What did you say?"

"Let's get you out of here." He pulled her to her feet. "Can you walk?"

He felt her nod and led her from the room, careful to avoid Bobby's body which lay in shadow near the door.

"My eye!" Despite the searing heat of the steam room, Marcy shivered against him. "Where's Brant?"

"Almost there."

Cool air struck them as Jack flung the door open and staggered out. He didn't dare pick her up on the slippery floors in the steam room, but as soon as his feet found solid footing, he swept her into his arms and strode to the room where he'd left Brant. She buried her head in his shoulder, silent and quivering with fear or pain, he didn't know.

Police, guns drawn, and paramedics burst into the room as they reached Brant's side. "Denver police!"

The paramedics hurried to Brant who slumped against the wall.

Marcy tried to lift her head but he said, "He's all right. They've got him." He prayed the same would be the case for Marcy. Now that he had her in his arms again, he wasn't going to let go.

Bobby's head slid on the wet floor, and he lifted it with difficulty. Where was he? His vision was clouded and lightning split his skull. He blinked, but nothing changed. Then it came back. He'd dragged Marcy into the steam room and stabbed her with the syringe of serum. A wave of nausea overtook him, and he knelt to retch out the distilled contents of his stomach. What had come over him? Hearing Brant say Jack loved Marcy flipped a switch in his brain—add in the alcohol, and he went mad. The doctor warned him another episode was possible when he got stressed.

The events were still muddled. Was she dead? He pushed to a sitting position against the tile and rubbed the back of his head. No, Jack tackled him and took Marcy.

But where were they now? Surely, they'd called the police. His heart started pumping and adrenaline flooded his veins. He scrambled on the wet polished tiles and jerked the door open. Hearing voices in the training room, he ran in the opposite direction, still muddled from the blow to the head and the booze he'd consumed.

He punched the keypad, climbed into the janitor's closet and pulled the door shut, intending to wait until the facility cleared out. They wouldn't expect him to stay around after what he'd done.

Depending on where he'd hit her, Marcy wouldn't suffer any adverse consequences. He'd just meant to scare her. Brant would be fine, too. His season was over, and the serum only reacted under tremendous circumstances, such as the strain on the joints of a football player during a game. It was utterly benign unless mixed with certain painkillers and serious torque. That was the beauty of it, and how he'd gotten away with it for so long.

Now, he wasn't sure he would get away at all.

His breathing returned to normal, but he still felt every beat of his heart in his brain. Silence stretched out. They might have taken Brant in the ambulance.

As the fight or flight symptoms wore off, the same remorse he'd felt when Pete died pecked at his insides like a hungry chicken. Why couldn't he have kept his cool? He pushed wet hair off his forehead.

He promised himself he'd never snap again, but now he had, and look where it landed him. Holed up in the broom closet.

Marcy's words stabbed him like a knife through the heart. "I thought you loved us."

I do love you. His insides writhed and he puked. She'd said it herself: He was a murderer.

31

BOBBY CREPT FROM the closet like the snake he was, his clothes covered in vomit. The stench of wine and bile clogged his nostrils. The pain in his skull was almost audible, it screamed and pounded in his brain. He slipped in the mess he'd made, confused about where to turn. A footfall in the hall startled him. How long had he been sitting there?

"Farris, stay where you are." A uniformed officer pointed a gun at his chest. "Hands in the air."

His arms refused to lift, and his tongue protested movement. Another officer ran into the room, and together they slammed his face to the ground, cuffing his wrists behind him. A heavy knee bored into his spine.

A single word came from his lips. "Marcy?" His voice echoed off tile flooring. She was gone forever. Pete was gone and so was Lisa. The things he'd done reached up and clawed him, ripping the callus he'd built over his heart. Where was the triumph in this moment?

His head hit the counter behind him as they sat him up and read his Miranda rights. He wished he had the power to run; maybe they'd shoot him, and it would all be over. A just penalty for his crimes.

"When will they know what's wrong?"

A nurse stood her ground outside the waiting room door. Jack wasn't family, and he wasn't allowed in the Emergency Room. "The doctor is doing an evaluation on Mrs. Farris now. I can't release information on her son."

"I understand." He sank to the couch behind him. The swollen tissue and blood around her eye worried him. He'd had to restrain himself from punching the wall when she explained how Bobby had stabbed her in the eye with the syringe.

Seeing his distress, the nurse paused and donned a soft smile. "When I know something I can share, you'll be the first to know."

He ruffled his hair. They hadn't even let him ride in the ambulance because he wasn't family. That was a problem he meant to rectify as soon as possible. He'd never wanted anything more in his life.

A clumsy prayer, more like a plea, bumbled from his lips, and he realized his prayer had already been answered. He'd asked God to spare her life, and he'd been a part of the answer. Maybe God used people to keep his promises. In that case, he would be glad to be on His team.

An hour later, the nurse came out and stood before him. "They're keeping her overnight for observation."

"What are they observing?"

"Her eye and a head injury are the greatest concern. If she does well, she can go home in the morning."

He exhaled. "Is she in pain?"

"They've given her some medication to help. Why don't you head home and return in the morning. I'll tell her you were waiting."

"When will they know if she'll regain sight in the eye?"

"Sorry, sir. I just can't tell you that information."

There was no avoiding the press. Once the story broke, the headlines were heavier than an entire defensive line. If the Internet could explode, it would have.

NFL players injured by trainer. Trainer suspected of murder.

He understood better than anyone, but this time he'd face them. For her. For the last year, he'd wrestled with himself over interviews and sponsorships, believing that he had nothing more to offer. Today was all about Marcy and what she'd gone through, and maybe it was one step closer to rebuilding what they had.

Standing next to the Farris' lawyer, Jack pushed back from the microphone, holding a hand up to deflect the barrage of questions the press shot at him like arrows. He'd volunteered as spokesman for the family, even though he squirmed at the thought of facing the press again.

He leaned to the microphone. "In response to recent events

surrounding the NFL scandal, the Farris family has asked me to act as spokesman. They've been through a terrible ordeal and ask for privacy as they deal with the circumstances surrounding the arrest of Bobby Farris and the death of Peter Farris. I would like to put all legal questions, to the family's attorney, Reginald Nitt." The moment he stopped for breath, questions peppered the silence of the big room.

He held up a hand. "As I said before, I defer to Mr. Nitt and Denver police for further questions about Mr. Farris and any charges he may or may not be facing."

"Jack can you tell us if Mrs. Farris has a comment?"

He smiled calmly at the reporter. "Mrs. Farris wishes me to send her deepest condolences to the players and families affected by this tragedy. And, she thanks the community for the outpouring of love and support she and her family have received."

"How did you feel about finding your name on the infamous list of injured players?"

He knew this question was going to come up sometime. "I can't change the past. It's part of my story now."

More reporters peppered him with questions, but he again deferred to Mr. Nitt.

"We do want the public to know that the death of Peter Farris, which was at one time ruled a suicide, is now being investigated as a homicide. Please allow the family time to grieve this loss again. A memorial fund has been set up for Peter Farris and the players who have been victimized. To share your thoughts and prayers with the players who were victimized, please visit Fallen Football Heroes dot org. You can also visit the NFL website for a link."

Flash bulbs exploded in Jack's face. There had been a time he'd enjoyed the attention, and maybe he would again, after a time. For now, he'd done what he set out to do for the family.

He breathed a sigh and headed for the parking lot, eager to get back to Marcy and the kids.

Murder and assault were among the charges the Denver police pressed against Bobby, but seeing him weeping like a baby as they shoved him into the police car hadn't given Jack the satisfaction he thought it would. It would be easy to hate the guy if he'd been stubborn or spat in the cop's face. However, the crushed look on Bobby's face made Jack's stomach squirm. Rumor was, he had some kind of mental illness. One would certainly think so, to have murdered his own brother.

Jack checked his watch and started his truck. Marcy was waiting for him at home. She'd been so strong as the details had poured out, and so forgiving to him. He thrust down the ache in the pit of his stomach when he thought of her husband's flagrant affair with Lisa Sparks and Bobby's longtime deception. She'd been through so much, yet maintained the grace he'd admired in her from the beginning. She proved, without a word, that her trust was in God. And Jack thanked Him hourly for her safety. His little conversations with God were becoming easier.

He pulled into Marcy's driveway, memories rushing in. A week ago, he was ready to throw in the towel on his life, to give up like he thought Pete Farris had. Now, thanks to Marcy and Coach Black, life looked brighter. There was room for God in his life somewhere, and he would find it. Marcy deserved a man who honored her. And he longed for a chance to unburden himself and trust God with his future. It'd been weighing so heavily, he'd almost forgotten how to live.

Marcy's weak smile met him at the door. "How did the press conference go?"

He kissed her cheek beneath the eye patch. She hadn't taken down the Christmas decorations, but the house smelled like she'd been baking. "Didn't you watch it?"

She shook her head. "This is a no media zone."

He followed her to the kitchen. "Understood. How are the kids holding up?"

She sank into a kitchen chair. "It's such a painful deception. I don't know if we'll ever get over it."

"You will. I'll be here to help you." He tilted her chin to look at her eye, but couldn't see beyond the patch. "How's the eye this afternoon?"

"The patch itches."

"So no pirate jokes?"

She shoved him playfully. "Where's the fun in that? I could make you walk the plank."

The warm fragrance of her hair brought a smile to his lips as he kissed the top of her head. "I just hate to see you hurting."

"He hurt you more than any of us, Jack."

Jack shrugged. "You can't put toothpaste back in the tube, babe. Besides, I wouldn't have met you if I was still playing." He raised an eyebrow. "Kind of a compliment in a way. They only took out the best players."

Three ACL reconstructions later, his career was sacked. But his confidence was returning.

"I'm thinking it would have been best for you to never have met any of the Farris family." She pulled her wrap close.

He stroked her shoulder. "I wouldn't trade our soap opera for anything."

That got a smile. "Did we ever have a date that didn't end in tragedy?"

"I don't think so, but I've got lots of free time."

Part of her wished Jack had stayed longer, but the other part knew she needed some time alone. Marcy's head throbbed and she tried not to rub the patch on her eye. It would heal more quickly than her heart would. Breaking the news to Carter had taken its toll, but she felt confident he'd rally. He'd asked to come out and stay for a while, but she'd declined, knowing he had his own life to sort out. Haley had a fitful day, but was finally in bed. She knocked on Brant's door. "It's Mom. Can I come in?"

He opened the door. "Sure."

She stopped in the doorway and gasped. "What have you done with my son? This place is so clean!"

"Very funny." He plopped down on the bed, and she sat next to him. "How are you feeling, Brant?"

"Like an idiot."

His response surprised her. "Why?"

"I should have known what Uncle Bobby was doing. I'd seen the pictures of Lisa and saw his little laboratory downstairs, but never put it all together. I should have protected you."

Marcy stroked his hair. "It was never your job, sweetheart."

"Since Dad died, everyone always said I was the man of the house."

"They were wrong to put such pressure on you. Our family is entrusted to God."

He swiped tears from his eyes with his fist. "Where was God when Uncle Bobby put extra pills in Dad's bottle? And gave him the injection?"

Like some questions, this one didn't have concrete answers. "He didn't have to take the pills, you know. Bobby banked on the fact that he would, and he was right. God doesn't interfere with man's free will."

Brant smiled at her. "Is it wrong to be glad he was murdered?"

She understood his question and had wondered the same thing. "Dealing with the stigma of having a parent who committed suicide is gone now. I don't think that's anything we shouldn't praise God for, even if it is a little morbid. We can't bring him back, but maybe we respect him more." She was finally able to shelve the guilt that had plagued her since she'd found him dead. She understood Brant perfectly.

"I'm sorry for what I said about you after Christmas." He stroked her knee. "I love you, Mom."

"Love you, too, Son."

Brant smiled, and she ruffled his hair. "Get some sleep. We'll talk more in the morning."

He yawned and nodded. She wondered if sleep would ever come easily again.

She drifted through the house, wishing Jack had stayed after all. After a sweep of the main floor, she spotted a tall shadow on the front porch.

"I think we're alone, now." Jack's voice broke through the stillness as she stepped out. He leaned back against the concrete steps in front of Marcy's house and blew a frosty ring of breath into the darkened night sky. The stars stretched out like a blanket on the chilly January night.

Marcy snuggled between his legs on the lower step. "Finally. I thought the camera crews would never leave the lawn."

He put his arms around her and laced his fingers with hers. "They'll be back."

She sighed. "We've lived through a whirlwind and survived. Brant's going to be ecstatic when you tell him your plans for the players' assistance organization." She was so proud of him, knowing he'd faced the press for her. And with all the calls he got from current and former players, she was sure his non-profit to help ex-players adjust to life after football would be very successful. Helping coach the Thompson Valley High School football team, he'd said, was an added extra.

"I hardly believe it myself. I'm pretty excited."

She leaned into his thigh. "This feels like trying to wake after a nightmare."

His fingers massaged her shoulders, tracing patterns through her thin sweater. "Makes you wonder how you could be so close to him and not see it."

She shivered. "I can't wrap my mind around it." She'd been close to pursuing a relationship with him.

"A man can get mixed up in his priorities sometimes."

Marcy leaned into him. He sounded like a different man, if he did have a long way to go. "He would have killed me if you hadn't come along." Her voice snagged in her throat. "I think his other intentions scared me more than the syringe." She pulled her sweater closer.

He sat straighter and pulled his arms from her shoulders. "You didn't mention that before. He try anything?"

Her laugh rang through the neighborhood. "Nothing you haven't tried. And he didn't get away with it either."

He tugged her ponytail so she had to look into his face. "How dare you say that of the Gentleman Linebacker?"

A playful grin encouraged him. "I take it back." She turned and knelt in front of him. "Nothing *I* wouldn't try." She put her hands on either side of his hips and kissed him, allowing her lips to express her appreciation for the man he was. His hands massaged the small of her back, bringing her closer.

He squeezed his legs around her waist, trapping her in the triangle. "I hope you mean to keep that up." He stole a kiss on the base of her neck.

She grinned. "If I keep you guessing, will it keep you humble?"

He cocked his head in consideration. "I'd like to be humble, but I'm afraid no one would notice."

She laughed. "Humility isn't something they teach in the NFL."

"But I'm learning."

She turned around, sat down and looked up at the stars. "That you are."

His hands found the knots in her shoulders and warmth spread over her body. She groaned when he found muscles that rebelled and rolled her neck. "I'm not sure how to move on from this."

"You were the one who told me to trust God."

Her head snapped up. "When did you decide that was the way to go?"

"I think it was coming on for a while, but I knew when I couldn't find you at the stadium. I might have strength enough for myself, but I can't trust someone as precious as you with just anyone. I recognize your beauty at its full worth, knowing who takes care of you."

Her heart fluttered. When had she ever heard such a compliment?

"You know what the Bible says about men?"

"Do I want to know?" Since when did Jack read the Bible?

"It is not good for man to be alone." The promise in his eyes melted any doubts she'd had.

"Coach told me the Bible was full of wisdom for life. I don't plan on being alone much longer." His arms encircled her waist, and she melted against him as he found her mouth and explored the possibilities of his prediction.

Breathless, she pushed back. "I have my limits."

"I think that's what I love most about you." Her heart shot fireworks as he buried his hands in her hair and kissed her cheek. "Kiss me good night."

"So soon?" Disappointment pricked her.

He pulled her to her feet and dragged her body close until their hips met and his mouth was inches from her. Electricity tingled through her shoulders and into her stomach. "I want you more than my next breath, Marcy. I'd love to pick you up, kick the door open and carry you inside. But you're worth every agonizing moment."

She practically melted into a puddle at his feet. "The play clock is ticking."

The End

RED ZONE SPONSORED BY THESE FINE BOOKS:

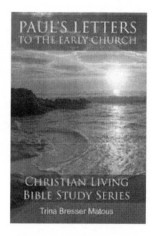

Made in the USA
Middletown, DE
24 September 2018